Twins

Bari Wood was raised in the American mid-west and graduated from Northwestern University. She is the editor of Drug Therapy Magazine and has also worked as an editor and bibliographer with the American Cancer Society. She lives in New York with her husband.

Jack Geasland is an American journalist specializing in medical affairs.

Previously published by
Bari Wood in Pan Books

The Killing Gift

Twins

Bari Wood and Jack Geasland

Pan Books in association with **Heinemann**

First published in Great Britain 1977 by William Heinemann Ltd
This edition published 1978 by Pan Books Ltd,
Cavaye Place, London SW10 9PG
2nd printing 1979
© Bari Wood and Jack Geasland 1977
ISBN 0 330 25354 9
Printed and bound in Great Britain by
Hazell Watson & Viney Ltd, Aylesbury, Bucks

The monkey rope was fast at both ends;
fast to Queequeg's broad canvas belt, and
fast to my narrow leather one.
So that for better or for worse,
we two ... were wedded; and should poor
Queequeg sink to rise no more, then both
usage and honour demanded, that instead of cutting
the cord, it should drag me down in his wake ...
Queequeg was my own inseparable twin brother ...

Moby Dick

July 1976

Kathy was sure it was Michael. She ran across the room, and grabbed the phone on the third ring. It was John Anders.

'I can't pick you up in time, Kathy. I don't think I'm going to get out of here before six,' he said.

'No?' She sounded so unhappy he laughed.

'Don't worry. I'll meet you there.'

'Where?'

'At Maggie's. I thought you were disappointed because I couldn't pick you up.'

'I was – I am,' she lied. 'I just forgot we were supposed to go to Maggie's.'

'Kathy, are you all right?'

'Yes, of course. I'm fine . . .' She couldn't remember her last full meal, and she'd had a headache since Monday; but if she told him that, he'd come running, and she had to be alone when Michael came back. If Michael saw Anders come into the building, or heard Anders' voice through her door, he might get frightened and she'd never see him again.

'I'm sorry, John. I don't think I can go.'

'Kathy, nobody's seen you for a week; they're starting to wonder.'

Let them wonder.

'I haven't seen you for a week. What's going on?'

'Nothing. I just don't feel . . .'

'If you're not here by seven, I'm coming to get you.'

She didn't answer.

'I mean it, Kathy.'

She thought fast.

Michael could rest here alone on the couch, and look out through the glass wall at the stars, the way he used to. He wouldn't be frightened away by being alone . . . he would be frightened away by Anders.

'I'll be there, John.'

'Good.' She started to hang up, but he was still talking.

'Kathy, I love you.'

He waited for her to say that she loved him too, but this time she just couldn't.

'I'll see you at seven,' she said.

As soon as she hung up she was sorry that she'd agreed to go. It was already five thirty. She hadn't washed her hair for days; it was limp and greasy, and she had no idea what to wear.

She tried Michael's number again, but there was no answer.

Ada Klein was almost eighty and she had to admit that her senses weren't what they had been. She couldn't hear well; her sight was getting worse every year; and she realized she might sometimes imagine things to fill the gap her waning powers left. But she was sure she wasn't imagining the smell. It started yesterday and at first she hoped she wouldn't have to complain. They always looked at her sadly whenever she did, then at each other as if to ask what could you expect from the old lady. There were four other apartments on the floor besides hers, and she had been sure someone else would complain before she had to. But it was still there this morning and it was worse. The July heat wave had driven most of her neighbours out of town, and she was alone on the eleventh floor with that terrible smell.

She called downstairs again, but nothing had been done by afternoon and she was sure it was getting worse.

Kathy wrapped a towel around her wet hair, opened the closet, and slid hangers along the bar. All the dresses were beige – light beige, dark beige, honey beige, grey beige . . . Then, in the back of the closet, she saw the old blue dress she'd worn the night she left Michael. Bad luck dress. She'd lived the worst night of her life in that dress, but it was the only thing she owned that wasn't some shade of beige; and maybe its luck had changed by now. She decided to wear it.

She fixed herself a gin and tonic and called Michael again. No answer. Yesterday she'd let the phone ring eight or nine times until she got the day girl at the service who told her that the doctors were out of town and wouldn't be back until next week. But if it was an emergency she could call . . . Kathy knew the girl was wrong; they hadn't left town – they couldn't – but she walked up to Seventy-second anyway, then across to the river. She stood alone in the heat with the park behind her and looked up to the eleventh floor of number 22 Riverside Drive. There was a light on in the living room, and a line of water dropped from the air-conditioner down the side of the building. They hadn't left. She thought about going up – just walking in on them. But Michael had said a week; and it had only been four days.

'Mrs Klein, we've checked the incinerator' – Tom Jonas sounded patient – 'and there's nothing.'

'But didn't you smell . . .'

'Not in the service area.'

'What about in the hall itself?'

'There's nothing in the hall that *could* smell,' Jonas said.

Mrs Klein thought for a minute while Jonas held on at the lobby end of the house phone, trying not to lose his temper. She wasn't usually a complainer, not like some of the others, but this had been going on since yesterday . . . that was all she talked about . . . the smell.

Mrs Klein said, 'What if there's something in the vents . . . a dead rat or something? Wouldn't that smell up the hall?'

She was right, it would. But he wasn't in any mood to admit it, and he sounded indignant at her suggesting dead rats in *this* building.

At seven thirty Kathy's hair was combed out and she was dressed, but she looked tired and thin, and the blue made her look even more haggard.

It was so hot outside that sweat stained the underarms of the blue dress by the time she walked the half block to Central Park West to get a taxi. Leaves hung limp over her head and the still air smelled of rotting vegetation. She hailed a cab, and told the driver to pass 22 Riverside Drive on his way to 4 East Sixty-eighth Street.

'That ain't on the way, lady.'

'I know that. Just go by there, please.'

He did, and as they got closer she began to sweat more, wondering what she'd do if she looked up this time and saw that the

9

windows were dark, and the air conditioner was turned off. She couldn't imagine it, like years ago, when she wondered what she would do if Michael married somebody else, or just decided he didn't love her.

The cabbie made a U-turn as she told him to, and stopped across from number 22. She leaned out of the window, her heart pounding in her ears, and looked up. The lights were on; the trickle of water continued from the air conditioner. She sat back and wiped her face with a Kleenex, then told the cabbie to drive on.

Mrs Klein knew that her senses might be playing tricks on her, but Muriel Levy was only sixty-two – she ran her own business on Seventh Avenue, jobbing women's purses – and the first thing she mentioned when she came over for her Sunday afternoon Canasta game was the smell.

'Maybe Mr Jonas will believe *you*,' said Mrs Klein. 'He won't listen to me.'

'I'll tell him when I leave,' she said.

'Maybe you could tell him now?'

'Why?'

'I don't know, Muriel . . . I . . .' Suddenly Mrs Klein's eyes were full of tears. She hadn't cried for years, since her husband died, and Muriel stared at her dumbfounded.

'Ada, what's the matter?'

'I don't know . . . But I think something terrible has happened . . . I'm frightened . . .'

Muriel Levy grabbed the house phone.

'Mr Jonas, this is Muriel Levy. That's right,' she said, 'I'm at Mrs Klein's 11B. Something is rotting in this hallway, and I want you to get your ass up here right now.'

Alice Boyer, Maggie Calhoun's secretary and official greeter, frowned when she saw Kathy. Then she took out her compact and patted some powder on Kathy's forehead.

'The heat's showing.'

Kathy laughed and started up the curving staircase lined with Degas pastels on grey silk wall covering.

'John's here,' Alice said. 'He's been downstairs looking for you three times already.'

Kathy nodded.

'When're you going to put him out of his misery?'

Soon, she thought. After tomorrow, after Tuesday at the latest, Michael and I won't bother John or any of you again.

'He looked so . . .' Alice searched for the right word.

'Whipped,' Kathy said.

'No, Kathy; just anxious.' Alice disapproved of the way she treated Anders, they probably all did.

He was coming for her now, as fast as he could across the pale carpeting, past the paintings that glowed on the wall and dwarfed the guests. She was surprised again at how good-looking he was, how neat, and how bland compared to Michael.

Handsome, kind, rich, gentle John.

He kissed her. 'You look like hell.'

'Thank you.'

'Kathy, what's the matter?'

'It must be the heat.'

He didn't ask any more questions, and went to get her a gin and tonic.

People greeted her with handshakes and a few words, but she knew that at this point she was probably something of an embarrassment, and that as soon as she was gone they would talk about how terrible she looked – the way they used to talk about Michael. She remembered once, years ago, overhearing Al Weiss ask Kramer, 'Where dya suppose Ross got that suit?' And Kramer had said, 'Max's of Canal Street – every suit in the house twenty-seven fifty – none higher.'

That was before David came back with his Paul Stuart three-hundred-dollar third-floor suits and thirty-dollar main-floor shirts, and his Dunhill ties, and Gucci shoes. She used to wonder where David bought his underwear. For a second, the old hatred got to her in a way it hadn't for years, and she leaned against the wall under a Cézanne that was supposed to be insured for two million dollars. Maggie was waving Kathy over. But on her way past Minnie Lasker, she heard Michael's name and stopped.

'Michael's been gone for months. But David wasn't through

until last week. John tried and tried, but David didn't even turn up for the hearing. Bastards! I *thought* I saw one of them on the street. But I couldn't tell which one. I used to be able to tell them apart . . . especially when Michael got so thin. Now I hear they're both . . .' She paused, and Kathy couldn't stop listening. '*On* something . . . Seconal's the educated guess. Both of them. And they've *still* got patients.'

Al Weiss and Will Grandeson saw Kathy and looked away, embarrassed, but Minnie was oblivious.

'Can you imagine,' she said, 'those – junkies delivering a baby?' Finally she noticed their discomfort, turned, saw Kathy and blushed purple: but she kept on talking in the same tone, at the same rate.

'Oh, Kathy, I'm so sorry. But it's . . . it's . . .' Then she stopped. 'I *am* sorry,' she said quietly. 'Michael was a good doctor.'

She was on the verge of tears and Kathy looked at her bowed head, thinly covered with black-grey kinky hair, and said, 'Forget it, Minnie. He'll be everything he ever was again. You'll see.'

The minute the elevator doors opened on eleven, Jonas knew that Ada Klein wasn't crazy. He knew what the smell was and he had to try and find out where it was coming from. He kept his mouth open and went down the hall. As he passed each door, he realized that except for Ada Klein and the Rosses everyone on the floor was out of town. He stopped in front of the Ross twins' apartment. He closed his mouth for a second, and knew, as soon as he did, that this was where it was coming from. He got back down to the lobby as fast as he could and called the police.

The servants were just setting up the buffets in the far room, and Kathy was dancing with John when Alice Boyer broke in and told Anders that there was a call for him.

'Nothing important I'm sure,' he said, and he turned back to Kathy.

'It's the police, John,' Alice said.

'Probably selling subscriptions to *Redbook*.'

'I think you'd better take it.' Alice looked frightened. Kathy stepped back. Something must have happened at the hospital. A fire maybe, or maybe a bomb scare; there'd been bomb scares before.

'Okay . . . I'll be back in a minute, Kathy. Save me some caviar.'

She wandered into the dining room, but she wasn't hungry. The bathrooms were occupied, so she went up to the third floor to use Maggie's. She was feeling queasy from the gin and tonics and she sat on the toilet with her eyes closed for a few minutes. Then she combed her hair and put on more mascara, but the makeup only accentuated the circles under her eyes, and made her look paler. She thought she'd never looked so bad in her life. Then she smiled into the mirror because she'd never been forty-three before. She didn't care as long as she had Michael.

Michael.

She stared at her pale, worn reflection and suddenly put it all together; the phone ringing and ringing while she waited at the other end . . . the police . . . Michael.

She was shaking as she opened the door.

The music was still playing and Mary Hughes was coming up the stairs. She didn't look as if she'd just heard something shocking. Kathy made herself walk normally down the stairs and into the dining room. People were lined up near the omelette chefs, giving their orders; the huge coated salmon glowed under the lights; steam rose from the rice, the creamed shrimp. Roast beef waited to be carved. Everything was normal except that Maggie wasn't there. Neither was John. Neither was Bill Friedman. Kathy turned towards the hall again, fighting panic. Down another flight. She heard voices and opened Alice's office door. They were around the desk. Maggie was standing with her back to the door. 'I don't think we should tell Kathy yet,' she said.

'Tell me what?'

Anders stood up and came towards her. No one said anything until he'd put his hands on her shoulders.

'Tell me what?' Kathy was trying to control her voice, but it shook.

'The police just called, Kathy.' He was stalling and she knew it.

'What did they say, John?'

He didn't answer. She dug her nails into his forearm, through the sleeves of his jacket and shirt. He flinched and tried to pull away, but she held on.

'Kathy, please.'

'What did they say?'

Maggie answered because Anders couldn't.

'The twins are dead, Kathy. The police just found them.'

Amazing. They found him while she was listening to Minnie Lasker – dancing with John – talking to Maggie, or Beth, or Al. Had they touched him yet, or was he still as he had died?

'They want me to go . . . to identify . . . it's difficult . . .' Anders said.

'Oh,' said Kathy, 'I don't think so. They never looked alike, not to me.' She turned to Maggie. 'Did you think they looked alike? I didn't . . . nothing alike . . .'

She held on to Anders and started to cry.

Anders breathed through his mouth trying not to think of the smell coating his mouth. Friedman had gotten sick in the hall, and had been sent downstairs to wait with Kathy while Anders was let into 11A. The living room floor was a foot deep in garbage that glowed with the colours of the labels of cans and TV dinners and the shine of aluminium foil and bottles against drab brown paper bags. The old furniture was still there; he remembered it from other times – and the drapes Kathy had had made, grey and greyer print, hanging sodden in the air-conditioned chill, and under everything, the carpet – which he remembered was grey too – squishing under his feet as he picked his way through the debris to follow Detective Mayer down the hall to the bedroom. To his right was Michael's chair, a gift from Kathy. How did he know that? Maybe she'd told him; maybe Michael had. Someone had shit in it a long time ago. Anders looked away, and told himself to keep his eyes on Mayer's back, not to think of what he was stepping in, past the bathroom where he could see bottles in the sink, too many to count as they went by – to the bedroom, where they'd found them.

One of the twins was lying on his side on the bed wearing a pair of boxer shorts, and nothing else. Anders walked around to the side to see his face; but the features were soft, smeared, and the face was starting to bloat. The other one lay next to the bed with one hand on the mattress as if he had been trying to climb up. He was wearing a checked shirt and a pair of wash pants. He might have died an hour ago, a few minutes even, because his face was still clear and fine.

'It is the Rosses?' Mayer asked.

'Yes, it is.'

'Do you know which is which? The doorman thought the one on the floor was Michael, because he was sure he'd seen Michael in those clothes.'

In spite of the smell and garbage, Anders leaned over and looked at the man on the floor.

Filmed eyes stared up at him – Kathy's Michael, his old enemy.

'Yes, I think it's Michael.'

'How old were they?' Mayer asked.

'Forty-three. Can I touch him?'

'What for?' Mayer asked, suspicious.

'Just to close his eyes.'

Mayer nodded, and Anders, lost for a moment in grief he never expected to feel for Michael Ross, forced the corpse's eyelids down. When he straightened up, he saw a wallet in a cleared space on the table next to Michael, and on top of it, a little brass manta ray. It looked as if one of them meant to take the ray and wallet together the next time he left. The figurine was a caricature with crossed eyes that made the fish look bewildered.

'What happened here?' It looked as if he were asking the corpse.

'The autopsy—'

'No, I mean this.' Anders waved his hand to encompass the room.

Mayer shrugged.

Anders looked down at Michael, then again around the room. Ice-cream cartons, empty cake boxes and soft-drink bottles, as if they'd been having a party – a child's party – for months. Anders' skin tingled. Mike and Dave Ross, the twins, together in the middle of all this, eating cake and ice cream, having a party in their underwear. Only the little brass ray didn't fit for some reason. It was shining and clean; a token from some other time.

Mayer touched his arm. 'Dr Benson's waiting to talk to you.'

'Yes, of course.' Anders looked at Michael again; then he followed Mayer out of the bedroom.

Mayer stopped in the hallway. 'Uh – just a question or two before we see Dr Benson?'

Anders nodded.

'We found lots of bottles around,' Mayer said. 'Some labelled Seconal, some labelled Desoxyn. Benson tells me Desoxyn's an upper, and Seconal's a downer. Right?' Anders nodded again.

'Then there's one we can't figure out at all.' Mayer took a bottle out of his pocket. It was empty, and it was labelled Dilantin.

'What would they want this for?' Anders asked.

'We don't know. Neither does Benson. He said it isn't an upper or a downer.'

'No,' Anders said. 'It's an anti-convulsant.'

'A what?'

'For seizures, convulsions, like from fever, or . . . or . . .' He stopped, thought for a minute, then said, 'Or from drug withdrawal.'

'Is either Seconal or Desoxyn the kind of drug you withdraw from?' Mayer asked.

Anders looked at him. 'You're a cop, Mayer. You know what Seconal is. Don't test me.'

Mayer shrugged. 'Gotta "test" everybody. How's Seconal withdrawal?'

'Bad.'

'Bad enough to kill?'

'Sometimes.'

'And it causes convulsions?'

Anders nodded.

'So you'd take Dilantin . . .' Mayer prompted.

'If you'd stopped taking Seconal and didn't want to have convulsions.'

Peter Benson, the chief pathologist for the Medical Examiner's office, was waiting for them in the living room. He stood in the middle of the mess like some kind of greeter, smiling, holding his hands in front of him, and apparently oblivious to the smell because, Anders noticed, he was breathing through his nose.

'Dr Anders, it's a pleasure.'

Anders couldn't believe Benson had said that.

'It is the Ross twins, isn't it?' he asked.

Anders nodded.

'I've heard of them of course. One of them won the Calhoun Award a year or so ago. Right? Let's see that was—' Benson rolled his eyes as he searched his memory.

'Michael,' Anders said.

'Yes,' Benson said pleasantly as if they were sitting in a cool clean restaurant, having a drink together; something tart, a rum and tonic, with lime in it. 'Michael. Of course I never saw the Rosses when they were alive, but the resemblance must have been remarkable.'

Anders didn't answer.

'Absolutely remarkable.'

Even Mayer was getting restless.

'There are resemblances that you don't think about, that you would never see ordinarily,' Benson was saying. 'The shape of their arms, for instance; and the way their finger and toenails grew; the pattern of body hair. Absolutely amazing.'

'I don't see what's so amazing about it,' Anders snapped. 'They were identical twins.'

'Of course. But I've had twins before.' Benson sounded like a teacher talking about students instead of a forensic pathologist talking about autopsy specimens. 'And they're not as identical as you'd imagine. Oh, I know they are in theory, but in life variation is inevitable.'

He sounded as if he'd run down, and Anders turned away, but Benson started talking again. 'It's like a template for a design. Everything that comes out of it should be the same, but never is – not even in dyes, not even in identical twins.'

'Yes . . . yes . . .' Anders thought if he didn't get some fresh air, he was going to faint, and he must have looked it because Benson took his arm.

'Here, are you all right?'

Anders shook his head. 'No, I'm not.'

17

'Quick, quick,' said Benson kindly, and he took Anders' arm and paraded him past Mayer and out the door to the hallway.

Anders collapsed on the bench in front of the elevator, and put his head down until the blood came back to it. Then he looked up at Benson. 'What happened to them?' he asked.

'I don't know. But I don't think it was suicide.'

'Why?'

'The Dilantin. We found an empty bottle. You don't take a full bottle of an anti-convulsant if you mean to overdose on Seconal.'

'But they might have had the Dilantin in reserve in case something went wrong and they couldn't get Seconal. Maybe they took it gradually.'

'No. According to the label it was purchased last Wednesday.'

'When did they die?'

Benson shrugged. 'The one on the floor probably died a few hours ago.'

Michael had been dead a few hours. He was probably still alive when Kathy got to Maggie's. Anders hoped she would never find out.

'I think the one on the bed was dead by the time the Dilantin was bought.'

'But why would Michael buy Dilantin if David was dead? And why would he take a whole bottle of it? And if he did, why didn't it work?'

'And if it worked,' Benson said, 'then what killed him? How-why-how-what. Lots of questions, Doctor.'

'But what do you think?'

'I think it wasn't suicide.'

Beth Friedman helped Anders get Kathy undressed and into bed. He gave Kathy a shot of Librium and stayed with her until she passed out. Then he called her mother, who said she'd get Sam home from camp and down to New York in time for his father's funeral. The next day, they faced the press; he and Gargan and Cross and Maggie Calhoun's PR man. The questions were pretty mild because no one really knew yet what had happened to the twins, or how long it had taken to happen. Anders knew they'd get worse tomorrow.

Afterwards he went back to Kathy's and poured her drinks, and listened to her talk and cry until she was drunk enough to fall asleep, while he sat, then lay down next to her.

Sometimes . . . tonight . . . she was all that mattered to him. He dreamed about giving up the hospital directorship, and telling Maggie Calhoun and Arlene Vale, and S. Gardiner Reese III, to take their money and their hospital, and go to hell, and he'd take Kathy and Sam away, to Maine maybe; buy a practice in Presque Isle or Bangor. Then he shook his head because he hadn't practised for twenty years and even then he'd hated it – the doctor who hated sick people.

He watched Kathy for a while, then he got up and went to call his service. Even with the air-conditioner going full blast it was muggy, and he had, along with the sweats, a feeling of dread that followed him to the phone.

The service told him that Peter Benson had called fifteen minutes ago, and had left a number and message to call back. The message was labelled urgent.

Anders didn't want to call Benson; it was almost one o'clock in the morning and no one called at that hour with good news. He went into the kitchen and poured some vodka over ice, added lime, then made himself a cheese sandwich. He trimmed the bread, smeared mayonnaise on one side, mustard on the other, and even thought about slicing tomato on it . . . slowly . . . to take time because in an hour or so, it would be too late to call Benson back. But he'd finished the sandwich and drink, and it was still only one fifteen. Washing up took him to one twenty. Finally he went back into the living room and sat down on the brown velvet couch and looked out of the glass wall at the sky. He waited until the ship's clock chimed the half hour, then he dialled Benson's number.

'Dr Anders? I'd almost given up.'

'What is it you want, Doctor?'

'We just got the report on the tissue samples we'd sent to Ithaca for tests.'

'What the hell are you talking about?'

'We've been using new toxicological tests when autopsy results aren't clear. As in the case of the Ross twins. We send the tissue to Ithaca, because we don't have the right equipment here, and

19

my assistant just called me with the results.'

'Couldn't it wait until morning?'

'No, it couldn't. I'm afraid the press will have the information by morning, and I wanted you to be able to prepare—'

'Prepare for what?' Anders' hands were freezing.

Anders heard Benson take a breath.

'Michael Ross died of withdrawal. We didn't find a trace of barbiturate in his gut or tissue. Our office will therefore conclude that he died of withdrawal and relative malnutrition.

'But someone injected enough barbiturate into David Ross to kill an elephant.' Benson paused.

'Why "someone"?' Anders asked. 'Couldn't he have done it himself?'

'No, first of all because we didn't find any needle tracks.'

'No needle tracks, no injection,' Anders said.

'Not necessarily, Doctor; David Ross had haemorrhoids.'

'Most men his age do.'

'Yes, quite. The point is that haemorrhoids bleed, and you'd probably never find needle tracks in that kind of friable, sanguineous tissue.'

Benson waited, but Anders didn't say anything, so Benson went on.

'That isn't all, Doctor. David Ross had a lot of barbiturate in his stomach, not enough to kill him, but certainly enough to put him out.

'Which means that someone else injected the drug into the haemorrhoid and that David Ross was asleep when he did it.' Anders held his breath. 'In other words,' Benson said, 'the twin on the floor murdered the twin on the bed.'

Anders hung up without saying goodbye, and went into the bedroom, Kathy was asleep, lying on her back.

He drank his vodka and watched her. 'Michael killed David,' he whispered.

She didn't stir.

It was almost two, the papers would be on the stands by six or seven, the phone would start ringing early, and she was going to need all the rest she could get because tonight would be her last untroubled sleep for a long time.

He took his drink back into the living room; he knew he

should sleep too and he took off his trousers and shirt and lay down on the couch.

Suddenly he sat up, chilled. Seconal wasn't an anaesthetic, and David was only asleep when Michael injected the drug, not unconscious. The pain of the injection must have been excruciating . . . at least sharp enough to wake him up. That meant he would have seen Michael with the empty needle. He would have known what Michael had done. He would have known that he was dying.

Did he plead with Michael to get help? Did he beg Michael to tell him why he'd done it? Or did he already know?

part one

chapter one

'Sadel, *he* can see them now,' Danny's mother said.

Sadel nodded, and took the twins' ice cream away, brushed back their hair and straightened their ties. The other women and children watched.

'The ice cream'll melt,' David said. No one paid any attention to him and the twins were led down the Pereras' long hallway to the old man's room.

As soon as Michael saw Salvatore Perera, he sensed disaster. The old man was leaning over, talking to the twins' father, and he was holding a glass of tea with a napkin wrapped around it. Their father was drinking tea too, nodding and listening. The twins waited. Michael thought of grabbing David and running away, down the hall, and up the stairs to their room where he'd shut the door, and get them both into the bed. They'd pretend they were asleep, until the party was over, until the old man went back to Brooklyn. But the old man wasn't going back to Brooklyn. He was Danny Perera's grandfather, the pride of the family, and he'd come to live with the Pereras for good. He'd be here from now on, right underneath Michael's room, day and night. Michael wanted to hold David's hand, but they were too old; he wanted to cry, but he was too old for that too.

Their father saw them and waved to come over. Then the old man turned, smiling at them, his lips red and wet inside his beard; but when he saw them, the smile stiffened, as Michael knew it would, then died. The twins stopped just a few feet from the old man's chair.

'Come kiss Danny's *zaida*,' their father said. 'He's been look-

22

ing forward to meeting you.' But the old man held up his hand and shook his head, and Michael knew he didn't want them to kiss him.

Everybody in the room knew that something was wrong and they shifted nervously; Sam looked at his sons, then back at the old man, not understanding. Even David didn't seem to know what was happening. Only Michael and the old man understood each other and they stared at each other until a sac closed around the two of them, and Michael felt as if they were the only ones in the room.

The old man's eyes were blue, not watery pale like Danny's and Danny's father's, but bright hard blue . . . cold. Michael began to see things in the old man's eyes; an empty sky stretching across a frozen ocean, the core of a glacier, split and exposed to melt in the sun. The old man inhaled on a long yellow cigarette; smoke came out of his mouth, made a gauze around his beard. 'Twins,' he said softly . . . 'twins.' Michael didn't move. 'Same clothes,' said the old man, 'same face, same house, same everything, right?' He had an accent, but Michael understood every word. 'Same school too, same class, same friends.' No one moved. 'And when you grow up what will you be?'

David answered for them. 'We're going to be doctors.'

The old man waited for Michael to say something, but he didn't. Then the old man asked, 'Will you go to the same college?' David nodded emphatically. 'And to the same medical school?' David nodded again.

The old man smiled, but Michael knew he didn't mean it. 'And when you grow up, will you marry the same woman?' David had started to nod again, but then he stopped, uncertain; the old man went on relentlessly, 'And will you live in the same house and father the same children?' Then in the same tone of voice, still staring at Michael as if David weren't there, the old man said, 'Get away – you must get away from each other. Do you hear me?'

Then he seemed to remember himself and his voice lost some intensity; he said something in Yiddish about sorrow, then back to English. 'In the old country, they say twins are cursed . . . not one person, yet less than two . . . that's what they say. But we believe in escaping curses, don't we?' Michael's eyes filled

23

with tears that spilled onto his cheeks. The old man must have seen the tears and felt sorry for Michael, because he stopped looking at him at last and turned to his father.

'Two such fine boys . . . you want them to grow up to be individuals; husbands, fathers, *menschen* . . . separate them now, as much as possible – or they won't grow up . . .'

Michael watched the crack in the ceiling over his bed. It had been plastered over, painted, but it still came back. He liked watching it. Sometimes it was a bare tree with spindly limbs; sometimes it was a river on a map with tributaries. Tonight it was a road with tiny side roads, and he watched imagining the villages and cities it went through, and where it finally ended – at some border he could cross. His eyes closed and, lulled by the light sound of David breathing in the next bed, he fell asleep.

He dreamed that he was back in the old man's room, except that in his dream the room was full of smoke and he couldn't see anything. He knew David was there, and that he had to find him before the old man got back. He looked everywhere, but he couldn't find David, he called him but there was no answer.

Then he cried for his brother until he heard the door open, and knew the old man was coming into the room, hidden in the smoke. He forced back his sobs until he throat ached, and he waited, terrified, for the old man to touch him. The old man wrapped his arms around Michael with chilling gentleness; his mouth was against the side of Michael's face. Then the smoke cleared, and there was David in the middle of the room bending over to tie his shoe laces as if he couldn't see his brother or the old man.

'No,' Michael gasped, helpless.

'Get away,' the old man said.

'No,' Michael cried again.

'Get away from him,' the old man whispered, pointing at David. 'Get away. You'll die if you don't; he'll kill you if you don't.'

The old man let him go, and Michael wanted to get away from both of them, but it was too late now because he couldn't move. He was afraid the old man was going to say the same things to David, and he tried to warn his brother – only to find that he couldn't talk either. But the old man's message was only for him, because he was gone and Michael was alone with David. David turned at last, saw his brother, and started towards him. Only it wasn't David. This twin was prettier than David, beautiful, with long thick curly eyelashes and wet, red lips. Then he blinked, a clicklike movement of his lids that made him look like a doll.

Michael was frightened that it was happening to him. His own face was getting stiff and he could feel the flush turning his cheeks red like David's; his teeth were wood, splinters that would tear his tongue, and if he didn't get away the same thing would happen to the rest of him. But it already must have, because he was totally paralysed; legs of painted wood, arms too; even his lungs, because he couldn't breathe. Only David could move. He was gliding closer and closer to his paralysed brother, and Michael knew in an instant that the old man was right. As soon as his twin reached him, he would kill him.

Michael woke up crying, covered with sweat. David ran across the space that separated them and got into Michael's bed. He held him close, whispering, asking him what was wrong. When Michael told him about the dream, David didn't say anything. Michael pulled him closer. 'Rock me,' he begged.

David stroked his brother's back, then unbuttoned the shirt of Michael's pyjamas. 'You're all wet,' he said, and he got the shirt off, then took off his own, and wrapped the blanket around both of them. Then, he gently pulled Michael's pyjama trousers down, then his own, so they were bare, lying against each other as David rocked them. He was ready to fall asleep again, but Michael wasn't.

'Don't stop. I'm scared.'

'You want me to get Ma?'

'No. Just stay with me.'

He did, but Michael went on sweating until David was wet too. At last Michael fell asleep, and David held him until he thought it was getting light; then he let himself fall asleep.

Michael had the same dream the next night, and the next. Finally they told their father, and he took Michael on his lap, 'Do you think David would hurt you?' he asked.

Michael shook his head, and Sam noticed that the boy had

dark circles under his eyes, and had lost weight in just the wfe days since the party.

'Of course he wouldn't . . . he loves you . . . Say it . . . it'll make you feel better . . . say, "David wouldn't hurt me".'

'David wouldn't hurt me.'

He hadn't thought David would. He didn't know what he thought or why he'd had the dream. The words helped . . . and before he fell asleep he watched the crack in the ceiling, and said over and over that his brother would never, never hurt him. He didn't have the dream for a week, but then it came back; and he had it again and again after that – every few weeks until the winter they were thirteen, when the old man died.

Sam went to the hospital to help Aaron Perera with the formalities of his father's death, while downstairs, the Perera family prepared for *shiva*. Sam got home in time for dinner. It was Friday – blessed day to die, he'd murmured, and they had *challah* for dinner, soup, and roast chicken. But that was all there was to their Sabbath: the candles were lit without prayers, the bread passed without blessing. Michael couldn't eat. He kept thinking of the old man lying alone in the chapel. He wanted to be happy about it . . . but he had a lump in his throat, and he was afraid he'd cry if they went on talking about the old man. 'Wonderful death,' Sam kept saying. 'The covers weren't even messed up.' Michael had to keep his head down. They'd think he was crazy, crying for the old man. David was watching him. Finally Kelly cleared the table, and clucked over his full plate, but she didn't say anything. Sam went downstairs to fill out a *minyan* for mourning, and Sadel took her coffee into the den to listen to the radio. The twins circled the table, and the radio in the den played 'Somewhere I'll find you.'

'C'mon,' said David. 'Mr Keen's on.'

'I can't.'

David waited.

'I've got to go down there,' Michael said.

'What for? The body's at the chapel.'

'I just want to see . . .' He didn't know what to say . . . to see the room empty, the bed bare, the drapes drawn . . . all traces of the old man erased? Then he'd never have the dream again.

'You really want to?' David asked.

Michael nodded.

'Okay, let's go.'

The Pereras' front door was open; the twins went down the hall past the living room where their father sat with the other men; past the dining room where the women sat, looking livelier than the men, and to the back hall that led to the bedrooms. Michael opened the first door, smelled stale tobacco smoke, and knew that this was the right room.

'Wait here,' he told David and went inside quickly and shut the door after him. It was his nightmare room, everything the same, except that the old man's clothes were folded neatly across the bed waiting to be given away. The closet was empty, except for the old man's shoes, which custom said had to be destroyed because no one was supposed to walk in the dead man's shoes. The old man's *talis* and prayer book waited on his dresser. His underwear and handkerchiefs and shirts filled the dresser drawers. Michael looked at everything, touched everything, but he didn't move any of it, until, on the table next to the old man's bed, he found a gold cigarette case engraved with the initials SMP – Salvatore M. Perera. Michael held the case in his hand, rubbed his thumb across the gold, and was about to put it back on the table when the door to the room opened and he saw his father silhouetted against the light from the hall.

'Michael? Mike, are you in there?' Without thinking, Michael put the cigarette case in his pocket, just as his father found the wall switch and turned on the bright overhead light.

'Michael, for Christ's sake! Michael, you're thirteen years old.' Sam fell back on Michael's age, because he didn't know what else to say. 'You're thirteen; you're five feet five. I love you. I love your brother. Don't be afraid.'

Michael waited. His mother sat across the table watching.

'That's four years since it happened, Mikey, and it still bothers you enough to make you sneak downstairs like a thief. Why?'

Michael didn't answer.

'It never bothered David. Why should it bother you?'

Another unanswerable question. Why could David swim so well, play touchball, make friends, get girls to laugh, and he couldn't? They could start a list of things David could do that he couldn't and not be finished by morning. David was watching him and he looked away. He knew how much David hated the comparisons. David expected them to be alike in every way. 'One egg,' their father had said when they were young. 'One sperm – identical chains of chromosomes. Wonderful!' And he'd hug them, one with each arm, so they were mashed against each other, and he'd kiss them, and hold them until they would start to squirm.

'David never thought it was a curse,' Sam said.

'I know.'

'David never dreamed about it.'

'I know.' Sam rocked a little, watching his son. 'Remember, Michael, he was an old man, from Poland.'

'Danny said they're Spanish,' Michael reminded his father.

'Maybe in the fifteenth century they were,' Sam said, 'but in this incarnation, Salvatore Perera was Polish. The point is that he couldn't even read English. So what are we talking about? What are you letting drive you crazy all these years . . . an ignorant old man's careless talk? That's all it was. Try to remember the way it really was.'

Michael tried. They'd told him often enough. The old man was wearing grey, not black as Michael thought. His beard was soft and white – angel hair, David called it – not grizzled as it was in Michael's memory. And the room hadn't been full of smoke.

Then Sam said, 'Do you remember what the old man said?'

Michael didn't answer because he knew what they'd told him, and what he remembered, and they were different.

Sam said, 'He told you that if you and your brother weren't separated you wouldn't grow into mature men. He didn't say that David would hurt you. David's your brother, your twin! Of course he'd never hurt you.'

No answer.

'Well, would he? Would David hurt you?'

'No.' The old formula.

'If you believe that, then why does it still bother you? Why did you go down there?'

'Because I thought if I went down there, if I saw the room . . . I . . .'

28

'You what?'

They all waited, his mother, his father, and David; even Kelly stood at the sideboard waiting to see what he'd say.

'I don't know. I thought I'd feel better.'

He was clutching the cigarette case so hard, he was afraid he would bend it, and he made himself take his hand out of his pocket.

'And do you?' his father asked.

'Yes,' he lied, 'much better.'

He hid the cigarette case in his junk drawer, all the way in the back where he thought no one would find it, then he got into bed and was looking intently at the crack in the ceiling when David came back in the room from the bathroom. Michael closed his eyes. David watched him for a while, then pulled back the covers and got into his brother's bed.

'Don't . . . let me alone.' Michael got as far away from him as he could, but the bed was too narrow, and when he tried to get up, David held on, laughing, and pulled him back. David poked his ribs, while Michael fought, starting to laugh too; David ran his fingers over his brother's belly until Michael doubled up laughing and yelling and fell across David's body. Sam pounded on the wall and yelled at them to shut up. Quietly now they heaved and fought on the bed. Michael tried to break free and David held on . . . never hurting, but always shifting his grip to keep his hold. Finally Michael collapsed next to David, and threw his arms around his brother, wondering what it was like for people who weren't twins, who were alone at night in their beds. The brothers were quiet and Michael could hear a truck rumble past on the highway, heading upstate with the driver alone in the lit cab, driving all night on the dark roads. Michael relaxed, and his breathing slowed to normal; David untied his brother's pyjamas and reached inside. Michael giggled and pulled away, but David reached again. 'Don't,' Michael whispered.

'Why not? You usually like it.'

'Not tonight.' He didn't know what else to say, not with the old man just dead, because this must have been part of what he meant. But David had gone too far. Michael was too excited to stop him, and when David guided Michael's hand inside his pyjamas, Michael stroked David the way he wanted him to.

Afterwards, David watched Michael sleep. He didn't really want to touch him again and was a little ashamed of what they'd done. But he couldn't help himself and he leaned over, careful not to put his weight on Michael, and kissed his brother's neck. Michael turned his head, but he didn't wake up.

chapter two

David watched Don Santore's arms slicing the water. The drops caught the sun, and blinded David. He closed his eyes and forced himself to breathe slowly, to keep his arms moving easily. Santore was giving it everything, and they still had a quarter of a mile to go. David looked again, the other boy was already starting to slow down. On shore Michael and Arnie were two blurs against the fir trees. Other swimmers splashed, but they were behind him and losing distance. Only Santore was left, and he wouldn't be for long. David came up for air; then down again, eyes open. So clear he could see the bottom; up, the sky, sun and trees . . . and Michael.

Easy, easy . . . he was abreast of Santore who kept splashing, arms working madly, but losing ground anyway. Easy! David slid ahead. He could hear yelling on shore. His father and mother, and Michael. He kept going until he couldn't even hear the other boy splashing. He was all alone on the lake. He ducked his head and couldn't hear the crowd. Another few yards. Michael was waiting.

'He's pretty good,' Arnie said.

Michael didn't answer. David was going to win again. David was first in their graduating class; he won the National Scholastic Essay Contest; he won the chess tournament; and the best-looking girl in school told everybody she was in love with him. The Rosses were at the lake because David just won the Toque Premed Scholarship, which would pay his college tuition, and their father rented a cabin right next to the Kleins at Kiamesha Lake in the Catskills to celebrate. Now he was going to win the swimming race. Michael squinted into the sun and watched his brother's arms pumping against the water. David was getting closer, another few feet ... to his right, his mother was jumping up and down, waving her hands, yelling for David. His father was blushing, looking around to see if the other men were watching his son. Michael held the towel. 'C'mon, Davey!' he yelled with the others, but for Arnie's benefit. He was really thinking about the water itself, and about the woods around it. They walked in them yesterday, and the woods were so quiet he found himself stopping and making David stop every few feet to listen.

The yells peaked. Michael could hear his father's voice. David stood up, waved, and waded towards him, and Michael started to wave like the others and smile.

He wrapped David in the towel, rubbed him, helped him dry his hair. His skin was chilled and smooth.

'You feel like a goddamn fish.'

'Smooooth,' said David, 'How'd I look?'

'You looked okay,' he said, looking past David to the woods.

David and Arnie both called Michael, but he didn't answer.

They stood at the edge of the woods, trying to see into the trees, and calling his name. He knew he should call back, but he didn't. They came a little closer. If he moved, they'd hear him; if he didn't, they'd see him in a second. He was ready to give up and come out when the wind started to blow and the tree branches made enough noise to cover the sound of his footsteps. Without knowing he was going to do it, he started running – not towards David and Arnie, but deeper into the woods. He stopped when the wind died, and listened.

'Michael . . . Michael . . .' came through the trees. David sounded desperate and Michael knew he should go back. But the minute the wind started up again, he ran again, away from the road and his brother, on and on. Even when the wind died and the forest was quiet, he kept running because he knew by instinct that he was too far away for them to hear him. He kept on until the path ended in a sandy patch at the edge of the lake.

He was in a cove. What he could see of the far shore was empty. A bird with long spindly legs stood in a patch of reeds near the beach and watched him.

'Hello bird.' It didn't move.

He looked up, then back into the trees, then across the lake. There was no one else around. He spread his arms and started circling with his head back, faster and faster until he got dizzy and fell on the sand. He rolled over on his back and started pulling his clothes off. When he was naked, he let the breeze from the lake dry the sweat on his body. Then the breeze died, and he lay still in the heat, sweating again. He wondered if he'd ever been alone before, and then thought he probably hadn't. Something about the quiet and solitude of the moment gave him an unexpected physical pleasure, and he reached down and touched his penis gently, then more firmly, stroking himself, arching his back to feel the light tickle of sand, thinking about David, about being alone, and finally about the girl Arnie had promised to get for them. Michael hoped she was like the waitress in the resort dining room who had heavy breasts and a round belly. He came in slow heavy spurts, his heart pounding so hard he thought for a minute that he would faint.

Then he grinned to himself as he started to fall asleep, thinking how he would look to someone who came upon him unawares – lying naked in the sun, sweating, and with a pool of semen drying on his belly. When he woke up, he went into the lake, swam, washed himself off, waded to the edge of the cove, then hid in the reeds and looked across the lake. He could see the cabins they were staying in, but the lawn was empty, and he realized that even though it was still light, it was getting late. The pine trees that rimmed the lake cast shadows, and the lights were on in the big dining room. He hunched down in the reeds so no one could see him, and he watched the far shore, feeling the water against his skin. David came out of the main house, ran across the lawn out onto the pier, and looked across the lake, right at the clump of reeds Michael was hiding in. Michael thought his brother knew he was there, even though he knew David couldn't see him.

'Michael . . . Mike . . .' David called. Not loudly, but his voice carried eerily across the smooth surface of the lake. It frightened the little bird, and it tucked back its legs and flew off over the trees. Michael didn't move.

'Miiiichael,' David cried.

Michael stood up wearily and started wading towards his brother. He swam, and waded again, until David couldn't wait any more and he jumped into the water, clothes and all, and waded out to meet Michael, reached him, hugged him. 'You're freezing,' David said, trying to warm his brother's body with his own. 'Where are your clothes for God's sake?'

'Back there.'

People came out of the main lodge, and David took off his shirt and tied it around Michael's waist to cover him.

The girl Arnie found for them wanted five dollars. She seemed a little frightened of the twins and she wanted Arnie to go first. But Arnie said he wasn't ready. 'You do it, Mike . . . go ahead.' David shoved Michael forward and he stood in front of the girl. There was a breeze that moulded her slip against her breasts and thighs and she looked very pale, a little unearthly in the moonlight. Arnie said she looked clean and kind of grey. But she was pale blonde, and much prettier than Michael had expected.

'Would you take off your slip?'

'Too cold. I ain't wearing nothing underneath. Besides what if someone comes along?' Michael wilted slightly at the thought and looked around. She stood still and he finally walked up to her and put his arms around her and kissed her. He felt her breasts and down between her legs, but he didn't know what to do next. She started to laugh, which jiggled her breasts and belly, and he held her tighter.

'You're just a bunch of little babies, ain't you?' Michael thought she was about seventeen, and they were sixteen. Not so much younger. But he had to wait until she took his hand and guided it under her slip while she grinned up at him in the moonlight.

'Now lie down.' His touch excited her and he knew she liked him.

David watched his brother's face change with what she did to him. He watched her uncover Michael's body, watched her hands sliding on him. Michael's head moved from side to side.

'Please,' he begged while David watched. 'Oh, please now—'
But she waited, grinning at him.

'Now?' She asked laughing. David watched in a trance.

Michael begged again, 'Please – please – please—' She lay back in the grass and pulled up her slip.

At first, David wanted to look away, but he couldn't. Hurry, he thought. Jesus, Michael, hurry, because I can't wait another second.

Then Michael finished, and rolled away; but Arnie's eyes were a little mad too, and he started for her. David shoved him away so hard Arnie fell. David wanted her right after Michael, and he knelt between Junie's legs, while Michael lay next to them in the grass in the moonlight watching what she was doing to his brother.

David pushed her back and forced her legs open. 'I don't want to hurt you,' he said. She laughed and sounded as crazy as he felt. David turned his head to the side so he could see Michael whose eyes looked huge in the dark and whose head was backlit by the moon.

They laughed like kids all the way back to Kiamesha. They stopped at a place called Jim's just outside of town and got some beer to drink in the back of Arnie's car; then drunk, crazy, hugging each other, the twins left Arnie alone, ran across the lawn together dancing and shouting and collapsed on the cabin steps. David raised the beer bottle and toasted his brother.

'Because you did it. Oh, God. Michael Ross, King of Kiamesha.'

'Amazing.'

'Amazing,' David agreed.

Michael was so tired he could barely stay awake long enough to wash and get into bed. He shut his eyes, ready to slide under the covers, his feet turned out, his legs too, relaxed against the mattress.

Then he thought of David on top of Junie right after he had finished – at the moment when he felt most tender and wanted to hold her close to him, there was David, looking crazy, and Junie laughing as David pushed her back. Michael squeezed his eyes shut to get rid of the picture, but as soon as it dissolved, for the first time in years he saw the old man, leaning towards their father, holding a glass of tea, talking and nodding, all the time looking at Michael. Only now the old man didn't look frightening. He had a worried frown on his face as if he were sorry about what he had to say, but he was going to say it anyway because he cared so much.

As soon as they got back to New York, Michael went right to his desk and opened the drawer. The junk was still there. He hadn't added or taken away anything since the old man died, but the cigarette case was gone. He pulled the drawer all the way out, and moved everything around, but it wasn't there. He knew that David had taken it, and that if he confronted him, he would tell the truth: *Sure, Mikey, I took it. I hated him for frightening you like that. It bothered me thinking about its being there, as if you still believed your dream – oh, I threw it in the river. Maybe it'll wash up on some beach in Portugal. Or maybe a fish swallowed it, and it'll end up on somebody's dinner plate.*

chapter three

Sam sat alone in the kitchen, while everyone was still asleep, drinking his coffee from a glass, which Sadel never let him do at the dinner table; and reading the Jewish paper, which Sadel didn't like to have around.

Michael cornered him there while David was still asleep.

'I want to talk to you, Dad.'

Sam reluctantly put down the paper. 'So talk.'

'It's about medical school . . .' Michael stopped and Sam drank his coffee and waited.

Sam looked closely at his son.

They'd both made CCNY dean's list four years in a row, but it had taken more out of Michael; he looked tired. Sam pushed the glass of coffee towards his son, and Michael took a sip. 'You want some toast?' Sam asked.

Michael nodded, and Sam made the toast, while Michael talked haltingly.

'So,' Sam said, 'which is it? You're not sure you want to be a doctor, or you're not sure which medical school you want to go to?'

Michael laughed and shook his head. 'I'm not even sure what I'm not sure about.'

'Terrific, but something, right? Something sticks?'

Michael nodded, chewing his toast.

'Okay. Then let's take one thing at a time. What's wrong with medicine?'

'Nothing I can tell you about.'

'Doctors make big money,' Sam said.

'Some don't.'

'That's because they're schmucks.'

'How do you know I'm not a schmuck too.'

Sam laughed, 'I don't know. In fact I think you are, just like me. But your brother isn't. He'll look out for both of you, and you'll do terrific. Besides, what'll you do instead, Mikey?'

Michael wondered what his father would say if he told him he wanted to be a truck driver, to drive the new diesels and refrigerator trucks until his arms bulged and his eyes had a permanent squint from looking into the sun or into the headlights of on-coming cars.

'Maybe I don't have to go to State?' Michael asked.

'Where would you go instead?'

'NYU. Columbia.'

Sam shook his head. 'I can't afford it,' he said.

'But I could stay at home if I went there. You'd save my living expenses.'

'You'll stay with your Uncle Yast if you go to State, and I'll still save your living expenses.'

'What if I got a scholarship?'

'If you get a scholarship, I'll be very proud. But I think you know it's not easy.'

Michael finished his toast and coffee while his father watched him, then Sam asked, 'What about your brother?'

'He's happy with State.'

'Would he be happy with it if you weren't there?'

'I don't know.'

'Then you haven't talked to him about it yet?'

'No.'

Sam realized then that Michael was trying to get away from David. He didn't think Michael even knew that was what he was doing; but he was. Sam drank his coffee, his eyes narrowed against the steam. This one was the quiet one, the morose one. Yet it was David Sam felt sorry for, suddenly very sorry. He thought of Arnie's wedding – parents and grandparents, and the twins all at one table, all having a good time, until Michael saw Arnie's cousin Ida, a bleached blonde with brown eyes, curly hair and fat little ass. And Michael had to dance with her.

One dance, two dances – David kept watching. Michael was close to her all right, and if Sam had been her father he wouldn't have liked it; but they were young, and a little hot, so what? It was David's reaction that bothered Sam. David was jealous; not the mean kind, but painful jealousy, and sure enough, when Michael laughed and rubbed his cheek against Ida's, Sam saw David blink, and grimace as if the pain were physical. Sam took pity on him.

'Go cut in,' he'd said. 'I don't like the expression on that girl's father's face.'

What would happen to David alone at State? Four years without Michael. He wanted to ask Michael to wait, just let Davey get through the first couple of years, then Michael could go his own way.

Sam looked at his too thin, handsome son. No, it was too much to ask. He couldn't sacrifice Michael to David. Old Perera had been right about that much. Sam said, 'Don't do any of it unless you want to, Michael. Be a janitor if that's what suits you, no matter what I say, no matter what your brother says. You understand me?'

Michael nodded.

'It's January,' Sam said. 'If you're going to apply for a scholarship, you'd better do it.'

Michael nodded again, and left his father alone in the kitchen.

Michael left the building on York with his application and walked past the hospital wings and annexes to the river. It was still snowing and he went to the library to get out of the cold. He needed two references at least, the woman had told him when she'd given him the application and list of scholarships. No, she'd told him, he couldn't pick the award he thought he wanted. Just fill in the application, get the references, and have his adviser call Dr Walters; and they would nominate him for the awards they thought would be best. He sat down at one of the reading tables, his feet in a puddle from his boots. One of them must have a hole in it because his sock was soaked. It was dry in the reading room and the register blew hot air practically in his face. He wiggled his toes to get his feet warm, and looked at the application. She'd given him two. 'In case you mess one up,' she'd told him. Which he would almost certainly do, considering how long and complex the questions were. There was a whole page just for his father to fill out.

He had to get references and he thought Sokolow would give him one; Sokolow taught physiology which Michael liked. Michael called him.

'Sure Ross – No, you can't get all the way here by subway. Take the Lexington to Eighty-sixth.' He did, and then walked through the snow to East End, thinking that now there was a hole in the other boot too. He was soaked by the time he got to the building where Sokolow lived with his wife and infant son. They didn't have much furniture, and the place was dirty . . . slip covers torn, bare floors dusty, books piled everywhere. The kid crawled on the floor playing with an onion, while the wife, who was tall, big-boned, blonde and handsome, stared at Michael – at his face, his hair, his neck and on down his body, to the damp trousers that stuck to his legs. A few times, he was sure she was looking at his crotch, so he crossed his legs, trying to concentrate on Sokolow who was drinking coffee, apparently oblivious of his surroundings and of the way his wife stared at their guest.

'It isn't up to me to say, Ross. But I think Cornell's the best in the country, maybe the world. Harvard's for the WASPishkeit – no heart. To learn the heart of medicine you need New York, not Boston, not Chicago. But a scholarship? That's rough.' Sokolow talked while his wife stared. Michael uncrossed his legs; her eyes fastened on his fly, and he started to sweat, until, between the melting snow, and sweat, he was wet through. Even his T-shirt was wet. Sokolow kept talking and the kid threw the onion and it hit the wall with a liquid thunk. Onion smell filled the air, and Michael started to shiver.

'Hey, Ross, are you okay?'

'Sure, sure. Fine.' The room was stifling and Michael looked at his watch desperately. 'I've got a class . . .'

Sokolow didn't seem to have heard him.

'Of course it's much easier, if you're going to specialize and know in what. Everybody's ready to give money to specialists.'

Sokolow sounded bitter, and Michael almost asked him what was wrong with specialists. Then he realized that that was the question Sokolow was waiting for, and if he asked it, he would be there until nightfall. So he said, 'I've been sort of thinking about gynaecology.'

Had he? He liked women, he had a good touch with them, and with David to do the talking, and him to do the touching – he shook his head because he was thinking like it was all over, like he'd gone to State with David, specialized with David, set up practice with David, and somehow, everything in between had already happened . . . a billion decisions he couldn't remember having made.

He stood up, 'At least that's what I've been thinking.'

Sokolow stood up too. 'Well, it ups your chances of support, and in the end, you can do whatever you really want anyway. Who can stop you?'

No one.

'So, I'll say that, gynaecologically, you're a real whiz' – Sokolow grinned – 'which I understand isn't far from the truth anyway.' The wife grinned too.

Michael wanted to tuck his shirt in, but he didn't want her to see him do it; he didn't even want to ask her where the bathroom was, although he had to go; his hair was still so wet, and he would have liked to dry it. But he didn't want to use their towels. He even felt stupidly bad about leaving that page of his application here, as if it would be sullied by staying in their house.

'Don't worry, Ross. I'll give you a copy of what I write, so you can get a little conceited.'

Michael shook hands, said thank you, and got to the door.

'Take the Eighty-sixth Street crosstown,' Sokolow told him. 'Right on the corner.'

Michael waited for half an hour, but the bus didn't come. *It was stuck in the snow somewhere, its wheels spinning helplessly, until the wind blew too hard, and it tilted slowly over on its side, like a dying animal.* He shook his head to clear it, and realized that inside his wet clothes, his skin felt hot and tender. He touched his forehead; it was hot; his feet were soaked and freezing and there wasn't a taxi in sight. He started walking. It was after three by the time he got to the park, and he realized that he hadn't been really dry since early morning. Halfway into the park, he knew he was sick. His head felt cottony, and the touch of his clothes hurt his skin. He also knew that, if he stopped, he would have the shakes so badly he'd be lucky to be able to walk. He grinned. Orange juice, chicken soup, and no Sandy Gordon or Sandy Gordon's roommate; no switching, not tonight. Wonderful, because he didn't even like Sandy Gordon; he didn't even *know* Sandy Gordon or any of them. The only one he knew was David. Now David could have them both . . . slick, smooth, sweet things . . . why didn't they ever clear the paths in this park? He was up to his ankles in snow all the way across the park. Poor Sokolow. Michael wanted to lean against the lamp-post because his neck and legs hurt, but he didn't dare stop.

David was waiting for him, as if he knew just when he would arrive. Michael leaned on the iron railing that bordered the raised foyer.

'What the hell happened to you?'

Michael grinned and went down on one knee because, as the warmth of the room touched him, he started shaking so badly he couldn't stand. 'I got lost in the snow,' he said.

David was running to him, across the room and up the steps. Now his arms were around him, lifting. 'Mike . . . Mike . . .' His voice far away. If Michael hadn't felt so lousy physically, he'd have felt guilty – like an adulterer. But it wasn't consummated. Not yet, he thought, David, I haven't cheated yet.

When their mother came in from the kitchen, she put both hands to her cheeks. 'What happened to him?' In Yiddish.

'What's he been doing? What's wrong?' More guilt; a fever of guilt. He smiled at David, 'Just investigating,' he said softly. *To see if I could get away from you,* he thought. 'Looking at my options . . . a little foreplay . . .' Then he closed his eyes and refused to open them again, no matter what anyone said.

He had pneumonia. Why didn't David? David wasn't a schmuck, David didn't get pneumonia. They gave him aureomycin, which made him even sicker, and every time he opened his eyes – which he did as little as possible – David was there. David in a sweater. David in a shirt and tie. David in his pyjamas. One night – he knew it was night because the little lamp shaped like a pig was on, the only light in the room – he could see David's shadow against the wall, a long, black line.

His fever and the winter seemed to break finally on the same day.

'A warm day in February,' David said. 'Can you stand the light?' Michael nodded and David pulled up the shade.

David coached him and he took the make-ups in March. He would have to finish in summer school instead of in June with the rest of his class, but he would graduate in time to start medical school in September. The weather stayed sunny, and one unusually warm day towards the end of February, he took a long walk in the park. When he got home there was a letter waiting for him from the Dean of Admissions of Cornell Medical School saying that they had received a letter of reference from Abraham Sokolow, PhD, of CCNY, but had no record of any application from Michael P. Ross. Would he please advise.

Please advise.

He sat on the foyer steps watching the pattern of sun on the rug in the living room. He didn't know what had happened to the application; it was probably still in his winter coat. He went to the closet and looked in the pockets, but it wasn't there. Then he looked in his dresser, in his briefcase, even in his old desk drawer. It wasn't there. He kept telling himself that it didn't matter, that he was weeks too late to apply even for admission, much less for a scholarship. But he went back to the coat, and this time he turned out the pockets. They were empty; not even a gum wrapper or a piece of Kleenex.

part two

chapter four

They were way downtown somewhere: East Broadway – Chrystie Street – Essex Street? Where else did they have baths like this any more? Michael was half naked, and David was helping him take the rest of his clothes off.

'Where are we?' Michael groaned.

'Does it matter?'

'I'm pissed.'

'If you mean you're drunk, that's true.'

'I mean I'm angry!'

'At whom?'

Michael wasn't sure. The room, the white metal lockers, white tile walls, white tile floor, shifted smoothly one way, then another. He tried to grab David, to shake him and tell him how angry he was; but David had oil on his skin and Michael's hands kept slipping. Then he was naked, and David wrapped a towel around his waist, and took his hand.

'C'mon, Mike. It'll help.'

'I told you I'm mad.'

David led him, and Michael followed.

He was sure that if they stopped for a second he would be able to remember who had made him so angry, but they kept going; tiled walls slipped past.

'Listen, David, I didn't want to do it.'

David laughed. 'You could've fooled me; could've fooled the girls too. You sure looked like you wanted to do it.' A white door opened in front of them, and the steam folded over him, clogged his nose and mouth. He couldn't breathe; he'd die in here. He tried to tell David, but David pulled him down onto a bench that was so hot he was sure it burned all the skin off his ass right through the towel. Then David pushed him back gently until he was half lying on the bench, and lifted his feet up.

'I'll be right back,' David said.

David was leaving and they hadn't discussed how angry Michael was. He started to call him when he heard someone laugh and he realized that he wasn't alone, that he didn't know who or what was hidden in the steam. He lay back on his bench, trying to see into the mist, but he couldn't and he closed his eyes.

When he came to, David was pulling him to his feet.

'I'm still pissed,' Michael said.

'Me too because I can't carry you, so walk for Christ's sake!'

'I can't go on like this . . .' which was such a ridiculous thing to say, they both laughed.

'Please, can't we stop, David? Please let's talk about it?' Michael asked.

'About what?' David put his arm around his brother, supporting him, gently, solidly.

Michael tried to think of what they had to talk about. 'The girls,' he said. That wasn't it, but it was a start. A big man wearing nothing but a towel and a *yarmulke* walked by, and the twins giggled.

'What about the girls?' David said. He started pulling Michael again.

'I don't like it.'

David stared at him.

'I'm all fucked out,' Michael said.

'You should be.' David led. They were moving again, and Michael couldn't talk any more. He hadn't said it, whatever it was, and it seemed to lodge in his chest like bad food that wouldn't go down or come up.

They went through another door where a short muscular man waited next to a table. David brought Michael to him, like an offering, and they got Michael onto the table under a round yellow light. The eye of the god, Michael thought, watching them cut out his heart. David's hands were on his legs, straightening them; then he wasn't touching him anywhere and Michael couldn't see him. He was alone with Muscles.

Maybe *he'd* listen. 'We've been doing it too long; that's it.' He finally had it, and David wasn't there to hear. 'Too long and always the same. Always the same girl for both of us. Listen.' The masseur's hands were locked together, covered with cream, and coming down under the god's eye, right in the centre of Michael's chest.

'I need one of my own,' Michael said.

'Sure you do,' said the masseur. 'Everybody does.'

The hands touched him, palms down; then they spread, slid and rubbed. Michael closed his eyes, laughing because he was sure it was going to tickle, but it didn't; and as the masseur touched places no one had ever touched before, Michael felt a relief so profound he thought he'd pass out.

Then he was turned over so that his arms dangled from the table. He could tell this man everything. He could tell him how tired he was, how much the past four years had taken out of him. Don't send your kid to medical school. It's shit. It'll kill him.

He woke up in his own bed, terribly thirsty and with a headache. David brought him tomato juice, and aspirin, and supported his shoulders while he drank.

It was the sixth month of their residency, and Michael was due on duty by ten. David helped him up, made coffee, gave him more juice and aspirin, and he felt a little better by the time he got to the hospital. Friedman saw him in the lobby and shook his head.

'You're on maternity?'

Michael nodded miserably, and Friedman laughed, careful not to do it too loudly. 'You'll do okay, Mike. The babies don't give a shit; the women are busy with the babies; and the only really sick woman on that floor doesn't know her own name much less whether or not the resident has a hangover.'

He meant Michael's prize patient – a pregnant junkie who was a couple of days away from labour, and mumbled blindly at the walls and ceiling, then screamed until they gave her a shot. Friedman called her the cucumber because of her pallor. She had no other name, no ID, no visitors. When she was calm, Michael kind of liked her, and she liked him.

'Hey, darlin',' she said when she saw him, 'you look like she she got the best of it.'

'She did.' Michael smiled.

'Ain't got none left for me?'

'Not a drop.'

'You know I could do you real nice for fifteen bucks.'

'I don't have fifteen bucks.'

'Fifteen wouldn't help me anyway,' she said sadly and Michael wondered if anything would help her.

He examined her as gently as he could, but she wiggled, and teased him, and once or twice he was afraid he would hurt her.

James Romer, chairman of OBGYN, was waiting in the hall.

'How's she doing?'

'Two fingers,' Michael said. 'I think it'll be tomorrow. But maybe tonight.'

'Foetal heartbeat?'

'Strong.'

'Which one are you?'

'Michael.'

'You look like shit, Michael.'

Michael didn't know what to say.

Romer sighed. 'Go take a nap. I'll tell Sheila to page you in the lounge if she needs you.'

It was snowing. Perfect sleeping weather his father used to say. Sam had died over a year ago; quietly in his sleep, and the doctor said it was a freak, that he should have lived another fifteen years.

Michael half sat, half lay in the chair, and closed his eyes.

His father would have known the questions to ask. 'If you're mad, it's at someone, Mike. Who? Who're you mad at?'

His last thought before he fell asleep was that it had to be David, and he was sure he'd remember why when he woke up. But when he did, there was a woman standing next to the chair, looking down at him. At first he was confused, thought it was Junie because she had blue eyes and pale eyelashes. But she was a stranger. He tried to sit up, but his head pounded.

'I'm sorry,' she said. 'I didn't mean to startle you.'

She went on staring at him. She didn't smile or move, and he couldn't think of anything to say. He wondered how long they'd be there before someone came in to take her away and make him go back to work. Someone was coming now – John Anders, the chief resident. Michael shook his head to clear it and the pounding receded as Anders came into the lounge, right up to her, as if he knew her.

'It's all right, darling,' Anders said. 'Nothing important. We can go now.'

Darling? Michael saw the delicate almost washed-out look she had; she was just Anders' sort. She'd stay crisp in the summer, never sweat and turn pink after five minutes in the sun.

Anders saw him, then saw the way she was looking at him. 'Kathy?'

Michael wondered if she'd gone to Groton too, or if that was only for boys. He giggled, and she laughed with him as if she knew what he was thinking. Anders was left out; he knew it, and he didn't like it.

'Hello, Ross.' He sounded very cold, and Michael knew he should struggle to sit up, nod politely and call him Dr Anders. She was watching. He'd never made love to a woman who looked like that. He thought how smooth her skin would be, cool and powdery. Her fingers were long and thin, and her hair was thick, dark blonde. Michael went on staring at her, as if Anders wasn't there.

'What's your name?' she asked.

'Aren't you going to tell the lady your name?' Anders sounded nasty, and Michael felt like a child who deserved to be reprimanded.

'Michael Ross,' he said obediently.

Anders took her arm, and started to lead her away. Michael finally sat up. 'What's your name?' he asked.

'Kathy Field.' She was embarrassed, and laughing at the same time, and he wondered if she'd tell him her phone number in front of Anders; maybe call it to him from down the hall near the elevators while everyone watched.

At the door, she turned and smiled at him, then she followed Anders out of the lounge and down the hall.

Michael expected to forget her.

He went back to see the cucumber; he had lunch with

Friedman, called his mother, then David. But he kept finding reasons to pass the lounge, and every time he did, he looked to see if maybe she'd come back and was waiting for him next to the moulded plastic chair he'd slept in.

He didn't know why he kept thinking about her. She wasn't his type at all. He went into the lounge and got a cup of coffee from the machine.

Finally he looked in the phone book. There were three K. Fields; he called them all. One was a man, one was a dry cleaner, and one didn't answer. He looked at that address – two West Sixty-seventh Street. Good address. Miss Field had money.

He called her twice during their once-a-week Chinese dinner. She was probably still with Anders, somewhere in the city. He kept watching the door as if he expected to see them walk in. But this wasn't Anders' territory – too far uptown. *Anders was with her in the sixties somewhere – at the Carlton, Carlisle, Westbury, Pierre. They were dancing and drinking champagne cocktails, while she laughed at the little sugar cube, at the bubbles, at Anders' club tie, at his tight little ass. Once more around the floor, Anders was saying, then we'll go someplace quiet, just the two of us.* The waiter took Michael's full plate away.

'Anything wrong, Mike?' David was looking too closely.

Michael shook his head. 'Still thinking about the *shiksa* in the lounge? Anders' girlfriend could mean trouble for us, Michael. Maybe you oughta forget this one.'

'I'm not going to forget her. I'm going to see her again.'

David raised his hands in surrender. 'You want to see her, we'll see her.' Then he grinned, and almost asked Michael what he thought would be the best way to get her into bed with them. But he didn't, and late that night, David woke up and saw Michael standing at the bedroom window, looking out at the little court with its straggling tree. David decided he didn't like Miss Field and the effect she was having on his brother.

'You actually saw one of them?' Susan Kramer grabbed Kathy's arm and steered her away from the others. 'What was he like?'

'What do you mean one of them?' Kathy asked, tolerating the other woman's grip because she wanted information.

'They're identical twins,' Susan whispered, and Kathy started to laugh. Susan let her go.

'What's so funny?'

'It's hard to imagine two men looking like that.'

'Good, huh?'

Anders had been watching them, and he started across the lobby, wondering what Susan said to make Kathy laugh. Susan told him, 'We were just talking about the famous Ross twins.'

Anders looked sour. 'Their fame is not all medical.'

'No?' asked Kathy. 'For what then are they famous?'

Susan smirked, and before Anders could interrupt, she said, 'For fucking, my dear. Everybody and anybody.'

The curtain bell rang and they had to go back inside.

Afterwards they went to the Colony, and Kathy drank too much, trying to forget the face of the man in the lounge. But as soon as Susan got up to go to the toilet, Kathy followed.

'How do you know that about them?'

'About the fucking?' She laughed, but her eyes were sharp, watching Kathy in the mirror. 'You must have been impressed.'

Kathy asked again, 'How do you know?'

'From the nurses, my dear. Who talk as much as they fuck – which is saying something.' Then she turned to face Kathy. Her husband was Nathaniel Day Kramer, as New England as Kathy was, family as good as hers, better than Anders'. But he was a short, thin, unpleasant man who never trimmed the hair in his nose or ears, and had never, in the six months that Kathy had known the Kramers, caressed his wife or expressed any affection for her in public. Maybe he did in private, but Kathy was sure Susan would be just as happy if he never touched her. Someday she'd ask Susan why she married him. Then she thought she wouldn't because at this minute, and probably for a long time to come, she couldn't care about anything except Michael Ross.

'Why all the interest in the Ross twins, Kathy?'

'I'm not sure.'

'Which one did you see?' Susan asked.

'Michael.'

'Okay, okay. What was he like?'

Kathy wondered how much she could tell this woman. She wanted to tell someone, because she'd never felt like this before.

48

She wanted to tell Susan that he was like a mosaic angel in a church in Istanbul. 'Middle Eastern,' she wanted to say, 'except for the fine bow of his mouth and, oh, Susan, his eyebrows and hair are black, and his eyes are so dark I couldn't tell pupil from iris at first – square, heavy jaw – square chin – pale, sallow – and he needed a shave.' She couldn't say any of it, and she blushed, and Susan laughed at her.

'C'mon, Kathy. I'll never tell.'

'He was the best-looking man I ever saw.'

Susan sat still, now watching the mirror. 'So I've heard. Dark. Right?'

'Very dark.'

'And thin?'

'Thin.'

'You're still blushing. Love at first sight?' Susan really laughed at that, and Kathy giggled, but just to keep her company.

Then Susan said, 'There really are some nasty stories about their sex habits, Kathy.'

'Good,' Kathy said.

He called Kathy at eleven the next morning.

'It's Michael Ross. I'd like to see you again – tonight.'

She laughed. 'That's clear enough.'

He waited, not seeing anything funny, and when she spoke again, she sounded serious too. 'I'm in class tonight until seven forty-five, but I could meet you wherever you say.'

'What sort of class?'

'Painting. We have a model in the evening.'

'You're an artist?' That didn't go with the way she looked. He thought of artists as short and dark; they didn't wear suede shoes and carry kid gloves, and they especially weren't seen with Groton, Harvard, East Side John Anders.

'Yes, I am.'

Both of them tried to think of something to say next and couldn't. Finally Kathy got frightened that he was going to change his mind, and she asked, 'Where shall I meet you?'

'The Blue Angel on Fifty-fifth Street. About eight. Okay?'

'Fine.'

She called her hairdresser and browbeat him into cutting her hair without an appointment. Then she pulled every dress she owned out of her closet, hated them, thought about buying something new, and told herself she was being silly. She looked at the clock. It wasn't even noon and for the first time in years she wondered how she could stand waiting until eight.

chapter five

David was combing oil that smelled like dead roses into his hair.

'Jesus, that's awful,' Michael said. 'I can smell it over here.'

'Yeah . . . sexy. Here, you use it too.'

Michael held out his hand and David shook a few drops of the stuff onto his palm and Michael smoothed it through his hair. 'Pheew!' It turned his hair to coal; waves and curls shone. 'Gorgeous!'

David leaned closer and looked into the mirror.

'You're sure we don't look like Fon Gool in some fuck film?'

'Ah, but we do. We'll keep our socks on and force them to commit unspeakable acts.'

'Think Miss Field of Vassar, Boston, Newport is up to unspeakable acts?'

Michael turned away from the mirror.

'C'mon, Mikey. It's still early. Call her. I'm telling you that Harriet is adorable. Wait till you see her. You'll thank me.'

'Forget it, David. I'm meeting Kathy in an hour.'

I'm meeting Kathy. David turned away.

'Whatever you say. But you'll be sorry.'

The cabdriver stared at them all the way up to Seventy-second Street. The doorman in Marianne's building stared at them. Harriet, the roommate, stared at them; then she smiled.

'Oooh! You're twins.'

'We're not twins,' Michael said.

'We do it with mirrors,' said David, and he stretched out his arms in front of him. 'Mooooha ha,' he moaned, staggering stiff-legged into the apartment, imitating Frankenstein. 'Mooo-hoooha . . .'

Harriet backed away, smiling, but a little uncertain.

Michael followed. 'Don't be frightened.' She was a little fat dark thing, absolutely his type. Her hair was black and curly, her eyes were huge and dark, and when he got her against the wall with David watching and grinning, he realized that her breasts were soft, and just the half hug hardened her nipples.

'I have absolute control over my brother,' he whispered to her, pushing her harder against the wall. Oh, god she was delicious! He could smell her cologne – heavy sweat stuff, a little apricotty – and under it her own smell. With her it would be totally familiar; he'd fuck her until he was weak and a little sick; then he'd take the other one too. He looked over at her quickly; nice, hard-faced, hard-bodied bleached blonde with dark eyes and lots of orange lipstick. He already knew how she'd feel; nothing strange, nothing new. She matched the dead-rose hair oil. He pushed Harriet harder, concentrating on her hips, and he brought his face close to hers, smiling; she giggled.

'I'm free next weekend,' he said to her.

'Me too.'

'I thought you might be.'

David watched.

'What about tonight?' Harriet asked.

Michael started to step away, but she held on. He could feel her thighs through his trousers, fat, round, soft.

'Yeah,' said David. 'What about tonight?'

'Hey, either you've got another date or you haven't,' said Marianne, protecting her roommate. Michael let Harriet go.

'Everybody's entitled to a mistake,' he said.

He'd betrayed the woman in the lounge. No, that wasn't right, he thought. He didn't even know her.

He and David and Marianne laughed all the way downtown in the cab. He knew David wouldn't mind, so he sat close to Marianne, feeling the muscles tense and relax in her thighs and hips as she moved, leaning first against David, then against him. She liked having the two of them on either side of her, and

51

Michael thought of how nice it would be to take her someplace right now.

He stretched against Marianne because he was so hot, and so angry at himself for not listening to David, who sat grinning at him on the other side of the blonde as if he knew exactly what was going through his brother's mind.

Maybe Miss Field had gotten tired of waiting. They were already fifteen minutes late; the club was smoky and dark, and people tended to forget that they were in public when they went there. Maybe she'd be embarrassed and leave. Then he'd call Harriet. He'd even pay for her cab downtown, and oh, what a time he'd have with her. With both of them.

David too.

He looked at his brother and shook his head. David laughed, 'Next time.'

'Next time,' Michael said, 'I'll do what you tell me to.'

But Kathy had waited. He saw her sitting alone as soon as they walked in; too well dressed, too thin and too pale.

'So that's the woman in the lounge,' whispered David happily. 'You didn't tell me she had leukemia.'

'And wearing beige,' Marianne sneered, feeling outclassed, 'to match her hair, eyes, skin and teeth.' David laughed. The hatcheck girl took their things and they followed another couple through the uneven aisle of tables to where Kathy waited for them.

The minute she saw them she stood up, which was stupid, she thought, because she should have planted herself foursquare for this meeting. Expect twins, Susan Kramer had told her, identical twins; but she still wasn't ready to see two of them coming towards her through the haze of cigarette smoke – two Michaels, with a tall overdressed blonde. Kathy held on to the table and tried to smile, but none of them smiled back. She was supposed to marry John Anders in April, but she couldn't now because she'd – what? – fallen for one of two men who were so much alike she couldn't tell them apart. Why tell them apart? Why not have both! But how would we manage that? Her mind slid towards how they could, and she blushed and looked away.

'So demure,' David said, as they reached the table.

'How do you do?' Brilliant Kathy.

'I'm David.' She had to look up at him. David. He took her hand and held it. 'And this is Marianne Lansky.' Kathy nodded. 'And of course you already know Michael, don't you?'

His voice was soft, and he held her hand gently, pressing his thumb into her palm. She'd read that people's knees turned to water, but she'd thought that with her twelve generations of New England ancestors she would be immune. But it was happening to her, because if this one was David, then the other was Michael. *Her* Michael. He was trying not to look at her, and she didn't blame him because she knew exactly what sort of expression she had on her face, and she tried to arrange her features to look like they usually did – cool, polite, interested. Her hand came up to her throat as if someone had tried to steal her pearls. A stupid gesture she couldn't help making.

'I'm sorry,' she said. Sorry for what? Idiot, she told herself, moron.

Michael didn't say anything, but David leaned close to her. 'Sorry for what?' he asked softly. Kathy stared at David.

'Sorry for what?' he asked again.

'That I couldn't tell which one of you was Michael at first.'

'At first? Can you now.' David leaned even closer, and she had all of Michael's attention too.

'Oh, yes, I can now,' she lied.

'How?' David asked.

'Why, your expression.' The minute she said it she thought it was true. David looked sharp, smart. But Michael's eyes were soft, as if he'd come from a very old race of men. She remembered thinking, when he first opened his eyes and looked at her in the sunlight in the lounge, that she wouldn't have been surprised if he didn't know English. If it had been David in the lounge, she wouldn't be here now, and she began to wish it had been, because she was already afraid that this wasn't going to work out.

They drank. She noticed that the twins drank vodka – Michael straight and David with orange juice. Another difference.

David and Marianne talked about the hospital.

'Did you hear that Gargan and Weiss were setting up together?'

No. David hadn't heard. Michael didn't listen.

'Oh, yes. Fabulous office from what I hear. On East Sixty-seventh yet. Less than a block from Fifth. Bought the whole house.'

'Fantastic.' David positioned himself so that his thigh was against Kathy's and he pressed gently.

'That's what everyone says, and they're having Sloane's come in and do the whole thing.'

Michael ordered another drink. He didn't ask Kathy if she wanted one. He seemed to have forgotten she was there, but stared at the people dancing or at the table cloth.

'I'd like one too,' she said softly.

David grinned. Marianne looked at her as if she'd done something rude, and Michael ordered for her, then went back to watching the dancers. The pressure of David's thigh increased.

Kathy stood up. 'I'll be right back.' And she got to the ladies room as fast as she could. There was a line for the toilets and she was afraid she'd wet her pants from the liquor and nerves, but just when she knew she couldn't make it another second, it was her turn. After she finished she splashed water on her face, then sat on one of the little red boudoir chairs in front of the mirror, because she was frightened of facing them again and wanted to go home. She was sure she could get out the back.

These places always had back doors through the kitchen into an alley where she'd cry standing next to the garbage cans. Then she'd call John, and they'd go someplace quiet where the food came in small, expensive portions. They'd drink just enough; then they'd make love while she stayed pleasantly detached, watching him from above his head while he heaved away with a kind of abandon that she was sure embarrassed him as soon as he came. She looked in the mirror. 'Just the look of Michael excites you, doesn't it?' she asked herself, 'even his twin excites you,' although she had a feeling that he hated her already. She combed her hair, left the room, and stopped the first waiter she saw.

'Is there a back entrance?'

He raised his eyebrows and shook his head; she took out a five-dollar bill.

'Through the kitchen,' he said, nodding towards double swinging stainless steel doors.

She went through the doors. A young boy who was shaping chopped meat into hamburger patties looked up at her.

'The back door?'

'Right around the counter – down the little hall there.' She went where he told her to. A man lifting a basket of fries from a vat of fat stared.

She walked down the hall and out into the back open court, where sure enough there were garbage cans all around her. Just ahead was the entrance to a building hallway that was lit so she could see the street ahead through the door. That would be Fifty-sixth Street. She crossed the court. The building door was open . . . then she stopped. 'Shit . . . oh, shit . . .' She hit the door with her fist and hurt herself. 'Shit!'

She looked up past the fence, above the buildings at the sky. It was freezing, and she had forgotten her coat. She laughed and went back inside. The boy shook his head when he saw her and so did the waiter. Michael was sitting at the table, still watching nothing, and David was standing up with Marianne ready to lead her onto the dance floor. Kathy knew at once which was which.

She walked up to them.

'We thought you'd gotten lost,' Marianne said nastily.

'Lost,' David echoed, touching her arm.

Then he led the blonde out onto the floor and Kathy sat down next to Michael.

The tempo of the music changed and the lights dimmed until the room was almost dark. David danced Marianne past the table, while Michael watched. His brother's hair oil gleamed in the half light of the dance floor spots, and his eyes were black holes. As he passed, Michael leaned over and put his hand on Kathy's thigh.

'This is the first of the dry hump numbers' – David's words, purposely vulgar. His voice even sounded different. 'Care to dance?' She didn't answer. He squeezed her thigh. 'What's the matter, no humping?' He saw her smooth the gloves in her lap. They were beige leather, to match her dress and purse, and they looked worn in the palm and he thought she'd tear them if she wasn't careful. 'I mean, it makes a good start for the evening.'

She looked up at him. 'Let's get out of here,' she said.

He sat back stunned, 'But what about—'

'Without them,' she said. 'Just the two of us. Alone.'

Clutching the gloves for dear life, she stood up and walked away as if she were sure he'd follow. He looked for David, but he was at the far end of the floor in the dark, out of sight.

Just the two of them, alone.

They were all the way over on West Sixty-seventh Street, walking into the lobby of a fine old building with faded 1910 murals and elevator cages made of iron twisted to look like vines and drooping flowers before Michael realized that he had left David alone with Marianne without even telling him where he was going. Without even finishing his drink.

She led him into the elevator, then down a hall and into a room two storeys high with a slanting glass wall through which he thought he could see the whole city. He walked over and stood in front of it; but she turned on the lights and the view disappeared in the reflection.

'Turn them off' he said.

She did, and the city came back. He could see the lights on the Hudson to his right, and Central Park to his left. He realized that while the floor number was only ten, they were really twenty or twenty-five storeys high.

'Some view,' he said. He didn't realize that she'd come up behind him until he felt her hands on his shoulders.

'Take off your coat,' she said. He did, still watching the lights outside.

'Can anyone see in here?'

'Only from an airplane,' she said.

She laid his coat over the couch. 'And your jacket,' she said. That surprised him and he turned around. The lights were still off but there was moonlight, streetlight, lights from the signs and other buildings, and he could see her clearly. She had taken off her shoes, and without them she wasn't nearly as tall as he thought she was. He took off his jacket as she walked towards him, and he thought as he folded it over the couch next to his coat, that he was alone with her. David wasn't there, neither was David's girl, there was no one giggling on the couch or in the bedroom, no one would walk in. They were alone. He wasn't sure, he would have to think about it later, but he thought this might be the first time in his life that he had ever been alone with a woman.

She kissed him, but he held back, waiting.

'Take off your tie.' It wasn't a command in any sense, she even added 'please' as an afterthought, which made him smile. He did as she asked; he also reached down and pulled off his loafers although she hadn't asked him to. Now they were both in stockinged feet, and she was still completely dressed. He wondered what would happen next. He wasn't able to do much himself at this point; he was adrift in being alone with her.

Except for her instructions to him about removing his clothes, they hadn't said anything, and now she went back to kissing him, while he stood suspended waiting to see how far she would go, and what he would feel.

She unbuttoned his shirt, pulling it up out of his trousers and away from his body. Then she slid her hands under his T-shirt and rubbed his bare skin, lightly, making him shudder a little. She got the shirt off, with him helping as little as possible, then she bent her head and rolled her tongue against his nipples. He got immensely excited, an erection ready to break. She went sliding her lips across his chest, sinking down and leaving a trail of moisture midline on his body. Then she got to his belt.

'Will you help me?'

They got all of his clothes off, and he realized how strange it was for him to be naked while she was still dressed; but he knew that in her mind he was the beauty, the prize, so this way was really appropriate. She went on kissing, licking down his body, and she finally took his penis all the way into her mouth. He wanted to laugh for a second, because he was sure if he didn't lie down or at least sit, he would fall on her. But he couldn't say anything and he let her go on until he was ready to come, then he sank down on his knees next to her.

'Please,' he said, 'I have to lie down. You too. And take your clothes off. Please. Because I want to do the same thing to you.'

chapter six

David went to the men's room to look for Michael. Michael wouldn't just leave like that. His drink was still there, and so was Kathy's. The men's room was empty and David went back to the table. Marianne was getting restless and wondering why David was so concerned about where his brother was. David ordered another drink and gulped it, then one more . . . still no Michael.

Marianne got drunk enough not to care who or where Michael was. David was almost as drunk, but he took her home with him anyway, and halfway there he realized what a fool he'd been – Michael was probably home waiting for him now.

But when they got there the place was empty. He went from the kitchen, where the apartment entrance was, to the living room with its stretch knit slip covers and 9-inch TV on a chrome stand, into the bedroom. No Michael.

He didn't think he'd ever been alone with a woman before. As soon as he realized that Michael wasn't in the next room with his date, or in the next bed, the sounds from the kitchen – Marianne making coffee, Marianne mixing drinks, Marianne taking her clothes off – became sinister. If she started on him now, he wouldn't be able to do anything. He stretched, trying for some semblance of excitement, but he didn't feel anything except betrayed. He called Marianne's number, hoping she would stay in the kitchen so she couldn't hear him.

Harriet answered. She sounded as if she'd been asleep.

'Hello, is Michael Ross there?' He pitched his voice very low.

'No, no one's here.'

He hung up just as Marianne came into the bedroom.

He lay back on the bed and watched the shadows on the ceiling from the streetlights. He heard car wheels slipping on the ice, and faraway voices, a horn.

He closed his eyes and turned over so he was facing Michael's bed.

She sat down and started rubbing his back. He groaned sickly and she jumped up.

'Hey, you okay?'

He shook his head. 'I feel sick.' She backed away. He groaned again, praying she wasn't the kind who'd bring a wet washrag, sponge his face, and hold his head until he was better. She wasn't.

'It's getting late,' she said. He kept his eyes closed and didn't answer. 'Maybe I should go home?' Still no answer.

'You sure you'll be okay?'

He rolled over onto his back and lay with his arms and legs spread, trying to look as if he'd passed out. He heard her go into the kitchen to get dressed, then he heard the door open and close. He waited, still not moving. Everything was quiet, she was gone. He rolled over and looked again at Michael's empty bed. Then he got up and called Kathy Field's number. No answer, but he knew Michael was there anyway.

David went into the kitchen, opened the window, and crawled out onto the fire escape. He breathed deeply and leaned against the railing, with the cold cutting through his jacket. But the fresh air didn't help. He was frightened.

He twisted restlessly and damned Michael under his breath, then aloud to the courtyard.

'Goddamn you, Michael!' He heard a window open and saw a head stick out. 'Shut up, up there.'

He knew he was jealous; he also knew that that was a nice normal way to feel. She was a pretty girl.

He made himself say it aloud.

'She's a pretty girl.' But being jealous meant being angry, not frightened, and he was frightened. Of what? He tried to examine his feelings calmly, and he closed his eyes and put his head back against the iron.

It wasn't Kathy Field who scared him. It was Michael being alone with her. David had always been there. Michael's body and feelings were David's, but tonight things were happening to Michael that David didn't know about, maybe that he couldn't imagine, couldn't share.

So what? So fucking what? Why should that frighten him?

Across the way he heard people talking and laughing; the court echoed with a party, and he realized, as the voices surrounded him, that Michael had been trying to be alone for a long time. Ever since David could remember – almost.

What if he liked it – with her – with someone else? What if he left? He would take all the feelings with him, and David would be alone.

He was sober all of a sudden, and didn't want to be. He crawled back into the kitchen.

'Fuck.' He drank out of the bottle. What kind of drunken shit? He *could* feel; he had all sorts of feelings. He'd go out now, go down to the Argus and talk to his friends; he had feelings for them. Then he'd find a girl. It was only twelve fifteen. He took off his jacket and his tie and put on a sweater to prowl in. He'd leave his feeling like a snail trail from one end of the East Side to the other. First to the Argus to his dear friends.

The phone rang, and he ran to it, knocking over the bottle; he was so sure it was Michael that he almost said his name when he answered. But it was someone asking for Michael; a man with a metallic voice that David didn't recognize.

David looked up at the clock, almost twelve thirty, and Michael hadn't even called. Fuck you, Michael!

'Sure, this is Michael Ross. Who's this?'

Michael left her half asleep. He kissed her, rubbed his cheek against her chest, down her belly. 'Scratches,' she complained faintly. He smiled at her, kissed her again. It was hard to leave, but he made himself get out of bed and he pulled the covers up over her. He did everything quietly – opening the bedroom door, closing it. He was naked, and he felt odd standing in front of that huge window-wall putting on his clothes. He did that quietly; the door moved on oiled hinges, and closed without a sound. He stood close to the silent elevator man, descending in the soundless cage, and out into the freezing, quiet, empty street.

'OOOOheeee!' he shouted. 'Whoooopeee! Hooooraaay!'

He started to run towards Central Park West. A patrol car slowed down, and he did too.

At Central Park he picked up a cab. 'Take me home.' Then he laughed.

'Okay, smartass. Where's home?' Michael told him and the driver tried to stay grim all the way across town while Michael babbled about what a beautiful winter it had been, how clean the snow was staying this year, about how sure he was that John Kennedy would turn things around, and they were in for a brighter tomorrow. 'Don't you think so?' He leaned over the front seat and looked at the cabbie and the cabbie looked back and grinned in spite of himself. 'You just got laid, didn't you?' he said.

Michael nodded. 'How'd you know?'

'You can tell. Good, huh?' he asked.

Michael looked serious, then smiled, then serious again, and the cabdriver roared.

'Oh, my!' was all Michael could manage for an answer.

He ran up the stairs, and banged the door open so hard he was afraid he'd broken it. 'David!'

No answer.

'Daaaaviddd!'

Then he realized that the place was freezing and he ran across the kitchen and shut the window. He looked around, but he knew he was alone. He hung up his coat and sat down at the kitchen table; twelve thirty. Where was David? Someone had spilt the vodka, and he wiped it up. There wasn't anything left in the bottle and he searched for something to drink, but all they had left was a small bottle of Mogen David which he couldn't remember buying. He drank what was left in it, then went back to the table. Where was David?

He went into the bedroom. It was empty and cold. His bed was smooth, but he could see the dent in David's where he'd been.

He went back into the kitchen hating being alone like this, longing for his brother. David was still with Marianne, probably at her place. Michael imagined them all sitting around her kitchen table drinking beer or coffee and talking about the hospital.

He wanted to talk to somebody too.

He couldn't sleep and he couldn't stand sitting there alone any more, so he got his coat and went back out into the street. It was dead freezing and every sound cracked in the air. He looked up and down the street sure that any second David would round the corner, or that a cab would pull up with David drunk in the back, so that Michael would have to help him upstairs, get his clothes off, and put him to bed while David mumbled about Marianne's iron legs breaking his ribs.

Michael sat on the brownstone stoop until he was so cold he was shaking. Still no David. But he couldn't go upstairs alone again, so he went to the hospital to see Friedman – or joke with the cucumber – or just see somebody.

Friedman was at that station reading a sex manual 'for married men', he said. 'It's different when you're married.' He grinned. 'You have to learn how to fuck without a hard on.' Then he put the book down and stared.

'You're Michael.'

'Clever.'

'Not David.'

'Brilliant.'

'Then it's David who's upstairs.'

David! Michael smiled. He'd found him.

'What's he doing upstairs?'

'Impersonating you for one thing.' Friedman watched Michael.

'I don't unders—'

'The cucumber's in labour this minute. And when Romer called you to come help, a Ross turned up and started helping.'

Friedman kept watching.

'He said he was you.'

Michael turned his back.

'How's she doing?' Michael asked the wall.

'Word is that she's dying.'

'And the kid?'

Friedman shrugged, 'Probably the same.'

Michael took the elevator up to eight, she was in delivery room three. The card outside the door was blank where the patient's name should be; the doctors were listed as Romer and Ross.

Michael looked through the glass inset in the door. The room was green and the poor cucumber looked unconscious and ghastly in the fluorescent light. Romer was standing to the side, and it was David who was sitting on the stool between her legs – David as Michael. It was an amazing impersonation, especially from a distance, through the glass. David touched her the way

Michael would have; his gestures were Michael's; when he looked up and said something to Romer and nodded, it was Michael's nod. And Michael knew that, if the door were open, he would hear his own voice, his own words. He put his head down, and tried to remember the feeling he'd had two hours ago when he was with Kathy Field. Two hours ago, he'd been like no one else in the world, standing naked in front of the window in the light from the moon. He'd been a unique, separate man. The way she'd touched him, everything that happened between them couldn't have happened if he'd been anybody else in the world. He thought he'd never forget the feeling, and now, watching his brother being him, he couldn't even remember what Kathy looked like.

Romer looked up, but Michael ducked below the glass in the door, then backed away and went downstairs. He passed Friedman without saying anything and went into the cucumber's empty room. The bed was still turned back as if she'd just gotten up to go to the bathroom, and there was an open book on the stand next to it. He walked around the bed and picked it up; it was a paperback Dr Spock.

He opened her drawer. Nothing, except the Kleenex and toothbrush and toothpaste they gave to clinic patients. No dusting powder, no little dolls or games or other books. He shut the drawer and went to her closet where a cheap cotton dress and threadbare unlined coat waited.

'If she makes it, I'll buy her a new coat,' he whispered. 'Let her make it – a new coat, I swear.'

'Hey, Mike,' Friedman was holding the phone. 'McGraw just called. She had a boy.'

'How are they?'

Friedman grinned, 'She's yelling for some junk.'

Michael came and shook his hand, then they went for the floor flask in the bottom drawer of the main desk. Just as they were raising their glasses to toast her, the elevator door opened and James Romer and David got off. Michael jumped up smiling. He wanted to run to them, to hug David, and he started to come around the desk still holding the flask. Then he heard Romer laughing. 'So you're not Michael after all!'

'Nope.' David shook his head, and laughed too. Romer put his arms around him, and there was something odd about the look on his face.

'It's late,' Romer said, 'but we could get a quick drink—'

No, Dave. It's two thirty. I want to talk to you. Don't go with him. Come home.

David looked right at Michael then back to Romer as if Michael weren't there at all. Friedman was suspended under the station lights watching, his book forgotten. Romer and David walked away together talking, heads close, and Romer's arm around David, his hand in the middle of David's back.

'You better watch that,' Friedman said.

'I don't know what you're talking—'

'Then you're the only one in the place who doesn't. James Romer's a homosexual, with a penchant for young residents.'

'Jesus! I better warn Dave.'

'David knows. I told him a long time ago.'

Romer was so blond David had to look closely to see his eyelashes. Even his eyes were pale; the hair on his arms shone like gold and his hair was cut so short that David could see pale scalp through it.

They'd had a lot to drink, but David was still sober and he thought Romer was too.

'Listen, Dave, I know good doctoring when I see it, and you were good.' He smiled. 'Are you that good under your own name?' The smile softened and David looked down. 'I do okay. We *both* do.'

'I can't guarantee anything; the competition is brutal, but you'll have my recommendation. That counts for something, Dave.' *I'm a big man*, he was saying. They drank while David thought. Boston was two hundred and fifty miles away from Kathy Field. 'There's only one fellowship?' he asked.

'There's only one Baylis. But there are lots of fellowships—' Romer stopped then said, 'Thinking about your brother?'

David nodded.

'Ever been apart?' Romer asked.

'Never. But he's good. I'm sure he can find something in Boston if I go.'

'Yes, if you want him to.'

The pale eyes looked into his in the candlelight. David knew they were drawing up rules, but he didn't understand the game yet. Romer was waiting.

'I won't go without my brother.'

Cold flicker. 'You may not go anyway, Dave. I told you the competition is rough.'

Rule one: David was supposed to go alone.

Best to get things clear in the beginning.

'I won't go without my brother.'

The two men looked at each other until Romer shrugged and signalled to the waiter. David wondered if it was for the bill, which he knew meant the end of the game, the end of the fellowship. Or another drink, which meant round two. The waiter stood, hands folded.

'Two more Wild Turkeys,' said Romer. David relaxed.

Then Romer said, 'You can't spend your lives together, David.'

'Why not?'

'Because you can't. Don't you want to get married, have children?' Another rule to be made. David grinned, liking the game.

'Not particularly.'

'Why not?'

'I don't know.' He tried to sound as if he were saying less than he meant, and suddenly realized that he was. He didn't want to marry anybody.

'What about Michael?'

He didn't answer.

'You know you're good-looking men. Maybe Michael's a little melancholy, a little restless, but women want him, don't they? Even that crazy, dear little junkie asks me about him.'

'Our careers are very important to us. They mean everything . . .'

'Bullshit.'

David drank. He knew he should walk out on this pale son of a bitch, fellowship or no fellowship. But what would happen if they stayed here and tried to go on as they were? Michael would get more involved with Kathy, and David would— What would David do? Dry up and die.

This faggot was giving him a way to get Michael away from Kathy, away from everyone. Okay, Boston. He smiled, a soft hinting smile, and leaned back so his legs stretched under the table to touch Romer's. But he quickly moved them, as if it were an accident.

'If Michael wants to get married, he'll get married, Jim. For the moment, I think he'd like to stay with me.'

'It's dangerous, David.'

Suddenly David was angry. Why couldn't people just leave them alone? 'Why is it dangerous? We're thirty years old. We're MDs – good ones. Don't you think we know what we're doing.'

'I don't think you're doing the same thing.'

'What's that supposed to mean?'

'Just a feeling that maybe Michael might not be so interested in Boston after all.'

'Fuck you, Romer.' David stood up to go, but Romer grabbed his arm.

'Don't go, David. Maybe we can work something out.' He was excited, his pale eyes shining in the candle flames. 'It's the right spot for you. No matter what happens between you and Michael – or between you and me.'

David tried to get free, but Romer held him; Romer closed his eyes for a second and then released David's hand.

'We can't work anything out without Michael,' David said.

'Would he say the same about you?'

'Of course.' *Would he?*

'Then we'll work something out with Michael.'

David was impressed with the neatness of the experience. He didn't feel as if he had to run to the shower; he didn't feel as if he'd lost anything, or betrayed anyone. Yet he'd been more excited than he'd ever been, because the man knew where to touch, when to stop, when to go on – better than any woman had ever known, better than he knew himself. He expected guilt, but felt less guilty than he ever had. Romer lay next to him, his eyelids tissue thin, slightly blue. David touched his chest and Romer opened his eyes and smiled.

'It's late, David.'

'Would you like me to leave?' David asked, knowing the answer.

'No.'

He was thinner than Michael and had almost no hair on his chest or arms; even his pubic hair was fine, like the hair on his head. His eyes were practically white in the dim light from the hall, and shadowed. David started to laugh.

'What's so funny?'

'I was thinking that, except that you have a cock and balls, you're so different from us you could be another species.'

'Could I?' Romer asked softly. David closed his eyes. It was familiar – in a way something that happened a long time ago when he and Michael were children, when nothing they did was wrong; when they would always be together.

chapter seven

This was the fourth night in a row David had been out alone. Michael waited; he walked the floor, and tried to read, then to sleep, but he couldn't. He called Kathy. No answer. He called Friedman but he was out too.

Finally he got the telephone book and sat with it in his lap without moving. Go ahead, he told himself, pick a name, call somebody. *How'd you like to have dinner with a lovely twin?* Ah, but twins are never lonely.

Finally he opened the book to the Rs and there it was: Romer, James D., MD, East 72 Street. Nice address, very nice.

He dialled and waited while the phone rang again and again. 'C'mon, you faggot son of a bitch; you're not asleep. Answer the phone.'

Friedman had said, 'Look, Mike, think what you want to think. You asked me and I told you. They're lovers. I don't know how long; a month, maybe more. Shit, Mike, don't look like that.' Poor

Friedman had actually paled, and Michael had tried to reassure him, *still not believing it. David and James Romer. David and Jonathan.*

On the seventh ring, Romer picked up.

'Hello.' What was David doing now? Standing behind him as close as he could get, reaching around the front of his body. 'Hello.' Romer was jiggling the key. Michael put his hand over the mouthpiece so there was nothing at the other end but dead air. Something rustled; then Romer said from a distance, 'There's no one there.'

Then Michael heard his brother's voice, 'A breather.' David laughed. He hadn't really believed it until he heard David's voice.

He hung up before Romer could and sat next to the phone for a long time, held there by what he had learned.

He kept seeing David and Romer together. He saw them by the lake in the moonlight and David had that crazy look on his face. Then they were in front of the glass wall at Kathy's; but it was David and Romer alone. Michael wasn't there. He was excluded.

The phone rang and he jumped.

'Mike?' It was David, but Michael couldn't answer because he wasn't used to the new picture of his brother and he didn't know yet how to talk to this David.

'Mike? Mike, are you there?'

Finally Michael said, 'Yes, David, I'm here.'

'Anything wrong? You sound funny.'

'No, it's okay.' Then he realized that he might sound as if he were giving some kind of dispensation. 'I mean, I'm okay.'

'You sound odd as hell.'

No answer.

'Were you worried?' David asked.

'Uh – no.'

'Well, I just wanted to let you know, I got myself a real beaut here.'

Yeah, Michael thought, a beaut.

'And I don't think I'll be home.'

Michael knew that all he had to do was tell his brother that he was worried, or lonely, or just ask him to come home, and David would do it. But he said, 'I hope she's terrific, Dave.'

'Mike, are you sure you're . . .' But Michael hung up.

He had to get out of there. David might call again, and he'd beg him to come home this time. Or even worse he might call them. That'd be a conversation: 'Dr Romer, it's Michael Ross, little Michael Ross. Is my queer brother there?'

Michael grabbed his coat and ran out into the street. A drunk had turned over the garbage cans. They rolled and scraped in the wind, and the garbage stank up the whole street. He kept going past Madison, to Fifth to the hospital.

Inside everything was quiet; a distant bell rang as he waited for the elevator. Then nothing. He went up to six, trying to find Friedman . . . somebody. But Walters was on, and he was sound asleep, sitting straight up in his chair. Mrs Emory smiled and shook her head, and Michael tried to smile back.

She leaned across the desk. 'Are you all right, Doctor?'

Why the fuck did everybody keep asking him that? Sure, I'm fine. Terrific. I just found out that my brother's a fag. He's making it with James Romer – *the* James Romer. Star queer. Right now, this minute. Otherwise I'm fine . . . just fine . . .

'Sure,' he said out loud. 'It's very cold.'

'Yes. Cold.'

It wasn't any better here than it was at home. He had to get away, and he almost ran to the elevator.

The car on the left stopped for him, and he got on and pushed two, but it stopped at five – and the doors opened, but no one got on. Five was cardiac with greenlit scopes and screens; the elevator stopped on four too, and again the doors opened and this time two nurses waiting for the up car stared at him. He thought how huge the place was, galleys, broom closets, the ORs on seven, delivery and nurseries on eight, the clinics on the ground and labs in the basement, stretching up ten floors and out for two square blocks – lounges, gardens, rooms. There were probably a thousand TV sets in the building, and God knows how many respirators and defibrillators. How many thousands of bottles, and hypos, straps to hold patients down, linen to cover them, and to hide them when they died.

On three the elevator seemed to give up, and the car stopped, the doors opening and closing. Michael didn't want to get stuck in the thing, so he got out. As soon as he did, the doors closed smoothly, and he was left alone. He couldn't remember ever having been on this floor before. He heard a noise that he couldn't identify, a whooshing that sounded like hundreds of people walking in rubber shoes. The lights were dimmer here, and there was a bad smell he couldn't identify.

Ahead he saw the lights of the nursing station and he walked towards them. But just before he got there a starched woman came out of nowhere and blocked his path, and what with the smell, and the whooshing, and the dim light, he was a little frightened of what he'd see when she raised her head and the light showed her face. But she was just a plain, middle-aged woman.

'Can I help you?'

'What is this?'

'You don't work this floor.'

'I'm on the maternity service.'

'That's on six. You are on the wrong floor.' She turned to go.

'Please, what's that noise?'

She pretended not to hear, and kept going, but he followed her.

'What's making that noise?' He was embarrassed to ask about the smell for some reason.

The woman turned back, looking annoyed.

'This is special service. The patients here are terminal. It's the respirators that make the sound. Most of the patients here are on respirators.' She paused and when he didn't move, she said, 'Most of the patients on this floor have cancer.'

Michael went back there the next morning. The nurses walked on crepe feet or sat quietly and the *whoosh*, *whoosh* was the only noise. The smell was terrible at first, but he walked around until he got used to it. Then he went into the staff lounge to get some coffee and there was Matthew Gargan, drinking coffee and looking over some reports.

'What're you doing here, Ross?'

'I got off the elevator by mistake on this floor last night and I wanted to see what it's like in daylight. It's a little frightening at night.'

'It's even more frightening when you can see what's going on.'

'I don't know; it's sort of peaceful.'

'Of course it's peaceful, the patients on this floor are dying.'

'The nurse told me.'

'Mostly of cancer.'

'She told me that too.'

Gargan looked at him. 'Doesn't that bother you?'

Not as much as he thought it would.

Now that neither of them was talking, Michael could hear the respirators breathing in their own rhythm. The smell was even here in the lounge, faint but definite; and he wondered if it would cling to his clothes like a woman's perfume; if Kathy would notice it, or David, or people in the elevator. He'd have to ask Gargan.

Gargan smiled. 'Bothered or not, you're interested, aren't you?' Michael nodded, and Gargan said, 'That's what happened to me once. I didn't understand it either; then one guy I knew – an oncologist too – said it's the quiet that pulls you in. Upstairs they're bitching about the food, about how much weight they've put on, about how this hurts, and that pulls, unwilling to put up with the mildest discomfort for ten seconds. Not here – altogether different perspective here.'

He could use a different perspective. 'What kind of gynaecologic problems do you get?'

'Cervix and ovary mainly. But we do get some odd ones.'

'Cure rate?' Michael asked.

'Zilch. Getting better on cervix, but that's because we're finding it earlier. Ovary's just like always— Say, which one are you?'

'I'm Michael.'

'Are you the one who wrote the paper on ketosteroids and ovarian cancer, or was that your brother?'

'It was me.'

'Nice piece of work, Ross. Very elegant hypothesis. Did you know that the library lends out Xeroxes of it?'

'No, I didn't know.' Michael had almost forgotten about that paper and he liked Gargan's knowing about it, and respecting it. It made what David was doing with Romer seem a little less important. He smiled at Gargan, sat down and relaxed a little.

Then Gargan said, 'Is it you or your brother who's up for the Baylis?'

Michael didn't know what he was talking about, and it must have shown, because Gargan said, 'The Baylis – Harvard – Boston Baylis. Fellowship of fellowships. Don't tell me you've never heard of it. It must be your brother David. Right?'

Michael couldn't answer.

'Hey, Ross, are you okay?'

Michael nodded.

'Jesus, I hope I didn't say the wrong thing.'

'No. I'd forgotten, that's all. What're his chances?'

'Terrific. He's got Romer in his camp, and Romer's a star. Besides, Romer's going too; and they're going to want to keep him happy. I mean, if he relies on your brother to help him . . .'

Romer with David in Boston. For how long?

'How long is the Baylis?'

'Three years,' Gargan said.

Whatever happened to Michael always showed. It must be showing now because Gargan looked very concerned.

'Hey, are you sure you're all right, Ross?'

'What kind of work will they be doing?'

'Romer's taking over the fertility clinic. Your brother would be doing the backup investigation. Of course everybody gets real sentimental about babies, so there's always plenty of money. I don't mean to complain; cancer pulls in the dough too, but everybody gives, then runs away, like they might catch it. It's not like babies for the barren . . . lots of tears over that . . . as if we needed more people in this world.'

Michael stood up. He had to hold on to the back of the chair.

'Hey, Ross—'

'I just stood up too quickly. I'm fine.'

'Listen, Ross, there's a lot of cancer money around. Thousands. Good fellowship right here, the ACA awards it. It's got lots of prestige, and enough dough to keep a man and his wife—'

Michael interrupted him. 'When will my brother know?'

'About the Baylis?'

Michael nodded.

'Any day now, I imagine. Look, Ross, you really should think about the ACA thing. It's good for about four thousand dollars—' Michael didn't know what to say, and Gargan went on talking. 'Just think about it. Don't ask anybody either, because you'll get a load of shit about how miserable it is. Which it is. No question. But there're good things too. Sometimes you win, and nothing's better, because the odds are so steep against you. Mainly, it's quiet. Death's not what people think. It's very quiet mostly.'

Michael still didn't answer. Then Gargan said, 'Have you and your brother ever been separated?'

'No.'

'This might help. I mean it's very involving; personal problems get to seem pretty small. Sex, money, even separations; you get a different perspective – like your patients. Ask anybody, and they'll tell you Matt Gargan's the nicest guy around.'

chapter eight

On Thursday morning G. Newcomb Streeter called David to tell him that he had just been awarded the Baylis Fellowship for the Advancement of Knowledge of the Diseases of Women. When he hung up, David stayed by the phone so long Nat Kramer came out of the lounge and asked him if he'd had bad news.

'No. I just won the Baylis.'

He didn't have to explain what that meant, and Kramer hit him on the back, and shook his hand.

'Boy! Terrific, great! C'mon, Dave, I'll buy you a drink.'

'Sure, Nat, why not?'

He hadn't told Michael, he hadn't even told Romer. But he needed a drink.

They went to the Argus and the bartender asked where David's better half was – meaning Michael – which some asshole at the bar thought was so funny he laughed on and off all the time Dave and Nat were in there. David had one bourbon while

Kramer talked about all the problems he was having with his wife, and wishing he could go back to Boston. ' 'S'where I come from, you know.'

David didn't know.

'Great town, Dave. You'll really love it.'

'I haven't told Mike yet—'

'Jesus, Dave, I'm sorry. Why don't you call him now? Jesus, it's too bad in a way.'

'What do you mean?'

'He's going to miss you.'

'He's going with me, Nat.'

'But I thought . . .' Kramer looked at David, then said, 'Sure, that'll make things a lot easier for both of you.'

David wouldn't let himself think about what Kramer had said. He had to get to the bank before three or they wouldn't have enough to go to a decent restaurant, and tonight he and Michael were going to celebrate. On the way he stopped for another quick bourbon, then afterwards he had still another. Bourbon was Romer's drink, and David was starting to like it. It had substance; he held it up to the light while the bartender watched.

'Substance,' David said. 'Real substance.'

'Yeah.'

'I'm going to Boston forever.'

'That's too bad.'

Someone was watching him from the end of the bar. David looked over and saw a young blond man, extremely handsome, beautiful, prettier than anybody in the world. Were his lips rouged? No way to tell until he kissed him. Not here. That was going to have to end; David had another bourbon and nodded a silent good-bye to the young man at the end of the bar. But the man misunderstood and came over to sit next to him.

David decided the colour was definitely rouge.

'Hi,' said the blond.

'Hi,' said David.

'Buy you a drink?' the blond asked, which was totally unexpected, because David thought he'd have to do the buying. The guy's pants were tight, and his cock looked enormous, even

74

soft. David eyed it, then smiled and lifted his glass in another silent toast. The blond followed suit.

'You know,' David said, 'I'm a fledgling.' It was almost three thirty. He'd known about the Baylis since two and he hadn't told anybody yet except Nat Kramer whom he didn't know very well and didn't like. Maybe he'd tell this guy.

'Fledgling what?' asked the man.

'Queer. I just got my first blow job from a guy last month.'

David thought that would drive him away, back to his end of the bar or off to the toilet to put more rouge on his lips. But the man laughed, and David noticed that his eyes weren't pale like Romer's but bright blue, and his lashes were dark. Mascara? David looked, but he couldn't tell.

'How'd you like it?' the man asked.

'Loved it.'

'Did you do it too?'

'Yes.'

'And?'

'Beautiful.' He thought he'd never said anything that he meant more.

Their knees were touching and now it was too late, because David wanted all the rest of it. He could wait a little longer to tell everyone, another half hour.

'What's your name?' he asked the blond.

'My real name is Herbie, but you can call me Alex.'

They laughed some more, knees pressing harder, and David was having a hard time keeping his eyes off the man's crotch.

'Mine's David.' One more drink and they'd go. But where? Herbie-Alex was getting quite bold with his knee work, and David was starting to think about the men's room when he looked at the clock and saw that it was now after four.

'I have to go. I just won an award, and I gotta have some kind of celebration.'

'What sort of award?'

David told him, and Herbie-Alex congratulated him, then kissed him on the cheek; he was a little drunk too. David looked past his head through the window of the bar and saw that it was still light. March already, spring coming. Spring in Boston, with

Michael. He was so frightened for a second he felt a little dizzy. Herbie-Alex touched his shoulder. 'Easy, David. Bourbon getting to you?'

David looked at the other man expecting to see a doll's eyes, cold, erotic, disinterested; but the other man's face was kind, the blue eyes soft and concerned.

'No. I just don't know what to do to celebrate.'

'Do you have someone to celebrate with?'

'My brother, Michael.'

'Do you like him?'

'What?'

'Your brother. Do you like him? You should celebrate with someone you like.'

'Yes. I like him a lot.'

Herbie-Alex smiled, and David thought he was really sweet.

'Then you get a bottle of champagne, and some caviar, and pâté, and you bring them home to him and you can both get a little drunk together. And maybe even cry a little.'

'Why should we cry?'

'Because you have to go to Boston, and leave your brother whom you like.'

'Oh, no. He's coming with me. He has to come with me.'

'Then you can really celebrate.'

'You bet. Where can we get the right stuff around here – the caviar and the rest?'

Herbie-Alex said, 'At my place.'

By the time David got home, the made-on-the-premises pâté had come unwrapped and smeared the bottle of now warm champagne and the jar of caviar. The french bread smelled of pâté and so did the cheese. Michael watched him unwrap the mess; and every time he tried to help, David waved him away.

'What's the champagne for?'

David meant to pour before he told him. He planned to stand under the ceiling light, raise the glass, and tell his brother all the good news. How they were going to have a new life together, just the two of them; no Romer – he'd tell him that – and no Kathy.

But he was still wiping the mess off the bottle when he said, "I got the Baylis, Michael.'

That was that.

Michael took the bottle away from David and opened it for him and poured the wine.

'You're going with me, Mike. I rented a house, not rented it yet, but I have a line on it. Talked to the woman today. A month's deposit and it's ours. It's got a garden, and a sunporch. And we'll each have our own room and bath, Mike.' David laughed. 'Shit, we're thirty, and we've never had a room each.'

'What do I do there, David? Keep house for you?'

David held on to the sink because it was starting and he couldn't face it without holding on to something. Then he realized that it had really started a month ago – with Kathy; he knew she would lead to this. If he couldn't win now, then it would go on and on. He couldn't think how long. Would he, he wondered, know so much if he weren't so drunk and so fucked out? He grinned down into the sink. Blown out, he corrected himself.

'There's a fellowship there for you. I applied, pretended I was you. Romer helped me.'

'Pretended you were me? That's getting to be a habit, isn't it?' David didn't answer. 'Did we get the fellowship?'

'Not yet. But Romer says we will. So you've got a job, a place to live . . .'

'David, I'm not going.'

Don't say it. David had put his finger to his lips.

'I'm staying here.'

Too late. What could he say? No you're not? He smiled in spite of everything. *I forbid it*!

Michael wasn't finished.

'I'm going to marry Kathy.'

'Michael, don't. She's not worth it. Listen, she can't do anything for you, that—' He stopped. Michael came close to him, but David turned away.

'She can't do anything for me – what? What were you going to say, David?'

'That she can't do anything for you that a hundred other

77

women can't. Here, in Boston, in Dubuque. What difference does it make?'

'It makes a difference to me.'

'You love her!'

'Yes.'

'So you stay, and you marry her; and what'll you do then? Clip Kathy's coupons?'

'I've applied for the ACA Fellowship. Gargan's helping me, and he thinks I can get it.'

Another shock! David wanted to tell Michael that he couldn't take it; nobody could. They'd seen what could happen. There was a guy named Berger they'd heard about in medical school who'd been an oncologist for ten or twelve years, and who finally went to pieces in the operating theatre during an extended radical hysterectomy. Apparently he'd actually started crying, right there in the middle of the surgery, and had torn out several fistfuls of his hair before they could restrain him. David looked at Michael's hair. Like his own it took a real tug just to pull out one strand.

Taking that fellowship was the worst thing Michael could do to himself, and David would tell him so – as soon as he was sober. He poured more champagne.

Michael stood up. 'I don't want any more champagne, Dave.'

'What about dinner?'

'I'm not hungry right now.'

'What about the other stuff?'

'I'm not hungry.' Michael went to the closet and took out his coat.

'Where are you going?'

No answer.

'Please, Michael, where are you going?'

They were facing each other, both wondering what was going to happen next when the phone rang. They laughed, because it was so silly; then David picked it up.

It was Romer. 'I can't talk now.' David put his hand over the mouthpiece, and called to Michael, 'Please wait, we've got to talk.' Then into the phone, 'Yes, Jim; yes, I heard.'

Michael tucked his scarf inside his coat and put on his gloves while he watched his brother. The champagne was still open on the table, and the bag of goodies waited next to it.

'Yes, Jim. Streeter himself called me. Of course – thrilled.'

Michael opened the door.

'Mike, please wait – oh, please—'

Michael smiled as if nothing special were happening. 'I'll be back later.' David started to hang up, but before he could, Michael got out the door and ran down the stairs.

He kept running when he got to the street. At Eighty-sixth, the bus was just leaving Third, and he put on extra steam to get to Lexington before it did. He just made it, and sat panting in the back while the bus ran west. At Fifth, where the bus entered the park, he got off, watched it on its way, and then ran in its track along the walk that lined the transverse. His coat flapped out behind him. The wind caught his scarf and tore it loose, so that it streamed out too. His hair blew flat against his head. Bare trees laced the sky. He ran all the way to the middle of the park then stopped and leaned against a tree trying to catch his breath. It was done.

He wasn't going to Boston; David was. He was going to marry Kathy. Michael couldn't catch his breath, and he knelt at the foot of the tree, and put his head down to ease the pain in his chest and side. He tried to understand how he felt. Then he laughed and wheezed at the same time because he wasn't even sure how to feel what he felt.

He turned and walked slowly out of the park, and back across Eighty-sixth Street. David was gone by the time he got home, and it was very peaceful undressing alone, washing, getting into bed alone, and reading until he fell asleep with the light on and his book open on his chest.

David thought about it all the next day and he finally decided to try to make Kathy understand what she was doing – not just to the twins, but to herself too.

He didn't want to sound rehearsed, but he didn't want to fumble either. He'd tell her what it meant to be twins, how they'd never been separated, and weren't meant to be. He'd explain that it wasn't a question of choice, any more than their conception had been.

He knew it was important for him to be relaxed, charming,

reasonable. The irresistible older brother – by thirteen minutes, he'd tell her – and he knew exactly the kind of smile he'd have on his face. He planned carefully. Michael was due there at eight, so he'd get there at seven fifteen. That way there wouldn't be too much time for Kathy to argue or to get bored with what he was saying.

It was only six, and David was nervous. Understandably, he told himself, and he went into the Argus. He meant to have only two drinks, just to relax, but Si kept pouring, and by the time David left there to walk to the bus stop, he was a little tight. He bought Life Savers so Kathy couldn't smell liquor on his breath. Then, because it was late, and his time was running out, he took a cab.

Everything started out fine. She opened the door, knew who he was at once, and she put her hand to her throat like the heroine in a silent movie confronting the villain. Good. He wanted her to be just a little afraid of him.

'I thought we should talk, Kathy. Because you're about to fuck up my whole life.' He hadn't meant to say that or anything like it. He could hear the desperation in his voice, and he cursed Si for letting him drink so much. She just stood there with that hand raised to ward him off and for the first time in months the way a woman looked began to excite him.

'May I come in?' he asked softly.

'Of course.' She stood aside. It was seven thirty. He had thirty minutes. 'Maybe a drink?' he asked.

She gave him bourbon, then sat across from him, waiting. They drank while he looked around. Her paintings lined the walls in this room. Michael had told him that he hated them. David looked at them, and hated them too. There were people in most of them, individuals that David knew he would recognize at once if he ever saw them, yet their features and bodies were smooth, bland-looking. They sat alone, or across from another person, staring blindly at each other, or out of windows onto frozen silent streets where the trees were motionless and people were paralysed in the act of walking. Everything was silent in the paintings; windows opaque; the houses, trees and people were isolated. He knew it was morning in all of them –

eleven o'clock – but he didn't know how he could tell.

'Do you like them?' she asked after giving him time to examine them.'

'No.'

'Do you think they're bad?'

'I don't know. No, they're good. I mean you know what you're doing.'

'Yes.'

He asked for another drink and watched her pour it, trying not to stare at her breasts. But she saw where he was looking and she blushed. Pale honey with golden rose cheeks. She was pretty all right.

'Sit here?' he said. Very soft voice, it sounded sexy even to him.

She stood. 'I think we'd better talk if you want to. Michael will be here in a while.' He shrugged.

'I don't think you should marry my brother.'

'Why?'

'Because he'll leave you for me in the end.'

'I don't believe you.'

'Look at me, Kathy.' She looked down, and he got up and stood close to her. 'C'mon, babe,' he said as gently as he could. 'It means a lot to both of us. Look at me.' She looked up and they stared at each other. 'You see Michael, don't you?'

'No.' She tried to look away, but he caught her chin and forced her to face him again.

'Keep looking, Kathy. Eyes, nose, mouth, even our bodies. Look at my arm, Kathy.' He turned her head and held out his arm. 'Push up the sleeve. I can't do it myself.' She didn't move. 'Go ahead, Kathy, push up my sleeve.' She did. 'Higher,' he said softly, and she pushed it higher, exposing his forearm to the elbow. He still held her chin, so she had to look or close her eyes. He rolled the arm so she could see the underside, which was pale and shot with blue from the veins that corded as he clenched his fist. 'Make him show you this,' he whispered. 'Identical. Even the way the veins go. See?' He let go of her chin and took her hand, rubbing it against the veins. 'One egg . . . one code . . . one man. He'll come back to me all right. And what'll happen to you when he does? You don't need the hurt, baby, and you don't need Michael. There're a million other men who'd want you. You're so lovely.'

He kissed her. Her eyes were open, staring at him. Her hand was still on his arm.

He wondered if Michael kissed her like this and if she looked at him the way she was looking at David, eyes huge, and blind, so close it hurt, and he had to close his. He wanted to tell her that nothing was the way he'd planned, but that, no matter how crazy and out of hand things had gotten, he wouldn't hurt her.

He kept kissing, pushing her lips gently with his own until he could get his tongue between them. He made himself move so slowly it was almost painful, one hand holding the back of her head, and the other – so slowly – to the side of her breast so that his thumb touched her nipple. She tried to pull back, but he held her head still working his mouth against hers, and she stopped struggling.

She was frightened and excited all at once. Hurry, she thought, hurry, right here on the floor, David's face covering Michael's mind, Michael's arms around her, while she dug her fingers into David's back; David's will driving Michael's cock. Hurry, because he's going to be here in a minute and she'd have to take them both on. Any minute Michael would open the door . . .

She pulled back with all her might. David wasn't expecting it, and she almost got free, but he managed to grab her around the waist and pulled her back.

'Please, David, please let me go.' He ignored the cry and mashed her against him, but she scratched him, digging in with her fingernails until blood ran down his face, and pain blinded him. He forced her to her knees. Then he got his arm across her throat so she had to lie back or choke. She tried to scratch him again, but before she could he hit her in the face and grabbed her hair. He had her helpless then, because he could use the hair like a rein. He went back to kissing her, his lips still soft. He was on top of her working his hand up her skirt and she stopped struggling, waiting for his first touch. He slid his finger into her. 'Slowly,' he whispered. 'I won't hurt you.' He was dizzy; he'd come once already and was ready to again. At first she let him do what he wanted; then she tried to make it easier for him. She felt him pulling her skirt up and she helped him. She was saying his name and he kissed her again, his fingers sliding and circling as her hips started to move. She reached down and gently rubbed the underside of his penis.

'Easy,' he whispered, 'I'll come . . . easy.'

He eased himself into her, and she arched up to get him deeper. He was where Michael had been; he was doing what Michael had done. He kissed her cheek, her neck, her shoulder. He'd never been so gentle, never felt such tenderness for any woman or man. Then he heard the door open and knew Michael was there watching. For a second he thought Michael would lie down next to them, and when he turned his head he'd see his brother stretched on his side, leaning on his elbow, his eyes shadowed while he enjoyed watching, waiting his turn.

But Michael grabbed the back of his collar and jerked him to his feet. That left Kathy lying on her back, Michael and David stood suspended, staring at her while she knelt and pulled her skirt down. Then Michael saw the red mark on her face where David had hit her. He saw the scratch on David's cheek, and the slickness of her secretions on his hand; he raised his fist like a club.

'What – Mike, are you going to hit me?'

Michael didn't move, then he dropped his hand to his side, and he let go of his brother.

They were waiting to see what he would do next. She was kneeling, still out of breath, pale from shock and excitement, and David was pale too. Michael knew that if he left now they'd be back at it before the door closed. He wanted to ask David why he wasn't with Romer, he wanted to shout at him, to call him a faggot, then he realized how crazy that would sound after what he'd just seen. David came closer. 'Mike . . .' Michael started to sweat because he was afraid that if his brother touched him he'd hit him in the face – his own face – and keep hitting until the blood ran out his nose and mouth.

But David didn't touch him; he turned instead to Kathy, who hadn't moved. Her cheek was swelling where he had hit her. She hadn't put her underpants back on yet, and David knew she was naked under her skirt. He remembered a movie they'd seen, where a bunch of soldiers raped a little girl and her mother in a cathedral. The grainy grey film came back to him in stills – mother and daughter standing in a stream afterwards, while the mother held up the daughter's skirt and splashed water on her, trying to get her clean. Kathy looked like the daughter – bewildered, frightened, pitiful.

David didn't want to leave her like this because he hadn't meant any of it; he wanted to put ice on her cheek, help her wash, tell her how sorry he was, that he'd make it up to her – to both of them. Then he saw her looking at Michael as if he wasn't in the room, and without meaning to he said, 'Don't look so pitiful, Kathy. You loved it.'

Sweat rolled down Michael's face, and David saw him clench his fist, but he couldn't stop. 'That's why you didn't hear him come in, isn't it, Kathy? Because you were loving it. Right, baby? Every second of it.' He couldn't look at her any more, but he went on talking. 'Don't feel too bad, Kath. We share everything, don't we, Mike? Everything.'

Michael hadn't moved and David knew that the longer he stayed, the more he said, the worse it got. He had to get out of there.

'I'll be downstairs,' he said.

Michael didn't answer or look at him, and David's bravado broke and he stammered, 'D—don't be too long, it's raining.'

He made himself concentrate on getting out of there – to the elevator, down across the lobby, and out in the rain. He crossed the street to stand protected under a marquee, and looked up at her window. He could still see them together in grey, like film pictures he couldn't stop. *Kathy was crying now, and Michael was helpless, wondering what to do. Whether to leave; whether to stay and comfort her; whether to stay and make love to her. He was crossing the room, gently pulling her hands down, and putting his arms around her, rocking her gently against him, the way David had sometimes rocked Michael when they were young, and Michael was sick, or had hurt himself.* The pictures kept coming. *She'd stopped crying now. Michael was stroking her hair. Now he was kissing her, softly, the way David had kissed her.* David wanted to be there with them, watching, the way Michael had watched, standing in the foyer, until they turned out the lights, and left him alone in the dark.

'Waiting for someone?' David turned. It was the doorman.

Asshole question. 'My brother,' David said.

'Does he live around here?'

'No, but his boyfriend does, right across the street. You've probably seen him – blond, about six three. Wears a picture hat and elbow-length gloves.'

The doorman walked away. David went back to watching the window.

Nothing happened at first. Kathy didn't move, Michael didn't move. Then she started to cry and he went to her, and put his arms around her. She turned her head away, and he knew she'd never look at him again without seeing David, and he'd never make love to her again without remembering her under his brother – blind, oblivious, loving it.

David was everywhere now. Michael looked around. David's glass was still on the coffee table, and David might as well be there too, sipping bourbon from it and watching Michael try to comfort Kathy. He had really been there even that first night, when Michael believed that he was alone with her, that they were making love in the dark, in private. David would be with them tonight in her bedroom and if they married, David would be on their honeymoon. Michael had never been alone with her, and he never would be.

chapter nine

Mr Field smiled at Michael and held out his hand. Michael took it, and for a second wanted to squeeze the thin bony hand in his until Kathy's father was forced to kneel. Michael let go quickly, and picked up his glass.

'They must have been trying as youngsters.' Mrs Field sipped her champagne and leaned towards Sadel, who stared helplessly at the diamonds glittering in the other woman's ears. 'I mean the resemblance is so extraordinary.'

'Yes, extraordinary.'

More smiling, and they started toasting – to Michael and Kathy, to the future, to New York, to Boston, to medicine. Michael wondered what they'd do if he proposed a toast to cancer, and just then his eyes met David's and David grinned and raised his glass as if he knew what Michael was thinking. But Michael turned away and walked over to the suite's huge windows overlooking the park.

David put his drink down carefully and left the suite. He could hear Mrs Field telling Sadel how handsome her sons were, and when he closed the door behind him, he heard Michael laugh at something Kathy's sister Agnes said. But no one stopped him.

He didn't know what to do with himself, and he wandered through the lobby, and into the men's room, past the shoeshine chairs to the lounge where he could slick down his hair with Brylcreem, shave, spray his armpits, wash out his mouth, and powder his crotch all at the expense of the Plaza. He leaned on the counter and looked into the mirror on the wall. The attendant was sitting in a straight-backed chair, holding a towel ready. David stared at him in the mirror until the attendant shifted, and looked away.

'Moooohaha,' David gurgled at the mirror. The attendant gaped.

'Moooohoooo,' David moaned. He stretched out his arms and started to turn. The attendant tried to stay where he was; he even tried to smile as if he got the joke. David kept turning. 'Mooooo ...'

And then the man jumped up and ran out into the lobby. David turned back to the mirror as his face sagged. His skin looked grey, and there were circles under his eyes, under Michael's eyes too. The twins had been apart all week. Michael stayed at Kathy's every night except Wednesday, and then he got in very late and slept on the couch in the living room.

The attendant came back with the shoeshine boy who was almost seven feet tall and had knife scars on his neck. They stood at the door watching David, and he watched them. Then he looked at his own reflection. He looked mad even to himself. He tried to smile.

'Can I use the can?'

'Sure,' said the big one. 'Just don't throw no Kotex down it.'

David went into the cubicle, pissed, and washed his hands and face. The two men watched every move. He had to use a paper towel because the attendant wouldn't come near him. He left a dollar bill in the tip dish, walked out past them, waving good-bye, and out into the lobby. Then he leaned against one of the shop windows. It was three-fifty. Michael was marrying Kathy in ten minutes.

David tried to get through the ceremony by not listening. He could hear his mother crying in the background. He could see Kathy nod, smile, and bow her head. Michael's back was to him. Then he heard his brother's voice, and he had to listen.

'I, Michael, take you, Kathleen—' David was hypnotized. I Michael being of sound mind and body hereby bequeath . . . It went on, 'Forsaking all others . . .' They should amend the service for this occasion, David thought, because one twin couldn't forsake the other, because one couldn't forsake chains of chromosomes.

Her turn came and David stopped listening again. Then it was over, and Michael was kissing her. He'd never seen Michael touch her before. He backed out of the circle of guests, and headed for the room next door where a buffet was set up and waiters stood with trays of champagne. He took two glasses and went into the hall to the phone booth. He called Eastern, and they told him there was always room on the Boston shuttle.

'At eight o'clock?' The girl laughed. He might be the only one on the plane – not too many people going to Boston at eight o'clock Sunday night. He drank both glasses of champagne and called Romer.

'How's it going, Dave?'

'He married her.'

'Of course he married her. That's the point of weddings.'

David didn't answer.

'Nice party?'

'Expensive.'

'It should be. Her father owns half the town. Have a drink for me.' Then a significant pause, 'I can't wait to see you, David.'

He knew he should answer in kind. But he couldn't.

'I'll be on the eight o'clock shuttle,' David said.

'I'll be there.'

The ensemble started playing, and Michael danced with Kathy, then with her mother.

At seven Friedman made Michael switch from champagne to vodka, and he reeled to the men's room, splashed cold water on his face, combed his hair, and felt better. He looked better too and he was starting back to the party when David walked in, and closed the door.

'Michael, I'm catching the eight plane. I can't leave like this.'

Michael didn't say anything.

'I'm sorry, Michael, I don't know what else to say.'

He held out his hand. Michael didn't take it.

'Mike, please don't do this.'

They faced each other in the mirrors that lined the walls. If David hadn't had his hand out, Michael wouldn't have known which was his reflection.

'Please, Mikey.'

Michael didn't move.

'I swear to God I'll make it up to you,' David said.

'I don't know how you'll do that, Dave.'

'I have time. I'll think of something,' David said. He waited, then finally left Michael alone.

Michael counted to fifty before he went back to the party. The lights were dimmed and everybody was dancing except Mrs Field, who was left alone with the cold lobster. Michael could see from the way she was holding on to the table that she was very drunk. Gargan was there and some others from the hospital. Only David was missing.

He looked everywhere. David was gone. His eyes made another sweep of the room.

'David . . .'

'I beg your pardon?' A very tall, bony woman was standing next to him, holding a plate of lobster claws.

He ran. She stared after him; others turned to look too, but he kept going – down the stairs so fast he was afraid he'd fall, and across the lobby to the fountain entrance just as David was about to get into a cab at the corner of Fifty-ninth and Fifth. Michael just wanted to say good-bye.

'David!' The wind was too strong; he'd never hear.

David turned just as a bus blocked his view of the door.

'Shit!' Michael screamed and tore around the bus. 'David!' Then David saw him, turned and ran too and they met in front of the fountain, laughing, both out of breath, hugging each other.

'John Gilbert and Greta Garbo!' Michael held David tight against him.

'Olivia de Havilland and Leslie Howard,' David gasped.

Michael had to think: 'Charles Boyer and Ingrid Bergman.'

David started talking so fast it was hard to understand him.

'I don't know what got into me, Michael. I swear I don't. I'd never hurt anybody; I wouldn't hurt her, not on purpose. I wouldn't hurt you. I'm sorry. I was desperate.'

Michael kept saying, 'I know, I know.'

'Where are you going tonight?'

'Upstate. Killarn. I'll call you. Where'll you be?'

'Boston.' David hesitated, then added, 'At Romer's. It's in the book.'

Then, as Michael was about to step back, he felt his brother's lips on his cheek. The touch found a nerve that sent a shiver down his neck and across his body. He pulled back and stared at David, but David kept smiling.

'I'll talk to you tonight, Mikey. You can tell me how wonderful it was.' Then he looked serious for a moment,

'Congratulations, Michael.'

'Thank you, David.'

David found another cab, and Michael watched his brother get into the back seat, and turn and wave. Then the light changed; the cab drove east on Fifty-ninth, and Michael suddenly felt bereft, as if no one had told him that David was leaving, as if they'd decided only this minute to part and he was suddenly alone. He waited until the cab disappeared into the traffic, then turned to go back to his wedding party. He could still feel his brother's touch across his belly and groin.

David waited until one, but Michael didn't call. Romer was in the kitchen making hot toddies to celebrate the beginning of what he called their Boston period. The phrase made David think of menstruation.

He called their mother; she was half asleep.

'They're at Lake Killarn Lodge, Davey. But it's their wedding night. You shouldn't call.'

'You don't understand, Mother. He said he'd call me.'

'Oh, Duvele' – her old name for him – 'he was just saying that. He won't call tonight.'

He promised her he'd wait until the next day to call, but as soon as she'd hung up he called Killarn.

'Dr and Mrs Ross don't have a phone in their cabin,' the desk man told him.

'That's ridiculous. He's a physician. There's got to be some way to reach him.'

'I'm sorry. He told us that they weren't to be disturbed.' Then the voice sniggered. 'It's their wedding night.'

'You don't understand, it's very important that I talk to the doctor.'

'No, sir. *You* don't understand. There's no phone in their cabin, and it's a long walk just to reach them.'

David grabbed the phone off the antique inlaid table, yanked the cord out of the wall and threw it across the room.

Romer came rushing in from the kitchen.

'Dave, what's the matter? What happened?'

David stared at him dry-eyed, wondering how long he could take this man with his hot toddies, his metallic voice, and his fine old furniture.

'Sorry, Jim. I got the phone cord wrapped around my foot, and I tripped. Hope nothing's broken.'

part three

chapter ten

'If I lost as many patients in a year as you do in two weeks, I'd be on Seconal twenty-four hours a day,' Friedman said.

'Then you'd lose them even faster,' Michael answered.

They were having breakfast in the basement cafeteria.

'You look like you haven't slept for a week, Michael.'

Michael didn't answer that.

'And you're too thin.'

Still no answer.

'Let me get you another roll.'

Michael nodded because it was easier than arguing. He'd tell Friedman that he'd eat it later, and take it away with him wrapped in a napkin. Lately a lot of the morning rolls had ended up in the nearest waste can.

Friedman came back with a trayful: 'Orange juice for vitamin C, the promised roll with genuine corn-oil oleo, and a dish of prunes to keep you regular.' For himself Friedman brought two cheese Danish and an egg-salad sandwich. Michael finally laughed, and Friedman smiled and sat down again.

'What's on for today, beautiful?' Which wasn't such a joke, Friedman thought, because the lost weight had hollowed Michael's cheeks and given him an almost feminine beauty. Friedman told Kramer that if he were a faggot – which he said he would be if he could ever get it up again – his choice would be Michael Ross.

'You'd have a better chance with David.'

'I don't like David.'

'Why not?' But Friedman couldn't say why. Maybe, he told

Kramer, because he liked Michael so much, and he couldn't feel the same about both of them. 'Like you have to have a favourite Ross. You know what I mean?' Kramer said he had no idea what he meant.

'Bad day,' Michael said. 'They're operating on Carol Arland.'

'What did they decide to do?' Friedman asked.

'Pelvic exenteration.'

Friedman paled. 'Then we're going to the movies. *North by Northwest*'s playing on Eighty-sixth Street. We'll have lunch at the dime store, then we'll eat popcorn and wash it down with vodka. My treat.'

'Gargan wants me there, Bill. She's going to be my patient.'

'What're her chances?'

Michael looked at the clock. 'I'll take this with me.' He wrapped the roll in a paper napkin.

'What about it, Mike?'

Michael shrugged. 'I don't know. She could live – if you can call it living.'

Friedman tried to smile. 'She'll catch up on her reading.'

'Yeah.' Michael stood up to go, then turned back.

'Bill, come with me.'

Friedman looked down at what was left of his sandwich, 'Jesus, Mike, don't ask me.'

Michael started to say please, but he saw the expression on his friend's face and he touched his shoulder and left. All the way down the hall from the cafeteria he tried not to think of David. When he reached the phone booth near the elevator, he stopped. A nurse was inside, and Michael stood where she could see him and tapped his foot impatiently. He looked at the clock and saw that he had ten minutes to go. The nurse was winding up, nodding, turning her back to say good-bye, or maybe I love you. She left the booth and Michael took all the change out of his pocket, and counted out enough for Boston. The booth smelled of her perfume, and he wanted to leave the door open, but the corridor was full of carts being wheeled up and down, so he had to shut it and stand surrounded by her scent.

The call went through, and the phone was ringing in Boston. In a second he would hear his brother's voice. Seven fifty. They were awake at Romer's house, having coffee in his breakfast nook overlooking the Beacon Hill garden. Michael could see Romer sipping his coffee and watching his lover cross the room to answer the phone, watching the slide of his back and the globes of his buttocks with that sensual, appraising look he had.

'Hello,' David answered. Michael held onto the little ledge. He hadn't even meant to call.

'Hello?' David sounded worried. 'Hello, hello.' Suddenly he knew it was Michael. 'Mike, Mike? It's you? Hello. Answer me, Michael.' Michael shook his head. I'm sorry, he thought. I don't know what's the matter with me. Then he hung up, and went out of the stifling booth into the corridor. He had six minutes, and he was afraid he'd be late, but the elevator was waiting, and he rode up with a bunch of nurses and interns who eyed each other like contestants in a sporting match.

Carol Arland's body was shaved and exposed under the green light. A line was drawn the length of her abdomen, and Clark, the star, was waiting for the anaesthetist's okay. Michael was the only one in the theatre, and they couldn't see him clearly from the floor, so he closed his eyes.

Someone sat down next to him.

'Hey, Mike, you don't want to miss a minute of this.' Friedman was sitting there grinning at him.

'Bill, you didn't have to—'

Friedman shrugged. 'Who knows? I might have stage three cancer of the cervix some day.'

'You don't have a cervix.'

'Don't quibble.'

The anaesthetist signalled Clark, and he came forward. Her bare skin looked disembodied, meat laid out to dry. Clark raised the knife, and Michael held the sides of his chair and made himself watch.

Gargan had told him it would be bad, but nothing had prepared him for what happened next. Clark must have thought that small suturing was beneath his dignity, because he just cut, and kept on cutting until everybody and everything around the table was covered with blood. Friedman and Michael looked at each other, both white, both fighting nausea. Blood spurted until Gargan and Kramer were soaked, but Clark kept cutting.

Finally the great man finished, and stepped back, arms raised like a magician at the end of his act, while Kramer and Gargan moved in to keep what was left of the woman on the table from bleeding to death.

Michael leaned forward to try to get some blood back into his head. He looked up in time to see Friedman stumbling blindly for the toilet which some savvy architect had put only a few feet from the last row of seats. Michael looked back at the body under the light one more time, then he followed Friedman.

'Jesus,' he said after they'd been sick and were splashing their faces with cold water, 'Jesus, I'm sorry, Bill. I had no idea it'd be that bad.'

'Me either. Don't tell me she's going to live? You don't really think there's enough left . . . Oh, Mike, I'm sorry . . .' Michael ran back to the cubicle. His throat and nose were raw, and he felt as if his whole body were collapsing back to front, leaving nothing in the middle.

When he came out, Friedman said, 'I want my breakfast money back.'

At five they brought Mrs Arland to her room. Michael sat with her until five thirty when he had to make rounds. He came back at six, and for a moment, standing there in the doorway and looking at her, he thought she was dead. Then he saw her chest move. The catheter bottle dripped. He returned at six thirty, but she still had that terrible pallor. He stood next to the bed and watched for a few minutes. Then he read her chart. By seven thirty she was flushed in stripes. He came into the room again and watched; the stripes faded and left a colour more or less lifelike. He pulled a chair next to her bed and waited. Fifteen minutes later her eyelids fluttered and he went to find her husband, who was waiting in the lounge. The husband leaned over her bed; he'd been drinking and Michael could smell it across the room. Gargan with his sixth sense of when the patient comes back to life was at the door.

'Carol, honey.' The husband breathed fumes into his wife's face and she opened her eyes. She saw him, and looked past him; then she saw Michael and tried to smile. Her eyes closed and she was out again.

Gargan nodded at the husband. 'She'll come in and out for a while. It'll be hours before she is coherent. Then she's going to be in pain, and we'll probably sedate her again. So you might as well go home, Mr Arland.'

Her eyes were open again, but they were blank and dry-looking. Michael noticed that she had freckles and light blue eyes like his brother's lover, and that she must have once been very handsome. Again her eyes swept past her husband as if he were of no consequence and came to rest on Michael.

He almost ran out into the hall. But Mag Stapleton's assistant was waiting for him with Carol Arland's file. He pretended to study it, but the words blurred, and all he could remember from the chart was that she was forty-two and had one child.

It was the next day before Michael had a chance to look back in on her. Her eyes were closed and he thought she was asleep until she reached out and touched him. The back of her hand was stabbed from too many IV entries.

'Is my husband here?' she whispered.

'I don't know. I'll look.'

'No, don't do that. I want to talk to you. Will you sit down?'

'You should rest.' He didn't want to talk to her.

'Please bring the chair.'

'I have to put your chart back.'

He went to the station and refiled her chart. Then he gave himself five minutes of just standing there with his arms hanging at his sides and his eyes half closed so that the far wall, the floor, and the doors looked slightly blurred.

Finally he turned and went back to her room.

'It's about – about what they did to me,' she whispered.

Michael pulled the chair over and sat next to her.

'About everything that they took out. I talked to Dr Clark, and he said that' – she was blushing – 'that my husband and I could never make love again.'

Michael didn't answer.

'What I'm worried about is whether or not Dr Clark told my husband.'

'If Dr Clark said he'd tell him . . .'

'I'm sure he did,' she said. 'But my husband was talking as if he didn't know.' She blushed even deeper and Michael was surprised that she had enough blood pressure to blush at all. 'He's an outspoken man, my husband, and he might have been joking around just to make me feel better. But maybe he wasn't; maybe he still doesn't know.'

Michael rearranged her Kleenex and water carafe without saying a word.

'Could you find out?' she asked. He unknotted her bell cord. 'I can't stand him joking about it and maybe thinking that when I get out . . .'

He made himself look at her. She was still blushing, but her eyes were dry.

He stood up, 'Are they giving you enough pain-killer?'

'Yes,' smiling, 'I feel very floaty. You know?'

He nodded, and she waited.

'I'll talk to him this afternoon, Mrs Arland.'

At five exactly Arland came out of the elevator. He was a big man, much taller and broader than Michael.

'Mr Arland, I'd like to talk to you.'

He wasn't carrying flowers or books, or anything from home the way the other husbands did. But she'd been in and out of the place so often, and for so long, that maybe she already had everything she needed.

'Sure, kid, what's the problem?' He had a loud voice and Michael led him to the lounge and got coffee for both of them.

'Tastes like shit,' Arland said. Michael nodded; they were both extremely uncomfortable.

'I don't know how much Dr Clark or Dr Gargan told you about your wife's operation . . .'

'They said that they were going to . . . to sort of gut her.'

Michael scalded his tongue on the coffee.

Arland went on, 'They said it could save her life.'

'Did they tell you they had to remove the upper portion of her vaginal canal?'

'No.'

Fuck Clark, thought Michael, fuck Gargan.

'They should have told you, because what they did means that she can never have sexual intercourse again.'

Arland put his paper cup down on the plastic table; it started to leak and Michael watched the ring it made, not wanting to look at the man next to him.

Then Arland said, 'Is that what we're sitting here and pissing our pants about?'

Michael nodded.

'I haven't screwed Carol in over two years,' Arland said. 'Not since her hysterectomy. I couldn't get used to the idea that they'd taken everything out. She didn't seem like a whole woman any more.'

Michael thought of her clear, fine blue eyes and the smooth, slightly freckled skin.

'No reflection on her,' Arland was saying. 'She's a nice woman; used to be pretty.' She still is pretty, Michael wanted to tell him. She was pretty for the past two years, you prick.

'And she always was a good mother.'

Michael was nodding, standing up and backing towards the door.

'But I just couldn't do it. I mean literally couldn't. I know she felt bad about it . . .'

'Excuse me, Mr Arland. I'm a little late.'

'Sure. Thanks for telling me anyway.'

When Michael returned at seven she was awake, but they'd just given her some Demerol and she was smiling gently at him.

'Are you married?' she asked him.

He nodded.

'Is she pretty?'

He didn't know what to say, but she didn't wait for an answer. 'Did you tell him?' she asked.

'Yes.'

'How did he react?'

Even through the Demerol haze, her look sharpened and Michael thought her whole body tensed. He looked at her for a minute, then, inspired, he said, 'He took it very badly, Mrs Arland. I called one of the nurses in and we both sat with him until he was calm enough to see you.'

She nodded as if it were the answer she expected, then closed her eyes.

✱

Friedman and Michael went to Wong's where Michael drank steadily until eight. Then he called the floor at the hospital and was told that Mrs Arland was still more asleep than awake. She'd been given her full dose of Demerol and would hold in limbo until morning. He and Friedman continued to drink until ten. Friedman had eaten about six meals that day, and snacked on egg rolls while they drank. Michael had had coffee, nothing else, and by ten he was too drunk to walk straight. Friedman took him home and got him upstairs while the doorman called ahead, so Kathy was waiting for them at the door. She smiled, polite Boston, while they got her husband's collar and belt loose, and she asked about Beth as if they'd met in the lobby of the Carlton while she was on her way to have her hair done. Michael passed out sitting upright with his hands folded neatly in his lap. He hadn't said anything since they left Wong's. In fact, Friedman was sure he hadn't said anything for the last hour they were there.

'Would you like some coffee?' Kath asked.

'Sure. Got any cookies?' When they were in the kitchen Friedman asked, 'He's having a lot of trouble sleeping, isn't he?'

She nodded, measuring the coffee, 'And eating,' she said. 'I've tried every recipe published to find something he just couldn't resist.'

'Pussy,' Friedman said.

'I've tried that too,' she said. They both tried to keep straight faces, but she broke first, and then Friedman. They laughed wildly while the coffee water boiled and steamed up the windows, and Michael began to snore in the living room.

They stopped finally and Friedman asked, 'How long has it been since their mother died?'

'About six months. I'll never forget that funeral – Michael with David next to him every minute: "Now there's just us, Mikey. Now we're all we've got".'

'Christ! Did he say that?'

'Not in so many words. But he has other ways of expressing himself. For instance he refuses to sell that mausoleum on Riverside Drive, and it was left to both of them, so Michael can't sell it unless David agrees.'

'Why not rent it out?'

'David says whoever rented it would ruin it. You should've heard him. "Think what they'd *do* to the *furniture*, Mikey. And to Dad's *rug* and to all the *books*".' She imitated David's voice so well, Friedman felt a little uncomfortable.

'What does he want?' Friedman asked.

'He wants him and Michael to live there. But he can't have that, so he'll settle for what he can get.'

'Which is maybe you and Michael living there.'

'Oh, Bill, I don't want to. I love this place. Why should I live in that old people's home just because David Ross is sentimental about his father's rug?' She sounded close to tears.

'The fellowship doesn't help, Kathy; Michael should resign it and go back to general gynaecology. Gargan can take it because he's got the thickest hide on the East Side, but Mike's a cream puff. He dies a little with everyone of them. They hurt – he hurts. Their husbands cry and he feels their loss and desire. It's just not for him.'

'It isn't only the job, or his mother dying, or the apartment,' Kathy said.

'What else?'

'David just won't leave him alone.'

She poured the coffee and brought cream and sugar. He could see she was trying to decide how much to tell him.

'He calls Michael every Sunday, except when he pretends to forget or to be too busy.'

'What's so terrible about that?'

'He doesn't forget. He's testing to see if Michael will call him.'

'And does he?'

'Always.'

'What does David say to him during these calls?'

'He tells him how happy he is in Boston. He tells him about the garden he and Romer have, about the house on Cape Ann, about the restaurants they go to, and the fancy parties. He tells him how much money he's making, how all his patients are healthy, happy and pregnant. About his tailormade suits, about his newfound taste for this and that; about what a cultured, tasteful, intelligent, aristocratic homosexual he is since he had the discretion to leave his wretched brother with his wretched wife.' There were tears of anger in her eyes. Friedman listened.

'Then he starts in on how much money they could make in Boston, how many patients they'd have if they set up there – together of course. He talks about office rents, about the parks, about the beautiful society women. About what a nice house they'd have together.'

'Together? What about you and Romer?'

'We'd be discarded, I suppose.'

'He can't have Michael in Boston and in the apartment. He can't have both.'

'He doesn't want both. He wants Michael – here or in Boston or wherever he can get him.'

Just before Friedman left, he leaned over and looked at Michael asleep on the couch. He looked very young, his face was smooth, his eyes rolled beneath his lids. Friedman wondered what he was dreaming about.

'It's a connection you and I can't even begin to understand,' Charles Snyder told Friedman.

Snyder was Co-Chairman of Manhattan's Psychiatric Department and had been one of Friedman's favourite advisers at Columbia.

'The twin in Boston sounds like the dominant, and he won't let Michael go. Meantime, Michael's trying to be himself – something besides David's double.'

'He is himself.'

'Maybe, but he doesn't know that. Michael Ross has a confusion the rest of us don't. For most of us, there's ourselves, and then there's everyone else . . . "them". We can differentiate; we can act for our own good when threatened. We can say "It's him or me," and know what we mean. But Michael can't. There's someone in the world so much like him he probably can't tell his own good from his twin's. Think of the confusion when David wants Michael to do something that Michael thinks might be bad for him. How can he decide whose side he's on?

'Then there's the sheer comfort of their being together. When Michael's with David he's probably never frightened, never lonely. He probably sometimes feels that together he and David can do anything. Maybe even save the women . . . so maybe Michael feels guilty, as if he's letting his patients die.'

'All doctors feel that,' Friedman said. 'Except shrinks, who always have another chance.'

'Not always. Losing a patient over the edge is like having them die. Worse maybe, because you keep thinking you should be able to do something.'

'Does it sound like Michael Ross is going over the edge?'

'Not like that, no. He might have a breakdown – maybe a bad one. But it sounds like he could make it back.'

'What about the other one?'

Snyder shrugged, 'I don't know. He sounds pretty classic. The deserted twin . . . brother . . . mother . . . father. Holding a note that poor Michael can never pay.'

'What happens when David tries to foreclose?'

'I don't know. He may never try, or he may wait for circumstances to do it for him. Don't forget, Michael's got the roughest job in medicine, and every time he loses a patient he's pulled closer to his twin; to the one person in the world who won't judge him.' Snyder lit a cigarette and watched the smoke. 'From what you tell me, it's Michael who's the maverick. Most twins stay together, not just out of convenience, but because they're perfect company for each other. In a way, David is the abused one. He expected his brother to behave normally, to stay with him. He probably waits too.'

'What's he waiting for?'

'For Michael not to be able to live without him any more.'

chapter eleven

'Mike, it's David.'

Michael laughed. 'I recognized your voice.'

'I'm at the airport,' David said.

'Where are you going?'

'I'm where I'm going, Mike. I'm at La Guardia – Mike, are you there?'

'Yes.' Michael felt weak and his heart was pounding. 'I'll be right there. I'll take a cab.'

'Hey, easy.'

'Why easy? Don't you have time?'

David laughed, 'I've got the whole weekend, Mike.'

Amazing. Michael needed David, and there he was.

'Let me hang up and get out there for Christ's sake.'

'No, meet me in the park by the fountain.'

Michael started to protest, but David cut him off.

'Bethesda fountain, half an hour.' Then David said softly, 'Just half an hour, Michael. That's all.'

Michael left a message at the Art Students League for Kathy. Then he changed his clothes, but he was still early. He left the house anyway, and crossed the park at Sixty-seventh. When they were kids, they used to play here. The park had been lovely then, clean and quiet and they used to pretend they were in the country. Most of it was ruined now. The ground was covered with broken glass and torn paper. People walked their dogs in the grass.

The fountain looked the same from above, but close up, he could see cigarette butts and tinfoil in the stones.

He leaned against the edge of the fountain, waiting. Most of the other people around the fountain were black or Puerto Rican, and a few of them were staring at him. He realized that he was well dressed, that he was wearing a watch, and that the only other whites were a couple of ragged-looking hillbilly types. He looked up towards the street, then at his watch so they'd know that someone else was coming, that he wasn't alone. But two of them didn't seem to care, and they separated from the others and walked towards Michael.

One was black with straightened hair that stuck out over his ears; the other one was hillbilly – pasty-faced with red-rimmed pale eyes. Michael tried to stay calm; he took inventory. He had about seventeen dollars in his wallet, plus the watch his father had given him when he graduated. It was gold and might satisfy them if the seventeen dollars wasn't enough.

They were getting close. The hillbilly had some front teeth missing, and he looked grey and sick as if he'd been protein-starved for twenty years. Michael smiled in spite of himself.

'You say one of your attackers had protein malnutrition and the other was a black with straightened hair?' The two cops would look at each other. 'That's not much of a description, Doctor.' Then he'd tell them about the missing teeth, and – wait – the black was wearing a leather jacket with Indian designs on it, surely that helps . . .

The others were watching, looking forward to what was going to happen. They wouldn't help him. Michael was trapped. Behind him was the fountain; to his right the stairs to the street, but they were too far away. The bridle-path tunnel was nearer, but he thought that if they got him in the dark, they'd kill him. Out here, they'd take the money and watch, and maybe draw a little blood. The lagoon was on his left. Absolutely trapped.

'Michael! Hey, Mike!'

David was standing at the top of the stairs, waving both arms, his coat caught in the wind, blowing out behind him like a cape. The two men stopped and everybody looked up. Michael waved, laughed with relief, and started to run to David.

The two men and everybody on the plaza stared at the twins. Michael saw that they were startled, a little frightened, which they should be, he thought, because he was suddenly huge, invincible. He could run across the stones to his brother so quickly his feet skimmed the ground. He was stronger than all the men standing in the park put together.

'Count Dracula, I presume.' Michael grabbed David. Everybody stared – he hugged him – they kept staring. 'Jesus Christ!' he whispered. 'Did you bring the silver bullets?' David held him closer.

'I am the silver bullet,' David said, 'and what the fuck is going on here?'

'A little would-be mayhem.'

The two men stood, cold and impotent, watching the twins.

David said, 'What's the matter? You never seen twins before?' Then he said, 'C'mon, Mike, let's get out of here; I told the carriage to wait.'

•

They stopped first at Stampler's bar, an old-time favourite where they used to bring women; and Michael was so excited the alcohol seemed to leak right through him and he had to piss again and again.

David laughed at him. 'One more time and you're going to come out of the can an old man, squeezed dry. Drink up, we've got to go.'

No, it was too early. 'We've got time. I told Kathy we'd be back in a couple of hours.'

'Kathy! We're not going there, Mike.'

'She's expecting us.'

'Then call her and tell her to stop expecting us.'

Michael flushed. 'I can't do that, Dave.'

'Not even to see and be seen by James Holmes?'

James Holmes was the 1958 Nobel Laureate in Medicine and Physiology. Michael stared while David pulled a card from his wallet. It was an invitation to the home of Dr Holmes, for David Ross and guest – for tonight – for right now.

David put the invitation back and finished his drink. Michael noticed that his brother's wallet was stuffed with money.

Holmes owned a house on East End Avenue in the eighties; it was a mess. Drapes hid packing boxes; some of the glasses had straw in them, and the pictures on the walls didn't match the light spots on the paint. The place was enormous; the twins climbed four floors looking for people they knew, and saw that the stairs went up at least one more floor, but a folding gate blocked the stairwell.

'I wonder what they keep up there,' David commented.

'Or who?'

Michael had forgotten the impact the two of them made. Everyone they passed stared at them, especially the women, and Michael looked for the prettiest the way he used to before he met Kathy. The great doctor was holding court on the second floor on a huge down couch before an unswept fireplace. Pizzas dried on a round oak table nearby. Three half-gallon bottles of vodka stood in a row on the window seat along with some bad wine, also in half-gallon bottles, and plates and plates of damp crackers. Michael had to half-bow to shake hands with Holmes because the man was so short and had sunk so deep into the down pillows.

Holmes thought he recognized Michael's name. 'You must be thinking of David, my brother.' Michael nodded across the room to where David was talking intently to a young blond whom Michael recognized as the Coronary Research Fellow. Holmes looked over, remarked on their being twins, then shook his head. 'No. It's Michael Ross I'm thinking of.' Dark, bright eyes stared at him. 'ACA fellowship, right?'

Michael nodded.

'Of course,' Holmes said. 'Matt Gargan talked about you. He said you're a miserable softy who had some cockamamie idea about ketosteroids and ovarian cancer prognosis.'

Michael smiled. 'I guess that *is* me.'

Holmes nodded at the pillow next to him, and Michael sank into it.

'You know my own work was concerned with hormones and cancer?'

'Yes sir. I think everybody in this room probably knows that.'

'Of course. That's why they're here, isn't it?'

'I'm sorry,' Michael said. 'I didn't mean—'

'You did, and you're right.'

David was still talking to the blond. They moved over to the pizza and wine, and David seemed amused.

Holmes said, 'Why don't you get us some vodka, and tell me about this ketosteroid thing.'

'You don't think it's cockamamie?'

'Matt Gargan's a nice guy, but short on imagination. I think you may have something.'

They talked for a long time; Michael got up once to get them another drink and a slice of pizza, which was now cold and hard, and they went on talking. Mostly about Michael's work. He was a little shy at first, but Holmes kept asking questions and soon Michael was doing most of the talking. He had forgotten how much he knew about the ketosteroids; he was looking forward to Holmes' questions, sure he could answer them. He knew that Holmes was impressed and he started thinking that it was all much more important than just the half-assed hypothesis of a resident in gynaecology; Holmes obviously thought so. Finally

Michael told Holmes how much of it was based on Holmes' early work, and Holmes – James Holmes, Nobel Laureate – blushed because he was pleased at being one of Michael's sources. It was a good moment, and Michael toasted it silently with the vodka. Then he told Holmes he'd read most of his recent reports.

'That work,' Holmes said, 'stretches back into the thirties; that's how long ago I started. Of course, we didn't have computers then to do analyses. We didn't have half the equipment you have today. A lot of time was taken up with stupid scut work that no one has to do any more. You're a clinician now, aren't you?'

Michael nodded.

'Ever do real lab work?'

'No.'

'You'll have to if this starts looking really important.'

'I was just interested in using the ketosteroid measurements as a clinical tool, Doctor.'

Holmes looked closely at him. 'What if it turns out to be more than just a "clinical tool"? What if it has more basic implications. You'll have to take a broader look at your whole approach.'

Michael didn't know what to say. David was circling them, and watching. Other people were watching, too, wondering who the guy was who was monopolizing Holmes.

'You'd better think. Hormones are my field. I've spent half a lifetime trying to understand their role in normal and in pathological development. And I think you've hit on something. The ketosteroids—'

David was leaning over the back of the couch pretending to listen, but when Holmes turned away to pick up his drink, David mouthed 'Let's go.'

Michael shook his head, but David pointed at the blond, and then at the door. Holmes saw him, and smiled.

'Your brother's ready to leave'.

'I guess so; we're already late.' Which was true. It was after nine and Kathy didn't know where he was. Holmes took out his card and handed it to Michael. It wasn't even engraved.

James T. Holmes Ph D
Department of Endocrinology
Kay Shahn Institute of Cancer Research

Then his office address and telephone number.

'Call me tomorrow . . . no, that's Saturday, isn't it?'

Michael nodded and smiled.

'Call me Monday. We'll have lunch. There's an Institute dining room of sorts and they have good soup.'

Michael shook hands with Holmes.

'I've always had luck with softies,' Holmes said.

David and the blond were waiting in the entrance hall, looking at their watches.

The blond claimed to have a horror of subways so they took a cab downtown.

'I've got to call Kathy.'

'You can call her from Fred's,' said the blond.

'Who's Fred?' he asked David.

David shrugged and the blond gushed, 'He's a dress designer who makes totally millions and who always has somebody totally fabulous at his parties. Last time it was Lauren Bacall, and the time before that it was one of the Rothschilds.' The blond, whose name was Dick Winters (David called him Cock Summers), talked all the way to MacDougal Street where the fabulous designer had his fabulous loft. Michael hated him by the time he got out of the cab. He was even a little annoyed at David and refused to go upstairs until he'd called Kathy. She was worried and angry and ended the conversation by telling him if he weren't there by ten, he needn't bother to come home at all. David said it was an open invitation to stay out all night, and the blond looked arch.

Michael felt like a child beside them because they didn't have to call anyone to explain where they were and what they were doing. They pushed open the door to a hallway reeking of garbage, up a hundred stairs and into the biggest room Michael had ever seen. Half the ceiling was a skylight from which plants drooped like moss in the half light. The floor was covered with plastic tile coated to look wet, and the furniture – what there was of it – was close to the floor, soft-looking, with lots of pillows.

There must have been fifty or sixty people there, but the place was so big it seemed half empty. Most of the men were younger than the twins and very good-looking. It was hard to tell how old the women were or what they looked like under the makeup. One woman stared at them as if she wanted to cross herself. Many of the guests wore sunglasses and someone had put sunglasses on one of the African masks that hung on the walls.

Some people were dancing, mostly barefoot, and some were sitting on the couches and pillows, smoking and talking or just staring off into space; and some were necking. There was a sleeping balcony half of which was a huge mattress and some were moving around on it, but it was too dark to see what they were doing. The blond took David's arm and led him around, and Michael followed, not knowing what else to do. A young, very handsome man came up to him and began talking about the beatific vision of today's youth. He looked beatific, about eighteen or nineteen, and was smoking grass. He offered Michael a reefer, and Michael looked at David, who nodded.

'We'll share it.'

It was a miserable-looking thing that got soggy quickly, but they smoked it down until the paper glowed and burned their fingers. When they finished it, the blond gave them another and watched David light and inhale. David smiled sleepily at Michael and the blond half sat, half lay on the pillows next to them. Michael kept thinking that it was very late, three or four in the morning and couldn't believe that it wasn't midnight yet. Kathy couldn't be really pissed, not if he got home by midnight.

He looked around, but Lauren Bacall wasn't there.

'I'm Fred.' A tall thin man stood over him. Michael got up and left David sitting with the blond, who had his arm around him.

Fred put out his hand, and Michael took it. 'I'm Michael.' Fred shook it until Michael's eyeballs rattled, but he kept smiling. They weren't going to make an ass out of him – not until midnight.

'That's my brother.'

Fred looked down at David.

'My twin,' Michael said.

'I can see that,' Fred said.

'We heard Lauren Bacall was going to be here.'

'She cancelled at the last minute. Cramps.'

'Oh god,' Michael said. 'That's terrible.'

'I'm glad someone understands.' Fred gave Michael another reefer and led him away from David. Michael tried to pull away but couldn't, so he looked back to be sure that David could see where he was being taken. But David's eyes were closed and the blond was kissing him on the mouth. Michael snapped himself front and kept his eyes on Fred's back.

When they were a little way from the others, Fred turned around.

'Your brother looks all fixed up.'

Michael didn't say anything.

'Are you straight or gay?'

'What?'

'Do you want a woman or a man?'

Michael took a deep drag on the reefer. 'A woman, I think.'

'Too bad. You're pretty. Anybody ever tell you that?'

'Everybody – all the fucking time. Beautiful is what I hear most.'

Fred nodded. 'Everybody's got his cross.'

He led on and Michael followed. They stopped in front of a woman who had messy black dyed hair, a long white face, and huge dark eyes rimmed in black.

'This is Mary Jane, Michael.' Fred laughed wildly. 'Honest to God, that's her name, Mary Jane.'

'How do you do, Mary Jane? I'm Michael Ross.'

She had a long straight nose, and thin, well-moulded lips. Her eyes were very dark and she was pretty. In fact, as Michael looked around he realized that most of the people were pretty. Probably nice too. He avoided looking at the corner where he'd left David.

He put his arm around her and she took his reefer and took a drag. He really wanted it back, but he mustn't be mean. She was wearing false eyelashes around those incredible eyes.

'Allen Ginsberg lives a block away,' she said.

'Who?' Not that it mattered.

'Allen Ginsberg; "America I'm going to put my queer shoulder to the wheel." Allen Ginsberg.'

'Oh, yes.' He didn't know what she was talking about, but he thought her voice was nice and the way she barely moved her mouth when she spoke was charming.

'What do you do?' she asked. The same question he would have gotten uptown. Things weren't so different after all, except that everybody here was so good-looking.

'I'm a doctor.'

'Of what?'

He had to think what she meant. That certainly wasn't an uptown question.

'Medicine,' he said finally.

She stared at him sadly as if he'd admitted some defect. 'Are you Jewish too?'

'Yes.'

'So'm I.' She sighed. 'Mary Jane isn't my real name. Is that your twin brother over there?'

Michael nodded without looking and Mary Jane began to laugh. 'He sure doesn't act Jewish. You should see what that guy's doing to—'

'I . . . excuse me.' Michael moved away from her and headed towards a closed door that might be the bathroom. The walls went up forever, the floor was frozen, and he could slide where he was going, pushed by the wind, gliding without effort, a figure of incomparable beauty, wearing a cape of black silk that blew out behind him. He opened the door. A woman was sitting on the toilet with a shiny black jump suit bunched around her ankles. A man was standing across from her, talking to her, and holding two glasses. They both turned and looked at him.

'I'm almost through,' she said.

The light above the sink shone on her breasts and thighs, and Michael suddenly became immensely excited. He shut the door and turned right into Mary Jane who was standing behind him; he actually hit her with his penis.

'I'm sorry,' he said.

'Come with me,' she whispered, and she took his hand while he glided behind her on the ice to another door that opened into a moonlit room full of tables and shadows. There was carpet underfoot and he had to walk normally. He heard rustling, and people breathing. They weren't alone in the room. Mary Jane led him to one of the tables – or was it a sideboard? He could see dishes piled on the top; he must be careful. She positioned him so that he was leaning back against the table-sideboard-buffet. She opened his pants so tenderly he wasn't sure it was happening, took out his penis and guided it into her mouth.

Everything changed colour. He was afraid her eyelashes would come off and he'd have to explain the false eyelashes caught in his pubic hair.

The door opened and David came into the room. Michael could see him clearly.

'My little brother,' David said softly.

Michael thought it was perfect that David was there too, with this lovely girl. He smiled at his brother and shook his head because he felt so good. David smiled back, and leaned against the wall to watch.

'Hey, Dave.' Michael looked at David until he wasn't aware of anything except his brother's face and the fact that he was going to come in a second.

chapter twelve

Someone was singing 'My time is your time.' They went on to 'I've got you under my skin . . .' Then another voice: 'Songs from the forties – the golden oldies . . .'

Michael opened his eyes – the television set was on, but the picture was rolling and he closed them again quickly. When he woke up again, it was daylight and the picture was steady. Dave Garroway was looking at the camera . . . at Michael . . . and chatting as if he could see him. Michael reached over and turned him off, shading his eyes. He was in their old room at home on Riverside Drive, but he didn't remember getting there. He was face down, half off the bed, looking at the floor, and he thought of the old man's room just downstairs. The Pereras had moved a couple of years ago. He didn't know where.

David came out of the bathroom.

'C'mon, get dressed. I'll make some coffee. The last boat leaves at ten.'

They'd done something so bad they had to leave the country, and they'd signed on for a three-year whaling voyage that left today – at ten. 'What boat?'

'From Sheepshead Bay. We're going fishing.'

'We can't do it all in one weekend.'

'We can try. C'mon, get dressed.'

Michael called Kathy while David drank the coffee. When she heard his voice, she hung up.

The twins took the same subway to Sheepshead Bay that they used to take in the summer with their father. When they got there, they bought beer and salami sandwiches the way they used to, and Michael called the hospital from a telephone booth on the dock.

'Dr Ross, Mrs Arland's been asking for you.'

David climbed up the gangway to the fishing boat.

'Nothing wrong. She just wanted to see you. Would you like to talk to her?' Mag Stapleton's voice made it clear that she thought Michael should talk to her. But the little boat hooted, and David was waving.

'You're sure she's all right?' Michael asked.

'Yes. Everything's stable physically.'

'I'll be there tonight tell her.'

Stapleton seemed reluctant to break the connection.

'Dr Gargan's been asking for you too.'

'C'mon,' David yelled. The boat hooted again.

'Anything special?'

'No. Just wondering where you've been.'

Shit! The one weekend he had alone with his brother. Why couldn't they leave him alone just for an afternoon? Was it too much to ask?

The captain was yelling something at David, gesticulating, and David was waving and smiling, trying to get them to wait.

112

Now David was shouting at Michael again and Stapleton said, 'Mrs Pollack's been looking for you too.'

'I thought she was going home.'

'Not 'til tomorrow, but she wants to say good-bye.'

The big good-bye, Michael thought; she was a nice woman.

'And Dr Friedman too—'

'I'm sorry, Mrs Stapleton. I've got to go.'

'But when will . . .'

'I'll call this afternoon; maybe stop in later. As long as nothing's wrong.'

'Nothing's wrong, but there . . .'

The captain was pulling at the gangway; the boat was going to leave without him. David ran along the rail to the opening, waving and yelling.

'I'm sorry, Mrs Stapleton . . .' He hung up, yanked the booth door open and ran to the gangway just as it started to shift. David grabbed his hand and with a heave pulled him over the gap between plank and deck onto the boat.

They caught four small flounder, which they gave to the captain. Then they got back on the subway, cold and wind-burned and rode home through the spring afternoon.

'Do you remember the last time?' David asked. 'The year before we went to school.'

'Sure. Was it in April too?'

'That's it. April, when the blues hit.'

They were fishing for porgie and they drifted into a huge school of them. If Michael leaned over the side and strained his eyes, and if the boat hit the swell the right way he could see them – millions of them he thought, all the way down to the bottom of the ocean.

'They're going somewhere, Doc,' Captain McLaine told their father. 'Or maybe they're running from something. One thing, they sure ain't biting.'

They tried everything. Squid, mackerel, lures, smelt. But nothing worked. Captain McLaine shook his head, and talked about trying the Montauk grounds, when David saw the water roiling in the distance and what looked like an island of silver-blue backs shining in the sun. 'Look, Dad, look!' he shouted and the other fishermen ran to the rail and looked too.

'*Jesus fucking Christ!*' yelled Captain McLaine. '*It's the blues. Mother of God!*'

At first Michael wasn't sure what was happening. He kept watching the water, and thought he could sense the panic of the millions of little fish that surrounded the boat as the island of silver came closer and closer. Then the blues hit; the sea heaved with the big fish. His rod bent double and he reeled up a struggling blue fish that had swallowed the bait and hook. McLaine came with his knife, cut the fish loose, and rebaited the hook. He was laughing, and his eyes shone.

'*Not that you'll need bait; their blood's up; they'll bite on anything.*' *They did. On bare hooks, on pieces of paper. They pulled them up one after the other, some with half-eaten porgies still in their mouths, too greedy to pass up the shine of the hook, even though they had their prey. They came in wave after wave into the school of porgies, until the men were pulling the fish in through chunks of bitten-up flesh and blood slick.*

It sickened Michael, and he stopped, and when David saw he wasn't fishing any more, he stopped too. But the men had a wonderful time. They drank and pulled in blues until their arms were tired. They thought having the twins on board had changed their luck, and they kept calling them something, but Michael couldn't remember what.

'Good luck Jonahs,' David said as if he knew what Michael was thinking. 'Do you remember that?'

Michael nodded and smiled, but he was beginning to feel uneasy. David went to wash up, and left Michael alone for the first time that day. He called Kathy again, but she didn't answer. Then he called the League where they told him that Mrs Ross was there but had asked not to be called to the phone unless it was an emergency. Was this an emergency?

He wanted to say yes, that he was getting frightened, and that he had to talk to her, because it was getting out of hand. He wanted to hear her Yankee voice with the hint of dialect ask what was getting out of hand. He knew the minute she said that, he'd be fine. He'd go home and they'd have dinner together and then maybe make love. He might even tell her about last night. It wasn't important. He had been high and wasn't even sure he'd had an orgasm.

Mrs Stokes asked him again if it was an emergency.

'No.' He was sweating as David came back, wiping his hands. 'No, it isn't an emergency.'

'Is it Kathy?' David asked.

'No. She's not home.'

'No dinner waiting, no home fires burning. Good. C'mon.'

'C'mon where?'

'Trust me.'

He followed Dave out of the house and down the street to Broadway.

'Dave, where're we . . .'

David raised his finger to his lips. 'Trust,' he said. 'A little trust.'

At Broadway they turned downtown to Seventieth and there, at the Avis West Side office, David rented a bright blue Ford Falcon.

They drove across Sixty-fifth to Second, then across the Fifty-ninth Street bridge to Queens. The long spring sunset was under way as they headed out Queens Boulevard to the Long Island Expressway entrance. Michael sat suspended as his brother drove him farther and farther out towards the ocean.

He didn't keep track of the miles or of time. Queens ended, and Long Island began. They turned south towards the ocean and kept going. Michael saw signs for the Southern State, then for Jones Beach and Fire Island. But they passed them and kept going. Twilight came. He was hungry, but it didn't seem worth mentioning because he knew David wouldn't stop. Finally he saw a name he recognized – Haney – and he knew where they were going.

David knew he'd caught on. 'We won't make it for sundown,' David said, 'but close enough.'

They turned at the Haney exit and in what was left of the light, Michael could see sand on the road. They drove through Haney, out another sandy road and turned into Montefiore Cemetery. There were other cars there, other people visiting relatives' graves for Havdallah. The twins walked across the smooth grass to the edge of a patchy field that rimmed the cemetery. There, although visibility was getting very poor, they collected as many stones as they could find, then went back to the cemetery path and out towards the trees that spread over the tombstones. They found their mother's and father's graves without any trouble, arranged the stones as a token of their visit – to greet their parents' shades. Then they sat together on the grass next to the markers, in the cold April evening, and talked quietly.

'Have you decided about the apartment?' David asked.

Michael shook his head. 'Kathy doesn't want to move in there. She doesn't say so because she's worried about me, and she'll do whatever I want, I guess.'

'Why is she worried?'

'I don't know.'

'It's the work, isn't it?'

'Maybe – maybe a little.'

'Have you saved any of them?' David asked.

'One woman had stage-three ovary, and something happened – no one seems clear what – but just when they thought she was terminal, she went into remission. They sent her home last week. But of course she could be back to die in a month or two . . . or maybe it really is a remission. Who knows?'

'But except for her . . .'

'They all die.'

The twins were quiet for a while, then David said, 'You know, Mike, I needle you on the phone on Sundays because I miss you so much.'

'I know.'

'But a lot of what I say is true. It's a better life there. Better work. Better pay. Kathy would be at home, near her family.'

Michael tried to read David's expression as he said this, but it was too dark to see clearly.

The quiet was insidious. The feeling of being in the country, alone together without ties, was specious. The clean grass and fresh air were in isolated patches.

Michael started to sweat, although it was very cool. The clouds were dark grey against the sky. To his left he could see the lights of Haney. They were a hundred miles from New York, from the cancer ward, from Kathy. He thought if he listened, and if David would just stop talking, they might be able to hear the ocean.

Then David said, 'We'd be together, Mike.'

Michael lay back in the cold grass and looked up at the sky. *We'd be together.* He was so tired.

'We could sell the apartment, buy a house,' David was saying. 'More social life . . . people give more parties.' Then he laughed. 'You won't get as many blow jobs in the dining rooms – too many ancestors staring down from the walls.'

Michael laughed too. Then David lay down next to his brother, close, but not touching; and without saying any more the brothers watched the sky.

They said good-bye at the bus station. The driver razzed them, 'Hey, is one of you going to La Guardia or are you going to stand there necking all day?'

Michael could see that the sight of the twins embracing made everyone uncomfortable and he pulled away from David.

'I hate leaving you to face it alone,' David said.

He meant Kathy and the dying women. Michael looked up at the clock. Another minute or two and he'd have to go back to his wife.

'Dave . . .' It was almost out.

David, don't leave me.

David waited, halfway between his brother and the bus, next to the grey concrete ramps where the empty buses stood forlornly like old horses in stone stalls.

Michael smiled shakily. 'Have a good trip, Dave.'

David sagged. 'Thanks, Mike.'

When he was settled in his seat on the bus, and Michael was left behind on the ramp waving, David took out *A Study in Scarlet*, which he was reading because Romer insisted that he couldn't claim to be civilized until he'd read Sherlock Holmes. He sat with it open on his lap while Long Island City, then the phony expressway park raced past the window. He didn't even try to read. He'd waited a year, and for a second back there he thought the waiting was over.

If she were angry, if she were cold, if she tried to make him feel guilty, he'd get on the next goddamn plane to Boston and she could spend the rest of her life playing with herself.

It was twelve thirty, Sunday. He hadn't seen her for almost two days. The elevator crept.

'Missed you, Doctor. Been away?' The elevator man looked at his wrinkled shirt and trousers.

'Far away.'

'Really? Where?'

'Greenwich Village.' The elephant's burying ground.

'That's not so far.'

Michael leaned close to him, breathed on him, glad he hadn't brushed his teeth. The man flinched. It's the dark side of the moon. 'It's farther than you think.' You can get a blow job without touching – no hands, no kissing.

He went down the hall while the elevator man watched. He didn't have his keys and he'd have to ride down in defeat if Kathy didn't answer. But what if she did, and then closed the door in his face? Or worse, what if she had decided to get back at him? What if Anders was there now – her revenge? *Michael would ring the doorbell, while the elevator man watched, and John Anders would open it, naked with a hard on that stretched out into the hall, almost to the far wall.*

Michael didn't know what to do.

The elevator door was still open. Why didn't somebody ring for it? But it was Sunday; they were all gone, or asleep, or dead. He made himself ring the bell and heard Kathy coming across the floor and up the step to the little entrance balcony. Then she opened the door.

'You should always ask who it is,' he said. He heard the elevator door close, and Kathy started to cry.

'I thought you weren't coming back. I was so frightened.'

He was inside, with his arms around her before he knew what was happening. His face was against her neck, then in her hair. He stroked her back to quiet the crying. It was a near thing, he wanted to tell her, a near thing, but he'd made it. He was here.

chapter thirteen

Michael had breakfast with Friedman, and told him about the night in the Village while Friedman rolled his eyes and pretended to wipe drool off his chin. 'Oh God! And what were they doing on that mattress?'

'I never did find out.'

'Asshole! Send a man to a boy's work, and what d'ya get – disembodied lips and tongues.'

'No, she had a body.'

'What's its telephone number?'

Michael grinned. 'I didn't ask.'

Friedman clutched his head. 'It doesn't matter. I'm too fat to go to parties like that. One look and they'd shut the door in my face. Did you ever hear of a fat man at an orgy?'

'Never,' Michael said.

'Don't let me have anything for lunch except three Bloody Marys and a bowl of wonton soup. Promise?'

Michael raised his hand, and swore.

Everything was quiet on three. Mrs Arland was asleep, and Michael almost woke her up, because he knew how glad she would be to see him.

But she looked peaceful, her colour was good, the IV clear. He stood for a second and looked down at her, not thinking anything except how fine her skin was, how pretty she was, asleep, with some of the strain gone. He had a feeling as he looked at her that she was going to make it. That years later she'd come back to visit him as an old woman and they'd have dinner together, or a drink. He left her asleep and went to say good-bye to Mrs Pollack, who was going home to die. Her husband wouldn't be there until three, so he helped her put her things together; a couple of books with tattered bindings and an old blouse and skirt, some dusting powder and a stuffed plush seal.

'Goodness, you'd think I'd collect more in all this time, wouldn't you?'

'People usually do,' Michael said. He folded her robe for her because she had bony metastases to her spine and she was wearing a brace. He thought of the cucumber's few things, and wondered how she was. She'd cried when she found the coat in her closet and asked everyone who had put it there; but no one knew. He'd heard from Social that she'd given the baby up for adoption and had been arrested and sent someplace not long afterwards for pushing.

When Mrs Pollack was ready, Michael went downstairs with her and Mr Pollack, said good-bye to them quickly, not wanting to watch them go out the door and get into a taxi. Then he went into the Hadassah gift shop in the lobby and bought a small gingham dog they had on the counter and took it upstairs. He went right to Mrs Arland's room, thinking he'd leave it on the table next to her bed, so she'd see it as soon as she opened her eyes. Her door was open, and the surgeon, Clark, was in there examining her. He hadn't even bothered to pull the curtain around her bed, and she was exposed to anyone passing in the hall. The wounds and the tubes coming out of them were horrible, worse now in a way than they had been the first day. Her face was turned away, so she didn't have to look at Clark, and her eyes were closed so she couldn't see Michael.

Clark looked up. 'You might as well come here, Ross. You won't see too many like this.'

At the mention of his name, she screwed up her face as if she didn't want to think of him watching what Clark was doing to her.

'I can't right now, sir. I . . . I'll be back in a minute.'

He backed out into the hall, and leaned against the nurse's desk. Friedman came out of the lounge, 'Hey, Ross, what's with the toy dog?'

Just then, Michael saw David come around the corner and head for the elevator.

'David?'

David didn't answer; he kept going. Michael walked after him.

'Dave.' No response. David reached the elevator and pushed the button.

Michael started to run. 'David, wait!'

Friedman tried to grab him but missed. 'Mike, what's . . .'

A nurse was in the way. Michael was coming right at her, and she jumped back against the wall.

The elevator door opened, and the crowd shifted to make room for the newcomer.

'Daaavid.' Michael cried. He was still holding the gingham dog.

Friedman bowed his head; the nurse sagged against the wall; the elevator crowd stared, and a dark man Michael had never seen before turned to face him as the elevator doors closed.

Snyder was looking forward to seeing Michael Ross; he knew exactly what to expect; he knew exactly how to act; he knew he'd impressed Friedman, and he enjoyed remembering what he'd said. He even thought of doing an article on twins and self-partisanship.

But the minute he saw Michael, his self-satisfaction evaporated and he was left thinking that he wasn't usually such a fool. This man wouldn't fit any theories; he wouldn't make a pattern for an article; and he wouldn't be a nice easy case that Snyder could use to pat himself on the back on bad days. He was like everybody who'd ever walked into his office; lonely, vulnerable, and probably in pain. He watched Michael carefully as they shook hands. Very vulnerable, Snyder thought. And very, very good-looking. Burdensomely good-looking. It was hard to think of there being two of them, and he wondered how absolute the resemblance was.

Michael was restless and he kept asking for water. He looked right at Snyder, not like some whose eyes had to keep moving, but Snyder could tell that the contact was conscious and required some courage. Snyder also realized that Michael Ross was badly confused, raw, and Snyder was going to have to watch himself every minute.

Michael talked without interruption, and Snyder listened and smoked.

Then Michael said, 'I know my brother. I couldn't make a mistake. I saw him.'

'I believe you.'

'But it wasn't him.'

'You had an hallucination, Michael.'

Michael hadn't told Snyder he could use his first name and he couldn't remember Snyder's first name, so it would be Michael and Dr Snyder, which annoyed Michael.

'Bill told me that you and your twin were very close,' Snyder said.

'We still are.'

'But *you're* married.'

'That's right.'

'Do you and your brother still see each other often?'

'As often . . .' he stopped.

'As often,' Snyder prompted.

'As possible,' Michael said softly.

'Does your brother live alone?'

'No. He has a lover.'

'Any chance that he'll marry her?'

'It's . . . it's a man.'

Snyder could see how much that bothered Michael and he decided not to let it go.

'Have *you* ever had a homosexual relationship?'

No answer.

'It's quite common. When you were a boy—?'

'Yes, I did.'

'With your brother?'

'Yes.'

Snyder put out his cigarette and lit another. They had to start sooner or later, and Snyder believed sooner was better.

'It must have been quite an experience,' Snyder said, leaning back and doing his best to look casual, 'a little like having sex with yourself.'

Michael started to sweat.

'I never thought of it as having sex,' he said.

'No? What did you think it was?'

'Fooling around.' Sweat rolled down his ribs.

'Did your mother dress you alike?'

'Yes.'

Poor bastard, Snyder thought.

'You two don't dress alike any more, do you?'

'No.'

Then just as Michael was starting to relax again, Snyder asked, 'How do you feel about the other man?'

'You make it sound like a love triangle.'

'Isn't it?'

Michael stood up. 'I told Bill I'd see you. I've seen you. Thank you, Doctor.'

'Michael, don't get pissed.' Snyder shook his head. 'I'm sorry; I don't want to say the wrong thing to you. You're jealous, he's jealous. That's what usually happens between siblings. Please sit down, Mike.'

Michael didn't move.

Snyder looked up at him. 'You've got to start handling the twin thing sooner or later, Michael.'

'I'm doing fine.'

'Not if you're hallucinating, you're not.'

Michael sat down.

'You're having trouble sleeping too, aren't you?' Snyder said.

'Yes – a lot.'

'Do you take anything?'

'No.'

'Sex help?'

'Sometimes; sometimes not.'

'I'm going to give you a prescription for secobarbital. Seconal. It'll help every once in a while.'

'I won't be able to work the next day.'

'Does the work still mean anything to you?'

'Of course.' Michael stopped, and then said after thinking a minute, 'It means a great deal to me. I'm good at it.'

Snyder nodded and smiled at him. 'I know how you feel; I'm good at mine too.'

'Do your patients—' Michael almost said 'die,' then he realized that didn't apply, so he said instead, 'Do your patients recover?'

'Almost all.' Snyder handed him the prescription. 'Taking this stuff once in a while won't hurt, but only on that basis. A lot of pharmacologists I respect are beginning to think it's addicting. Besides, if you take it steadily you'll get rebound, so only occasionally. Okay?'

Michael nodded, and Snyder said, 'Just knowing it's there "in case" helps some people.'

Then he said gently as Michael stood up, 'Take all the help you can get, Mike. There's no crime in it.'

At the second session Snyder told Michael to call him Chick. 'I know, it's a shitty name, but that's what people call me. You don't smoke, do you? Does it bother you?' Michael shook his head, 'Thank God,' and Snyder lit up. 'Where did you and David grow up, Michael?'

'New York; Riverside Drive.'

'Jesus Christ!' Snyder said. 'I lived on Riverside too. From about forty-two until forty-nine. But I'm older than you.' He looked at Michael's record. 'You're thirty-two. I'm forty. My dad hit it rich during the war, and we graduated to the suburbs.'

Talking about the forties reminded Michael of the old man, Perera, and he told Snyder about the dream. He was surprised that he still remembered it so clearly and could describe it so well. Snyder sat enthralled, and when Michael had finished, Snyder shook his head. 'Wooden splinters for teeth. That's gorgeous.' Michael grinned. 'I'm really happy you like it. It's the first time I ever enjoyed talking about it.'

Snyder laughed. Jesus, he thought, I like this guy. Let him be okay; let him get loose.

Then Snyder said, 'How long since you've had the dream?'

'Years. Not since high school.'

'And your father and brother told the same story about what the old man had really said?'

'Exactly the same.'

'But you saw it as horrible, threatening . . . a curse?'

'Yes.'

'Do you see any parallels between the dream and your hallucination?'

'Only that David was in both of them.'

'There's more. Think about it. I mean, try to see what you did in both cases.'

'I was wrong about what had really happened both times.'

'Yes. But how were you wrong?'

'I don't know.'

'You distorted reality to satisfy your desires. But the desires have changed.' Snyder put out his cigarette, lit another and smiled. 'If only they would stay the same. How easy it'd be to pick a wish, and give yourself seventy years to grant it.' He laughed, then turned serious, 'The first time, as a child, you changed the world to reflect your need to get away from David. But you've gotten away now, haven't you?'

Michael nodded.

'How long has it been?' Snyder asked.

'Two years,' Michael answered softly.

'Now you change the world again. Right? To fit the new need.'

Snyder waited, but Michael didn't say anything; and finally Snyder said, 'According to the book, *you*'ve got to tell *me*, Mike.'

'You're saying I want David back.'

'I think that's what *you* were saying by seeing him when he wasn't there.'

By the third session Michael realized that he was looking forward to seeing Snyder; the past two weeks he'd been sleeping a little better and he'd decided not to get the Seconal.

This time Snyder had a dead pipe held upside down in his mouth, and he stalked around the desk and looked out of the window a lot.

'I'm trying to quit smoking – fucking ridiculous fucking idea from the fucking people who pay for your fucking fellowship.'

'You don't sound like you're doing so well.'

'Fuck it.'

Snyder took out a cigarette.

Michael looked at him for a second, then said, 'Don't do that. We can go get a drink if you like. I'll buy. Or better yet, I'll make up some livid, vivid sexual experience that'll keep you so enthralled you won't think of cigarettes for a week.'

'This experience – do we have it together, or do you just tell me about it?'

Michael turned red, and Snyder laughed. He leaned back in his chair, still laughing, lit the cigarette, then asked, 'That bothered you, didn't it?'

Michael nodded, then laughed. 'Not as much as I thought it would.'

'Have you had any homosexual experiences as an adult?'

'No.'

'Have you wanted to?'

Michael thought, 'I don't think so. I've been curious sometimes, and—'

'And what?'

'Maybe like you said, a little jealous of David.'

Good, Snyder thought. Michael could say that easily and directly. He had thought it would take much longer. He still had to be careful though, very careful.

Michael opened the magazine idly, flipping the pages while the cafeteria's Friday lunch mixture of Campbell's clam chowder and vegetable soup cooled. The story was called 'The Twins Who Found Each Other' – supposedly true. He usually avoided stories and articles about twins, but this one was stuck between the decorating ideas and recipes, and looked harmless. It was illustrated with colour pictures of two pretty blonde girls who were labelled 'Dead Ringers'. He hated that phrase – dead meant dead. He wasn't sure what ringers meant. It always made him think of shrouded corpses playing horseshoes.

'They were separated at birth . . .' But one knew she was a twin, just knew it. She had dreams and saw visions which reached their peak during puberty, but kept on even through college, and even after she got her own apartment and landed a 'high-paying' job as a copywriter in a small advertising agency. Then one day a co-worker asked her if she'd been in Albany last week.

No, she'd never been there – born, raised and still living in Trenton, New Jersey.

Well then, there was a dead ringer for her who was a copywriter in an advertising agency in Albany. Same face, same job. It couldn't be coincidence.

She went to her adopted parents. No, they didn't know anything about a twin. She went to the hospital she'd been born in. No, they couldn't give out such information. She went to the adoption agency. They couldn't help her. She threw herself into the bureaucracy, going from office to office, filling out forms, cajoling, crying, threatening, once even bribing. Seven months later it paid off. She did have a twin; she even knew what their names had been. Only she didn't know and couldn't find out what her twin was called now.

The twin's persistence started to make Michael uneasy, but he kept reading.

She called the agency in Albany. Yes, there *had* been a woman there who fit the description, a copywriter, but she'd quit some time ago. How long? About seven months.

They didn't say it, but Michael knew the Albany twin had quit the same day, maybe the same hour, that the Trenton twin had started her search. She was trying to get away. Michael's soup was getting cold.

Then the Trenton twin quit her job and went to Albany.

Run . . . hurry . . . Get away, Michael pleaded with the Albany twin.

The people in Albany gave the Trenton twin the other one's name and address. She went there.

Michael held his breath.

Barbara was gone, but one of the girls in the building knew her boyfriend. The boyfriend said she'd headed upstate. Glens Falls was his guess.

At Glens Falls the telephone office knew her. She'd moved though, about four months ago. They didn't know for sure, but there was talk of Schroon Lake.

At Schroon Lake everyone was fascinated and sympathetic. But there hadn't been extra work there for months except on the Northway construction. She probably went on north.

The Trenton twin was exhausted and frightened, but as persistent as ever. *Where north?* Shrugs – Plattsburgh, Burlington, Montreal? Wait, try Lake Placid; there's the new lab which opened up there, and the Whiteface Ski Area. Try there.

Thirty more miles north through the Keene valley and farther into the mountains. It was fifteen below and snowing.

Michael tried to eat the soup, but it was cold and he wasn't hungry any more. He could see the Trenton twin on the lonely winding road, alone in her car, nothing ahead but blowing snow; nothing behind but life as a singleton. Did she think about driving off the road into one of the gulleys?

At Placid the trail ended. Her twin was there all right, holed

127

up in some cabin out on the Whiteface road. Go about three miles; you'll see a lumber road off to your left. She was with a man. Looked all neat when she first came there, then took up with a man from Tupper Lake – lumberer in the summer, worked on the Northway in winter. But no account anyway.

She found the place. It was about a quarter of a mile off the road – she had to walk through the snow. It was surrounded by pines, and there was an outhouse.

Her sister – her twin answered the door. The magazine didn't say how the found twin reacted, but they went back to Trenton together. The Trenton girl got her twin a job at the same agency so they could work together, and they rented an apartment so they could live together.

The Albany twin was caught.

' "Caught" was your word – not what the story said? Right?' Snyder asked.

'Yes.'

'And you found the story very disturbing?'

'Very.'

'I don't have to tell you that you identify yourself with the Albany twin, and David with the Trenton twin?'

'Yes.'

'And you're afraid he's going to "catch" you.'

'I guess so. But I know I'm distorting again.'

'I don't think you are, Mike.'

Michael didn't move.

'From what you've told me,' Snyder said, 'that's exactly what David is trying to do, and if you're not careful he'll succeed.'

Snyder watched Michael's face, but he couldn't tell what he was thinking.

'And he'd probably do anything to "catch" you.'

'David wouldn't hurt me.'

'Not directly. No, I don't think he would. But he'll profit from anything that does.'

'What is that supposed to mean?' Snyder looked at Michael. He still seemed calm.

But they were getting too close, and everything from here on was a risk. Snyder tried to calculate but couldn't; he'd told himself that Michael Ross wasn't someone he could figure; all he could do was trust his instinct. With someone like Michael, every word was a risk, every gesture. Still, Snyder knew he had to take them, or he might as well stop wasting their time and Michael's money. He took a deep breath, which he hoped Michael wouldn't notice, then he spoke as evenly as he could.

'What that means is that everything that wounds you, depresses you, defeats you, is David's ally. You've left him; you're running and he wants you back. But you don't know how to protect yourself. So if something *does* happen – like the Carol Arland thing – you've got to turn to David, conjure him up if he isn't there.'

Michael didn't say anything.

'But that's exactly what he wants to happen – for you not to be able to make it on your own.'

Michael was pale, and trembling with anger. Snyder knew instantly that he'd figured wrong, but it was too late to go back.

'He's waiting for you to fail,' Snyder said softly, 'so you'll finally find out how much you need him.'

'That's absurd.'

Snyder didn't answer because he'd gotten much too involved with this man, cared too much about him, and he was afraid anything he said would be the wrong thing. So he sat helplessly while Michael's anger deepened.

'You've been listening to that fat son of a bitch Friedman.'

'He's your friend.'

'David's my brother.'

Finish it, Snyder thought. My brother, my twin, myself.

'He wouldn't hurt me; he'd do anything to keep me safe and happy. You just can't understand that, so you try to make him look bad.'

'Mike, please, I didn't mean—'

'You did mean. You and my wife and Romer, and all the rest of you who want one of us for yourselves. What do you think Friedman wants – *really* wants – with me? Go ahead, tell me. You're the goddamn witch doctor.'

Michael waited, but Snyder didn't dare answer.

Michael wouldn't leave it alone. 'Well? C'mon, Chick, answer me. What does Friedman want – and maybe even you a little;

129

maybe it isn't just a joke to make me feel comfortable – what do you want?'

Snyder stared at Michael. 'More important,' he said, 'what does your brother want?'

Michael was on his feet heading for the door.

'Michael, don't go. For Christ's sake, Mike! It's out of hand – the hallucinations – they'll happen again. Michael!'

But Michael shut the door behind him, cutting off Snyder's voice.

chapter fourteen

Michael couldn't sleep. At one he gave up and went into the living room to stare out at the sky, and at one thirty he called Friedman.

'Did I wake you?'

'At one thirty in the morning,' said Friedman hoarsely. 'What makes you think that gay old, slim old, gorgeous old Bill Friedman would be asleep?'

'I did a terrible thing today, Bill.'

'So what else is new?'

'I mean it.'

'It'd better be something really special.'

'I walked out on Chick Snyder. After I – I told him that I thought you had a yen for me.'

Silence. Then Friedman started to laugh. 'I'd do it, I swear to God, if I could just figure out how, but I'm too fucking fat to get down there.' They laughed until Michael's sides ached, and his eyes burned. Then he went back to bed and slept the rest of the night through.

The next day Friedman tried to talk him into going back to see Snyder again.

'I can't, Bill. He made it sound like my brother had it in for me. That's shit. I know you don't like David.' Friedman opened his mouth, closed it, opened it. 'You look like a fish, and don't bother to lie. You don't have to like him. But you've never tried to make him sound like a villain.'

'I can't believe Chick would be so stupid.'

'He made my seeing him a betrayal.'

'What kind of asshole shit is that?'

'It's the way it is, Bill. I won't listen to anyone try to make David sound bad.'

It was a warning and Friedman knew it.

'Maybe you could see someone else?'

'No. I feel okay now.'

'Now you do, but that last thing scared the shit out of you. Out of me too. How do you know it won't happen again?'

They sent Carol Arland home at the end of April. 'So far so good,' Gargan said. 'No evidence of recurrence, no metastasis.' Michael brought her a plant to take home with her. He kissed her good-bye and left before her husband got there.

Mrs Pollack died at the end of the month, and it turned cold. Then they brought a twenty-five-year-old woman down to three. She'd been classed preterminal for weeks with a malignant teratoma of the ovary metastatic to the lungs – very rare, and apparently very deadly because she died three days after they moved her. Alberts, the chief resident in pathology, came up a few minutes after they called downstairs. Michael was waiting for her mother.

'Be sure to get autopsy permission. It's a real messy thing, teratoma.'

Michael knew about it vaguely. Teratoma was a fairly rare tumour, usually benign, that had other tissue elements in it. Sometimes highly developed elements – hair, teeth, fingernails. A gorge raiser, Friedman would call it.

'They're gentile,' Michael said. 'I'll get permission.'

'Good. You know there's a theory that a teratoma is a twin that didn't make it.'

Michael didn't say anything.

Alberts went on, oblivious. 'The idea is that something happens to the twin while it is an embryo – before it has a chance to become anything like human. It stops developing and becomes part of the other twin – and the twin that finally gets born becomes the host.'

Michael's face was smooth and expressionless.

'It usually stops growing,' Alberts said, 'or if it does grow again, it's usually benign.'

'But this time—' Michael said quietly.

'Ah, this time, yes. This one's malignant all right. Real rare. Can't wait to get at it. It spread too, didn't it?'

'Yes,' Michael said, 'to her lungs.'

'It should be interesting to see what kind of tissue we find there,' Alberts said.

Michael kept thinking about the tumour Alberts would dissect tomorrow; not a twin, he told himself, just screwed-up tissue that had gone its own chaotic way. But no matter what he told himself he couldn't sleep.

The next morning he went to the Pathology Lab right after rounds. Alberts was there drinking coffee and smoking. The door to the autopsy room was closed, but someone was working in there because Michael could hear voices.

Alberts smiled and waved at the door. 'Got a real beaut this morning. Lung granuloma. Industrial origin, we think.'

'Did you finish with the other one – the teratoma?'

Alberts flipped through cards waiting on his desk to be filed. 'Margaret Alvarez,' he read. 'Teratoma, malignant. Primary, ovary. Metastases to both lungs. Final diagnosis, bronchial obstruction due to tumour.'

'But the tissue in her lungs. Was it like the other?'

'You mean did it have hair and teeth in it?' Alberts smiled. 'Teratoma gives everyone the willies the first time,' he said.

'Well, did it?' Michael asked.

'No. But it was still the same tissue type as the primary.'

'Then it was the other one, the thing in her ovary, that was the twin?'

'Not twin, *exactly*, Mike.' Michael wondered if Alberts knew he had a twin. 'Just developing genetic material – that might, *might* have been a twin – if, if, if. As it is, it's just weird tissue. Want to see it?'

Alberts didn't wait for Michael's answer. He went to the line of files against the wall and brought a large manila envelope back to one of the tables and turned on the light. 'You're not interested in the photomicrographs, are you?' Alberts asked. Michael shook his head. 'Too bad,' Alberts said, holding a slide up to the light. 'They're beautiful.' Michael didn't say anything. 'Okay, okay,' Alberts said. 'All you clinicians are gross.' He laughed at his pun, and Michael smiled weakly, trying to look amused. Alberts shuffled through the contents of the envelope. A hundred pieces of paper, Michael thought. Reports, tumour descriptions, slides, and she was just as dead. He wondered why they bothered.

Finally Alberts held up a colour polaroid print. 'Here it is,' he said. 'Gross tumour, right after our first slice.'

Michael looked at it under the light. It took him a few seconds to orient himself. 'The white globs?' he asked Alberts. 'Teeth,' Alberts said happily. 'Some are just bits of teeth, but some completely formed even to the bottom ridges. And see the dark whorls there? That's hair— Hey, Mike, are you all right?'

Michael was backing away from the table towards the door. 'It's late,' he said. 'I should have been upstairs.'

Alberts had gone back to his pictures and slides. 'What's really interesting,' he was saying, 'is the tissue we found in her lungs. Exactly like this – getting ready to become something – liver probably. Christ what a fuck up! Right? You want me to get you a copy of these. They're really something special. Markham said I should enter them—' Alberts heard the door close and looked up. Michael was gone.

Cancer's a little like a parasite, Gargan had said once, *but Jesus it's a dumb one, because it dies with its host.* Michael leaned against the cinder-block wall, trying to look as if he'd just stopped to think some perfectly ordinary thought. But the people passing stared at him anyway, and he moved on.

He couldn't forget it and now he was thinking about the teratoma dying with the woman – dead woman, dead twin. He stopped again. It was being alone at a moment like this that made it hard. He needed company. Maybe Friedman? But the door to Friedman's office was closed. He'd gone home. Michael got into the elevator and went down to three, but Gargan wasn't there. Even the lounge was empty. He began to panic and imagined himself riding up and down in the elevator all day, and all night until someone – Kathy – called the police, and they found him there. He was also exhausted, and he hadn't eaten anything. He thought he'd go home, get some sleep, and maybe a sandwich. Then he'd feel better. But he knew he wouldn't sleep – not now – and not tonight. He wasn't sure he could face that – the dying parasite, and no sleep. He remembered his father talking about this or that customer who seemed to have long streaks of bad luck. Jobs he'd call them, and he'd say it wasn't fair. Michael could actually hear his voice: 'No one should have to bear all that.' *He* shouldn't have to bear it either. At least he should be able to sleep. He went into the men's room and into one of the cubicles. There he wrote out a prescription for Seconal, and smiling and shaking his head at himself for feeling like a criminal, he left the room and went down the basement hall towards the pharmacy. He was almost there when the door to the outpatient clinic swung open at the end of the hall, and he saw David walk quickly down to the street door, and out of the hospital.

Michael got to the door and out into the street in time to see David turn up Fifth. Michael ran after him in the drizzle, wearing just his sports jacket and in a few minutes he was soaked through and cold, his hair plastered against his head.

At Ninety-sixth David turned east, and started walking faster, as if he knew Michael was coming after him and he wanted to get away. Michael matched his pace, but he couldn't seem to gain on him. Across Madison, and then at Park, Michael missed the light and had to run through the traffic. Still oblivious, David went on to Lexington, and Michael was afraid his brother was heading for the subway where he'd surely lose him. Sure enough, David started down the stairs. Michael followed.

Signs pointed 'Downtown'. David turned and Michael raced after him.

The train was in the station; David got on and Michael ran for it. He slammed into a woman in a pink slick coat and her whole body turned with the force of his shove. He jumped onto the train, the last car, just as the doors closed.

Michael looked around. David wasn't there. On to the next

car, and the next, still no David; then one more; the train stopped and he was about to get off.when he saw his brother just ahead. Now he had him; no way he could get away from Michael this time. But before he could reach him, the train pulled into Forty-second Street and David got off. Michael followed, shoving his way through the people waiting to get on. The crowd was solid on the stairs. He started pushing, afraid that he'd lost him finally; then, just ahead, he saw David's checked coat and thick black hair. He was trapped by the crowd the way Michael was, and they had to stay there, stuck just a few yards away from each other, moving as the crowd moved – up the stairs and onto Forty-second.

Michael followed David all the way to Seventh Avenue, where a marquee advertising live burlesque made him think madly of dead burlesque – a line of white draped bodies, lying in a row across the stage. David kept going past young boys who stared at him up and down, then did the same to Michael as they passed. Women with hair teased into helmets and thick false eyelashes, looking like insects, simpered at him. Finally David missed the light and had to stop. Then Michael caught up. It had taken him so long, that he didn't know what to do for a minute. He touched his brother's shoulder: 'David.'

He turned and a man Michael had never seen before stared at him. The stranger was wearing powder, eyeshadow, mascara, everything. He smiled when he saw Michael. 'Who? David? Sure, honey,' he lisped. 'Or Bill, or Fred, or anything you want . . . so pretty . . . ijjummms . . . wijjums.'

Michael was going to puke right there.

Lipstick smeared the man's mouth, and his hair was dyed dead black. The make-up had collected in the creases on his forehead, and at the sides of his mouth; his eyes were dark, full of intelligence and spite.

'You want David?'

Michael couldn't answer.

'I'll be David, babykins.'

Michael filled the prescription for Seconal, took two of them, then tore the label off the bottle and put it on the top shelf of the medicine cabinet.

He closed the medicine cabinet quietly and, in case Kathy was in the next room, he flushed the toilet; but the bedroom beyond was empty and he went to the phone and dialled David's number. He let it ring and ring, but there was no answer.

part four

chapter fifteen

Rosa Scheib's office was in a short West Side backwater – Eighty-seventh Street between Columbus and Amsterdam – that was new to Kathy. There was no receptionist or secretary, and Kathy showed herself in when Dr Scheib called her. She took Kathy's hand, 'Congratulations, Mrs Barker,' she said. 'You're going to have a baby.'

Lila Barker had been Kathy's roommate at Middlebury.

'What about the spotting?' Kathy asked.

'Not enough to worry about; everything looks fine.' Dr Scheib sat down and started to write.

'I don't like to give iron tonics. They don't agree with a lot of women, and no matter what the drug companies say, natural is best. Do you mind liver?'

Kathy shook her head.

'Good girl,' Dr Scheib beamed at her. Kathy felt like a traitor. 'Liver at least twice a week and more often if you can stand it. Spinach too. Put it in salad if you get sick of it cooked. It's delicious raw.'

Dr Scheib kept writing. 'Of course husbands can be a problem.'

Kathy looked up sharply, but Dr Scheib kept writing. She couldn't know who Kathy's husband was.

'If he gets too difficult, have him call me, and I'll explain about the liver and spinach.' She was a good doctor, Kathy thought. 'Take two aspirin if you have a headache. Otherwise nothing I haven't prescribed. Not even Alka Seltzer. Anything can reach the baby, and you don't need to swallow a lot of crap just because you're pregnant, you understand?' Kathy nodded.

Then Rosa Scheib looked closely at her. 'You don't seem very happy, Lila.'

'I'm all right,' Kathy said. 'Just a little surprised is all.'

Dr Scheib laughed. 'Why surprised? What did you think was going to happen?'

Kathy could have spent the rest of the day telling Rosa Scheib what she had thought would happen on the day she found out she was pregnant, and how different the reality was going to be.

'Don't worry,' Dr Scheib said. 'The problems will work themselves out. And no matter how scared and worried your husband is tonight, by tomorrow he'll realize that he's going to be a father, and he'll be glad.'

Kathy wanted to laugh, because Dr Scheib had it all wrong. Michael wouldn't be glad; he wouldn't be sorry either. He wouldn't care one way or the other. She couldn't get over the idea that he'd gotten her pregnant during one of the few, joyless times they'd made love during the past few months. He was cold, even when he was in her, disengaged, and she was left alone under him, a little frightened, and just wanting him to get finished, so she could get out from under his weight.

'I've never known a husband who wasn't happy finally. Now come. A little schnapps to celebrate.'

Dr Scheib opened the bottom desk drawer and took out a flask and two paper cups.

'*L'chayim.*' She raised her cup to Kathy, and Kathy drank with her.

Ten minutes later, with her prescriptions and a sheet of instructions, Kathy was out on Eighty-seventh Street looking for a cab. Across the street two women sat on a brownstone stoop on pillows, ignoring the cold. They were wearing short fake fur coats that showed the skirts of their flowered cotton dresses. When they saw Kathy's mink, they stopped talking and stared at her. She smiled and nodded, but they didn't smile back. The building they sat in front of was neat, freshly painted; they were both fat and dark and pretty, and she knew that upstairs behind curtained bay windows, opened a crack for air, their children napped or watched TV or played with other children. She knew that in an hour or so, they'd go upstairs to linoleum-floored kitchens with tiny windows over the sink, and start cooking dinner for their husbands.

She walked towards Columbus to get away from their staring, and as soon as she turned the corner, and knew that they couldn't see her any more, she crumpled up the prescriptions for vitamins and a laxative, and the sheet of instructions Dr Scheib had written out for her, and threw them into the nearest litter basket.

Friedman walked around his desk and stared out of the window towards the river. 'Kathy, you're asking me to kill my best friend's baby before he even knows it exists. I can't do that.'

'Do you think he's fit to be a father?'

Friedman didn't answer.

'Well, Bill, do you?'

'Kathy, give him a chance.'

'I've given him three years of chances. This baby is a mistake. He won't want it, and I don't want it.' That was a lie. She'd give anything to be one of the fat little women sitting on the stoop on West Eighty-seventh. 'I can't even sleep any more.'

'That's not a good reason to have an abortion, Kathy.'

'Michael doesn't sleep either, Bill. Some nights we lie next to each other waiting for morning, without saying a word to each other. Did you ever lie like that a whole night?'

Friedman kept looking out of the window, because he didn't want to face Kathy. Not sleeping meant rebound, which meant Michael had been taking the stuff for longer than Friedman knew. Months.

'Well, Bill?'

Barbiturate addicts made lousy fathers. 'Yeah, okay – if you're sure.'

'I'm sure. When?'

'The sooner the better. No sense in waiting.'

She wanted one day, knowing it was there. She'd skip class and go to a concert or to the movies. She'd buy a new dress or have her hair done. Then she'd do something light and silly – have lunch at the Plaza where she'd be bound to meet someone she knew, *Darling, you look radiant! Of course, she'd tell them. I'm going to have an abortion first thing in the morning.*

'Can we wait till tomorrow, Bill?'

'Sure. But it'll have to be late, about three.'

'That's fine. Tomorrow at three.' She stood up to go.

'Kathy, does David still call on Sundays?'

'Yes, unless Michael can't wait and calls him first. Or unless David comes for one of his weekends, or meetings, or workshops. He's here now, and that's where Michael is – with David.'

'Would you do this if it weren't for David?'

Kathy shook her head. 'Would anything be wrong with Michael if it weren't for David?'

Friedman didn't answer.

'What *is* wrong with him, Bill?'

'I don't know.' Friedman lied.

David Saul Ross, MD.

Then came Romer's name, then the lab assistant's. The affiliations were next. All at Boston General Hospital, all big-time.

Michael tried to read the abstract again, but the words kept blurring, so he concentrated on the names – on David's name. Someone came to the lectern, 'Dr David Ross . . . describe . . . results . . . clomiphene.' The speaker sat down and David got up from the front row. Michael hunched down in his seat. The man sitting next to him noticed – then stared; first at him, then at David, then at Michael again. 'You're twins,' he whispered. 'Aren't you?'

Michael didn't answer.

'I didn't know Ross had a twin.'

'Lights please,' David said. The lights went out.

'Amazing,' said the man next to Michael.

'First slide.'

The man ignored the slide show and went on staring at Michael in the blue light from the projector.

'Absolutely amazing,' he said.

Michael faced front without seeing, tried to listen and couldn't. Feelings reached him – David's confidence, the approval and interest of the audience. Then the light came on. There was scattered applause, and people were standing up. Michael was trying to get to the exit before David saw him. But the man was standing in the aisle, barring his way. 'Your brother gave a fine talk. He's becoming the expert in this, isn't he?'

Michael didn't answer.

'Are you a physician, too?' Michael nodded. He wanted to be polite.

The man didn't move. 'Twins often follow the same profession, don't they?' he said.

'Yes, I know. But we're not twins,' said Michael.

He had to get home – to Kathy. He felt flushed and needed fresh air.

'Just brothers? But that's remarkable! I've never seen such a resemblance between brothers, even between fraternal twins.'

'We're not brothers either,' Michael said.

The other man stared.

'We're not related at all,' Michael went on. 'It's just one of those freaky resemblances. Actually I'm an only child.'

He felt a presence at his side. He knew it was David and wondered if he had heard what Michael said. His heart was pounding, and he felt as if he were suffocating.

'Hello, Mike. I thought you said you couldn't make it.'

'That was some talk, Dave. Really terrific.'

David looked closely. 'Come on, Mike, let me buy you a drink.'

'Sure, sure.'

They walked up the aisle, around the man who kept staring, then across the huge lobby carpeted in maroon and beige squares, a thousand duplicate designs that made Michael dizzy to look down. The lobby was full of people, sitting on maroon plush couches and chairs, leaning against heavy carved tables, or standing near walls covered with patterned wallpaper, broken by mirrors, desks, doorways. Most of them were looking at the twins, one behind the other – exact replicas of each other crossing the carpet together. Except that David was full-faced, smooth-looking, wearing soft grey flannel that hung straight and perfect above long, slim, grey flannel legs, and Michael was too thin and looked tired. He had a headache, and he kept watching David's back, praying they'd reach the bar before he got too dizzy to walk.

Finally they were sitting in a dim corner and David ordered white wine for both of them without asking Michael what he wanted. Then he leaned towards Michael, who had to keep himself from leaning away.

'Look at you, Michael!' Michael took him literally and looked down. His sports jacket was old tweed, and hung on him. He smiled, raised his glass and toasted David, 'Here's looking at *you*, kid.'

David didn't smile or raise his glass in return.

'You look like hell,' he said.

'I suppose so.' He didn't have much of an appetite any more, and he was waking up with headaches. 'Brain tumour,' he moaned with mock lugubriousness. 'I have all the symptoms.'

'It's not funny.'

'No. I guess not.' He looked at David's excellent tailoring, his fresh haircut.

'That fellowship should be up for renewal soon. Right?' David said.

Michael nodded.

'Don't take it.'

Michael started to laugh because he'd almost asked, 'What's wrong with cancer?'

David didn't even smile.

'You could open an office, Mike. It's not an unusual thing for a physician to do.'

'Oncology and office practice aren't compatible.'

'That's what I mean – no more cancer. Listen, Mike; women get hundreds of things wrong with them that don't kill them – that you can treat, even cure. You don't have to hate what you do.'

Michael didn't say anything.

'Why go on with it?' David asked.

Michael was silent. He didn't know why. Maybe because it was the exact opposite of what David was doing. But he couldn't tell David that.

'Think about it, Mike.'

Michael finished his wine and reached for his briefcase. They'd been together almost half an hour. 'I've thought about it, Dave. Again and again.'

'Then why won't you listen to me?'

'Maybe I will.'

'Mike—' Michael had started to slide out of the booth, but David touched his arm. Michael sat still. 'I'll be through up there myself this year,' David said. 'Maybe we could even set up together.'

Michael felt a sudden cramp, from the wine, he thought.

'I have to go to the can, Dave.' He left the table before David could say anything. When he got to the men's room, he realized that he'd forgotten his briefcase and would have to go back for it; back to where David was waiting for him.

He leaned over to try and ease the cramp. His arms were too thin, and the cramps and diarrhoea were getting worse. He knew there was nothing seriously wrong yet, but the Seconal was wearing him down; another year or two like this and there'd be other signs, he told himself. Back pain around the kidneys, bloating; his ankles would start swelling if he sat too long. If he didn't make some changes, he'd start having real trouble by the time he was forty.

When he came out of the cubicle, he took two red capsules out of the medication envelope he now carried all the time. He swallowed them with water cupped in his hand, washed his hands and face, then waited for the few minutes it took for the inner tremor he could never quite place to ease. It was happening now – everything slowing down, opening out, flattening; the tension that kept his insides clutched lifted. The whole centre of his body was soft and smooth. Bones slid against flesh, organs slid against each other. His headache was gone, his eyelids closed softly over his eyes. He combed his hair gently; it was fine thread – black spider web. He put his comb in his pocket and went back to their table where David, restless and getting angry, was waiting.

chapter sixteen

'Bill, what's wrong with my brother?' David asked.

You are, Friedman wanted to say; and if you'd take a flying fuck to the moon, Michael and his wife would be just fine, there wouldn't be any abortion tomorrow afternoon, and I wouldn't have to spend the rest of my life lying to my best friend, wondering what his kid would have been like. He stared at David, and couldn't understand why people thought the twins looked so much alike. He didn't. David was handsomer for one . . . prettier, Friedman thought nastily, everything about him looked groomed – his hair, his clothes, even his nails. He was so angry at David that he couldn't talk.

David waited and finally Friedman was able to say, 'Michael's working too hard. All of his patients die and he cares too much. It's a bad mix.'

'Is it just the work?'

Friedman didn't answer.

'Is it?' David asked again.

Friedman looked around. It was almost three and the cafeteria was practically empty. No one was at the next table.

'No,' he said quietly. 'I don't think that is all.'

David waited.

'I think Mike's taking something.'

As far as Friedman could tell, David's expression didn't change. He didn't even look surprised.

'Taking what?' he asked calmly.

'I'm not sure, but I think he's on the upper-downer go around.'

'If you're right,' David said, 'then the downer could be a real problem, couldn't it?'

'Yes.'

'What do you think it is?'

'I'm guessing it's Seconal.'

Friedman saw a tic of something on the twin's face, but he couldn't identify it.

'It's addicting, isn't it?' David asked.

'A lot of people seem to think so.'

'How long does it take?' David asked softly.

'I'm not a pharmacologist, David.' He was going to scream.

David sensed the anger and took another tack. 'I've told him to give up the fellowship, Bill. I want him to go into practice. I think that's the only answer for him.'

Friedman thought so too.

Then David said, 'I even offered to set up with him.' He saw the look on Friedman's face and stopped talking.

Friedman stood up slowly, deliberately, and just as deliberately he dropped his spoon on the plastic-topped table.

'You want to help your brother, David? Then leave him alone. Just leave him alone.'

He didn't wait for David to answer; he walked across the cafeteria and out the door into the hall, knowing David was watching him.

Friedman couldn't forget David's reaction. He couldn't forget about Kathy and tomorrow, and he started thinking that the Rosses were taking over his life. He wanted to tell his wife about Kathy, but he couldn't. He did tell her about David. But David was Beth's favourite, so she defended him the way she always did.

'Of course David looked odd,' Beth said. 'You'd just told him that his twin brother was becoming a junkie.'

'I didn't tell him any such thing.'

'Not in so many words, maybe; but that's what it comes down to. So he's worried about Michael.' She was clearing the table in double-time, trying to get the pot roast into the kitchen before they ate any more of it.

'But that's just it' – Friedman raised his voice – 'I don't think he is worried about Michael – I think he was worried about not knowing what was going on.'

'That's a terrible thing to say.' She was standing in the dining-room doorway holding a dish towel. 'David loves Michael.'

'And Michael loves David if you can call whatever it is between those two love. That doesn't mean they wish each other well.'

'You don't really think David wishes Michael harm?'

He's done him harm, Friedman thought, whatever he wishes.

'Whatever he wishes for his brother, David wasn't upset – not the way you'd expect – and that expression on his face wasn't worry. It was more like – like satisfaction.'

Beth told him he was crazy, put the dishes in the sink to soak and went to her bridge club.

Friedman couldn't sit still. He turned on the TV, and couldn't watch it. He took out the pot roast, and ate some, though he didn't really want it. Finally he turned off the TV, and all the lights and sat alone in the dark, thinking about Michael, and trying to rationalize what he'd done. He'd told David what he suspected, because he believed it was for Michael's good; now he knew that it wasn't. Whatever his intentions, Friedman had given David ammunition to use against Michael, against Kathy, against that poor life he was going to kill tomorrow. The least he could do was tell Michael he'd talked to David.

Friedman turned on the lights, and called the Ross apartment. Kathy told him that Michael was still at the hospital and was due home any minute. David was there, waiting for him; had been there since seven. 'He should be home soon,' she said, 'David has to catch the nine o'clock or he'll miss his ride to Cambridge.' She sounded harried.

Friedman called Michael at the hospital. Michael sounded tired, his voice slightly thick, and Friedman wondered how much Seconal he'd taken that day and how long ago he'd taken the last one.

Friedman had suspected that Michael was on drugs because of his behaviour. He had sudden odd highs that had no basis, accompanied by nervous aimless movements – brushing at his cheek as though something were crawling on it, tearing paper that stayed too long in his hands. These alternated with stretches of inertia, forgetfulness, constant talk of being sleepy. Friedman suspected some sensory loss as well – less sensitivity to heat or cold – loss of libido. But he was sure there was no perceptual loss. Michael still thought as well as ever. Now as he watched Michael carrying paper cups of machine coffee across the lounge, he noticed other things – a tiny droop to his left eyelid, a fine tremor in his hands.

Michael sat down and handed Friedman his cup. 'I thought you were having dinner at home?'

'Had it. Forty pounds of pot roast and eighty pounds of noodles – that's because we're on a diet. Now I'm going to work it off by drinking coffee with you.'

'Okay, Bill. What's so urgent? It's seven thirty and Kathy's waiting for me.' Seven thirty, Friedman thought. David would have to leave soon if he was going to catch that plane.

'I had two nasty revelations today, Mike,' he said.

'Only two?'

Friedman didn't smile; he looked down at the waxed linoleum and thought what a cold lonely place this hospital was, and how it had made them all a little crazy. Then he looked up at his friend and saw a crease form between Michael's long black eyebrows as he waited to hear what Friedman had to say.

'I realized that you're taking Seconal,' Friedman said. 'And something else too – bennies I'd say. Too much of both. That's revelation number one.'

Michael began to shake. The paper cup trembled, and hot coffee spilled across the back of his hand. Friedman jumped up and ran outside to the nursing station where he got some Kleenex. He came back, took Michael's cup away from him and wiped the back of his hand as if he were a child, asking himself as he pressed the Kleenex gently against Michael's skin, why he was doing it. What was there about this twin that touched him, while the brother left him cold and a little frightened? No one else reacted that way to David – David was the favourite – Beth's favourite, Anders' favourite. 'At least *he* has some social presence,' Anders once said. 'Took both of them to a fund-raising lunch last month and all Michael did was drink and go to the fucking toilet. At least David could talk to people.' Not to me, Friedman thought as he ministered to Michael's hand; not to me.

'Better put some cold water on that,' he said aloud.

Michael nodded and went to the fountain. He soaked the Kleenex in cold water and held it to the back of his hand. The burning, which was frighteningly mild, eased and he went back to where Friedman waited and sat down. He couldn't bring himself to lie, so he didn't say anything. But Friedman wasn't waiting for an answer, he had more to say.

'Revelation two is even worse.'

'I can't wait,' Michael said.

'I told David what I suspected. I had to – he asked me if anything was wrong; and I couldn't take the responsibility of being the only one who knew. I've suspected it for months now – but I couldn't tell Kathy because it'd frighten her. She'd think I meant heroin or morphine – to her all drugs're the same. But David's your brother *and* a physician. I thought he would understand – try to help.'

'What did David say?'

'That's revelation number two. It didn't seem to bother him.'

Michael sat still. Friedman could hear the snack cart in the hall. They fed everyone too goddamn much. Poor chicks came out of Manhattan ten pounds overweight from all the custard and crap. He looked at the clock over the door. Almost eight – David would be gone by now. Michael still didn't move.

'Say something for Christ's sake!'

'How do you know how he felt? Did he say anything?'

'It was what he didn't say. He didn't ask how he could help; all he did was talk about how you and he could set up together. Like the drugs would give him some kind of leverage.'

'How can you think . . .' Michael wanted to be angry. 'How can you . . .' But it didn't ring true and he stopped, then leaned over and put his head in his hands. Friedman waited.

'Are you all right, Mike?'

Michael nodded.

'You want me to leave you alone?' Another nod. Friedman left the lounge, went downstairs and out into the street.

Michael knew Friedman had told the truth, and he tried to be angry again, this time at David. But he couldn't, because as soon as Friedman told him about David's reaction, he felt it too – he leaned back in the chair, he could feel it now – he closed his eyes. What had happened to David was happening to him.

Michael was with Romer; in Cambridge, having dinner at Gaby's right around the corner from their house. The place was full of blond men in tight pants who eyed him and smiled, finding

148

excuses to walk by the table. They were all freckled, with tight skin and pale blue eyes, and they all had long thin legs and little, held-in-looking asses. Romer – another pale, blond, watery presence – was trying to look sympathetic.

'What's wrong with my brother?' he was asking Romer. 'He hasn't been himself for months. Today he told someone that we weren't twins – not even brothers – that he was an only child. Something must be wrong.'

Romer was shaking his head, shifting his chair around to sit next to Michael, putting his hand on Michael's knee – his thigh. Michael pretended he didn't notice.

'I've tried everything,' Romer was saying, 'but it's no use. I think he's taking something. I think he's taking morphine. You have to take him back to New York – you have to look after him. They've asked for his resignation. He's alienated all our friends. I don't want him any more.'

Romer's hand getting higher and higher, openly stroking and Michael was surreptitiously sliding down in the chair so Romer could touch his penis.

'You're all he has now.'

The words brought an explosion of feeling so intense he thought Romer's playing with him had made him come.

Michael woke up, half lying in the chair, still with the feeling he'd had at the end of the dream – the feeling he knew David had had when Friedman told him about Michael and the drugs. Michael stretched, still feeling it, trying to identify it; it was most like elation, but even that was too mild a word; David was elated because Michael was faltering. He'd never thought it so clearly before, and he knew at once that between the drugs and the work, it would happen the way Snyder had said it would. He would be caught. He threw his cold coffee away, and went out to the phone at the nursing station to call Anders. It was already eight fifteen. David would be gone by now, which was just as well because Michael's resolve was still too young to stand much testing.

Yes, Anders said, he could give him a few minutes. 'But only if you can get here in ten minutes. I have an eight thirty engagement.'

Prick, Michael thought. 'That's fine, John. It's about the fellowship. It won't take long – I have to get home anyway.' For an even better engagement, his voice said.

As soon as David saw Kathy he knew she was pregnant. He remembered the exact paragraph in their new third-year textbook – 'The faces of pregnancy . . .' She had all the signs – dark spaces under her eyes, hollowed cheeks, easy flushing and a hint of veins under the skin of her face. He looked at her body; if she'd let him take her clothes off, he'd be able to see tiny white tracings across her breasts and hips. If she'd let him touch her, he'd be able to feel them. She leaned over to put his coffee on the table, and he could see the carotid artery throbbing in her neck, pushing the circulation that fed Michael's baby. He wondered what she would do if he touched it, and he reached up and held the tip of his fingers against the pulse. She stopped moving.

'Leave me alone, David.'

She flushed. He could feel the change of temperature in her skin, and the faster rate of her heart in the artery.

'Why haven't you told Michael you're pregnant?'

'How do you know?'

'It's my business to know.' His fingers slid down her neck to the ridge of her clavicle. He wanted to let his fingers slip down to her breast, but he made himself stop. If she moved a fraction, he would be able to feel her breast without willing to. But she stepped all the way back, out of reach.

'If you'd told Michael,' he said, 'Michael would have told me. So you didn't tell him. Why not?'

She didn't answer.

'You know something's wrong too, don't you? Something's wrong with our Michael?'

She went out of the kitchen and he followed her down the hall and into the twins' old room, which was now Michael's study.

'Don't you want to know what's wrong, Kathy?'

She turned and faced him.

'All right, David. What's wrong with Michael?'

'Friedman says he's taking Seconal. I think he's right. You suspect something like that too, don't you?'

The light here was softer than in the kitchen and she looked even better. He came across the room. 'You'd have seen the signs before anyone else, wouldn't you, Kath – diminished sexual pleasure, for one thing – bouts of impotence.'

'What's Seconal?'

'It's a kind of sleeping pill.'

'But he can't sleep.'

Friedman was right again. Michael was hooked. 'That's because he's taken too much for too long and it's beginning to rebound, which means he's dependent.'

'Dependent?'

'Maybe addicted. People mix them up, but they're not the same.' He was standing very close to her; she could smell the cologne he wore and the fresh scent of his shirt and hair. His face was fuller now than Michael's and his body was firmer and heavier. She'd never seen him naked.

'This used to be our room,' he told her. 'What did you do with our old beds?'

'They're in the guest room.'

They were almost touching, and she started to move back, but he put his arm around her to stop her. She could feel that he was excited, and she was afraid to move.

'You didn't tell him because you're going to get rid of it, aren't you, Kathy?' he whispered. 'Aren't you?'

She stood as still as she could.

'Very wise, Kathy; the smartest thing you could do.'

She was so excited she felt faint, and she could feel David trembling. He was going to kiss her, and she pulled away. He let her go.

'I won't tell him, Kathy.'

'You don't have much time,' she said.

'Don't I?' He was coming for her again.

'No. It's eight thirty. If you're going to catch a nine o'clock plane.' Nine o'clock of the last day she had with her baby, and David had ruined it, just like he ruined everything. She'd forgotten in the sexual excitement he made her feel how much she hated him.

'I'll fix you a sandwich before you go.'

'I'm not leaving until I see Michael, Kathy.'

'I thought you'd seen Michael.'

'He wasn't himself then.'

'What makes you think he'll be any more himself tonight?' He'd reached her as she turned away for the kitchen. He followed her. They were halfway across the room and David was closing the gap between them, when Michael opened the front door and stood in the gallery. Kathy giggled, because she knew how crazy they must all look. She wondered if David still had an erection, if Michael could see it.

Michael didn't even look at her. 'I thought you'd be on your way to Boston by now,' he said to David.

He looked terrible in the overhead foyer light, but his voice sounded deeper and stronger than it had for months, and Kathy came closer.

'I wanted to talk to you, Mike.'

'Talk! Don't be shy. You've talked to Friedman, you've talked to Kathy. Now talk to me, Dave. Go ahead, talk.'

David turned red.

'I talked to Friedman because I was worried about you, Mike.'

'Worried, David.'

'Mike, please.'

'It doesn't matter, because Friedman was wrong. I'm not "on" anything.'

'I'm glad,' said David. He didn't look glad.

'And I've finally decided to listen to you.' David held onto the railing that led up to the foyer because for one of the few times in their lives he didn't know what his brother was going to say.

'I told Anders I was resigning the fellowship, and going into private practice.'

Michael already regretted what he was saying. He wanted to take David into his study, have a beer with him and tell how much the work had meant to him; how sorry he was to give it up. Maybe, like Holmes had said, maybe he had some kind of talent for it that he'd never developed, and now never would. David would understand. But Michael made himself go on talking, and he kept his voice neutral. 'In fact,' he went on, 'Kathy and I are going to start looking for an office tomorrow, aren't we, baby?' Michael kept looking at David, 'Just like you said, Dave, my own office; full of patients who aren't going to die. But with what Ma left me, I don't think I'll need a partner.'

Kathy sat down on the foyer steps.

'I was offering more than money,' David said quietly.

'Oh, I know that. Much more. But I think I should try it on my own, David.'

David couldn't let go of the railing. He looked at Kathy and saw tears in her eyes and knew that tonight as soon as he left, Michael would make love to her, and she'd tell him about the baby. David thought that he would have given anything if he could have been happy for her; if he could have stayed the night in the next room and listened to them plan, then make love. He'd wait until everything was quiet, until Kathy was done crying, and Michael was done talking; and then he'd open the door to their bedroom very quietly, sneak in and stand next to his parents' old bed and watch Michael and Kathy sleep in the moonlight. He'd think about Michael's baby and then so softly she'd never know it, he'd lean over and touch her swelling breast, and kiss her tenderly on the mouth. Then he'd go around to Michael's side of the bed, and stay there next to his brother until the sun came up.

He couldn't look up.

'If that's what you want, Mike.'

'Yes, Dave. Exactly what I want.'

David passed Kathy and went to the door.

'David, don't forget your coat.'

She got it for him out of the hall closet, and stood ready to help him on with it, but now he didn't want her to touch him, and he took the coat away and put it on himself while Michael watched. Kathy gave him his hat and he put that on too. Then he reached for the door, but Michael got there first and held it open for him. Only then did Michael see what he'd done.

'Dave, I'm sorry.'

'What? What, Mike?'

'I . . . nothing.'

'I'll talk to you on Sunday,' David said.

'Not this Sunday, Dave. That's when you get the best office ads – Sunday. I'll call you in a week or so. Let you know how we make out.'

He watched David walk down the hall and ring for the elevator. He walked slowly as if his legs were stiff, and he stood with his back to Michael waiting for the elevator.

Mrs Klein next door was cooking dinner and the hall smelled of garlic. Michael realized that it was after nine, and he hadn't eaten. Maybe David hadn't eaten yet either. Of course he hadn't. He must be starved. He wanted to call him back, and they'd go to Schwartz's – just the two of them – and have dinner. But he didn't call. He waited, watching his brother's back until the elevator door opened, and David got on without looking back at Michael or waving good-bye.

David missed the plane and called Romer who was just getting ready to leave to meet him. 'The next flight's at eleven,' he said.

'Shit. I won't get to bed before two in the morning.'

'Don't bother. I'll stay in Boston and get the bus in the morning.'

'Sure you don't mind?'

'Not at all.' He minded very much. He wanted Romer – someone – to be there when he got off the plane, especially tonight.

'How'd the speech go?' Romer asked belatedly.

'Fine. Just fine.'

David wandered the airport, down empty ramps to empty gates where he could see, past his own reflection, the huge dark shapes waiting outside. He bought a book called *Intern*, by Dr X, hoping it would make him laugh. But when he went into the bar, he read the first few pages and found that Dr X wrote tight, grim prose about something he understood. David left the book in a litter basket, replaced it with an Agatha Christie, went back to the bar and drank double bourbons until they called his flight.

When the small jet took off into the night sky that reflected the airport lights, the darker horizon tilted and kept its tilt. David closed his eyes while everything heaved around him. When he opened them, they were almost past the lights of the city, and he wondered, as the world swayed this way and that, how long it would be before he came back.

As soon as Kathy was asleep, Michael went into the bathroom and closed the door. He opened the medicine cabinet and took the labelless bottle off the shelf. Then he closed the cabinet door and looked at himself in the mirror, still holding the bottle.

He looked exhausted, and he shook his head at his reflection. 'You sure as hell don't look fit to be anybody's father.' Then he smiled at himself, 'We'll see what we can do,' he told the mirror.

He opened the bottle, shook the few capsules left into the toilet bowl, then flushed the toilet and went back to bed. He knew that what he was trying was risky, and he decided he'd go to Friedman at the first sign that something was going wrong. But all that happened was that he didn't sleep that night – he didn't expect to – nor the night after. Kathy worried about his bloodshot eyes, and the almost staggering gait he acquired. But he slept a little the third night, the fourth even longer, and by the end of the week he was sleeping the night through, walking normally, and he had gained two pounds.

chapter seventeen

It didn't take David long to place Danny Perera. As the slightly breathy voice went on and on from New York – from Riverside Drive – David put a face together. A child's face – delicate, thin-skinned, that showed blue veins in a high forehead topped by thin sandy hair. Then he remembered Danny as a young man – balding by the time he was twenty – with weak blue eyes that watered and blinked. Finally, when he remembered the eyes, he remembered the old man – Danny's grandfather. *His* eyes weren't weak or watery; some throwback to a sturdier slavic stock that bypassed his son and grandson. David wondered if Michael ever dreamed of the old man now – the way he used to – and if the old man still scared him.

No, he thought. Nothing would scare Michael any more. All-together, East Side-practice Michael Ross. Unscarable, un-shakeable – husband and father, saviour of all women with minor gynaecologic complaints who lived on the East Side between

Sixty-ninth and Eighty-sixth. David carried the phone around his typically academic medical office as Perera talked. He looked at the dusty Venetian blinds covering a dusty view of the quadrangle and at the stained linoleum covering the tiny floor. True, there was an outer office, and a secretary – and for Boston General that said a lot. But Michael didn't know that, and the last time he'd been there – three or four weeks ago – David had thought he was gloating.

'Wait till you see my new place,' he'd told David. 'Five rooms and two bathrooms – one for the patients to change in, and one for me.' He'd smiled. 'I think I'll make Sally use the other one.' Then he looked around and stopped smiling – worried that he was sounding smug. But he was too excited and the subject came up again while they were having lunch at the faculty club – without Romer. 'The location's really perfect – Kathy found it from an ad – principals only, so we didn't have to pay an agent's fee. She's picked out wallpaper for the reception room and a new desk for Sally and one for me. Wait till you see the drapes – the carpet.'

Then he said, 'You know what I keep thinking about, David?' David didn't know. 'About what it'll be like someday when the kid sees it. I used to wonder why Dad used to bring us down to the showroom every chance he got, why he wanted everyone in the shop to see us. Now I know.'

Michael laughed, and David turned his fork over and over on the tablecloth. Wonderful Michael. No. Not so wonderful, according to Danny Perera.

'He wouldn't see my wife at all, David, and he practically hung up on me.'

'I'm surprised, Danny,' David said. 'After all, we were all children together.'

'That's what I told him, Davey. But all he would say is that he didn't think he could handle it. He wasn't seeing any more cancer patients. He was my last hope.' Perera sounded lost, 'I don't know where to turn now.'

'How did you hear about Mike?'

'Our surgeon – Matthew Gargan – he told us that Michael knew as much about this kind of cancer as anyone in the country – maybe in the world. Gargan didn't say Mike could cure her, you understand – nothing like that. Just that he might know something new.'

'If he did, he'd tell Gargan.'

'He can't tell anyone anything about Louise unless he sees her. And he won't do it. Says he's afraid. That's what he told me, David – on the phone – an MD. "I'm afraid," he says to me. Honest to God.'

So, David thought, he's afraid of something after all!

'Can you tell me what treatment she's already had?'

'Sure.' Perera began to tell him.

Poor woman, David thought, as Perera catalogued what had already been done to his wife. Perera sounded as if he were reading from a list, stumbling over the words now and then.

When he finished, David said, 'I'm sure you know there's not much more anyone can do, Danny.'

'I know that, Dave. But I just want to be able to tell her – to tell myself – that we've done everything there is to do. I don't want to wind up asking myself "What if we'd seen Michael?" Jesus, it's not a lot to ask. Maybe if *you* talk to him. You were always so close.'

Not any more, David thought.

'I'll try, Danny. We're not boys any more, and we've each gone our own way.'

It was nine thirty when Michael got to the office. Sally was already there, so he could ring if he wanted to. But he loved using the key. Morning rounds were a cinch now – three D&Cs, one prolapsed uterus, and a spontaneous abortion. Everyone would be on their way home by the end of the week. He smiled. The woman who'd lost her baby was very upset. She'd made it for five months and no one could tell her why she'd lost it then. But she was in good shape; 'Terrific shape,' he told her. 'You'll be pregnant again in six or seven months if you want to.' 'You're sure?' He'd laughed – laughed with a patient! Then he held her hand, realizing for the first time how pretty she was. She seemed to like the way he looked too, and she'd giggled a little. 'I'll even put money on it,' he'd said. 'What if my husband needs help?' Openly inviting. Careful, careful. Jesus, she was pretty though. And he'd never noticed. 'He won't. He'll do just fine.' Big smile, a little avuncular. Pat her shoulder. Careful, he thought, not with the patients.

He opened the heavy downstairs door and went down the polished tiled hall to the newly painted black door with a plaque reading: Michael P. Ross, MD. Still smiling because his patient wanted to screw him. She wasn't drugged, in pain, or waiting to die – he hadn't seen anyone die for months – she was a live, whole, healthy woman who wanted him.

He waved at Sally.

'Your brother just called,' she said. 'I told him you'd call back as soon as you got in.'

Michael kept going, across the waiting-room that Kathy had almost finished decorating. The walls were soft colours – lilac and mauve – with pale flowers twining in vertical strips.

'Very restful,' she'd said.

'Why not just blank walls – we'll save money.'

'There's nothing restful about blank walls.'

What did David want ? Why was he calling so early ?

Kathy had picked the desk, too, and paid for it – her office-warming gift she said. He never saw the exact price, but he knew it had cost a fortune, and he was proud of it. It was huge, solid mahogany, with a leather top and so many drawers back and front that he didn't think he'd opened them all yet. Every time he walked into his office, the desk's opulence surprised him. Kathy usually hated big pieces of furniture that took up so much floor space. But it was his desk. She'd bought what she thought he'd like, and she was right. He wished David could see it.

He hung up his coat, and sat down behind it. It was nine forty-five. Mrs Payne due at ten. False pregnancy – she was fifty – very false. She just liked seeing doctors – young ones who had to handle her, Friedman told him.

'Give her a long, gentle examination,' Friedman said. Friedman had been her last doctor, but she wanted to change because, Friedman told Michael, he was too fat, and she'd heard that Michael was very handsome. 'Use lots of Vaseline, and charge her twenty-five dollars a visit so she'll think she's gotten something worth having. A little Valium probably won't hurt either.' Michael would go along with everything except the Valium. Drugs still made him uneasy and he wasn't going to give anyone anything they didn't need. Friedman shrugged at that. 'Nice ideals,' he'd said, 'but they're going to want it – and they'll go to us'n's that'll give it to them.' Michael was too happy to argue, but he was sure that, by practising good medicine, he'd have all the patients he could handle.

He seemed to be right. It was only a few months since he'd opened the office, and he didn't have a free hour left this week.

Sally came in with some coffee. 'Did you call your brother, Doctor?'

He felt a little less jaunty suddenly. David was waiting for his call.

'Not yet, Sally. I'll do it now.'

He waited for her to leave. Then he put sugar in the coffee, stirred, drank some. It was ten to ten. He had time before Mrs Payne. He drank some more coffee. Finally he pulled the phone towards him, dialled long distance, and gave the operator David's number.

Danny Perera liked Matthew Gargan's office much better than Michael's. Gargan's had a solid long-established feeling that inspired trust; here everything was new; he could still smell paint and wallpaper glue. He liked Gargan's looks better too – Gargan was a big man, about fifty, balding and soft in the middle, and he wore very expensive suits that looked baggy and soiled. Michael was too handsome – better-looking than he'd been in his teens, and even then he – both of them – had turned heads. Now he was too tall, and slight – almost frail, as if he'd been ill, and his clothes were extremely neat. Not established-looking at all.

Yet, Perera had gone to a lot of trouble to be there, and he wasn't going to let inconsequentials bother him.

It had been many years since he and Michael had seen each other, and Perera still used the childhood name that David used to use.

'I don't expect miracles, Mikey. I know Louise is going to die. They all tell me she's going to; I finally believe them. She's going to die.'

Michael thought if he said that one more time, he was going to throw Perera out. But the man was so defeated, so pitiful-looking. Almost all his hair was gone, and the watery blinking eyes were covered by thick glasses. His shirt collar was too big and Michael knew that there were stick-thin arms in the sleeves of his jacket, and too thin legs in his trousers.

'But once it's over,' Perera said, 'I'm going to need the consolation of knowing that everything possible was done for her. If you could just see her – talk to her – maybe something will occur to you.'

'Danny, nothing's going to occur to me that didn't occur to Gargan. He's better than I am – whatever he says. He's been treating women like your wife for thirty years. I was only at it for three. And even that was too much for me. Believe me, I can't help her.'

'But I told her about you. She wants to see you. Look, maybe it can't help, but it can't hurt either.'

Yes it can, Michael thought. It can hurt plenty – because I can't, *can't* see one more dying woman. Why can't you leave me alone, you and my fucking brother? He looked at the top of his new desk, the leather smooth and polished; a closeup of his hand reflected in the shine, farther away his face distorted in length, ruddy from the colour of the leather. Fuck Danny Perera. Michael was going to stay right here at this desk until five thirty, then he was going to make his rounds on floors five and six, five and six only. After that he was going to go home to his wife and son, have dinner, watch television and go to bed. Gargan liked death – like Clark, like lots of people. Fine, then let them handle it. He was finished.

'I'm sorry, Danny.'

'But David said he'd talk to you. He said you'd do it for him.'

'David had no right to say such a thing.'

'But didn't he call?'

'Yes; and I told him what I'm telling you. It is not in your wife's best interest for her to see a physician who has no intention of treating her.'

He could have gone on saying no all afternoon – all night if he had to – except that the little man started to cry.

He didn't bow his head or turn away. One minute, he was talking to Michael, and the next, tears were streaming down his cheeks. He wiped his cheeks with the back of his hand. 'I'm sorry,' he said. 'I'm sorry.'

Michael didn't say anything. The tears kept pouring and finally Perera took off the thick glasses and started to wipe his eyes. He half smiled, shook his head, reached in his back pocket for his handkerchief and then looked straight at Michael.

The tears had cleared the whites, turned them bluish, made them sparkle, and suddenly Salvatore – not Danny – Perera faced Michael across the desk.

Michael's desk, the walls – Kathy's bookshelves, with his books and some of hers to fill in – and with them the illusion of safety he had in this room – his room – dissolved. He closed his eyes. All around him he saw the old man's room out of focus and in front of him the old man himself, leaning towards them, holding his glass of tea.

He opened his eyes. Danny Perera was wiping his eyes.

'I don't know what hit me, Mikey. You think you've gotten used to a thing and then it sneaks up on you.'

'Some things you never get used to, Danny,' Michael said. Nothing had ever been the same between the twins after that afternoon. The old man had been an angel, pointing them out of a mad Eden where there was nothing but each other. Without the old man, there might have been no wife, no son.

Perera wiped his eyes, blew his nose, and composed himself.

'How long ago did your grandfather die, Danny?'

'My father's father?'

Michael nodded.

'Oh, years – twenty years. Why do you ask?'

'Just wondered.' Then Michael asked, 'What room is your wife in?'

'Room 306.' A pause, then, 'You're going to see her?'

Michael nodded, 'But just *see* her. It doesn't mean anything.'

'Jesus, Mikey – Oh, Jesus Christ – thank you. I'll tell the kids, Michael. You'll be in our prayers this *Shabbos*.' He didn't ask why Michael had changed his mind; he thought it was because he'd cried.

He shook Michael's hand – actually wrung it with a strength that surprised Michael. Then he just stared at him, and for one terrible moment Michael was afraid the man was going to kiss him. But he settled for patting and squeezing his shoulder, and then, overcome again, he left Michael alone.

Michael called the service and told them he'd be on the third floor at about three, instead of back at the office. Then he said good-bye to Sally and took the elevator instead of the stairs. The scene with Perera had worn him out, and he dreaded the one to come. But he owed the old man's grandson the few minutes of his time it would take to see Louise Perera. He was superstitious about leaving such a debt unpaid.

The elevator doors opened on three – the greenhouse – 'Where they keep the plants,' Friedman used to say – and for the first time in four months Michael heard the noise of the respirators. He'd almost forgotten it. He'd almost forgotten the smell too, but now it was back, all around him, getting stronger as he passed from the elevator foyer into the hallway proper. They had fans and vents, a special air system for this floor and wick deodorizers in all the rooms, but the smell conquered all the devices.

When he used to come here every day, he'd gotten used to it, and there were times he didn't notice it at all. Now it hit him again, took him by surprise – sweet, fetid – cancer smell. He breathed through his mouth because he had no intention of getting used to it again. He was going to be on this floor for half an hour, no longer, and he planned never to come back.

Michael kept his mouth open all the way down the hall to the open door of 306 where he knocked on the door frame.

Louise Perera looked up at him, and he stopped in the doorway and stared at her. Danny Perera looked fifty; he was bald, grey-faced, skinny and short. If Michael had thought about what he expected Danny's wife to be, he would have pictured the sort of woman who marries a man who looks like that. And maybe Louise Perera had been that once. Maybe she'd been fat; maybe her colour had been bad; maybe she'd had a dull look. But now she was beautiful – the disease had eaten away all extra flesh, exposing the fine bones of her face, stretching her pale skin across sharp cheekbones.

'You're Michael. Danny's talked about you so much I think I'd know you anywhere.'

He was still too startled by her appearance to answer.

'Come in.' She patted the side of her bed. Her hair and eyes were as dark as his, stark against the pale face, white sheets. 'C'mon.'

He took a step into the room. She started lifting the covers off the dishes of her snack tray.

'We serve Sanka,' she said, 'and custard and rice pudding. Plus eggnog. You'd think I'd had an ulcer instead of something as exotic as cancer. Real cream for the Sanka. And what's this – cookies! Butter cookies, I'll bet. Not bad, but there's nothing like a prune Danish, is there? Maybe if I asked.' Then she smiled and he recoiled. Her four upper front teeth were broken, jagged. She saw the movement but kept on smiling. 'I had some kind of seizure and they had to break them to get the tube out of my throat – couldn't pry my mouth open. I guess I've got some jaw. Comes from years of nonstop talking' – still smiling – 'so when I clench, I really clench. None of the guys here will admit to having done it, and I don't blame them. Imagine having to smash an unconscious woman in the teeth with a hammer. They can't pay doctors enough. I mean, what can you pay someone to make up for having to do a thing like that?'

He came farther into the room; she poured the Sanka. 'They always give me two cups and someone always comes to drink the second one. Usually Margaret – Margaret Stapleton. She runs the desk. Crispest little woman I ever knew. Never sweats and her hands are always dry and cool; it makes such a difference. I'll bet you never thought of your nurses' hand temperature as part of the therapy. You wouldn't believe it, but she has three grand-daughters. I wouldn't have given her thirty-five, would you?'

Michael shook his head, thinking that Louise Perera was thirty-six and looked twenty. The disease again. Weeks of rest and nothing to worry about except staying alive one more day.

'Danny said you were reluctant. He's given to understatement, Michael, because you look terrified. Are you?' she asked.

No answer.

'I know I'm going to die. I don't expect any miracles, just a

163

little comfort, that's all. That Gargan's a cold piece of work. Not that I mind – he's a good doctor, and he tried to unbend, he honestly did.' She closed her eyes and leaned back. 'But I was another cancer on the hoof to him, and I think he got a little scared of liking me. I don't blame Gargan, but Danny's wretched. He needs someone to talk to about me, someone who'll sympathize.'

A cloud had blown past and the room was suddenly full of sunlight. He could see dust floating in it, the detritus of pounded pillows, linens, used Kleenex. The air was full of white dust. She had stopped talking and the room was very quiet; even the whoosh of the respirators seemed muted. There was one in here too; the sun revealed it, waiting in the corner – for her. He knew she would need it soon if she were unlucky. The best she could hope for was a sudden clot, moving at night while she was asleep, silently, unfelt, cutting off her oxygen. They wouldn't find her until morning because she wouldn't even have time to ring.

The last thing in the world he needed was to get involved with Louise Perera.

She let him stare past her at the bright window for a minute, then asked again, 'Are you?'

He looked back at her, 'Am I what?'

'Terrified.' He came all the way into the room and sat down on the edge of her bed, one leg bent up on the mattress so he could feel the warmth of her body through the sheets and light hospital blanket.

'Yes,' he said. 'I am.'

'Why?'

'Because I just can't be detached any more.'

'But that's just the point,' she said, 'Danny and I've had enough detachment. We need someone who cares – or at least seems to – especially Danny. Don't you see that in a few weeks he's going to be left alone with a lot of guilt? He's going to need professional comfort – someone who'll look sorry that I'm dead.' Why didn't she cry? How could she say these things so calmly?

'The trouble is,' Michael said, 'that I won't just look sorry, and Danny's guilt will be nothing compared to mine, because I'll be the one who couldn't save you.'

Neither said anything for a minute; she handed him the dish of cookies and he took one, looking at her intently. She looked back calmly, not shy or bold; just examining him in the same way he was examining her.

'You know,' he said finally, 'I'm a twin.'

'Danny told me. But he said your brother lives in Boston.'

Michael took her hand. It was tiny, without substance, dry-feeling; the back was spotted with marks from the IV needles.

Kathy's hand used to be the only hand he ever touched that wasn't stabbed and bruised.

'My brother called me and told me to handle your case.'

'Do you usually do what he tells you?'

'No, I usually try to do the exact opposite. Which is too bad because he told me not to take the cancer fellowship and I should have listened.' Neither of them saw anything strange about the suddenness or depth of their intimacy. The rushing sound, the metal device waiting in the corner, and the shining transparent IV bottle trying to supplement the little she could eat on her own, all made it clear that whatever happened between them had to happen quickly.

'Why did you take it?' she asked.

'Money, prestige. He had a big appointment and I didn't want to get left out. But he told me how bad it would be and he was right. You see, it was a clinical investigation fellowship.' He didn't think anyone had ever listened to him so closely before. Her face didn't change; there were no expressions of sympathy, no interjections to convince him she was listening.

He went on: 'The patients who are probably going to get better don't need clinical investigators because we already know enough about their disease to control it. The ones who came to me were – were – negative.'

She looked away. 'Like me?' she asked.

'Yes, like you. They all died and I finally couldn't handle it any more. I had a sort of breakdown and I gave up the fellowship.'

She was silent for a moment. Then her eyes filled. He moved

a little closer to her on the bed and watched her wipe her eyes, try to smile.

'You wouldn't be telling me all this if you were going to be my doctor, would you?' she asked.

'No, I don't think I would.' He wasn't sure why he had, anyway. Maybe because he knew she was going to die in a month or six weeks, and that, as soon as he left this room, he would never see her again.

'Nothing will change your mind?'

'Would you really want me to change my mind, now that you know how I feel?'

She shook her head. Someone must have just washed her hair for her, because it was shiny and soft, not dull and oily the way most of his patients' hair was . . . used to be. Now the women he saw undressed in the little tiled bathroom that opened off the examining room, next to the empty office. They put on paper gowns and if he went into the bathroom, there was a skirt hanging there, and a blouse. They folded their girdles and bras and left them on the little white painted stool. Their hair was always clean and sprayed. He could smell their makeup and perfume, and when he touched them, they were uncomfortable – embarrassed. They'd shut their eyes tightly, or stare at the ceiling, trying to forget what he was doing to them. Not like the women here; they didn't care any more what anyone did to them, as long as it didn't hurt too much. Drugs glazed their eyes, and when he'd rolled up their gowns he smelled alcohol or the cancer smell, or excrement. No cologne here, no hair spray. The women were lank, ugly, defeated.

Yet Louise Perera had clean shining hair and she was wearing mascara and a touch of lipstick.

'Your hair looks lovely,' he said.

'The Swedish lady comes to do it every other day. She has a special basin. But you must know all about her.'

He didn't know.

'The women on this floor don't usually bother.'

She ducked her head, and he suspected more tears, but when she looked at him, she was smiling. 'Last Sunday,' she said, 'they let the boys come to see me – they only let them come once a month – and the poor things stood in the door and stared and stared. Finally, Sal – he's ten – said, "Mommy, what happened to you? You're so pretty." And Ira, who's just six, didn't say a word, but he couldn't take his eyes off me, and when I kissed him good-bye, I swear he blushed.' She was smiling, as if her looks were a joke she'd played on her family. 'You see, my parents were orthodox, and I always wore a scarf or something to cover my hair, and never any makeup. Now, I realize I have to do something not to frighten people.'

He couldn't listen any more and he stood up so quickly he jarred the tray and the cups and dishes rattled.

'I have to go,' he said hoarsely.

'Of course. I didn't mean to keep you.'

He went to the door as quickly as he could, hoping she wouldn't say anything else. She didn't, but he stopped anyway and turned back.

'If there was anything I could do . . .'

'I know you'd do it, Michael.' Still smiling, the sun gleaming on her hair, on her pale smooth skin.

He almost ran down the hall to the elevator.

chapter eighteen

By ten the next morning Michael was in Bethesda, surrounded by the parks, plazas and buildings that made up the National Institutes of Health. Inside Building 31, corridors unrolled in every direction, some silent, some enclosing muffled noises. He followed numbers to Dr Reales' office where a short young man without a tie asked him to wait. The man typed raggedly while Michael waited, saying 'fuck' or 'shit' every time he hit the wrong key, which he did again and again. The magazines were months old with most of the articles torn out; the ashtrays were dirty; and the carpet was worn and needed vacuuming. Michael wondered if someone had planned this suite as a contrast to the plastic perfection of the rest of the place.

Benjamin Reales, director of the cancer chemotherapy screening programme, matched his office. He was short and dark with a pencil moustache and oily, curly hair. His sweater was only half tucked in his pants and he had a blob of something yellow – mustard? – front centre.

Michael gave him the pile of papers he'd carried from New York; duplicates of everything the pathology department had on Louise Perera.

Reales looked through the material once while Michael sat there. Then he said, 'I can't tell you anything for a few hours. It'll take time to go over all of this. Can you come back about three?'

Michael said he could.

'The chances are poor that the drug is even indicated at all,' Reales said.

'I realize that.'

Reales shrugged. 'I don't suppose you want a tour.'

'No, thank you.'

'Very wise,' Reales said, 'very wise. Avoid the cafeteria.'

'I will.' Michael opened the door. Then Reales said without looking up from his desk, 'I know about your work – the keto-steroid levels and what they indicate or perhaps predict. Some would call it elegant. A limp term. It's fine, creative work, fastidiously done.' Michael couldn't move. The door was open and the receptionist, who must have heard Reales, was staring at him.

Michael didn't have the heart to tell Reales the work would never be finished – at least not by him – so he just nodded, thanked Reales, and left.

He took a bus into Washington and wandered through the Smithsonian. He bought a picture book on dinosaurs for Sam and a string of Indian beads for Kathy.

Just as he was ready to leave the shop, he saw a small brass manta ray sitting on the glass counter. Its metal tail twisted above its flat triangular body, and it had tiny red beads for eyes that were set oddly, making the fish look cross-eyed and slightly bewildered. He bought it and had them wrap it in tissue and put it in a box.

Reales was waiting for him when he returned at three thirty.

'It's possible,' he told Michael at once. 'Definitely possible, although you realize, the risk is considerable, and she will almost certainly die anyway?'

Michael nodded, weak with relief.

'But our pathologist,' Reales said, 'has found what he thinks
are definitely embryologic elements in her tumour. At least
enough like it to make the treatment vaguely rational.' Vaguely
rational? Give with one hand, take away with the other. What
kind of science was vaguely rational?

Reales smiled wryly as if he'd read Michael's mind. 'I know it
isn't much,' he said.

You're fucking right it isn't much.

'But without it she has two, three – maybe four weeks left.
With it, maybe a week longer, maybe a month, maybe a year.
Who knows?'

What predictable spik horseshit, Michael thought. Now raise
your shoulders for us and say *Que será, será.*

Suddenly Reales leaned across the desk. 'What did you
expect?' he asked sharply.

'I don't know.'

'But more. Right? You want to come down here one morning
and bring back *the* drug, cure cancer and astound your friends
and patients.' Suddenly the little man looked tired, and his
voice softened. 'I wish I had it to give to you. But try this anyway. It won't kill her any faster than the cancer – and maybe,
just maybe – but don't tell her that. And do yourself a favour,
don't you think it either.'

Reales handed him the envelopes and a small brown package
wrapped, taped, and tied. 'Give this to Johnstone,' he said.
'He'll know what to do. Remind him about platelets – every day,
mention platelets. Her platelets are everything.'

Michael kept the package in his lap on the plane, feeling like
one of those couriers who carried things chained to their wrists
for safety. He was sure they had the stuff well packed, but he
couldn't relax or forget what he was carrying. Methotrexate –
the wave of the future.

As soon as he got back, he took the package to Johnstone.
Yes, Johnstone knew what to do – he'd been down there for a
full year. 'But be ready for a rocky time. This stuff's a real go-to-
hell cell poison – not just the cancer cells, either. Make her sick
as a dog.'

When Michael mentioned platelets, Johnstone looked very disgusted. Of course he knew what to do about platelets. Did Reales suddenly decide he was an asshole? Platelets! What was going to happen to her platelets? Poor thing. That's what would probably kill her. Platelets.

Michael called David, who sounded bored and kept saying how interesting it was. But as soon as they hung up, David went upstairs through the drafty, smudged-looking halls of Boston's professional wing to Romer's office. Romer was head of the department, so his floor was covered with worn, stained carpeting instead of linoleum, and he had a view of the street and viaduct.

They were still a secret to many, and David liked the idea; all around them there were people working who said, 'Good morning, Dr Ross. Good morning, Dr Romer,' never dreaming what went on between them. Sometimes at conferences, he would look at his lover – respected, deferred to, well-dressed; neat Jim; pale blond, even-featured Jim – and remember him in other poses – pulling David's hair, hurting him sometimes, once so hot he couldn't wait till they got home, but insisted they make love in the office. David had tried to get it over with as fast as he could because he was sure someone was going to come in and find them. Fine scandal that'd be – head of the department and his much-praised assistant professor.

Romer was drinking coffee and eating a doughnut, and when David told him what Michael was going to do, he whistled silently, spraying crumbs.

'Some imagination your brother's got. Very good – very, very good. I don't know if I'd have the wit to think of it, or the guts to try it.'

'You mean it might work?' There was something in his tone that made Romer look sharply at him.

'I don't think it'll work. By that I mean it won't do for ovarian cancer what it's done for choriocarcinoma. It won't cure the woman.'

'It won't?'

'I doubt it.'

'Then what's so good about it?'

'He could buy her some time – maybe a substantial amount –

months – perhaps more. No one's done this yet; we don't know what'll happen. But in theory it's a hell of a fine idea.'

'But just in theory?'

Again something wrong. Romer was quiet for a moment, watching David. Then he said, 'You know, Dave, you sound almost sorry that it might work, and relieved that it probably won't. You're a little jealous, aren't you? Used to having all the praise for youself. There's plenty to go around, Dave. Your work's worlds apart. And Michael's had a rough time. They couldn't get me into oncology for anything in the world,' he said.

David thought of trying to tell Romer that he wasn't jealous, but he didn't know how to explain how he did feel, so he didn't say anything.

Adele Samuelson was spread and staked like a hide in the sun when Sally came into the examining room and told Michael that Johnstone was on the phone with the results. Michael had been waiting for the call all morning, but he made himself continue working at his normal pace. It seemed like hours, but finally he finished, and while Mrs Samuelson was getting dressed he called Johnstone back.

Johnstone was from Maine, and he played it to the hilt.

'Ayeh, we got the platelet counts, leukocytes, lymphocytes,' a pause, 'eosinophils'. Then he started reeling off the numbers.

'For Christ's sake! I'm not a haematologist. I don't know the norms. Just tell me if it's okay.'

'Well, BUN says it's okay, but that was never much of a problem – SGOT, alkaline—'

'You son of a bitch.'

'Easy, Doc, easy now.' But Johnstone sounded happy, pleased with both of them. 'I can't find anything wrong enough to stop us. It's worth a try, Mike, definitely worth a try.'

Friedman didn't think so. He called right after Johnstone and insisted they have lunch. Neither could make it till three and by then all that was left was fried chicken, drying under ultraviolet light.

'Bill, you gotta be starving to death to eat that shit.'

'I'm starving to death.' He had Max add mashed potatoes and gravy.

Michael followed with his cheese sandwich and tea. 'Attaboy, Ross, show me how to stay thin,' said Friedman as he started eating. Nothing was said until he finished. Then he wiped his mouth, chugalugged a Coke, belched and sat back.

'I heard what you're going to do with the Perera woman.'

'Indian runners in this place.' Then, because he was afraid Friedman's feelings would be hurt, he said, 'I was going to tell you myself, Bill – this afternoon.'

'Why not this morning? Or yesterday afternoon?'

Michael was embarrassed.

'I know why, Mike. Because you know I'm going to tell you not to do it. It's the same story all over again. You're knocking yourself out to watch someone die.'

'It might help; there's some indication . . .'

'Sure, it might. But she's going to die no matter how much it helps. Everyone says so – people who know better than you. All you can hope is to buy her an extra week or two. And you still wind up with another corpse to your credit for all your trouble. I thought you were all finished with it.'

'I was, but her husband is an old friend.'

'I don't care if he's your mother.'

'He called David, and David called me.'

'Fuck David.'

'It isn't for them, Bill. It's for her.'

'The most dangerous reason of all.'

'Why don't you see her before you say that? Talk to her for a couple of minutes, and then come back and tell me not to try.'

'I don't care if she looks like Greta Garbo and talks like Groucho Marx – you shouldn't touch it.'

'Just see her, Bill – ten minutes – and I'll buy you a drink if you still feel that way.'

Friedman said, 'Ten minutes, for a free drink?'

Michael nodded.

'You're on.' Friedman left him alone in the cafeteria.

He wasn't back in ten minutes. So Michael left a message at the register and went to Johnstone's lab. Friedman found him there an hour later.

'I need a drink.'

They walked down the block to Wong's without talking. Michael waited until they both had their drinks.

'What do you say now?' he asked.

Friedman drank and winced. Michael waited.

'Okay, she's pretty – very pretty except for the broken teeth. In fact, she's a lovely woman, funny and sweet. She's maybe even special. She was trying to learn to knit when I got there, and I swear there was yarn around everything and she was laughing with the stuff twisted around every finger . . .'

He stopped.

'Stapleton was teaching her. But she said it was hopeless . . .' He stopped again.

Then he said, 'If she were ugly or stupid – I'd say try. But she's not. So how're you going to feel when she dies?'

'Like I tried very hard to save her.'

'You're sure?'

'Positive.'

'I think you're wrong, Mike. I think you're making a terrible mistake; but the drinks are on me.'

Michael didn't check in when he got back to the hospital because he didn't want to be interrupted; he got off the elevator on the third floor and walked through the smell and the sound of the respirators without even thinking about them. Louise was lying back with her eyes closed, but she opened them as soon as he came into the room. He'd only seen her once, but she already looked familiar to him.

She sat up. 'I thought—'

He put his fingers to his lips and she stopped talking. He wanted to sit on the bed again, but he took the chair instead because he had to be distant. What he said to her had to be perfectly clear because she had to understand the risks.

They started giving her the methotrexate the next day and by the end of the week, it was all over the hospital that someone at Manhattan was actually using methotrexate to treat ovarian cancer.

Teams of interns and residents came to Louise Perera's room every day while she was examined, X-rayed, punctured, and medicated. Every morning they counted her platelets and every night they gave her Compazine because the methotrexate made her so sick. At first, Michael was there only in the mornings and evenings, but soon he started visiting at odd hours when patients cancelled, or when Sally had scheduled a free hour. He became involved in the more mundane aspects of her care, things he never thought about before – whether the IV was clear, if she had plenty of ice water (although she told him that drinking water now made her sick to her stomach), if her sheets were smooth. Once when it was too warm in the room, he gave her an alcohol rub and for the first time realized how wasted her body was, and yet strangely beautiful. He felt a terrible pity for her which must have showed because she laughed at him when she saw the look on his face and whispered happily, 'The food here is ghastly.'

On Sunday, he waited to talk to Danny who left by six on weekdays. But it was the once a month children's visit, and Michael stood off to the side, watching her sons. They both looked like her, except that the younger one had blue eyes. They stayed close to Danny and Michael. He could see that they were a little afraid of their mother. It was easy to understand; she'd been gone a long time and now looked different to them. Their shyness, their ill-hidden fear, must have been terrible for her.

Michael wanted to explain to Danny that, although his wife wasn't any better, exactly, she wasn't any worse, and that was a kind of progress. But Danny wouldn't listen. He kept trying to hold Michael's hand, to tell him how grateful he was, how much they owed him – how they could never repay him – until Michael couldn't stand it any more and went home.

In a few days, he stopped noticing the broken teeth, and Louise Perera looked perfectly beautiful to him.

chapter nineteen

The Monday David called, Louise Perera had been taking the drug for two months and there was still no change.

'Hey, Mike, how's your star patient?' David asked.

'Holding on. No worse.'

'Well, that's something, isn't it?'

'Yeah, something.'

'I have to be at a meeting in Rye on Friday, so I thought I'd zip down and spend the weekend.'

When did David start using phrases like 'zip down'?

'Don't fall all over yourself,' David said when Michael didn't answer.

'C'mon, Dave. I always look forward to seeing you.'

'You sound a little down, babe.' And where did he get the 'babe'. Michael didn't feel down.

'Not too much for you, is it?' David asked.

'No, everything's fine,' Michael said, and thought that everything was wonderful.

That night when he wrote David's name across the weekend on his calendar, he realized that it was already April.

Ten months had passed since he'd opened the office – almost spring. The time had gone quickly – the best months of his life, he thought – the busiest anyway.

The East Side Jewish matrons had heard about Michael's looks, his brand-new office, and now about his 'amazing work with cancer', and the waiting room was packed every day that he was in. Half of the women had nothing wrong with them. They came to get out of the house, to see their friends, to read magazines – and to see and be examined by the young, good-looking doctor. Some even brought their children so they wouldn't have to pay baby sitters. He finally had Sally put a sign on the door and on the reception-room wall that read, 'Due to the nature of my practice, children under sixteen are not allowed in the office, except as patients.' That cleared the children out and some of the mothers. They were good-natured about it, and he hoped they'd come back if they ever needed a doctor.

It would be summer soon; most of his patients had summer homes, and they'd pack themselves and the children off to Long Island or Connecticut or upstate New York, leaving their husbands at home in the weekday heat, to eat out, drink too much, fuck too many strange women, and wait for Friday. Summer would be quieter and he would have more time to spend with Louise. He knew how dangerous that kind of thinking was. Reales had warned him; he'd warned himself. But he couldn't help it.

Kathy was in the shower and he was alone in the bedroom. He closed his eyes, rested his cheek against the cool, smooth pillow-case and let himself imagine it was summer, and that Louise was still alive. She'd have to wear a wig by then, because the drug was making all her hair fall out. 'My lovely hair,' she'd cried, while he sat next to her helplessly, telling her over and over and over that it would grow back – the loss wasn't permanent. 'I'm going to die, Michael. How will it grow back?'

He almost told her then that she wasn't going to die. The impossible was happening – the drug was working. She was going to live, to go home. But he didn't dare say any of these things to her; until now he hadn't dared to think them himself except in flashes that he couldn't help. Now he let himself go. Louise would live through the summer and by fall she'd be able to keep food down, and her hair would grow back, thick and dark. Early autumn was clearer in his mind than tomorrow. As soon as she felt strong enough, he'd take her outside. Her first time out in months would be with him. She'd have to hold on to him because she'd still be weak, but she'd be on her feet. She'd look at the leaves turning colour in the park and they'd sit on a bench.

He had to stop thinking like this; he'd go crazy if he didn't stop, because she was going to die, next month, next week.

'Are you all right, Michael?' Kathy asked, ready to turn out the light.

'Fine,' he said. He lay on his back, his eyes open in the dark, thinking about Louise.

By the end of five laps, Michael's lungs were ready to burst into the ugly blue water, his eyes burned from chlorine and his mouth tasted and felt bleached. He started the sixth lap, and realized, in the middle of the pool, that if he didn't get out, he'd drown. But he didn't seem to have any strength. He began splashing like a kid, arms and legs out of control – moving water but not his body. He stopped and tried to touch bottom, but he couldn't – the side of the pool looked as far away as ever, farther – he'd gotten turned around. He knew he should relax and tread water, until he got his breath back, but he couldn't seem to control his movements. His nose was full of water, his throat was too. He began to choke, and then to panic. Suddenly he felt David's body against his back, and David's arm came around his chest. Michael relaxed – he was being rescued. He let himself be towed a little way, then tried for the bottom again, and this time he could stand. He faced David.

'You all right?' David asked.

'Yeah, fine.' He was a little embarrassed. He could see page two of the *News:* DOC DROWNS IN NINETY-SECOND STREET Y POOL.

'You look scared.'

'I was.'

David laid his palm against Michael's bare midriff. People sitting around the pool watched them, even a few of the swimmers lifted their heads out of the water to see what the twins were doing. David pushed gently into Michael's flesh.

'Soft, love – too soft.' 'Love,' 'Babe,' 'zip down' – the new, Beacon Hill David Ross. Michael was suddenly unreasonably angry, and he moved back into the water so David wasn't touching him any more.

David shrugged. 'It's true, Mike. You need exercise, you're not that young any more.'

Michael looked at his brother's body, at the muscles around David's chest, at his flat abdomen. David looked down at himself proudly, poking his belly to show it was firm.

Michael couldn't stay angry. 'I told you once,' he said gently, 'You're the best-looking man I know.'

David grinned, lay back in the water and started stroking for the far side of the pool; midway he turned over and started swimming in earnest. There was something about his movement which let everyone know that he was serious about what he was doing and people on the sidelines started watching, while the other swimmers stayed out of his way. Michael sidestroked to the side of the pool – the shallow end – and pulled himself out on to the tile ledge. David kept swimming. At ten laps somebody started counting, and at twenty, other people counted too.

Michael leaned towards the girl sitting next to him. She was pretty, and she was wearing a red tank suit that showed her nipples, stiff from the water, the bulge of her mons, and small tufts of pubic hair. She had been watching both of them since they came into the gym. Now she was just watching David.

Michael wondered what she'd do if he just stroked the bulge gently. He smiled. A nice horny thought for the first time in months.

He and Kathy hadn't made love much since Sam had been born. In fact, the last time was a little dim in his mind; a couple of weeks ago anyway, maybe a month.

But now he was really excited.

David was good for him – or Louise was.

'Excuse me,' he said.

'Yes?' She asked. He looked down her suit and she sat up straighter, but she was smiling at him.

'How many laps is really good?' he asked.

'Oh, anything over twenty. I'm not sure what the record is. I've heard fifty, but most people are finished by ten or fifteen. He's at twenty-five. That's very good. How many did you do?'

He was relieved that she hadn't seen his splashing panic.

'I did five.' He wanted to tickle the hair curling around the elastic of her suit.

'Out of shape, huh?' Very sympathetic. He noticed that her forearms and legs were well muscled. She was in very good shape. He touched her knee lightly with the tips of his fingers, and he felt a tiny shudder run through her.

'Very out of shape,' he said sadly.

'You should work out.' He ran his fingers down the inside of her calf, feigning absent-mindedness, as if he didn't realize what he was doing. Everyone was watching David. She didn't move except to shudder again. Wonderful, he thought. He had spent a whole day examining women who were naked except for their shoes and a sheet, and now he was getting an erection from stroking some girl's leg. Wonderful. His fingers came around her ankle, and began rubbing the arch of her foot.

'That's why I'm here,' he said, 'to work out. Do you come here often?'

Maybe we could work out together in the locker room or in the shower – quickies at the Y. He hadn't felt this good in a long time.

Then she looked down at the hand sliding along her foot, and snapped her legs shut. 'Like a pair of jaws,' he told David later.

'You're married,' she said accusingly.

'Yes, I am.'

She stood up.

'Is he married, too?' She nodded towards David, who was still swimming. Michael stood up too. He did have an erection, straining against his trunks. She looked at it, then quickly at something on the far side of the pool.

Michael laughed. 'No, he's not married, but he's a homosexual.'

She jumped into the pool and swam like mad for the other side. He sat down again, still smiling, and wondering if the hard on, which now felt incredibly solid, would ever go down again. He pulled his knees up so no one would see it.

David had stopped the serious swimming. He was half paddling to try and cool down, but finally he stood up next to Michael's feet, held on to the tile rim, and gasped – head down, shoulders heaving.

'That was terrific, Dave. How many'd you do altogether?'

'You mean' – gasp – 'that you weren't counting?'

'No. There was a girl next to me, wearing a red suit that let everything out. And I've got a hard on which is beginning to feel like part of the landscape.'

David laughed and gasped until he started choking and Michael jumped into the pool to pull his brother's arms up over his head – the only sure way, according to their father, to stop someone coughing.

'Watch yourself in the shower,' David gasped.

They left the Y and walked, with their hair still wet. Michael moved closer to David, who was telling him about Boston. ' "I don't care if he is Jewish," she told her husband. "He got me pregnant, and we're inviting him to dinner." I swear that's what she said to the guy,' David said.

Michael laughed. 'You better watch yourself,' he said. 'You could wind up with a rifle up your ass.'

'Believe it or not,' David said, 'the husband was as happy as the wife. We had a good dinner and for the first evening in his life he didn't blame anything on the yids – out loud. Actually, I kind of liked the guy, and I took the dinner off the bill.'

David wanted to be asked, so Michael asked him, 'How much did you charge?'

'Six hundred.'

Michael whistled. 'I'd have to knock the husband up to charge that much.'

They turned towards Fifth, and David spotted the Argus, which used to be one of their favourite bars.

'C'mon,' David said. 'We'll have a drink to the good old days.'

At the bar they passed the Sunday drinkers, who stared at them. They went into the back room where there were booths and only a few other people.

David ordered double bourbons. 'You'd be amazed how much people'll pay without a whimper when it's something really important to them. Like a baby. How much is the baby you've always wanted worth?'

'That's too much money, David.'

Michael hadn't had bourbon for years. It tasted heavy and oily, and the glass seemed very full.

'No it isn't. They get a lot of my time and thought for the money – and they get a baby.'

'So what does the treatment include . . .' Six hundred dollars. Even if David saw only one patient a day it was a fortune. Michael tried to calculate how much his brother made a year. But he hadn't eaten since lunch and he was already a little high.

'Look, Mike. I don't just write out a prescription for Clomiphene. It takes weeks just to evaluate each woman's problem. Some of 'em are never going to get pregnant – ovaries dead – and you've got to separate them out because it's no good giving them the drug. Of course, most don't believe you when you tell them the drug won't work.' David finished his drink all at once, and ordered another round. Michael drank faster to keep up.

'And they usually go to see someone else; you hear about it – because it's like a small town up there, and some Dr Jones or Smith, or Adams – yeah, Adams – will call you and tell you that he's seeing your ex-patient.' David took another big swallow of the second drink as Michael just started on his. 'They're all called Adams up there, and they all went to Harvard. I think I'm the only Jew. There's one Guinea. I know the guy – Bardino, Frank Bardino. We have dinner together sometimes, but his wife heard about me and Romer, and we only see each other when she's out of town.' David took another drink, no longer bothering with the chaser. He was getting drunk. 'But even then he's uncomfortable – you know how it is?' Michael didn't know. 'Like I'd made a pass,' David explained, even though Michael hadn't asked. 'Shit.' David laughed. 'I wouldn't do that. He's short 'n fat, and what's left of his hair is greasy.'

'Do a lot of people up there know about you and Romer?' They'd never talked about it before; until this afternoon at the pool, he'd never said it aloud before. But now it was easy.

David shrugged, 'A few. Like a small town, I told you. Every doctor knows every other doctor. They can forgive me. After all I'm a Jew from New York, and no one's going to ask me to tea anyway. But Romer – Choate, Dartmouth Romer – how could he? His mother was an Adams, or maybe she was an Ely. I forget. So how could he?' David laughed and signalled Si for another round. Michael hurried to catch up.

'It must get lonely,' Michael said.

'Yeah, lonely.' Then David looked closely at Michael. He was waiting for his brother to tell him to come home, and Michael knew it. He gulped at his bourbon.

David went on talking quickly. 'It's not so bad,' he said. 'We're not the only homosexuals in Boston.'

'Good thing,' said Michael with mock gravity. 'Bad enough being the only Jew.' David laughed wildly, spraying the bourbon he hadn't swallowed, and Michael mopped his face, smiled, then started laughing too.

Si brought more bourbon – that made four drinks each and Michael was finally drunk enough to ask, 'Dave, why?'

'You mean why Romer?' Michael nodded. David hiccupped.

'I don't have to worry about getting him pregnant.' They laughed again until they couldn't any more. Then David stopped and shook his head, serious again. 'I like that kind of sex.' Michael wanted to ask what kind that was, but he couldn't, so he said, 'Sex is sex. It's all good.'

'Yeah, I guess.'

'Then why?'

David said, 'Because it doesn't tie me up. No wife, no kids. I stay free.'

'Free to do what?' Michael asked thickly.

David was so drunk he almost said 'to come back to you when the time comes'. But he caught himself and instead he shrugged again and waved vaguely.

'Tell me about Louise,' he said. 'All about her.' He saw the way Michael smiled, as if he'd been waiting for the chance to talk about her.

'This place stinks,' David whispered to Michael; Michael nodded slowly. 'Stinks,' he agreed. 'What's that sound?'

'Respirators.' David gave a mock shudder, then stumbled. Michael held on to him.

They were walking very carefully down the third-floor corridor towards the nursing station. Michael knew vaguely that he was late, but he couldn't see the hands of his watch clearly, so he didn't know how late. The station was empty and Michael and David moved past it, both listing slightly.

'Room 306,' he told David. 'If she's asleep, you just get to look at her, that's all. Just a quick look.'

'What's to look at?' David asked. He made Michael stop moving until he answered.

'You'll see,' Michael said. 'You'll see.'

Louise opened her eyes when they walked in. Michael held on to the wall near the door, and David walked to her bed, swaying slightly.

'Is this the one?' he asked.

Michael nodded.

'Hello, star,' David said softly.

She heard one voice, and saw two men with the same face in the half-light of the night lamp.

'Michael?' She sounded frightened, but Michael was afraid to let go of the wall.

'No, star,' David said, still softly, his voice like velvet. 'I'm David.'

Her hair was almost blue in this light – eyes huge, shadowed, dark; bones so fine he thought they'd break if he touched them; winged eyebrows, and – oh my, she had a cleft in her chin. David reached over to touch it and Louise shrank back against the pillows. That startled him and made him angry. She wouldn't shrink from Michael.

'I said you could look only,' Michael said.

'I won't hurt her.' David's voice was smooth, as if she were a pet.

Michael's scalp crawled. David went closer, sat on the bed.

'Michael, please,' she said.

Michael shook his head. 'It's okay. It's only David.'

'She knows I won't hurt her. Don't you, star?'

No answer. It was dark in the room and the door was closed. Stapleton would be coming in any minute . . . please come in, Michael prayed silently, not knowing why he wanted them to be interrupted.

'Michael's told me all the things he does for you. Well, maybe not all – not the secret things, star. That's still between the two of you – not to worry. But all the other things – the sweet considerate things. The little presents.' He spotted the brass manta ray on the bedside table. 'Like that. I bet that's from Michael, isn't it? So cute. Oh yes, he told me about the back rubs, and bringing you nail polish. Let's see.' He took the hand that wasn't connected to the IV, and held it to the night light. 'Scrumptious colour,' he said. 'He even told me about the wig he's going to help you pick out – so sweet. See how much he tells me. But that's to be expected, star. After all, I'm his twin.'

'Please,' Louise said, trying to sound calm.

David hunched next to her on the bed, casting a huge shadow on the wall. Michael watched the shadow.

'I'm so tired,' she told David. 'I'd love to talk to you tomorrow – after I've had—'

'Sure,' he said. 'No talk now. We'll just have a quick look and leave the star to rest. Right, Mike?' No answer.

'Now, just lie back and relax.' David's hands were on the sheet, starting to roll it down. 'We share everything,' he told her. 'Everything. Ah, you're not so thin . . .'

Michael got away from the wall. The floor tilted towards him, but he stayed on his feet. 'David, leave her alone.'

'Oh, this'll only take a minute.' David was stroking her neck gently with one hand, and with the other he'd started untying the front of her gown. She raised her hand, but the call button was out of her reach. Then he pulled open the nightgown, exposing her breasts. Michael reached the table, and pushed the call button.

David looked up. 'My, aren't we in a state!'

Louise covered herself with shaking hands.

'I'm sorry, Louise,' Michael said. 'We're both drunk. I'll take him home now.' She didn't answer.

David looked down at her. 'I guess little brother doesn't want to share after all.' She turned away just as Stapleton opened the door and turned on the overhead light. David and Michael stood blinking in the middle of the room.

'Is everything all right?' Stapleton asked. Louise kept her head turned.

'Sorry, Mag,' Michael said. 'I was just retying the bell cord, and rang by mistake. Didn't mean to make a fuss – I thought Mrs Perera would like to see my brother. You remember David?' Stapleton looked from one to the other without saying anything. Michael knew she could see how drunk they were. 'Some people enjoy seeing how much alike we are,' he finished lamely.

'And did she?' asked Stapleton drily.

'No. She didn't seem to,' Michael said. David didn't say a word.

'We were just about to leave,' Michael said.

'I think that's best, Doctor.' She followed them to the door and watched them down the hall to the elevator as if she were afraid they'd change their minds.

David walked stiffly, staring straight ahead. Michael turned once to wave at her before they got into the elevator.

He found a cab on Fifth and as soon as they were inside, David leaned back and fell asleep. When they got home, Michael helped him across the lobby, both silent. The elevator man grinned and watched their progress down the hall to the apartment. Inside everything was quiet. Kathy had left a light on in the living room. Michael eased David onto the couch and went into the bedroom. It was dark; Kathy was breathing evenly. Then he went back to the living room. David was out, head back, mouth open, half lying on the couch. His head was twisted against the arm, and his feet were on the floor. Michael put his feet up, and forced an embroidered pillow under his head to ease the strain on his neck. Then he opened the collar of his shirt and unbuckled his belt. David started to snore. Michael thought that he and Louise were the only two people left awake in the whole world. He turned off the lights and left the house.

This time he took the freight elevator to three. He stood in the shadows near the elevator and looked down the corridor. Stapleton was there. He leaned against the wall and waited. In about ten minutes she started her rounds. When she had checked Louise and was in the room next door, he walked quickly and silently down the corridor and opened her door. She was awake, her head propped up, reading *Travels with Charley* which he'd bought for her a couple of days ago. She closed the book when she saw him.

'It's Michael,' he said before she could ask which one he was.

'Drunk or sober?' she asked.

'Less drunk.'

He sat down on the bed next to her, the way David had done – the way he himself had done the first time he saw her.

'Michael, what was wrong with him?'

'A lot of things. He was jealous of you, and he's angry because he's afraid I'll be hurt if you die.'

'When I die.' He ignored that. Then he said, 'Mainly, he was doing what he knew I wanted to do.'

Nothing, no reaction.

'Do you understand me?' he asked. She looked down at her hand, at the closed book. Then she nodded.

'Do you want me to leave?' he asked. Still no answer.

'Do you?'

'No.'

He touched her cheek, her mouth, then he kissed her; he

could feel her body start to shake. He got up, pulled the curtain around the bed, then he came back and kissed her again. He opened her gown, then very slowly, not to startle her, he touched her breasts, stroked circles around her nipples, then took one in his mouth. He opened his shirt and leaned lightly against her so she could feel the hair on his chest touch her bare skin. She started to put her arms around him.

'No,' he said, 'don't move. Let me do it all.'

chapter twenty

The next day, Michael took David to the terminal to get the bus for La Guardia. They didn't say much; he felt as if David had already left, and the figure sitting next to him in the cab, and then on a bench in the terminal waiting room, was a ghost. Maybe David felt the same. Maybe he was really already back there with Romer, in small-town, Jewless Boston. The plane was at ten, and Michael watched the clock stick at eight forty-five, then eight fifty-five.

'About last night . . .' David began.

'Forget it; we were drunk.' Only five minutes to go.

'You went back there last night, didn't you?'

He knew David would keep asking until he got some answer.

'Yeah – okay. I went back,' Michael said.

David looked at him. Why did Michael think the eyes were empty, that this wasn't David at all, just someone who looked like him? As always, David knew what he was thinking. 'You wish I were anyone else and anywhere else, don't you?' he said. 'You don't want even me to know, do you?' Michael didn't answer. 'But I do,' David said. 'I know why you went, and what you did when you got there.' It was nine at last. David stood up.

He looked at Michael's bowed head, and wanted to plead with him to let it go, to forget her. He knew a dying woman when he saw one and drug or no drug, Louise Perera was finished. David knew the pain that was coming; he could feel it already if he let himself. 'Don't do it,' he told his brother

186

silently, 'don't.' But he couldn't say it. So he said, 'She's very beautiful, Mike.' He took Michael's hand, and then, for the first time in years, he put his arms around his brother.

As soon as David left, Michael took a cab all the way up Madison. All the elevators were mobbed, so he ran up the stairs to three, sweating and out of breath. Stapleton was waiting with a message that Gargan wanted to see him – 'as soon as convenient.'

'Oh, Mag,' he said to her, 'you didn't tell him that Dave and I were drunk, did you?'

'Of course not. No harm done. In fact, it – something – did her good. She got through her whole breakfast this morning – for the first time since she's been on this floor – and she sent me off to the galley for two cups of custard. I left her finishing the second one and looking forward to the snack cart. If you two have this effect often, you could hire yourselves out to haunt hospitals.'

Michael stuck the message from Gargan in his pocket, kissed Stapleton and tried not to run down the hall to Louise's room.

He didn't know what kind of reaction to expect, but she smiled when she saw him.

'Have some custard.' She extended a full spoon towards him. 'Go ahead. Mag says there'll be more on the snack tray, so you're not depriving me. Go ahead, Michael. No one can resist custard.'

'Louise, I . . .'

'If you say you're sorry, I'll throw the custard in your face.'

'I didn't hurt you?'

'Of course you hurt me. Everything's sore. I've been walking bowlegged and I'm just glad I don't have to cross my legs or do anything but lie here and eat custard. I asked for fish cakes and spaghetti for lunch, but I'm not too sanguine about my chances. Maybe if you talked to them— No, I guess not. Okay – poached eggs. Come and have lunch with me. *You* eat the fish-cakes.'

Stapleton came in and interrupted. 'Gargan called again looking for you.'

'Okay.' He waited for Stapleton to leave, then he asked, 'Can I come back tonight?'

'I don't know what they'll give me for dinner.'

'Louise, I'm serious.'

'It's the wrong thing to be, Michael. I'm going to wind up leaving you, no matter how much I love you.'

'I'll be back about eight.' He left before she could answer.

Gargan was in his office on the second floor. He was wearing his coat, ready to leave. 'Where the hell have you been?'

'With Louise Perera.'

'Yeah – Louise Perera.' Then he smiled and took his coat off. 'To hell with the meeting – this is too good to miss. Come with me.' He wouldn't explain, so Michael had to follow him without knowing where.

Gargan led him down the grey enamelled backstairs to the ground floor where the outpatient clinics, and the bio and radiation evaluation labs were. They passed bio, and went into radiation where Ted Kahn was waiting for them.

'I thought you'd gotten run over, Ross; I've got a lunch date. Sit over here.' He pointed to a chair in front of the hanging light boxes. Gargan sat next to him.

'Now, Ross, how's this?' Kahn slid four X rays into the lightbox clips. 'This is six weeks ago,' Kahn said. 'Four weeks – two weeks – and this – this is yesterday.'

Michael stood up and looked closer. Kahn looked at Gargan; they were both smiling. Michael saw the name taped to the bottoms of the negatives – Louise Perera – four times, and the dates. The X rays were all of her lungs. In the first there were several dark areas in the picture where the tumour had spread from her ovaries before the primary was found and removed. Lungs that couldn't support life was what the picture showed – the woman with those lungs was a few days away from needing a respirator. But in the second picture, the dark spots appeared smaller. Not definitely, just an impression of reduced size. In the third, the trend was clear. In fact, as Michael saw, that one spot had disappeared entirely, replaced by what looked like normal tissue. And in the fourth and last, all but one was gone, and it had gotten much smaller.

He turned to Gargan and Kahn. Their smiles had turned to huge grins. It was true!

'Oh, my God!' Michael said. 'Oh, sweet God.'

'Sweet, sweet God,' said Kahn.

'Amen,' said Gargan, rolling his hands and eyes in mock worship.

Michael grabbed Kahn's arm. 'What do I do now?'

'I don't know. You're the doctor.'

'It's never happened here before,' Gargan said. 'Call Reales. Call him – now – while I'm here so I can listen, too.'

Reales was ecstatic. Michael heard him yelling at the receptionist, 'It worked – I think the SOB brought it off – it worked. Platelets – what about her platelets?'

'Okay as of yesterday. I don't know about today; you'd have to talk to Johnstone.'

'Then what the fuck are you waiting for? Get Johnstone.'

None of them knew how to transfer the call, and Reales was too excited to do anything but scream for Johnstone, so they told him to hang on, and Michael ran down the hall, and back up the stairs to find Johnstone.

He came, mumbling every step. 'I did everything Reales told me to; she only needed four transfusions.'

Michael didn't tell Johnstone, like the others hadn't told him, and as Johnstone listened to Reales his eyes widened and he got the same idiotic grin on his face that the others had. He started writing, made Reales repeat something and went on writing while the others listened. Then he handed the phone back to Michael.

'Good one, Ross.' More back slapping. 'Real good one.'

'C'mon, c'mon,' Reales was yelling into the phone.

'I'm here,' Michael said.

'Okay. Now listen to me, Ross. The platelets are still important – don't let down on them.' God, the man was obsessed. 'But now the fancy stuff is over – now it's drudgery. The tumour – tumours – are necrotizing. They're being starved to death. That's good! But as they go, they leave unstable tissue – gaps – which means she's ripe for clots. She's got to be watched all the time – get stockings on her, get her out of bed, keep her as active as possible. Her nurse will do more for her now than you can. Johnstone has the rest.

'Oh, and Ross, you did a creditable job. It was an imaginative, courageous idea. If you ever get fed up with the medical-establishment politics in New York, you have a standing offer to try the medical-establishment politics in Bethesda.'

189

He saw Anders in the hall. They were too close for Anders to pretend he hadn't seen him.

'Hello, John.' Michael waited.

'I understand congratulations are in order,' Anders said.

How could anyone be so goddamn stiff? Michael tried to soften the scene by smiling. They were talking about Louise's life, and he was superstitious about bad feeling.

'It looks good for today, John. I hope it goes on.'

'Well, we'll see, won't we?' Anders said shortly, and walked around Michael and down the hall.

Michael wanted to tell Louise, but Gargan warned him against it. 'Don't even tell the husband,' he said. 'I know how it is. One of the best moments in life is telling a patient who thinks he's going to die that he probably isn't. I've had that privilege a few times, and it's heady stuff, Michael. But you can only expect so much of people. She's ready to die. The disease is unpredictable. Okay, we've got a remission that could last months – years – a lifetime. But it may also last only a few weeks. The point is, if you tell her now, and the disease recurs – which it probably will – then she's got to get ready all over again. She's over the worst of it, now; she's gotten over her anger, mourned her own death, said good-bye to her family – to everyone really.'

Except to me, Michael thought. She hasn't said good-bye to me.

'She's more or less at peace. Maybe thinking, as they do sometimes – and you know this too – that there's nothing so terrible to leave after all.' Then Gargan had looked out the window. There were hints of spring in the colour of the sky and park. 'It's a shitty time of year to die,' he said absently. He turned back to Michael, 'But she's ready. You won't help her by getting her unready. There's plenty of time for that.'

It was good advice because two months later she died.

Stapleton called Michael at four o'clock in the morning to tell him. He told Kathy what had happened and, amazed at how calm he was, he dressed and took a cab to the hospital. Danny wasn't there yet, although he had called to say someone from the chapel would be there to get her in an hour or so. They'd move her downstairs in a few minutes, but she was still in the room. Michael thought of turning the sheet down to look at her, then decided not to. He took the brass ray off the table and slipped it into his pocket. He left everything else the way it was and went back out into the hall, just as Danny stepped out of the elevator. Danny's eyes were red from crying, and he looked as if he hadn't bathed or shaved for days. He was a man who needed a wife, Michael thought. As soon as he saw Michael, he began to cry again. 'Where is she?' he asked, sobbing.

'In there. But don't go in, Danny. There's no point.'

'I want to see her.'

'Why?' Michael asked. 'She's really dead.'

Danny kept on crying and Michael put his arm around him and led him to the lounge. 'We'll have some coffee, Danny, and talk a little.'

Michael brought him coffee, and sat next to him. He smelled sour, and Michael wondered how Louise could have ever let this man do to her what Michael had done. But she hadn't known any different until Michael. Her mother and father were Old Country Jews who lived with other Old Country Jews in a community five blocks square in Brooklyn. To her, Danny had been big time, she told Michael – from Manhattan, Riverside Drive, and his parents owned their own apartment. That was the real stuff – the height of sophistication. Besides – he was Spanish. The cream. And he was a CPA who wanted to keep a kosher home, and belonged to the *shul* on Central Park West. 'I thought Danny Perera had everything,' she said.

Finally Danny stopped sobbing and Michael said, 'You know, Danny, we should do an autopsy.'

'That's out of the question.' Michael didn't want it done either, but he had to argue to ease his conscience. 'It could be very important. We really don't know what killed her.'

'Bullshit.' The profanity didn't go with the little man. 'Cancer killed her.'

No it didn't, he wanted to say. It was going away. I was beating it. It was something else – a clot, like Reales said to watch out for, or maybe a haemorrhage.

'It's exactly *how* it killed her that we'd like to find out.' Then the stock phrase, 'What we learn from her death might save other people.'

'I'm sorry, Michael. But we're religious people. You know that. Besides, you cared about her. I saw the things you brought her; she told me how you stayed with her, read to her, saw that she was comfortable. She told me all the things you did for her.'

Not all, Danny. She didn't tell you everything I did for her.

Michael started to choke. He jumped up and ran to the window before Danny could touch him. 'Mike, are you all right?'

'Yeah, I'm okay.' He looked out of the window; it was starting to get light. Behind him he saw the reflection of the hall. Two white coats passed the lounge door, pushing a table on wheels, heading for her room.

'Look, Mike, you're Jewish – maybe not religious, but still one of us. And she was your friend. You don't want her mutilated – you can't.'

'No, Danny, I don't want anyone to touch her.'

David hated the Cape Ann house, especially in May. It was cold, the wind blew constantly, and everything was covered with spray that left a sticky coating of salt behind when it dried. No matter how many times a day he took a shower, he still felt tacky.

The house didn't have central heating, the electricity was erratic and it was a long drive to town over bad roads. Romer loved it, more now than he did in the summer, and David thought that the place was a perfect gentile vacation spot. 'Remember,' their father had told them, 'they're a different breed. The *goyim* never enjoy themselves unless they're uncomfortable. If you make it too soft for them, they get frightened, or bored. Remember that. It'll be the same with the women . . . with your patients . . .' It was the day they graduated from medical school, and they'd just told him that they had decided to specialize in gynaecology. He was so proud, and upset by his emotions that they were all afraid he was going to cry. Sadel was actually reaching for her handkerchief when he started talking about gentiles, and how different they were.

Now David felt like them. He wanted to be uncomfortable.

Every day this spring he had gone out on the beach in the cold, morning after morning, even before Romer was awake. It was restlessness, the kind that left him tired and unable to sleep peacefully, always a little hungry and not knowing what he wanted to eat. He'd been drinking too much since he got back from New York, and at night he'd dream about Louise and what he'd seen of her body. He knew what the rest of her would look like, crossed by surgical scars, stained with radiation burns. But her breasts were like a young girl's and she was always naked to the waist in his dreams. Michael was touching her in the most intimate ways, even though they both knew that David was in the room with them, watching them. He'd wake up tired and strained from the dream, even when he knew that they were going to let him join them, that Michael was going to share her after all. He wasn't excited about it, just weary, and afraid he wouldn't be able to perform. The vague dread the dream engendered would stay with him all morning, even on the beach in the wind, with sand blowing around him, stinging his cheeks.

At about two in the afternoon he'd start drinking, and the dream would fade. Sometimes he'd drive to town with Romer; sometimes he'd walk along the beach to see Paul and Mark. They were lovers – both rich, both from good families, Romer told him, but he couldn't remember their last names. Paul loved to cook and David would sit in the grey-lit kitchen and watch him peel, slice, sauté, sprinkle herbs and read recipes, all the time talking softly about nothing while David drank, suspended. By nine, after seven hours of slow, constant drinking, he would be ready to try to sleep again.

But today for some reason he felt better, more peaceful than he had in years – maybe since he and Michael were children.

The feeling had lasted all morning and by two he still hadn't had a drink and didn't want one. He lay back on the beach and let the wind blow sand in his hair, inside his shirt, but it didn't bother him. He was even thinking he might fall asleep on the beach when the pain hit him. It was so shocking he sat upright; then it hit again – excruciating, horrible – he couldn't localize it. He waited for it to happen again, but it didn't. He only knew it had been there because he had the sick, trembling feeling that severe pain leaves behind. He stood up shakily and began to walk towards the house. Halfway there, it happened again, this time so strong it brought him to his knees, and for a moment he thought he was going to pass out. Then it stopped.

'Michael,' he whispered. 'Oh, Michael.' He lay face down, the wind tearing at the back of his jacket. He was getting cold, but he didn't move. He didn't know how long he stayed there – the sun was low and it was getting colder. He managed to stand and this time made it back to the house. Romer was in the kitchen starting dinner. 'David, what's the matter? You look sick.'

'No. I'm fine.'

'Your sister-in-law called about an hour ago. I thought you were at Paul's, but he hadn't seen you, and I didn't know where you were. She sounded pretty shaky; I told her I'd have you call.'

'Thanks,' David said.

It was four and with a charter to Boston he could be in New York by seven.

He needed help today – just for today – Michael told himself. Tomorrow would be better – it had to be. He left the hospital and went to a drugstore he'd often passed on Ninety-fifth and Madison. There were no other customers and the man behind the counter was reading a paperback. Michael had already written out the prescriptions and handed them to the pharmacist, who looked at them, then at Michael. 'You got some kind of ID?'

Michael showed him his hospital card and his society registration.

'How come you don't use the pharmacy at Manhattan – much cheaper for staff.' He was very suspicious; Michael made a note never to come here again.

'Line was too long,' he said. 'I'd've been waiting an hour.'

The man nodded as if he'd heard that before, then looked at Michael again. Michael wanted to turn away, but he made himself look back steadily.

'You all right, Doc?'

'Yeah, fine.'

'You don't look fine.'

'Just fill those for me, okay?' The man shrugged and went to the back.

*

Michael waited until he reached home to take the first pill. He was so tired he could barely walk down the hall, barely turn the key in the lock. He swallowed one without water right there in the hall. Then another in the kitchen, then another, this time with water to wash it down. He heard Kathy in another room and the baby was crying – but he sounded far away – in another apartment somewhere down the hall. Mrs Klein's baby? Michael grinned. Mrs Klein was sixty; how did she have a baby? Oh, oh, he dropped the glass. What a lovely noise the breaking made, sweet tinkling like bells. He wondered if the plate would sound as sweet if it broke. He reached for it . . .

Almost three, the cart was in the hall outside her room; George grinning, because he liked her. He's saved custard. 'Where's Mrs Perera?' 'I'm sorry, George—' That would be Mag talking.

Where did all the broken glass come from? Michael knew he should try to clean up, but he'd cut himself. Better wait. Just a small cut, but there seemed to be blood everywhere. Kathy was talking – or crying. Shut up – it's not that bad. I'll clean it up in the morning. Now I've got to sleep. Got to get the Seccies.

The bottle was in his pocket. He stood up, picked his way through the broken glass and china and went into the bedroom. Kathy was following; talking.

'Leave me alone,' he screamed.

He went into the bathroom and took the dear reds – one, two, three, or was it four? Four – *he was at the hospital by four; she was waiting for him—* Five or six of them, he wasn't sure.

Kathy was on the phone – Bill, she wanted Bill. What good would Bill do? She knew who she had to call. He just hoped she'd stop crapping around soon and do it. Before he died.

Michael was incoherent. But he recognized David, knew he was there, and that calmed him somewhat.

He lay back and stared at the ceiling. David went to the bed, sat down next to his brother and looked closely at him. Michael's eyes were blank, and as David watched, he brushed something from his cheek. Then he repeated the motion as if he'd missed it the first time.

'How long has he been quiet like this?'

'A couple of hours,' Kathy said. 'At first, he was a wild man.'

'This afternoon?' David asked.

She nodded. David remembered the pain.

'He broke every dish in the house, and I was so frightened I took Sam down the hall to Mrs Klein. But I was afraid to leave Michael too long. I didn't know what to do. Bill's in Rochester, and I didn't want to call anyone else at the hospital. I didn't know what he'd taken, and if they found something funny—' She stopped.

'You did the right thing,' David said. 'What happened then?'

'He calmed down, seemed quite reasonable for about an hour. Then he started to cry. Oh, David, I've never seen anyone cry like that before. He's lost other patients, and I knew she was important to him. But I didn't realize—' She turned away.

No, he thought sadly, of course you didn't.

David pulled his brother into a sitting position; he felt his neck, then brought his face close to Michael's while he looked at his brother's eyes; he moved his finger, and watched; Michael tried to follow it. Then, very deliberately, he slapped Michael's face hard. His head snapped, and as it did, David hit him again, backhand.

'Stop it,' Kathy screamed.

'It's all right,' David said to her quietly. 'Turn on the shower as hot as you think he can stand. Then look everywhere – his clothes, his dresser, his desk, everything. We've got to make sure he can't get any more. Bring all the medication bottles you find. But first the shower. Okay, Kathy? Then the pills.'

Michael was shaking his head as if to clear it. David reached into his bag, broke a smelling-salts packet and held it under his nose. Michael's eyes started to run and he coughed and shook his head again.

Kathy hadn't moved. David turned to her, still holding Michael upright, 'Go on, Kathy.' David was tired and closed his eyes as he stroked Michael's head. 'He'll be okay. Just get the shower going and make sure he doesn't have anything else to take. All right?'

She nodded, then left them alone together.

part five

chapter twenty-one

Michael knew what David would say. 'Calculated to intimidate – ignore it.' Michael tried. He was alone in a room that was fifty feet long and had French doors at one end that opened to a garden sloping to the river.

'Come with me, please.'

The butler waited at the door. Michael put down the magazine, picked up his bag, and followed him to a small elevator under a curving stairway. He could see paintings on the stairway wall, but he wasn't close enough to see what they were. David had been here before, many times, and he should have warned him. Kathy came here often too, but he didn't expect her to notice. Her family probably matched the Calhouns in money and they'd never discussed the Calhoun art treasures.

The butler ushered Michael into the elevator, then followed and pushed three. The elevator had six buttons. He could almost hear David whispering, 'Don't be scared, just the first and third floors are furnished; the rest is nothing but dusty bare floors and cobwebs.'

Michael smiled as the door opened and felt more at ease as he followed the butler down the hall to her bedroom.

'David, I'm sorry to be such a baby, but I was so frightened ...'

'I'm not David.'

She sat up from the pillows, holding the quilt to her chin. 'Don't sit up,' he said sharply. She lay back. 'And tell him to go.' She nodded and the butler left the room. He pulled a small armchair up to the bed and sat down.

'How much bleeding?'

'Where's David? I called David.'

'David's in Paris. You want to wait for him to get back?'

'You're Michael.' It sounded like an accusation.

'That's right. Now do you want to go on sparring until you lose the baby, or will you tell me how long you've been bleeding?'

'Just since this morning. Only a little, really – and I'm sure it isn't serious.'

'You're forty-two, Mrs Calhoun, and this is your first child – everything is serious.'

She was shocked into silence. David never talked to her like this; he was always the diplomat – a hundred words of explanation for everything that had happened during the six months of her pregnancy.

'Okay, now just relax as much as you can.'

He'd brought a plastic-coated pad with him to put under her to protect the sheet; David always used one of her towels and she suspected that he purposely chose the embroidered or monogrammed ones.

Michael touched her very gently, and she relaxed. But the touch was firm too, not tentative.

'Let me know if I hurt you – even a little. Don't try to be brave. Now relax, c'mon, let your knees fall back. That's it. Keep them that way – good.'

His fingers in one place, then another, so quickly and easily she didn't have time to think about what he was doing and when he finished he didn't rush away to strip off the glove and wash as if he'd gotten dirty. He took the glove off slowly, looking past her as he did it, thinking.

'It *feels* okay – competent – do you know what I mean?'

'Not exactly.'

'As if your cervix has the strength to hold the foetus to term. But there's bleeding all right.'

'I *know* that.'

'More than you're seeing right now.'

That frightened her and he must have realized it. Because he smiled at her for the first time and said, 'I think it's okay. I really do. No, no, let me do that.' He rolled her nightgown down and pulled the quilt up to cover her. 'You're not to do anything. Do you have a good maid that you can trust?' She nodded. 'Let her do everything for you. I don't even want you up to go to the toilet. I don't think you need a nurse, but a hospital bed would be a good idea.' He took a card out of his wallet. 'You can rent one from this place – the equipment is spotless, fairly new and it's reasonable.' He stopped, looked around and laughed. She began to laugh with him, but that made him angry.

'Don't do that. Don't laugh, don't jiggle, don't yell. Just take it easy for a while.'

'You're not used to dealing with people – certain types of people, are you?'

'No, I leave the "certain types" to my brother.'

'Why?'

'Because they're usually a pain in the ass. If the bleeding gets any worse – even slightly – call me immediately.'

Only then did he remember that he was still holding the glove. He went into the bathroom, flushed it away, washed his hands and, nodding once to her, he left without waiting for the butler to come for him.

She called John Anders as soon as the door closed behind him.

'What do you know about Michael Ross, David's brother. Kathy's hus—'

'I know who he is, Maggie.'

'Good. What else do you know about him? What kind of man is he?'

She hated asking for quick, glib assessments of people, but they often saved time, and Anders was an astute man.

'Michael Ross is a prick.'

'Why do you say that?'

Anders thought, then decided to tell the truth. 'He stole my girl. I was in love with Kathy years ago.'

Maggie'd seen them together at a few cocktail parties and fund-raising affairs, and thought he still was. Michael was never with his wife. In the years since the twins had set up practice together, they were always represented by David. Maggie wondered why, because now that she'd met the brother, David seemed a little tarnished – a little smooth. She thanked Anders and called Bill Friedman at North Shore.

She hadn't spoken to him for almost a year, but she always liked him and was sorry when he chose to leave Manhattan.

She didn't spend long on pleasantries. 'When you did your residency with the Rosses, were you friendly with them?'

'Yes, with Michael.'

'Not David?'

'No.'

'Why?'

Friedman laughed, 'Because I didn't like him.'

'Why?' Fascinating – Anders hates one, Friedman doesn't like the other. She was just about to get intrigued in the surface, social way she often did things, when Friedman's voice turned hoarse, vicious.

'Because he ate his brother alive – still doing it for all I know. And I liked Michael and didn't want that to happen to him.'

'Michael doesn't seem like a man who could be devoured by anyone.'

'No? How long have you been seeing David Ross?'

'About five years.'

'Seen him around town? At parties? At the hospital functions?'

'Yes, but I don't see...'

'And in the drawing rooms on Sutton Place and Fifth Avenue – when you mention your gynaecologist – everyone's heard of him, haven't they?'

'Usually.'

'Ever hear any of them mention Michael?'

She saw what he meant. 'Only as David's twin.'

'Don't you think it's odd that after five years you – certainly their most important patient, and the biggest contributor to their hospital – have only just met David's partner?'

'Why was I allowed to meet him now?'

'Only David can tell you for sure, but I would guess it was some kind of emergency. Right? Something that couldn't wait until David was available.'

'Yes.'

'I hope everything's all right.'

'It is. Fine.'

She called Doris Wayne. Doris had more money than Maggie

did, which was hard to imagine; and she was a dedicated doctor watcher – had even insisted that her daughter go to medical school, instead of to Miss Master's as all the Wayne daughters of the past had done.

She'd *heard* of Michael Ross, of course – he was David's twin brother – but she'd never met him. Then she giggled. 'At least not that I know.'

'What's that supposed to mean?'

'There's talk that they switch – you know – you talk to David in the office, but then if he's busy, it's the other one who actually examines you. So you never know if you "met" Michael or not.'

'They're not *that* identical.'

'Identical enough. Besides, you're not exactly looking into each other's eyes, are you?'

Maybe Doris was numb, but Maggie was sure she could tell the difference in touch, and as she thought about it, she was convinced that she had never been examined by Michael Ross before.

'Doctor, the cable office just called. Your brother will be on the eight-thirty flight from Paris – Air France 409 – and he'd like you to meet him.'

Michael was tempted to cable back that he had a delivery and couldn't make it. But he called Kathy instead and told her that he had to be at Kennedy and wouldn't be home for supper.

'Amazing,' she said bitterly. 'He lasted a whole five days.'

The meeting was scheduled for eight days; but although David was always insisting that he attend, he never stayed the full time. Five days was the longest – he was back usually after three. 'Nothing going on, babe,' he'd tell Michael. 'Bunch of dead asses telling us, one more time, what everyone's known for twenty years.'

'Then why go?' Michael had asked.

'Got to be seen, Mike. The biggest men in the country go to these things. It's always important that we be there.' Always 'we', as if Michael had gone too. 'That's how we get consults, babe. Have a few drinks with 'em, talk a little shop, buy 'em dinner, and we get the fat!'

Michael was in the International Arrivals building by eight.

Flights were coming in every few minutes, from what seemed like hundreds of airlines, and the waiting rooms, halls and bar were jammed. He waited almost fifteen minutes for a shot of vodka. He gulped it down as they were announcing David's flight and went upstairs to the walkway from which friends and relatives could look down as the passengers were herded through customs. The hall was mobbed now and the counters had lines stretching back towards immigration. Where was David? There were so many dark-haired men, a sea of them as far as he could see.

Then David came into the customs hall, and Michael waved. David saw him and held up a green card. 'I can go,' he yelled, and Michael went down the stairs to the customs exit just as David came through the door. They shook hands now, Michael couldn't remember the last time he'd put his arms around his brother, but right now David looked so rumpled, and tired, and so little like his usual smooth self, that Michael wanted to hug him. He held his hand a little longer than usual and then took his suitcase away from him. David leaned close to him, and whispered, 'We should give the crowd a treat and skip out hand in hand.' As always people around them were staring at them.

'You look beat,' Michael said.

'Yeah, asshole meeting. Asshole town. I could've bought a house for what a good dinner cost.'

He talked all the way to the city in the back of the cab; leaning back against the seat with his eyes half closed, while Michael watched him, and wondered if he was getting as grey as David, and if the hollows in his cheeks were that dark.

Michael didn't feel like going home and he and David ate together at Belle's around the corner from David's apartment.

Michael was tired too, and they didn't talk much; David was the only person in the world Michael didn't have to talk to and it was a relief to eat without saying anything, then lean back and have coffee together, and a drink, and wait until David felt like telling him about Paris.

David didn't look up to hearing that Maggie Calhoun, his star patient, had seen Michael and liked him – liked him a lot, a refreshing kind of attraction that had nothing to do with sex, and that he almost never got from women. He could have had all the sex he wanted from his patients; but after Louise died, he didn't care about it much.

He and Kathy had a sort of asymmetrical schedule that wound up with his making love to her occasionally, but it was a quiet business, and he wondered sometimes what had happened to the excitement she'd made him feel at first. Lately, when he thought about her, it was to wonder how little he knew her.

There were always books piled next to the bed, and Kathy read two or three a week, yet they never talked about them, and the titles, when he looked at them, didn't mean anything to him. She painted, belonged to a gallery, sold canvasses for sums that he thought astonishing – only last week one had gone for seven thousand dollars – and he went to the openings to be congratulated, to stand alone after the congratulations until one of the women or two or three of the homosexuals had had enough to drink to make a pass at him. Then he'd kiss Kathy, excuse himself and go home alone.

He expected Kathy to leave one day. When she did – when the marriage was really over – he might tell her about Louise, and ask her – from her point of view – what had gone wrong.

Belatedly David asked about Kathy, and as usual didn't listen to the answer. Then about Samuel – still without interest. He avoided the child, who, with a child's instinct for not being wanted, left David alone, too. It was almost funny watching the two of them ignore each other; except that Michael had hoped they'd be close, a family. The worst of it was that sometimes Sam seemed to confuse the twins, and he ignored Michael if Michael and David were together. Kathy blamed it all on David – 'He thinks David hates him, and he frightens Sam. And he thinks you prefer David to him.' 'Prefer David,' 'Do anything for David,' 'David means more to you than your wife and son.' Stock Kathy phrases for the last few years; too stupid to argue about. But it seemed to get worse and now there were times when the boy avoided Michael even when David wasn't around.

David waved at the waiter and ordered another Scotch. Then he settled back, ready for talk, 'What have you heard about the Calhoun Award?'

'Total silence,' Michael said.

'Not even rumours?'

'Only that it's going to you, Dave.'

'Good.'

'I saw Maggie Calhoun today.'

'Did you tell her you were me?'

'No. I told you, I'll only do that in the office – and only when it's an emergency.'

'You mean she didn't come into the office?' David asked.

'No.' Michael told him what had happened.

'So you went to her house? What's wrong with her?'

'She's bleeding.'

'Jesus Christ! Why didn't you say something?' It was an accusation.

'Thanks for dinner, Dave.' Michael stood up wearily. 'Call her tomorrow. I'm sure you can repair any damage I've done.'

But the next morning Maggie called before David could, and asked for Michael. They were both in Michael's office when the intercom flashed.

'Mrs Calhoun for you, Doctor.'

David pushed the call button. 'You mean for me?'

'Dr Michael, she asked for Michael Ross.'

'She thinks you're still in Paris, David, that's why she asked for me.'

'But I'm not in Paris, am I?'

'Then take the goddamn call.'

'Mag.' So much false heartiness. David only did that when he was frightened. Michael turned towards the window; he didn't want to watch his brother's contortions.

'It's David, dear. Yes, I got back early. Michael told me what happened. Has the bleeding gotten any worse? – Better? You mean it's less? – Oh, yes, that's wonderful – yes, yes, I'll tell him – Oh, I see. You *do* want to talk to him? Of course.'

He handed Michael the phone without a word. 'Yes, Mrs Calhoun, can I help you?'

Maggie sounded cool, 'Were you the Michael Ross who knew Bernard Reales in the early sixties?'

He couldn't answer for a minute because the question made him think of Louise.

'Dr Ross, are you there?'

'Yes, Mrs Calhoun, I am.'

'Call me Maggie.' It was a command.

'I'd rather not.'

Silence. He wondered if she had hung up.

Finally she said, 'You've been very rude to me.'

He softened, because she suddenly sounded on the verge of tears, and crying might make the bleeding worse. Besides, he didn't understand why he was so bent on alienating her. He was usually brusque – that was true – but never this rude. And she was their – David's – most important patient. Maybe that was what was behind his attitude; get her to hate him, and send her back to David before she made trouble between them.

'You're right,' he said to Maggie. 'I'm sorry. Yes, I did know Benjamin Reales. Why?'

'Dr Reales told me that you were the first man in this country to use methotrexate to treat ovarian cancer. Until then it had been used only to treat a rare uterine cancer called' – she hesitated – 'chorio—'

'Choriocarcinoma.'

'Yes. He said your results were responsible for its being used in other cancers, successfully in some cases.'

'My results were not very impressive. My patient died.'

'But the tumour shrank. The woman did live longer than expected. Right?'

'Yes.'

'Thank you.' She sounded relieved.

'I still don't understand—'

'You will. Now when can you come back? I don't want to be a baby, but there's still some bleeding.'

'You'll have to talk to David.'

'You don't understand. I want you to take care of me.'

'That's out of the question.'

'I have a right—'

'So do I. It's out of the question.' David was listening very closely now. 'Would you like to make an appointment with my brother?'

'I felt very comfortable with you,' she said. 'You won't change your mind?'

'No.'

205

'Very well. I'll talk to David.'

He handed David the phone and went into the small examining room where David's next patient was waiting. She turned her head and smiled.

'David, dear, Mary told me you've just gotten back from Paris. Aren't the prices dreadful?'

Michael put on a thin plastic glove, looked at her, then chose a speculum.

He couldn't remember when they'd started switching; it had been innocuous enough at first. 'Mike, just this one time,' David would say, because he was on the phone, or with another patient, or just going out. Michael had done it because it seemed silly not to – and David took it more and more for granted. But lately it had bothered Michael, and when the women gushed and called him David, he thought of the nights when they were young men, and he would wind up screwing David's date while David screwed his and the girls would forget which one he was and call him David.

'How are you for next Friday, David?' she said. 'I mean two weeks from today? You can't say no – Arlene Vale is coming and she's been—' The woman had to stop talking.

'Don't move,' he said. 'Tell me if this hurts.'

'Just a little,' she said softly. He always liked how the tone changed – all the brittleness gone, and they went soft, helpless; it made him feel helpless too, and tender, no matter who they were or how much he disliked them.

'Not a sharp pain?'

'No.'

'Stay the way you are. Don't move.' She put her arm across her eyes; a lot of them did that – a child's gesture. He moved the light, the speculum, he leaned and pressed; she shut her eyes.

'Okay, that's it. Get dressed, and I'll see you in my office.' He walked out and took the folder with him. David was waiting.

'I didn't find anything very significant. I think the ovary's still a little swollen, but only a little. No other inflammation; no pain to speak of.'

He handed him the folder. 'That was a very cryptic conversation you had with Maggie,' David said.

'Your patient wants you to have dinner two weeks from

Friday. I didn't say yes or no. Somebody called Arlene Vale is supposed to be there.'

'She's Matt Gargan's patient – been bitching about him for months according to Mary. Can't blame her. He has to wear two pairs of glasses just to see across the room. Now she's trying to choose between me and Kerry Matthews. Believe me, she'd be quite a catch. Her family controls West Airways; and she has a set of emeralds that are supposed to be worth—' Michael turned his back and started for the door.

'You were interested enough in Maggie Calhoun,' David said.

Michael stopped; walking out wouldn't help, David would only come after him, and they might as well get it over with now.

'Look, David, I'm not interested in Maggie Calhoun, and I don't know what she wanted. As far as I'm concerned she's *your* patient.' He left before David could say anything else.

chapter twenty-two

'I can't tell you how wrong you are,' Anders said. The three other men in the room shifted uncomfortably and looked at Maggie.

'Is it because of him, or his wife, John?'

'Do you think I'd let a thing like that sway me?'

'Of course I do,' Maggie said.

'What are you two talking about?' Tom Calhoun was out of time and patience.

'Tom, I think you are all making a terrible mistake,' Anders said.

'Well, you're entitled to think so. Now I'm through spending time giving money away, so if you'll excuse me. However Maggie votes is fine with me.' He kissed his wife and left the room.

Gargan and Weiss looked at one another; Anders was really pissed.

'Maggie,' Gargan said, 'if John feels that strongly about it, maybe we ought . . .'

'I don't see any reason for John to feel that strongly. Michael Ross did the work he's being cited for; nobody's denied that. He didn't steal the idea. He didn't claim credit that wasn't due him. In fact, according to Kramer, he claimed nothing; it was you who actually published the results,' she said, nodding at Gargan.

'Sure I did. Somebody had to do it. But I gave him full credit.'

'That's a good example of what's wrong with Michael Ross,' Anders said. 'Why didn't he publish? He knew how important it was. Why?'

'Because it wasn't important to him.'

'Exactly. He was too broken up by the woman's death to be bothered with anything as mundane as advancing medical knowledge. The Calhoun Award is a standard. The man who wins it should set an example for all the clinicians in the country.' Anders was getting warmed up. Gargan blew his nose. 'What kind of example does Ross set?'

'He was an imaginative, courageous clinical investigator,' Gargan said.

'Bullshit.—Excuse me, Maggie.' She waved her hand and smiled at Anders. She was having a wonderful time. 'He's a personality doctor. If he likes the patient he's great. But what would have happened to that woman – who died anyway, let's not forget that – if she'd been ugly or old?'

'Maybe nothing,' Gargan said, wondering how Anders knew she hadn't been. He didn't know why he went on defending Michael Ross this way. He didn't especially like him; he much preferred his brother. He could always talk to David about something – investments, the latest bestseller, the guests at Doris Wayne's dinner party, or at Maggie's cocktail parties. But Michael was silent on almost every subject except medicine – except gynaecology – that narrow.

But he was a fine doctor, no matter what he talked about – better than his brother, better than Gargan. And the Perera thing had been a brilliant bit of extrapolation. Michael deserved the award. If he'd been a little more personable, he probably would have won it – or something like it – years ago.

'You know what I think,' Gargan said. 'I think you're indulging in a little character assassination, John.'

'Maybe. But – what about the rumours?'

'I don't even want to think about them.'

'Why? Because they might keep him from getting the award?' He'd never seen Anders so vicious.

'No,' Gargan said. 'Because if they're false, they're not worth my time. And if they're true, then it's too sad to think about.'

'What rumours?' Maggie asked. This was the best award meeting they'd ever had.

Gargan looked at Anders; Anders burned and walked away.

'I'll just find out from someone else,' Maggie said.

Gargan shrugged. 'There was talk that he and the woman he gave the drug to were lovers.'

All the fun went out of it for Maggie. She leaned back against the pillows. Now she really was tired.

'I think we've said all there is to say about Michael Ross's personal life. The Calhoun Award is for excellence in clinical investigation, not for prudent sexual behaviour. Does anyone have anything to say about Michael Ross's *work*?'

'Only that whatever he started eight years ago, he's left for others to finish,' Anders said.

'That's usually the case,' Gargan said. 'Last year's recipient did exactly the same thing.'

'Can we vote now?' Weiss was two hours late for a golf date, and he still had to drive to Westchester.

Four voted for Michael, one against. There was a larger committee – ten professionals and ten lay volunteers – who had to pass on the executives' decision, but they were a rubber-stamp group. The award would go to Michael.

'Hi, Doc. What can I do for you?'

The man was bald. Would he know? But David was ashamed to ask anyone else.

'Those dyes that cover grey. They have them for men now, don't they?'

'Sure do. We got 'em to turn gradual, or you can do it all at once.' Very matter of fact. David started to relax.

'I think I'd like to do it all at once.'

'Your hair's very dark, except for the grey. And when you dye real dark hair, it tends to get a dead look. Know what I mean?'

David nodded.

'We got a new product that you paint on, just to cover the grey. That way most of your hair stays natural and shiny. You can use it on cotton for big areas – like your sideburns – and the rest you use a paint brush. Better for your hair too.' They matched the colour of his hair to a sample card. 'Perfect, just perfect,' the man said.

When David finished dyeing his hair, he turned, followed his profile, then the back of his head with another mirror. It looked good; he could pass for thirty-five easily – maybe thirty. He took a long shower, shaved, used cologne, powder, deodorant, all products he'd bought in Paris. He wore a soft blue lightweight pullover, grey slacks, black Italian loafers – like butter – and his new blue Hermes blazer. One more look in the full-length mirror on the back of the bedroom door. Perfect.

David always went early. The boys were younger, nicer; the after-ten crowd was rough, mostly queens and leather jobs and they frightened him. He found one almost at once – a slim blond that looked twenty-five but was probably older. He had pale eyelashes and a sprinkling of freckles that reminded David of Romer. He smiled, then came down the bar to sit with David. There were others watching David too, and a few stood nearby, ready to take over if his companion faltered, or David changed his mind. There was time, lots of it, years, before he had to start paying. They went to a booth away from the others and drank some more. The boy – David liked thinking of him that way, thirty or not – asked him if he wanted to smoke, but he didn't. They left before David was really drunk. He was still steady on his feet and had had enough to make it last longer without dulling things too much.

The boy's place was in a tenement, way west on Bleecker, but it was nice, small but neat, and the sheets were clean. He must have changed them today on purpose.

The kid was good; he did everything David wanted in a slow, sweet, half-passive way. Even the second time. David thought he could go on forever, that he was twenty-five too, seventeen, until he saw himself in the standing mirror the boy kept next to the bed. How tired he looked! How much grey splotched the hair on his chest and pubis. Compared to the boy next to him, his body looked old.

'What's the matter?' the boy asked gently. 'Did I do something wrong?'

'No,' David said. 'You're terrific. You really are. But I just got back from Paris last night, and I'm not used to the time change.' He lied. It had been over a week, but he hadn't been able to shake the lag, and he was waiting to hear about the award.

'Sure, I understand. Besides, it's never as good the second time; not for me anyway.'

'I've always felt that way too; but you think you sort of have to . . . perform . . . you know?' He spoke as if the boy had shown some special understanding of his feelings. But all he could think of was how old he looked in the mirror.

The boy brought him a drink, begged him to stay. He said he wanted to talk, needed to, and David made himself sit there and listen and answer. But he felt tired and soiled, and wanted to go home. Then the boy started in again, but lightly, as if he were thinking of something else. When David started to respond, the boy turned off the lights so they couldn't see their reflections, and David felt more comfortable.

Maggie Calhoun called Michael at nine. Kathy had put Samuel to bed and she was in the little room, painting.

'I hope I'm not interrupting anything.'

'No, nothing.'

'I'm calling about the Calhoun Award.'

He smiled. They wanted him to make a speech about David, or maybe introduce his brother. The awards were made by Maggie and Tom, at their home, and only the select were invited. Michael had been invited every year, because David insisted, but he'd never gone before. He'd go this year. He'd rent a tux, buy Kathy a new dress, and he'd get drunk with his brother. He was really looking forward to it. David had waited a long time.

'We voted this afternoon – just the executive officers – and the board has to vote before it is official, but that's pro forma.'

She paused. Trying to build suspense? Let her have her fun. Then she said, 'We voted for you, Michael.'

'What for?' He didn't understand. He thought she was making a joke.

'For the work you did eight years ago – when you gave Louise Perera a drug no one had ever used before for that indication—'

This was crazy.

'—for showing the kind of imagination and courage that are the foundation of effective clinical investigation.'

Crazy bitch.

'What about my brother? What about David?'

'We gave it a great deal of thought.'

'You didn't give it any thought, because if you had I'd be at the bottom of your list. I did one thing, eight years ago, which was half luck, half finding the right report at the right time. It had as much relation to clinical investigation as your ass does.'

Maggie was all propped up with pillows; she had a glass of pear brandy and a demitasse of Eloise's good coffee, and she was having a wonderful time.

'How can you do that?' Michael yelled into the phone, 'Jesus Christ, how can you? You've got a guy who's worked for years – on an important and difficult clinical area – successfully!'

Kathy had heard him yelling and came into the living room. He knew he was raving, spraying saliva into the air, but he couldn't stop. This bitch couldn't do this to David, just because she'd been turned on by Michael's rudeness.

'If it wasn't for David—'

He saw the look on Kathy's face and stopped. Calhoun didn't know what she was doing; she was ignorant. It was Gargan who did this, and Anders. Anders wanting to make trouble between him and David.

'I'm sorry,' he said. 'I shouldn't be saying these things, but what you're doing is wrong.'

'I don't think so,' Maggie said. 'This isn't a rich woman's whim. I talked to Dr Reales and he compared what you did to Huggins' first use of oestrogens to treat prostate cancer. And Gargan said it was courageous and imaginative.'

212

'What about Anders?'

'How the executives vote isn't usually discussed with the nominees, Michael. But I'm sure you know how he feels about you without my telling you.'

'Look, I'm not going to . . .'

'Talk to Kathy before you decide; after all, this is important to her too. And talk to David. He may be truly happy for you. There will be other years for David. Think it over and call me tomorrow.'

'There's nothing to think over . . .' But she had hung up.

Kathy stood watching him from the doorway.

'That was Maggie Calhoun,' he said.

'I know. She called me about it this afternoon.'

'Funny you didn't mention it.'

'I thought it would be better coming from her.' So she was in on it. It seemed John Anders was the only one on his side.

He smiled, which she misunderstood.

'I told Maggie, there'd be trouble,' Kathy said, 'but I was sure you'd be reasonable.'

'Will David be reasonable, do you think?'

'I don't care.'

'I do.'

'Would David care if the situation were reversed? Has he cared all these years while he went to meeting after meeting, to workshops and seminars, telling the world how great David Ross was, how much *he's* done, while you stayed here in the office with all the sterile, whining women. Sure he wanted a partner. Someone had to do the dirty work. If Maggie had called him tonight, would he have argued that you were being passed over?'

'Stop it, Kathy.'

He turned his back on her and walked down the hall to the den. She followed.

'Leave me alone, Kathy.'

'Why? You deserve the award. Maggie told me all about it. She said that you should have won a long time ago. It's for something you did alone, just you. Why is that so hard for you to face?'

She came close to him and looked up at him. 'What if there were no David and you'd just won the award? What would it be like then?'

'I don't know.'

'I'll tell you. We'd be celebrating now. Drinking champagne and thinking of ways to spend the Calhouns' fifty thousand dollars. We'd have called my mother, and Bill and Beth Friedman, and Matt Gargan, to thank him – and maybe even John and Al Weiss. Then we'd get a little drunk together.' There were tears in her eyes, 'And maybe we'd even make love to celebrate. If there were no David, this would be one of the happiest nights of your life!'

Drink champagne, make love, then wake the kid and tell him how wonderful his father was, while he blinked in the light wishing they'd let him go back to sleep. Michael smiled. Bill would wet his pants. *'Sure I'm glad. Shit, that's great! But I'm jealous as hell, too. Buy a yacht with the money, and invite me'n Beth for picnics.'* He couldn't remember the last time he'd talked to Bill.

It was a normal wholesome way to spend the evening in which he had won an award. But across the park, David was having dinner, or watching TV or maybe he was out. Maybe he'd gone to the Village. He did that a lot on Fridays.

And what did you do, Michael, when they told you that you had won the award that your brother had worked for – waited for – for years? Why I got drunk on champagne, called a man my brother hates and fucked my wife.

Kathy was standing so close he could smell the lemon rinse she used on her hair. She still looked young, just a few lines around her eyes, from smiling or squinting while she painted.

They were tearing him apart.

But she didn't realize what she was doing to him, and she went on, 'I got some champagne this afternoon, Mike. I thought you might want it – and peaches. Remember the night we left Sam with Ada and went off alone?'

They'd had champagne and peaches because Kathy had read about it in a book. He thought it was crazy, but it turned out to be delicious, and the combination – the two kinds of sugar – made them both a little crazy and they'd run out of the cabin, both

214

naked, and made love on the grass next to the lake. He remembered afterwards, thinking how smooth her skin looked in the moonlight.

'I could use a drink . . . sure,' he said. 'I'd love some champagne.'

He woke up at eleven thirty. Everything was quiet. They'd finished the last bottle in bed, and it was still on the night stand. He got out of bed without disturbing Kathy and took the bottle into the kitchen. Then he went to the hall bathroom and took a shower and went back to the bedroom; she was still asleep. He thought that he could still feel the heat her body generated, even halfway across the room. She turned over on her back; her neck and breasts were pale and smooth, cool-looking, and he thought for a minute that he must have imagined the fever.

He went to the nursery. Sam was asleep too, lying on his back, with his mouth open, his lips slightly puffed as he exhaled. Michael looked down at him and thought about the money. What, he asked his son silently, what will we do with the money? Sam snored lightly. Fifty thousand dollars! I know, we'll buy a summer house.

It was already spring; they'd start looking tomorrow. They could drive out to Montauk – the Hamptons. They'd spend tomorrow night at Guerney's and eat lobster. Sam had never had a lobster. He went into the kitchen in the dark and looked out of the window over the park to the river. He could wake Kathy and they'd start planning.

Kathy knew more about summer houses by the sea than he did. He'd make Sanka and find some cookies, wake her up with it, and they'd sit up till dawn talking about the house. The water boiled, he poured the Sanka and was looking in the cookie tin when the phone rang. There was an extension in the kitchen and he grabbed it before it could ring again and wake Kathy.

'Dr Ross? Dr *Michael Ross*?'

'Yes.'

'This is Sergeant Kemper, Sixth Precinct. You have a brother named David Ross?'

'Yes.' Ask something, he told himself. Don't just stand there saying yes.

'Has something happened to my brother?'

'Nothing serious. He's been in a fight – banged up a bit. Nothing we couldn't take care of here. Probably a few good kidney punches, and he'll piss red tomorrow. Otherwise he seems okay. He hasn't really committed any crime. We don't have the other guy – or *guys*, according to him. He says one of them's still laying for him. Says he bruised him pretty good. Anyway, whether it's the truth or not, we don't want to take any chances. You'd better come and get him.'

'Where are you?'

'Sorry. Tenth Street just off West. It's pretty empty around here, and if he is right about the guy laying for him – well – you understand. This is a pretty rough area.'

'I won't need bail or anything?'

'No. There's no crime as far as we're concerned – at least not one you could call arrestable in Greenwich Village. All you need,' the cop was saying, 'is some ID to prove you're his brother.'

And I won't need that when you see me, Michael thought.

The streets were empty, and he was in front of the red brick, columned Sixth Precinct in twenty minutes. The entrance was on Tenth. On West Street trucks were spread along the curb, hiding the docks and the river. There was a diner down by the docks, and a gas station – both closed. On Tenth there was nothing except the station house and a few dark open-air fruit and vegetable markets. Inside, the linoleum floor was pitted and stained, wooden benches lined the walls, and a few brightly coloured moulded plastic chairs were spotted around the lobby.

'Third floor,' Sergeant Kemper told him, and just ahead a lighted sign pointed to the elevators. He must have looked harmless because the cop at the desk nodded, but didn't stop him.

David was waiting for him, reading a copy of *Time* magazine and smoking a nonfilter cigarette he'd bummed from the sergeant, when Michael opened the door.

David had a bruise on his cheek that was turning yellow, and some dried blood on his upper lip.

'It only hurts when I laugh,' he said.

He didn't sound drunk.

'What happened?'

'Bloody nose, bruises and contusions, and I think a tooth's loose. Can't tell for sure, but I keep swallowing blood.' Michael sat down unsteadily.

'Open your mouth.' Michael saw a deep split inside David's lower lip where the membrane had been smashed against his teeth. It was still oozing blood. Michael gently touched all of David's lower front teeth, but none moved. David closed his eyes.

'Gentle Michael.' He opened his eyes, looked at Michael, and smiled. 'Michael of the healing touch,' he said softly, without a trace of irony. Then he closed his eyes again and leaned back.

'I had a wonderful time, Mikey – until that guy walked in. It was beautiful. That was some kid.'

Michael heard a toilet flush close by, a door opened and a large, meaty-looking man with red pitted skin and light blue eyes came into the room.

'Well, Dr Ross, that was—' He stopped. 'I guess you don't need ID, do you?'

'Sergeant Kemper, I'd like to take my brother home now.'

'Sure. Like I told you, we ain't holding him.' He looked from one to the other and must have seen the same respectability about Michael that the cop downstairs had seen, because he started talking to him, ignoring David, not even looking at him.

'I don't know how much truth there is to the "two guys" story,' he said just as if David weren't in the room.

'If my brother says it happened, it happened.' David watched them.

'Okay, Doctor, I didn't mean anything.'

'He's a doctor too, in case you're interested.'

David nodded to Kemper as if Michael were introducing them.

'I know that,' Kemper said. 'I'm just trying to be nice.'

'Nice?'

'You got it, Doc. I don't know who you are or what you do – besides looking an awful lot like your brother – but he ain't keeping very savoury company, and if that nice East Side address, and those letters after his name mean what I think they do, then the night man from the *News*, who was in the can with me just now, would just love to hear about it. Now I've kept your brother secluded until you got here, because I'm really a good guy; but if there *are* two freaks out there waiting to take him apart, there's going to be trouble. Newspaper-type trouble – which I'm sure you'd like to avoid – say by staying here till daylight – which you're welcome to do. On the other hand, if he's feeding us a load, you can all go home right now, and no harm done. See what I mean?'

Michael looked at David, 'Did you hear him?'

'Every word.'

'Well?'

David smiled, 'I lied.'

Kemper looked relieved. 'I guess you can go then.'

Michael walked out without a word; David followed, still smiling. At the door he turned back, 'Thanks for everything, Sarge.'

Michael was too embarrassed to thank the man. He just wanted to get out of there. On the ground floor he grabbed David before he could get to the lobby. 'Enough clowning. You didn't get cut up like that in bed.'

'Not exactly, no.'

'Then what happened?'

'An old, dull story, Michael. I was the dream trick, well dressed, prosperous, maybe a little desperate, and not so young. So the kid makes the connection, and maybe because he's not such a bad guy, he gives me a good time. Then, the second time around, just when I'm most indisposed, in comes the heavy to collect.'

He was almost happy to see him. Big guy, much bigger than the kid, and probably as strong as hell. But slow-moving, clumsy, a little dumb. 'Okay,' he said. 'Cover it up.' They watched David get dressed. The boy just threw on a robe. As David was putting on his jacket, his arms caught in the sleeves, the big guy hit him in the face. David sat down hard, blood running from his nose and lip. The guy was coming back and David's arms were still caught, so he hunched down and just before the fist made contact he

218

shoved his head into the big man's belly, hard as he could. The man stumbled and David got the jacket on, but the guy was recovering, coming back.

'I'll give you the money,' David yelled.

'Fuck you, you goddamn queer!'

Goddamn queer – the man was crazy. The boy was probably his lover. David looked to the kid for a clue, but all he did was shrug. The big man was swinging. David ducked and half hugged the huge body, not knowing what else to do. But it was a bad idea, because the man elbowed him in the kidney and the pain was so intense David was afraid for a second that he'd pass out.

He ducked, twisted, slipped free and jumped on the bed, insanely aware of his shoes leaving smudges on the kid's sheets. The kid was leaning against the windowsill watching calmly. Which was okay with David because if he joined in, David knew he would be finished, and he was frightened of what the big guy really wanted from him. Not money, that was clear. The lights were still off, but David could see their reflections in the mirror, both half crouching, shining with sweat. David feinted towards the mirror, and the big man, thinking it was a trick, started around the bed in the opposite direction. But David kept moving in the same direction and when he reached the mirror, he deliberately smashed his fist into it. The noise made them jump. David grabbed a pillow, pulled the case free, wrapped it around his hand and picked up the longest sliver of glass he could find.

The minute the man saw the jagged glass pointing at his middle, everything stopped.

David jumped off the bed and started backing towards the door, keeping the sliver aimed like a sword. They were both watching him.

'You ain't gonna make it ten feet from here, faggot.'

David swallowed blood, and realized that he'd already swallowed so much of it his throat was raw. 'You know,' he said to the man, 'you're in trouble.' The man froze.

'No,' said David. His voice gurgled slightly from the blood, but he was amazed at how calm he sounded, 'I mean in your head. You really ought to get help.' He was opening the door as he talked. Thank God, it only had one lock. The man was looking from him to

the shard still pointing and shining in the dim light. 'You're going to do something really terrible,' David said. 'I mean something you don't want . . .' The big one interrupted him.

'My Baby's out there; he's got a blade as long as your leg, pig shit, and he's gonna cut your nuts off.'

The door was open; David slammed it behind him and ran – but he was careful on the stairs because if he fell he might impale himself on the glass. He kept it all the way down the empty dark street to the corner. No sign of the big man's baby, no sign of anyone, and yet David was sure he wasn't alone. The other was there all right, somewhere, but maybe he didn't like the look of the thing David carried either. It looked mean all right, flashing as he ran under the street lights. One block, and he was still running, clutching his piece of mirror – two blocks and he wasn't even winded. His hair was blowing, his jacket was flapping behind him and even though he knew they were there behind him somewhere, coming on, and his mouth was full of blood and his back hurt, he felt as if he could run all night across the empty city, leaving them far behind. Three blocks and he saw a lighted doorway. He turned the corner and there was a police station. Wonderful! But for a minute he thought he'd pass it and keep running until he was on another dark street, then he'd turn on them and with nothing but a piece of glass, he'd face them down – kill them.

He made himself stop. He unwrapped the pillow case still covering his hand, now soaked with blood, and left it and the piece of glass in the gutter. He then walked as steadily as he could up the steps and through the lighted doorway.

'You think they're really out there?' Michael asked.

'Yeah. I don't know what "Baby's" like, but the big one's crazy – too mad to forget that I cheated him out of his fun – which I think involved razor blades and lit cigarettes.'

'You want to go out there?'

'Where's the car?'

'Around the corner. The front's for emergency parking, and I didn't think this was an emergency.'

'How far around the corner?'

'Quarter of a block, that's all. Look, Dave, maybe we should . . .'

'What?'

David was smiling and looking as crazy as the guy he'd just described.

Jesus, Michael thought. He's done something to his hair. It made him look young, and maybe because of the bruises and blood, or maybe because of the expression on his face, he looked wild too. Very handsome.

'You dyed your hair!'

'Sh! It's a secret. You ready to go?'

'I sure as shit don't want to stay here all night.'

The desk man stared after them. Outside Michael heard a car pass on the West Side Highway above them, then another, then nothing.

'Which way?' David whispered.

'Left.'

They walked to the end of West Tenth and turned on West. The trucks were black boxes on the other side of the street, throwing shadows that almost hid them. Nothing happened until they turned the corner. Then Michael saw two figures pull away from the truck shadows and start running silently across the street. Michael wanted to run too – the car was only a few feet away. But David kept the same pace.

He whispered to Michael, 'As soon as we get under the light, we'll turn on them.'

The two men were coming full speed and the twins lengthened their strides. At the street light's edge, they turned in unison.

The big man gasped when he saw their faces, and fell back.

The little one – but not so little, and very pretty, like a girl with soft curly hair and huge dark eyes ringed in blue eye shadow – just stared.

'You must be Baby,' David said. Then he hit the little one in the face so hard that Michael heard them both grunt. That was all he had time to see because the big one had recovered and swung at Michael's throat; Michael jumped straight up in the air because he didn't know what else to do and the blow landed on his clavicle. All the big man's weight was behind it, and Michael started to fall. He pulled himself to the side and his whole body came down on top of his left knee. The pain shot up through his thigh, into his torso, took his breath away. He knew

221

he couldn't move and there was another punch coming. An instant before it landed, he fell almost flat and the fist glanced off the top of his skull. The big man had put everything into the swing, and he kept going, his whole body arching and turning in the trajectory of his fist. Michael crouched, locked his hands together into one fist, and swung it from the ground right into the man's crotch. He felt the soft genitals smash against his knuckles and heard the guy scream.

'David! Let's get out of here.'

David had his arm locked around Baby's neck while Baby was kicking and digging his elbows into David's midriff. David put his knee against Baby's back and shoved. Then the twins ran.

They made it to the car just as the other two got to their feet and started moving. Baby managed to punch the window as they drove away, but the big guy stood rocking under the streetlight.

On the way uptown, they laughed so hard David's lip split open again and Michael could see blood in the corner of his mouth. They laughed past the doorman and all the way up to the seventeenth floor in the self-service elevator.

'He's going to have to take Baby with him everywhere,' Michael croaked, 'just to hold his balls up – but gently, so gently. God forbid Baby should sneeze.'

They examined themselves. Michael was going to have a bad bruise on his clavicle; the spot was already bright red and covered almost a quarter of his chest. His knee was a mess and he was having trouble bending and straightening it, but he was pretty sure nothing was broken. David thought Baby had broken one of his ribs. He took off his clothes; he was covered with bruises and his hand was pretty badly cut. Michael swabbed the split lip and knuckles with Merthiolate, and felt along his brother's nose to be sure it wasn't broken. Then he rubbed his back for him to ease some of the ache. Finally he covered him with a soft afghan David had folded at the end of the couch. Their mother had made it years ago, when they were kids, and they'd shared it until their parents bought them separate beds and insisted they sleep in them. David lay on his stomach under the cover with his eyes closed, and Michael went into the kitchen to make himself a drink. It was almost two, and Kathy didn't know where he was, but she was probably still asleep. If he got home soon, she might never know that he'd been out at all. He poured some Scotch, took a sip, then sat down at the kitchen table, smiling at the aches, at the satisfying strain he'd felt in his muscles, in his whole body. 'D'ja leave some for me?' David was standing in the kitchen doorway. Still naked.

Suddenly something – the distance, maybe the light, made Michael realize he hadn't seen David naked for years – since they were young. He was facing his own body, but a harder version – how Michael would look if he still swam, played tennis. David's thighs looked longer because the muscles accentuated them, and the hint of softness at his middle made his body easy, inviting looking. He was leaning in the doorway, and his cock hung to the side, reddened and thick as if he'd just used it. But he had – two hours ago – three. No longer than that.

'Plenty left,' Michael said. Don't stare; he stood up and went to the refrigerator to get ice and stood there with his back to David, taking a glass. Finally he had to turn around. David hadn't moved, but he was grinning so wide the lip had split open again,

'Christ, Mike, you look like you never saw a cock before.'

'It's been a long time.' Michael's smile felt fragile.

'Don't you ever look down?'

No answer.

'You know, Mike, you oughtta try a little urology – just so you don't forget there really are two sexes. I've always thought that was the real danger of straight gynaecologists; work and play get all mixed up. Now in my case—'

Michael was laughing, and the tension, whatever it was, was gone. They drank and Michael leaned back, tired, achy, happy, wishing he could stay right where he was for the rest of the night – no driving crosstown, no getting undressed again.

David turned out the light. The kitchen was dim, romantic, full of shadows. Michael was about to close his eyes when he saw David's shadow on the wall, coming across the tile, spreading against the sink and cupboards, only now his cock was jutting out like a club, huge and fierce, breaking the streamlining of his body.

Michael sat upright. He couldn't see the shadow, didn't want to look for it.

'David,' he said to the darkened room. 'They gave me the Calhoun Award.'

Nothing happened. Michael kept staring at the door through which the light was coming, until he began to wonder if he was alone in the room and had dreamed the shadow. Then David asked quietly, 'When did you find this out?'

'Tonight. Just a couple of hours before the cops called.'

'I see. What did they give it to you for?' Michael wished he could see his brother. He was standing to the side, just out of his line of vision.

'For using the methotrexate on Louise. Apparently I opened some kind of door for them. That's what the Calhoun woman said.' The Calhoun woman. He was trying to sound as if he hated her – to appease David, 'and they think what I did was some sort of breakthrough.'

David didn't answer.

'I haven't accepted it yet,' Michael said.

'Why not?'

'I was angry, didn't think I deserved it. And I – I wanted you to have it.' David laughed, and Michael finally turned around.

David said, 'If I thought they'd give it to me if you turned it down, I'd tell you to do it. But they won't. Maggie's a stubborn bitch and she has what she considers good reasons for not liking me.'

'For instance?'

David shrugged. He came and sat across from Michael on the plastic-covered kitchen chair, which made Michael shiver when he thought of the cool smooth stuff against his brother's balls.

'I think she likes to have fantasies about her doctor.'

'You look like pretty good fantasy food.'

'*Look*, yeah. But then she found out that I don't "perform", and what kind of fantasy can you have about a man who apparently doesn't fuck?'

Michael watched and listened, but he knew David was wrong. She had been as interested in Michael sexually as she would have been in Santa Claus. And he was sure she felt as little for David. Maybe it was just an excuse. He looked up at David, and David smiled.

'That sounds like horseshit, doesn't it?' he asked.

Michael smiled back. 'I think it does.'

'You know what Romer said when I told him what you wanted to do to Louise.'

Poor woman. Eight years and Michael still wasn't over it. 'He said that you had more guts and imagination than he did. He was right, too. Maggie is a smart woman, Mike, she did what she thought was right this time. I was only in the running because they just couldn't think of anyone else. It's been a slow year, and cancer's always the juiciest, because everybody's so scared of it – and they all feel so sorry for the poor schmuck who has to treat it.

'Besides if I can't have it, I really want you to. It's good publicity, and maybe it'll make up for all the years in that office . . .'

'You mean it?'

David looked surprised. 'Did you think I wouldn't?'

'I don't know what I thought.'

'Only thing – we gotta dye your hair, too, or everyone'll think you're my older brother. That's one night when I want everyone to confuse us – all the time.'

'I don't want to dye my hair.'

'Don't you like mine?'

Michael admitted it looked good, very good.

'Then why not? Do you *want* them to tell us apart?'

Did he? That night, when they thanked him and gave him money for trying to save Louise's life, maybe he didn't want to look like David.

David was waiting.

'I never liked the idea . . .'

'C'mon. You look like an old man, for Christ's sake. I'll show you.'

Michael followed him out of the kitchen and down the hall.

David was waiting for him in the bathroom in front of the sink. He was holding the bottle of dye.

'Now look at that,' he said.

David was right; he looked younger, better than Michael.

'Maybe it ain't just the hair; maybe you're just the best looking . . .'

225

'Maybe. But we'll never know until we try.' They were smiling at each other as David brought out the cotton and paint brush and opened the bottle.

chapter twenty-three

Michael went to the Sixty-ninth Street building where Chick Snyder's office was; he walked past the door, but it was dark, and the door was locked. He went back the next day, and the lights were on, but he didn't go in; instead he waited in the floor lounge, watching the door. Snyder walked in about six with an unlit cigarette in his mouth. He stopped when he saw Michael, then walked over to him, lighting the cigarette as he came across the room. He didn't smile, or hold out his hand.

'Don't tell me this is coincidence. I won't believe you.'

'It isn't.'

'You want to talk here, or make an appointment?'

'Both . . . I . . . I'm having some trouble . . .'

'I'm sorry to hear that.' Snyder sounded sorry and Michael relaxed slightly. 'Is it still your brother?'

'I don't know.' Michael looked at the floor, 'I'm tired,' desperately tired he wanted to say.

'You look tired,' Snyder said. 'Back, neck, everything. Right, Mike? Stiff and tired.'

Michael nodded and kept looking at the floor. Snyder had almost forgotten what a fine-looking man Michael Ross was.

'I've seen your brother a few times – meetings, parties – but never you. How come?'

'I never go.'

'Why?'

'I don't know.'

Snyder put out his cigarette, stood up, and took his date book out of his pocket. 'I won't risk your forgetting to call to make an appointment. How's next Thursday at four?'

'It's fine.' It was too long to wait, but Michael couldn't say so.

Then he asked, 'You're not still pissed at me about the last time, are you?'

'No. I don't think I ever was. I like you. The way Friedman does; in an odd way, I can't figure.' Snyder grinned, 'I even told my psychiatrist about you.'

'What did he say?'

'That I'm a repressed fag.'

Michael stared up at Snyder, wondering what it would be like to be able to think and say things like that about yourself.

'What did you say?' Michael asked.

'I told him that it wasn't like that. That there was something else about you that had nothing to do with sex. Feelings like that don't have as much to do with sex as most people think.' Michael remembered his brother's shadow on the wall.

'With what then?'

Snyder touched Michael's arm and for an instant Michael was afraid he was going to cry. 'It'll cost you fifty bucks to find out, Mike,' he said gently. 'See you next Thursday.'

Michael hadn't looked at himself naked for years. He couldn't remember the last time. He ran his fingers through his hair, squeezing out the extra water, dried his face and chest, then let the towel fall away so he was facing his body uncovered. He turned to the side, then back and looked at himself over his shoulder. Then front again. He leaned forward, then back, then from side to side, watching the muscles move. He came close to the mirror and looked closely at his face and chest. The bruise on his chest was fading, but his knee still looked raw and sore. He wasn't young any more, and it showed here and there. There was grey in the hair on his chest and belly, and the lack of exercise made his middle look soft. But he was thin – thinner than David. Too thin. He raised his arms and his flesh pulled tight against his ribs; he stretched up as far as he could reach, watching his body strain in the mirror, surprised at how much he enjoyed looking at himself. Kathy opened the bedroom door and stopped on the threshold.

He reached blindly for the towel, embarrassed, which embarrassed her too, and she looked around the room to keep from looking at him.

'You'd better get dressed,' she said. 'It's almost eight and you're the guest of honour.' She got out of the room and shut the door behind her without looking at him again.

Bill Friedman was the first person Michael saw when he and Kathy walked up the curving staircase to the Calhoun's reception hall. He must have been waiting for them, because he was right at the head of the stairs, standing away from the receiving line, holding a drink and smiling.

'Michael, oh Mike.' They shook hands and Michael pounded his friend's shoulder, both of them laughing, both surprised at how glad they were to see each other and embarrassed at being so glad. Bill was laughing at nothing and Michael had turned bright red and started laughing too, because he didn't know what to say.

'Shit,' said Friedman, fighting for breath. 'Why don't they let us hug and kiss like the goddamn broads.'

He grabbed some champagne off a passing tray and they toasted each other. 'Congratulations. Jesus, what a coup! I've told everyone on the North Shore that I know the famous Michael Ross. Hey, how do I look?'

'Fat, and wonderful.'

'That's how I feel. You know I'm forty-two – forty-two fucking years old and everyone says I don't look a day over sixty. It's the paunch that does it – that and not making too much money. Nothing like a struggle to keep you young. Kathy looks wonderful.' Michael watched her pale beige chiffon figure, elegant and faded, disappear into the reception hall.

'She's still one of the most beautiful . . .' Was she? John Anders was steamrolling across the huge room towards her. Other heads turned, slight bows from the women, smiles, waves. But longer looks from the men. A lot of them touched her as she passed. Then she was with Anders and the rest fell back. They were smiling and nodding to each other; he put his hand on her arm, bent his head to hear better, see her more closely.

'And you,' Friedman was saying. 'God, you don't have a grey hair on your head!'

'I just dyed it.'

'You what?'

'Crazy whim. David dyed his, and it looked so good—'

'Where is he?'

'Waiting for nine to make an entrance. He always says earlier is gauche and later is rude.'

'Chic David.'

'You two'll never get along, will you?'

Friedman looked closely at Michael, but Michael had already had two glasses of champagne and he wasn't angry.

'How are things with you both, Mike?'

'Things are good. I think he felt a little left out about this thing . . .'

'It couldn't happen to a nicer guy,' Friedman said.

Suddenly Michael didn't know what to say. Bill meant David; he was glad David got left out.

'I haven't seen Maggie yet,' Michael said, and he walked away.

Maggie was in a wheelchair, the skirt of her gown trailing down, covering the steps.

'Congratulations, Michael.' Kathy was standing nearby holding a glass of champagne, smiling, proud, smug. Anders was at her elbow.

'I'm glad,' Maggie was saying, 'that you finally realized how silly you were being about David. He's a good sport . . . a fine doctor.' She was trying to be gracious. 'So often we don't give people a chance to show how decent they really are.' She inclined her head slightly, a tribute to her own sentiments, then looked around, 'Where is he, by the way?'

'He'll be here any minute,' Michael said.

Her eyes went to the foyer as if she thought David might have gotten up the stairs without her seeing him.

Michael thought he saw David, then he moved and realized that he was facing a floor to ceiling art-deco friezed mirror, and he looked at himself, then at the room behind him.

He could see Kathy talking to Anders, laughing and looking up at him.

Lovely couple, Michael thought, perfect. He took another glass of champagne, drank it, watching his wife's reflection. He thought if she stood next to a tan wall, with her faded hair and constant beige, she'd melt into the plaster, and they'd never find

229

her again. He looked back at himself. Louise would never have faded; she'd be standing here next to him, wearing black or bright red and he'd have bought her so many diamonds to wear in her ears and around her neck and wrists she'd sparkle like crystal in sunlight. Kathy never wore diamonds; she said they were too much for her, that emeralds and pearls were her gems. She was right, Michael thought, as he watched the confident, deliberate way she bent close to listen, straightened up to talk; diamonds were too much for her. Diamonds were for Louise.

'Michael or David?' A tall handsome man, very pale, very thin was standing behind him.

'Michael,' said Michael. He took another glass of champagne.

'Congratulations.' He smiled. There was gold edging his front teeth.

'I don't...'

'I'm Jeremy Clark...'

He didn't offer to shake hands, but Michael didn't blame him ... Precious hands, worth half a million a year or more. Michael grinned at the hands, wondering if they were insured. Rubinstein's hands, Heifetz's hands ... and Clark's. Pelvic exenteration Clark, who'd butchered Carol Arland.

Clark was standing next to Michael and dipping a long silver spoon into the nondrinkers' punchbowl, which was full of something red and slick in which bits of orange and ice floated. Michael stared at Clark and at the spoon catching the light as it dipped, rose, and dipped again.

Clark's eyes met his, and he smiled and nodded. Michael turned and headed towards the parlour, where he'd last seen Friedman. Friedman was drunk too, grinning at an even fatter man Michael didn't know. They were standing against the wall of windows that looked out over the garden, and into the windows – so David once told him – of Mrs Rockefeller's dining room. He'd almost reached Friedman, funny crazy Friedman who'd protect him from Clark, when he heard David's voice in the foyer, apologizing for being late.

He turned before David could see him and walked as steadily as he could across the room away from his brother. Ahead a glass and chrome table almost hid a high-backed upholstered chair. He sat down in the chair and leaned back, so that he was partly hidden from the room.

There was a half-full glass on the table next to him, and he reached around and took it, drank what was left in it, then put it back on the table. Minnie Lasker went by, so drunk she was leaning on Al Weiss and saying, 'I thought the little prick'd stay home, and we'd miss our one chance to see David Ross eat a little shit.'

Friedman and Beth passed by, but Michael was in the shadows and they didn't see him. They were fat, Gargan was old, and Al Weiss in his Finchley suit looked like a defeated chorus boy. Somewhere to Michael's left, he knew that Clark was carrying his cup of red liquid and sipping, smiling, watching them all with his pale-grey eyes.

Kathy and Anders were probably still standing against the wall, across from the Cézanne, and Anders was leaning into her, while they talked about last week's concert or next week's gallery opening. There was Arlene Vale with a blond who wasn't over twenty-five and whom she'd take home with her tonight, and pay tomorrow. She'd probably tried to fuck David and couldn't. How many others like that? A lot, Michael thought, as he watched people break away from their groups, and head for the reception hall to see David – his brother – eat a little shit.

He sat still and stared straight ahead. Another waiter passed; another glass of champagne. He'd lost count. He closed his eyes and thought about all the cold, gruesome, deadly, lonely people collecting around David.

He knew he should be with his brother, but he stayed where he was without moving, afraid even to blink. When the party was over, he'd go to the bathroom, then come back here to this chair to sleep tonight, tomorrow night, and the night after. Until Thursday afternoon at four. He didn't think Snyder would mind his turning up in his tux.

'Hiding from someone?'

Michael saw his brother's tie first. It was slightly crooked. David had had to tie it himself, just an hour ago – alone, in his bare-looking, too-modern bedroom, working on his tie. The split lip was healing and Michael thought of them fighting together. Last night? No, the night before. Michael stood up and took David's hand, then, while everybody watched, he put his arms around his brother, and David, surprised, hugged him back.

'You're drunk,' he whispered in Michael's ear.

'Plastered,' Michael whispered back. 'And if we don't get this over with pretty soon I'm going to puke or pass out.'

David pulled away, but Michael held on.

'If you let me go, I'll fall on my ass.'

'Okay.' David held on, 'Shit, what do I do now?'

'Just hold on to me – it'll be okay.'

'But you've gotta stand up, make a speech.'

'I'll do it. Just don't let go of me.'

They cleared a small space in front of the windows and people stood in a semicircle. Maggie introduced the twins from her wheelchair, and polite applause greeted them as David helped Michael up the low step. Then the twins faced front and the audience stood still and looked at the two men. David started to speak.

'Maggie asked me to introduce my brother' – Michael was holding on to the lectern – 'since I've known him a long time.' Embarrassed laughter; everybody could see how drunk Michael was. David looked at him, shook his head, smiled and put his arm around him. Michael turned and stared at his brother.

'He's been doing a lot of celebrating; with good cause, because tonight he is being recognized as one of America's leading clinicians.' Michael leaned over the lectern. Kathy was pushing through the crowd, coming to get him, to take him away. Michael loved her for trying. But he couldn't stop looking at David's face. The crowd was absolutely still, no one moved or spoke, not even any rustling. They were waiting to see Michael take the award from his brother – his twin.

It was a satisfaction he wasn't going to give them.

He held onto the mike with one hand, and to his brother's hand with the other.

'I've had a great deal to drink,' Michael said softly; but the mike picked up his voice and the words boomed across the connecting rooms.

The waiter stopped carrying trays and stood still waiting to see what was going to happen next. Michael was squeezing David's hand so hard he was afraid he was hurting him, but David didn't try to get away, and Michael went on.

'Now I'm going to ask my brother, Michael, to take me home, before I do something he'll be ashamed of.' Suddenly they were all so quiet he wondered if they'd stopped breathing.

Then someone moved, not Kathy whom he thought it would be; she was still frozen like the rest. It was Maggie, wheeling to the ramp and looking up at him. She was trying to smile. Michael stared down at her from a great distance. She looked so confused he felt sorry for her.

'But I thought . . .' She stopped.

He leaned over towards her, still holding onto his brother to keep from falling, 'I'm sorry,' Michael said gently. 'I should have told you before. *He's* Michael. I'm David.'

Michael saw David's disembodied tux hanging on the closet door. He closed his eyes and turned his head. He was in his brother's bedroom. His jacket, tie and shoes were off; and he was covered with a light blanket.

He couldn't see him, but he knew David was in the room with him.

'I really fucked it up, didn't I?'

He knew Kathy was somewhere crying – with Anders rubbing her back, looking helpless, and wondering how to get her clothes off without her noticing. Michael laughed and David came over and sat down on the edge of the bed next to him.

'You're still drunk.'

'A little.'

'Don't worry,' David said. 'You were really wonderful; "He's Michael, I'm David!" Terrific. You gave every dead ass on the East Side something to talk about for a week; and I think that even though you left Maggie Calhoun covered with drying egg, she's a little in love with you now, and a lot jealous of both of us.'

That was true; they'd all been jealous. He remembered their faces as he walked carefully, carefully past them, holding on to his brother – down the stairs – and out the door onto the quiet street.

'You think I'll still get it.'

'Of course.' David stood up. He was wearing a long robe. The lights were off and the room was dim and full of shadows the way the kitchen had been the other night, and Michael realized that they were alone together again. He started to sweat. David stood next to the bed looking down at him, but Michael turned to look out of the window.

'Look at me, Mike,' David said softly. 'Look at me like you did tonight.'

Michael turned back and David untied his robe; he was naked under it and Michael started to turn away again.

'Don't, Michael.' Michael didn't move.

'Please, Michael, look at me.'

Michael looked again and after a while began to think he could lie there forever watching his brother's body.

'What's it like?' David asked.

'Like looking at myself.'

'But with a hard on. Right?' He started laughing, and Michael smiled and finally laughed too and shook his head.

'Let me look at you too,' David whispered, taking the blanket off Michael. 'I won't hurt you.'

'*Do you think David would hurt you?*' his father had asked when they'd talked about the dream, '*Do you?*' '*No,*' Michael said.

He relaxed; David reached around his body to unsnap his cummerbund, and Michael started to laugh. 'It'll take you all night to get all this crap off. Let me help you.'

They both started pulling at his clothes and laughing . . . 'Don't tear the cuff – easy, you're breaking my arm,' and they pulled his shirt off, then they got his trousers off, then his socks. But when David rolled up his brother's T-shirt and bared his chest, Michael couldn't help him. He was blushing and he moved only when necessary to let David get everything off. When he was naked, he couldn't watch David staring at him, and he shut his eyes and kept them closed until he felt his brother's hair touching his skin. He looked and saw David's head resting on his chest as if he'd suddenly gotten very tired, or very drunk and just couldn't hold his head up any more.

Michael smiled because they were going to sleep like this, and they'd wake up in the morning lying here naked, with hangovers, or maybe even still a little drunk. That was all that was going to happen. But then David raised his head and kissed Michael on the mouth. The split in his lip must have opened again, because Michael tasted blood and he suddenly remembered that he'd been hurt too; and the ache in his knees and from the bruises on his chest came back. He wanted to tell David that they were too old for this; he wanted to tell him that they couldn't be doing these mad, dark things when David couldn't even tie his tie straight. As soon as he said that, they'd laugh and drink some more. But Michael didn't say anything, and David moved his hand down Michael's body until he was holding his penis. Then his head followed. Michael could feel his brother's hair on his chest, and across his belly . . . And, so slowly, so tenderly – Michael had to smile at the care his brother was taking – David slid Michael's penis into his mouth. Michael already felt a slow ache of regret. Even as excited as he was – and he was more excited than he'd ever been – he couldn't forget all the people who'd think he was betraying them by doing this one thing that seemed so familiar, so right. He thought that he and David must have done this when they were children, and he'd made himself forget.

David shifted around so Michael could reach him. Michael explained silently to the others – Kathy, Sam, Friedman, Snyder – that he couldn't not do this any more, but that the act – he moaned, then cried – was almost beside the point – only a gesture of what they really felt for each other. Listen, he told them, I have never done anything so perfect. I have never felt such isolated, pointed sensation. His balls got tight, hard, ready to come. Not yet, he thought. Gently, gently. David knew what he wanted and slowed down, stopped, waited.

Sweet David, go on.

chapter twenty-four

Kathy needed an excuse to spend an evening alone with him, and she picked their twelfth anniversary. They hadn't spent an evening alone together in over a month, since the Calhoun party. Something was wrong and she thought tonight she might find out what. He hadn't made love to her since the party, and yet was more outwardly affectionate than he'd ever been. He kissed her when he came home and he'd started bringing her presents; but she knew he was having more trouble eating and sleeping than he'd had in years.

First she planned the evening carefully because if it was too lavish, he'd be on his guard.

She called Sally and made sure that Michael would be finished by six on the twenty-ninth. Then she got tickets for *Sleuth*, which everyone said was marvellous, and she made reservations at Café Nicolson, the most romantic place she knew. She hoped that after a few drinks and a light dinner in the shaded, fountained restaurant, they'd never use the theatre tickets.

She even bought a new dress – not beige, Beth Friedman told her, anything but beige. But she was still afraid that bright colours would overpower her, so she chose light blue, from Bendels, with the new low cowl neckline.

The day itself went on forever. Sam spilled things or broke them, and knowing somehow that she wanted him to hurry, he took twice as long eating his dinner as he ever had before. It didn't matter, she thought, because it was still only four thirty. She took a long careful shower, opened her new bottle of Chantilly, and a new box of stockings. She wore her mother's antique cameo earrings, no other jewellery.

When she was ready, Kelly nodded approval. Sam sat in front of the five-o'clock cartoons, pretending she wasn't there. He let her kiss him goodnight, but he wouldn't kiss her back. She wondered how children always knew when their parents were excited, and why they resented it so much. Finally it was five thirty. Sally would be gone; Michael would just be finishing, either with his last patient or going over records. He never left the office before six, except when he made early rounds – which wasn't today.

She took a cab across town, rolling up the window to keep her hair from blowing, smiling at her image in the cabbie's rearview mirror because she looked wonderful, and because she'd been married to Michael for twelve years and couldn't wait to be alone with him.

The doorman smiled at her and didn't bother to buzz. She used her key to let herself in because she wanted to surprise him, to appear suddenly at the door of his office in her new blue dress.

The outer office and waiting room were dark. David's lights were out and Michael's office was lit, but empty. His jacket was there, hung over the back of the chair; and his tie was on the desk. She picked it up, thinking that he usually wore his tie all day. Maybe he was in the bathroom. But it was empty and dark. Then she heard something rustling and another sound she couldn't identify at first because it was so unexpected. The noises came from David's office, and she went to it and pushed in the slightly open door. It took a second for her to become accustomed to the half-light but it was April, late twilight, and not yet dark.

They were twisted on the floor, their shirts and pants were open, their shoes were off, and they were moving in perfect time, like one animal. She heard the sound again and realized that one of them had moaned, or maybe they both had. Half of the shape on the floor was her husband, but if someone had put a gun to her head and told her to pick which, she couldn't have done it.

She was unable to speak or leave, and she couldn't go on watching, so she slammed the door. The stop – shock – recovery took a comically long time, but finally Michael was standing, covered, facing her. David stayed on the floor, open and cross-legged, as if he was just waiting for her to leave so they could finish.

'We couldn't wait,' he said, grinning at her. Michael just stared at her and she stared back. She had the tiny satisfaction of knowing that for that second, he wasn't thinking about David. Then he turned and looked at the man on the floor and back to her, as if he'd only seen them both for the first time.

'Oh, God,' he whispered. 'Oh, Kathy, no.'

No what? No, he couldn't bear her standing there? But that wasn't it. He meant no, he couldn't have been doing what she'd just seen. Looking at him now, she was surprised too. Only the man on the floor seemed to belong in the scene.

David called his brother softly, 'Michael,' but Michael didn't move or turn his head, and by the time Kathy looked away from him, she knew that he was seeing what she saw.

He saw that the twins weren't children; this place wasn't a garden; and whatever it was that he had been fighting had finally beaten him.

As if to flag his defeat, as she turned to open the door, she heard David call again softly, 'Michael.'

She walked the twelve blocks to John Anders' apartment. He had someone there, a woman she'd never seen before. She was tall and well built, but plain-faced and she actually pursed her lips when she saw Kathy, which Kathy wasn't sure she'd ever seen anyone do before.

Kathy walked through the living room to where she thought the bedroom was, while John followed helplessly, trying to get some explanation. When they were alone in the bedroom, she said, 'Get rid of her. I'll wait for you here.'

'I can't do that.'

She shrugged. 'I'll give you fifteen minutes. If you're not back here by then, I'll leave.'

'What is this? What's going on? For God's sake, Kathy?' She didn't even bother to answer.

Anders stood still until she looked at her watch. Then he went into the other room and closed the door behind him. He took the other woman's jacket with him. As soon as he was gone, Kathy started to undress. She knew that he'd waited years for this, and he'd get rid of the other one if he had to kill her to do it.

She took off everything. The Chantilly had permeated her clothes, and she could smell it as she pulled the blue dress over her head, then her slip. She lay down on the bed, closed her eyes

238

and saw Michael the way he was at the end – numb, shocked, defeated.

She stroked herself until she was wet because she didn't want anything to happen between her and Anders that even resembled tenderness. Then she lay still, her arms crossed behind her head, waiting. When he walked in, she heard him inhale sharply, then he came to the bed and sat next to her.

'Kathy—' He started to reach for her.

'I'm ready,' she said tonelessly. He froze. 'You do whatever you have to do to get ready, too. Don't touch me otherwise.' She wondered without much interest if he'd take it from her, but he did.

When he started moving in her, she couldn't think of anything except the brothers' bodies stretched against each other. Then she thought about killing herself – but she knew she wouldn't. There was her family, and her son – besides, she just wouldn't. Then she giggled.

'What's so funny?' Anders' teeth were clenched, he was so angry, so excited.

'I was thinking how much the paintings would be worth if anything happened to me.'

Then his voice became tender. 'Nothing'll happen to you, darling.' He slowed, stopped, waited. 'I won't let it.'

He began very slowly again and even though she didn't want to, she started to respond, which made her feel as defeated as she thought Michael must feel.

chapter twenty-five

Michael tried to make himself dinner and he burned himself frying the eggs, then spilled canned soup on the floor and tried to mop it up, but kept missing spots, and knew that he'd step in them in the morning.

He gave up and went out and bought some vodka and tried to drink the whole bottle; but even when he was reeling sick and ready to pass out, he couldn't forget the quiet. He dialled David's number; but when he heard David's voice, he made himself hang up without saying anything. The next night the quiet drove him out of the house and down the street to Carr's where they had a colour TV. He watched basketball and got drunk again, while a young girl sitting next to him watched the rim of his glass as it went to his lips again and again. Her eyeshadow was so thick it had smeared under her eyes, and so blue she looked as if someone had hit her. She smiled at him and leaned over so he could see her breasts. He left a ten on the bar, and walked out of the place. He passed the drugstore with its bank of telephone booths and he went into the D'Agostino's supermarket on Broadway. It was eight thirty and the place was almost empty. He filled a shopping cart with food the way he and Kathy did every Friday night. Fresh meat, and vegetables, and the special treats they used to buy when they were young. Anchovies, stuffed olives, canned Greek antipasto. All of a sudden there were tears on his cheeks and he quickly pushed the full cart to the back of the store near the meat scale where he leaned against the wall and put his head down. He didn't sob out loud, but people who passed saw something wrong and rushed away.

Finally he took out his handkerchief, wiped his eyes and face and began wheeling the cart again. This time he put back all the fresh food and bought frozen packages of TV dinners and vegetables, canned soup and canned spaghetti.

When he got to the checkout, the cashier helped him unload the cart, 'Looks like you're getting ready for a siege,' she said.

'What?'

'All that canned stuff – like you're setting up a bomb shelter.'

He didn't tell David that Kathy was gone.

He went home every night, ate canned or frozen food, drank and turned on the television for the noise. The phone always rang at seven thirty and again at nine. He knew it was David, and he didn't answer. One night – about a week later – the door bell rang, and he knew that was David too. Fortunately, he didn't have the TV on, so David couldn't be sure Michael was there. David rang, waited a few minutes, rang again, then went away.

The next morning David was waiting for him in the hall of their office building, ready to take him someplace quiet where they could talk. Someplace quiet would be David's apartment only two blocks away, and once they were alone there Michael was afraid he'd never be able to leave again. He turned around and went home. That night, no matter how much he drank, he couldn't sleep, and he called the next day and told Sally he was sick. When the phone rang, he knew it was David and he didn't answer, and again he couldn't sleep.

He wrote out and filled a prescription for Seconal.

He called Kathy. She hung up when she heard his voice.

Then he called Kelly and asked her if she'd come and clean for him, but she said she was working for *Mrs* Ross.

He hung up before she could say any more.

He changed the sheets, but forgot the top sheet, and found himself sleeping with the blanket next to his skin. He liked the feeling; it seemed warmer, and he decided he wouldn't use a top sheet any more.

He tried to find the laundry room, but there were no signs in the basement. He'd taken a lot of Desoxyn to wake up that morning. He was shaky and it was too dark down there, so he gave up.

The next day David kept walking past the open door of Michael's office. Finally he came in and shut the door.

'Michael, has Kathy left?' Michael's hands were folded in his lap. He didn't answer. David came around the desk while Michael sat still, staring at the far wall, trying to make a list of things he had to do after evening rounds. David touched his cheek. Michael looked at his brother's shoes, then again at the wall. He had to buy milk and coffee. He'd get Sanka because the other kept him awake. The freeze-dried wasn't bad . . . Kathy used to get it. David touched his shoulder gently.

'What are you fighting?' David said softly. Michael couldn't answer.

David went on. 'It only makes it worse. When you come to me you're not losing anything. Why can't you see that?' He put his fingers gently against his brother's lips. 'Mike, please,' he said. He sounded so hurt Michael couldn't pull away, and David leaned over him just as the door opened, and, over David's back, Michael saw Sally standing on the threshold. Michael tried to get up, but David misunderstood the movement and kissed Michael on the mouth. Michael's eyes were open and he watched her over the rim of David's head. It was too late. Sally had seen it, and Michael closed his eyes so he wouldn't see the look on her face. When he opened them, she was gone. The door was closed again and Michael knew he'd never see her again. He wondered if she'd tell other people? Probably her mother, maybe her son.

David stood straight.

'I'll lock the door,' he said, which made Michael grin because he knew it was too late. But he didn't say anything as David turned the lock and came back.

Michael wanted to touch him, but instead he stood up. 'I have to go.'

'Mike, please.' Michael could see how excited his brother was. Michael was too, and if he didn't get out of there it was going to happen again, right there on the floor with the drapes open and the sun streaming in so he could see everything, the way the hair on his brother's body was turning grey in spots as his was in exactly the same places. The shape of his brother's hips and thighs; even the sound of his voice. When David cried with excitement, it would be Michael's voice, and if Michael wanted to know how his face looked during orgasm, all he had to do was watch his brother's.

Michael opened the door, and the hall was empty.

'Please, Mike,' David called softly.

He shut the door on his brother standing alone in the middle of the room and went past Sally's empty desk – she wouldn't be back – the top of the desk was bare. Even the African violet she kept was gone.

When Michael got home, he called Kathy again, but there was no answer. He sat next to the phone for a few minutes, then he called the Fields' home in Boston.

Kathy's mother answered the phone, asked him to wait and left him praying that she'd gone to get Sam, and that he'd hear the boy's voice any minute. But she'd called Kathy's father to the phone.

'Listen, Ross, to me you've always been just what you come from – scum. In a better-run world, I'd have the pleasure of breaking your neck . . .'

'Mr Field, you have my son . . .'

'My grandson is safe. Just leave it that way or I will see that you never practise medicine again. My daughter told me what you did to her – what you are.'

Michael didn't know what to say.

'That'll be some scandal if it ever comes out. Do you think any woman would ever let you touch her again?'

Michael wanted to fight back, to tell him that if he lost his income, Kathy would lose hers. But Kathy didn't need his money; neither did Sam; there were the Field securities, Field trust funds, boxes and boxes of paper, and acres and acres of Massachusetts to protect his wife and son from ever having to look at him again.

'She told me that some of them were your own patients – women who relied on you, needed your help, trusted you.'

Michael laughed. 'Is that what she told you? That I was fucking my patients?'

Field choked when he heard Michael laugh, and hung up.

Michael decided to write Kathy, to tell her that he had a right to talk to his own son. He would be firm, but kindly too – hurt. Only he was very nervous. The conversation had upset him, and he took another red. But when it calmed him enough to think about what to write, he found that he couldn't hold the pen. He tried to write 'Dear Kathy' three times – finally just Kathy – but he couldn't do it; the lines on the paper were meaningless tracings. Finally he gave up and lit a cigarette. He lay down on the couch, watching the smoke curl out of his mouth and nose. He closed his eyes.

When he woke up, the cigarette had burned down across the insides of his fingers and the ash had fallen on his chest. A circle was burnt in his T-shirt, the hair on his chest had burned too, and there was a round red mark under it, starting to blister. He was shaking so badly he had to hold onto furniture and lean against the wall to reach the bathroom to wash the burns and put some penicillin ointment on them. He couldn't be alone much longer.

Michael put his windbreaker on over his T-shirt and left the apartment. It was very hot, and he sweated against the slick jacket. The sun burned his face and the back of his neck and drove him across the street into the park. He walked down to the river and looked across to the Palisades rising out of the slight haze in the air. The river moved silently in the sun, giving up a little coolness, and behind him he could hear children yelling and laughing. He looked north, facing the slight breeze, coming down from wherever the river began – from some little stream in the cool woods that you could jump across, drink from. He squinted – something around Eighty-sixth Street was catching the sun – something that looked like an island floating down the river, maybe from miles away, maybe from as far away as the Adirondacks. He imagined twisted branches and twigs, pine needles, stems and wild flowers held together with green algae, floating down past Albany and Bear Mountain, under the bridge, then out to sea. The island might end up at Montauk – farther – Bermuda, maybe even Newfoundland or Greenland, to be trapped in the ice forever. He watched it as it came closer; it was big – almost a quarter of a mile long – and reached almost to the middle of the river. It shone and rippled; he thought of an island of silver. But when it got close enough he saw the silver was the sun reflecting on the bodies of fish, thousands of them – dead and rolling in the current with their turned-up bellies silver in the sun. Something upstream had poisoned all of them.

A few of the children came out of the park to watch the island float by. They stood near Michael silently; one threw a rock into the mass and a patch of clear water appeared. But the bodies closed rank again at once. Then another rock was thrown, but the tosses were dispirited and the stones landed close to shore. Finally they all just stood there, until the current pulled the island of bodies out of sight. The children went back to their games, and Michael went upstairs and called David.

*

'Where the hell have you been? Florence Robinson's been waiting here since two.'

'Fuck Florence Robinson.'

'You're high again, aren't you?'

'Yeah, but I'm celebrating.'

'What do you have to celebrate?' Michael could hear the anger coming out.

'Bring some reds and some Desoxyn, and I'll tell you.'

No answer.

Michael said, 'Come on, David, bring the stuff here and I'll tell you why I feel so good.'

David rang the bell at six. Michael had picked up the empty soft-drink and beer cans, and the glow from the sun setting across the river hid the worst of the dust. He had taken a shower, and he was wearing a robe Kathy had given him last Christmas. He let David in, and went back into the living room, trying not to notice how neatly dressed his brother was. David followed him.

'Did you bring them?'

'Yes.'

David took the bottles out of his pocket, and put them on the table, watching Michael every minute, 'Tell me what you're celebrating,' he said.

'Can't you guess? C'mon, David. What am I doing alone at this hour – in an apartment that hasn't been cleaned for a month?' David looked around.

'She's gone.'

'That's right, David. She's gone.' Gone, done – kid and all.

David took a step closer.

Michael didn't move. 'I thought you might like to move in?' He waited, but David appeared too overcome to speak. 'It's what mother always wanted, David – us together, here. I don't know how Dad would have felt.' *Dear Dad, David and I are lovers; that's right, your sons make love to each other.*

'I would like to,' David said.

'Good. No sense in paying two rents, is there?' Michael picked up the Desoxyn then stood still and let David put his arms around him. It was exciting, wonderful.

'Undress, David. It's been so long.' David started taking off his clothes, and Michael had to watch him; he was still holding the bottle of Desoxyn.

When David was naked, he put his arms around his brother again. 'Michael, oh Michael.'

Sometimes Kathy would call softly to him like that, as if she were too far away to see him any more, and she needed to hear his voice.

Michael pulled away and opened the Desoxyn bottle.

'Don't. Not now. Come back to me. You don't need those,' David said.

'Sure, I do. They're terrific. Take one.'

David shook his head, trying to get Michael back and suddenly Michael wanted David to take them too. Why should he be the only one? They shared, didn't they? Wasn't that why they were here now, why Kathy was gone, and Sam; why he couldn't sleep or wake up, or do anything without his brother.

He held his hand out, 'Go on, Dave. Take them.'

David didn't move.

'Go on,' Michael said. 'Take them, and we'll finish together and go crosstown and pack your stuff and bring it here, Dave. We'll tell the service and the post office.' He laughed, rolling the tablets between his palms. 'We'll send a special delivery letter to American Express and we'll tell Con Ed, and the telephone company.'

He sank to his knees on the floor next to David, 'We'll need change-of-address cards for Paul Stuart, and Master Charge, and Bonwit's. Let me see – and Mark Cross, can't forget Mark Cross.'

'Stop it, Mike.'

'We haven't taken a vacation yet this year, have we?' Michael hadn't taken a vacation for years; he couldn't remember how many. 'But this year we will – together. Paris, London. We'll buy the tickets tonight. Or maybe someplace quiet – the Caribbean, the Bahamas. Maybe a cruise. Whatever you want. Go ahead, take them. You'll go three times without even getting winded. They're terrific. Take them. C'mon, Davey, take them. It's getting dark.'

Michael kept the tablets in his hand. They stayed on their

knees, facing each other. The air was red from the sunset, full of dust, hot and they were sweating.

'Take them,' Michael whispered.

'Why don't you *not* take them, Mikey?' David said.

'I can't do that.'

'Try,' David said.

Michael couldn't see the sense to that. David didn't understand – the dear reds, and these too, didn't cause pain, they eased it.

Michael said, 'I can't try.' Too much pain, as his father would have said, more than he should have to bear.

David must have understood without the words because all he said was, 'Are you sure, Mike?'

'Positive.'

David smiled at him, the wild smile Michael remembered from the night in the Village; then he opened his brother's hand to expose the pills. 'Three times?'

'Five times.' Michael laughed.

David leaned over and picked up the pills with his lips. Then he looked around.

'Use spit,' Michael said.

David sucked saliva in from his cheeks, and swallowed the Desoxyn.

'I love you, Michael,' he said.

chapter twenty-six

'Please, calm down, Mr Silver. Someone else is with your wife right now.'

'How can you let the son of a bitch walk around here? I tell you, he was drunk – or worse. She's lying there, dead white, blood everywhere, and there's Ross, leaning against the wall – because I don't think he could stand on his own – telling her she can go home if she wants.'

'Removing a physician's hospital privileges is a very serious step, Mr Silver.'

'Getting sued is pretty serious, too, Anders. And if she's lost our baby because of that bumbling junkie . . .'

Junkie. Anders was almost relieved that someone had finally said it out loud. '—I'm going to sue this hospital for a million dollars, and that shit Ross for two million.'

'I just talked to Dr Berger. Actually, Dr Ross was a little hasty . . .'

'Hasty!'

Anders went on as if he hadn't spoken, '—but that's all he was, Silver. The baby's solid. And according to Berger, your wife was never in any danger of losing it; Ross was *hasty*, that's all.'

'He was also drunk or high or something. And I'm reporting it.'

'To whom?'

'To you. And if you don't listen, then to anyone who will, including the newspapers.'

Anders hated Michael Ross, but he suddenly hated this man more. 'What do you mean by "listen", Mr Silver?'

'I mean get rid of him.'

Anders turned his back on the man. 'Thank you for stopping by, Mr Silver. I will certainly think about everything you've told me.'

'That's not good enough, Anders.'

'I'm afraid it'll have to be for the moment.'

The man stared at Anders' back and Anders didn't move. Then he heard Silver stand up and go to the door.

'I mean what I say. You bastards just got arrogant with the wrong man.'

Silver was an accountant – $15,000 a year – and as far as Anders was concerned, two steps above the janitor. He didn't bother to turn around. Silver walked out and expectedly slammed the door behind him.

Anders buzzed Lorraine.

'Page Michael Ross. I want to see him.'

Anders waited half an hour, then he called Kathy and cancelled their lunch date.

She asked him what was wrong. And he started to tell her, half wanting the satisfaction of hating Michael aloud in front of her. But the few times he'd done it, she had turned morose, and shut herself off from him for days. So all he said was that something had come up. She never asked any more.

As soon as he hung up, Lorraine buzzed him.

'Dr Ross is in emergency, Dr Anders.'

'I don't care where he is. I want to see him. There should be four other doctors on emergency.'

'No, sir. He's not attending. He's a patient.'

Anders half walked, half ran the block-long maze of corridors to the emergency wing. A young resident whose name he couldn't remember was waiting for him. 'He fell. There's nothing broken, but he's in bad shape.'

Michael lay on the table without moving. His eyes were closed and his pallor so absolute that for a second Anders thought he was dead. Then he saw the thin chest move shallowly.

'Mike. It's John Anders.' Nothing happened. He stood at the side of the table and looked at his old enemy. His ribs showed under the clean cotton of his T-shirt and his pelvic bones pushed against the sheet that covered him.

'Mike?' Michael opened his eyes, smiled, and Anders was overwhelmed with unwanted pity.

'I'm going to call Dave to come and get you,' he told Michael. Michael stopped smiling and shook his head.

'Please don't.'

'You don't want to stay here.'

'Just for a few minutes. I'll be better in a second. Maybe if you could get me something . . . a little Desoxyn would be nice.' Anders looked up at the young resident who was staring coldly at Michael. Now there'd be real trouble!

'Yes,' Michael was saying. 'Desoxyn'll do it. Then a few seconds right here; it's so clean here. But don't call David. Please. Promise me you won't.' He sounded desperate.

'Sure, Mike. Don't worry.'

Anders and the resident moved away from the table.

'What happened?' Anders asked.

'He fell, which is not surprising, considering how junked out he is.'

'What on?'

The young man shrugged and looked at Michael. 'Who knows with a head like that?' he sneered. 'The guy's been falling all over himself like an avalanche for months. Old bruises and cuts scarred over – real junkie-look to what's left of him. I doubt he weighs more than a hundred and twenty or twenty-five.'

Anders shook his head. Then the resident said, 'I hope you're looking upset because he's still here practising medicine, Dr Anders, and not because he's an old friend.'

The resident had a beard and long curly hair. His eyes were light, full of fire; he wasn't going to let the medical establishment get away with this.

Anders smiled. 'He's not a friend. As a matter of fact, I hate his guts. But he was once a good doctor—'

'Whatever he was, he isn't any more.'

Just like that. No quarter for Michael Ross. But the kid was right and Anders knew it. He sighed and wrote David's office number on a piece of paper. He looked over at the man on the table, but Michael's eyes were closed again, and Anders doubted if he could hear what they said.

'This is his brother's number. Call him and tell him to get over here. How bad is the damage?'

'He made hamburger of his knees, but nothing's broken. As for the other—' He shrugged.

'What do you think he took?'

'You name it,' the resident said. 'It's all the same shit as far as I'm concerned. Nembutal. Seconal, maybe Demerol. Comes to the same thing in the end.'

'No it doesn't. And you're going to make some kind of educated guess about whether this is barbiturate or an opiate. Then you treat it accordingly. And if you're wrong, smartass, and anything happens to him, you're going to wind up practising in Pakistan.'

The resident tried to keep the cocky look in place, but it was fading. 'How do I find out? You don't treat them the same.'

See? Anders wanted to say. See how easy it is to get scared.

'Try asking him,' Anders said, and he walked out.

David was in Anders' office half an hour later.

'Where's my brother?'

'Take it easy, Dave. He's down in emergency. I just talked to them and he's fine. You can take him home.'

David started for the door.

'I think we'd better talk first, David.'

David didn't stop, so Anders raised his voice. 'I'm dropping him from the staff, David.'

David stopped. 'On what grounds?'

'Where would you like to start?'

'I know we've been bad about the paperwork, and some appointments, John, but that's it. You can't . . .'

'Yes I can. I know no one's been hurt. But the talk's getting uglier every day. And today in rapid order, your brother turns up strung out, tells a woman who's six months pregnant and bleeding fairly significantly that she can go home – in front of her husband. Then he walks out, leaving havoc behind and falls flat on his ass on the steps of the main entrance. More bad luck! The resident who gets the case is a self-appointed protector of a helpless public who's not going to keep quiet about whatever it is your brother is taking. It won't be long before the boards pick it up – or even the papers. If he's still on the staff, still admitting patients, everybody's ass'll be in a sling, and he could lose his licence. So I'm putting him on leave. We'll make it medical leave – indefinite.'

David was pale and silent at first.

Finally he said, almost in a whisper, 'Then you'll have to put us both on leave, John. I won't stay here without him.'

'Why?'

'I just won't.'

'What'll you live on?'

'We still have an office.'

'With how many patients?'

David didn't answer.

'Stay here, Dave. I won't accept your resignation. Work it out another way. Michael will understand.'

David stood up. 'I want to see my brother.'

'Dave . . .'

'I have to see my brother.' He was a little frightening, and Anders stopped arguing and led the way. The smartass resident was waiting for them, leaning on the desk. He blinked when he saw the twin, but he didn't say anything.

'How is he?' asked David.

'Better.' The resident spoke to Anders. He avoided looking at David. 'He said it was Seconal, so I used ipecac. Called Reddy in the drug clinic and he said pumping's bad with barbiturates because you almost never get it all.'

'You didn't tell Reddy.'

'No. Your secret's safe.'

'Where is he?' David's voice was very tight.

'I had him moved.'

'Where?' Now David sounded dangerous. The resident looked at Anders.

'Just tell him where.'

'Room 804. He was trying to watch television when I left.'

This time Anders followed. And the kid came along, for laughs, Anders thought. But, to give him credit, Michael did look better. He was still half out, but not quite so pale. The TV was going in the background, voices and music filled the room and Michael didn't hear them come in. The minute David saw his brother, Anders saw his eyes close in relief.

'Mike,' David said softly. 'Mikey.'

Anders was suddenly embarrassed and he wished the kid weren't there to see this.

Michael's eyes opened. 'Dave, I fell down.' He raised his hand shakily and touched his brother's cheek.

The resident looked away, and so did Anders.

David trapped his brother's hand against his cheek with his own. 'How bad are you hurt?'

'It's my knees mainly.'

David rolled down the sheet and looked at his twin's legs; then he touched the hurt knees.

When he asked, 'Does it hurt?' Anders noticed that his voice was very soft and that every time David touched him, Michael smiled.

Finally David checked the bandages; then looked at and touched the bruised shins. He examined his brother's elbows, both slightly scraped.

'Can you walk?' David asked. 'Just to the street? I'll get a cab.'

'I think so.'

David brought his brother's clothes to the bed, and while Anders and the resident watched, he helped his brother dress.

'How's that?' he asked when Michael was on his feet.

'Okay, just fine.' Then Michael giggled. Anders and the resident looked at each other. 'Wonderful,' Michael said.

But as Michael passed Anders he stopped, and for an instant the wry, bitter, melancholy man Anders disliked so much was back.

'You said you wouldn't call him, John.' Then he walked slowly out of the room with David following to make sure he wouldn't fall.

chapter twenty-seven

David had somewhere to go every day. There were still some patients in the office and he was still on staff at the hospital, although that was going to end soon, because David wasn't just taking the stuff in the morning and at night any more; he was high most of the time, and it was starting to show. Anders would be after him soon, along with the committees, and the boards. But for now he had work.

Michael had nowhere to go. And one afternoon, he woke up and realized that he hadn't gotten dressed in almost a month. It was too hot to go outside he told himself when he opened the drapes and saw how dusty everything looked in the park. Men lay on the grass with newspapers over their faces, and everything had a still look that frightened him. He decided he'd get dressed anyway, and just not go out. But once he had on a suit and shirt, he felt different about it, and he decided to walk across Seventy-second to Broadway, then come right back. He took a raincoat to cover how thin he was. Outside, the heat felt good. Only a few people stared at him, and when he got to Broadway, he decided to go downtown. He took the express all the way to Thirty-fourth. He got off there, and walked through Macy's to get cool, because he was afraid to take his coat off. At Sixth he got back on the subway, and this time he thought about going to the end of the line, to see the ocean, and walk on the boardwalk, maybe all the way to Sea Gate. But when the train stopped at Delancey Street, he remembered his father taking them down there when they were kids, to buy clothes, and he got off, then walked east to Orchard. The streets were jammed, people eased past each other in the heat, talking, shouting over the horns, and the sidewalk was lined with cardboard boxes of clothing and yard goods. He walked close to the buildings, under the awnings, not looking at anything, just moving, feeling the closeness of the crowd, and listening to the confusion of noises. The insides of the shops looked cool and dark, and on impulse he went into one that sold yard goods. The bell tinkled as he closed the door, and an old man wearing a skullcap started to shake his head at Michael as if to say that the store was closed; but then a younger man came in from the back and asked him something in Yiddish. Michael wanted to answer in Yiddish. He used to know it; his parents had spoken it often, but he'd forgotten even the simplest phrases. He wasn't a Jew; he wasn't even a doctor any more; he wasn't anything except a twin. He suddenly felt so desolate he had to lean against the table which was covered with rolls of cloth – velvet and corduroy on this table, soft, warm naps of every different colour. He kept his head down. The young man watched him.

'Will you have some tea?' he asked in English.

Michael nodded. The man took his arm and led him to the back of the shop into a tiny linoleum-floored sitting room-kitchen. The floor was scrubbed and waxed. Michael could smell how clean it was. The man motioned Michael to sit on a painted chair, while he prepared tea. The old man sat in the corner, in the shadow cast by the refrigerator, watching every move Michael made.

He could imagine neat tiny bedrooms back behind the kitchen with eyelet curtains and all the windows open to an alley.

'Do you live here?' Michael asked.

'Lord, no,' said the young man. 'We have a two-family in Rego Park. My mother and father live upstairs, and my wife and I have the downstairs. We share the garden.'

So much information for one question. How could he be so open?

The man turned to Michael, holding a glass of tea in a napkin. How long had it been since he'd seen tea in a glass? 'Would you like a danish?'

Michael nodded, and the man put the tea on the table, and turned back; Michael was about to pick up the glass, when he suddenly realized that it was obscene for him to be sitting on their furniture, touching their cloth – for him to drink their tea or eat their food would be blasphemous. He jumped up.

'I'm sorry, I forgot something.' He ran to the door and out into the shop.

'Hey, at least drink your tea!' the young man called after him, but Michael kept going across the shop and through the door. The little bell tinkled, and he was out on the street blinded by the light and heat.

He ran back to the subway, but the stops weren't the same this time, and he got scared that he was lost, until at Seventy-seventh Street he got off the train blindly and came back up onto the street. He was on the East Side, and he had to get all the way crosstown before he would be safe. The distance seemed endless. He started walking because he didn't know where to get the crosstown bus. Then at the corner of Madison and Seventy-sixth Street, in the window of a long, dim, cool gallery, he saw a painting of his son. He was sure he'd imagined it, and he went past the window twice, then stopped; just wanting to see Sam's face – real or not. The man at the desk inside saw him, and Michael backed away from the window, found an empty cab and went home.

He went back the next day. The painting was still there. It wasn't a hallucination. He went closer while the same man watched, only this time Michael ignored him. He looked carefully at the portrait. It was Sam all right. In the corner, Kathy had signed K. Field. She didn't use his name any more, and he wondered what they'd told Sam about him. He had to find out. He had a right – Sam was his son.

He knew that if he called, Kathy would hang up, so he started walking west. Halfway across the park, he was afraid that he wasn't going to make it, but after sitting on the kerb for half an hour without moving, he was able to go on.

He had to tell the doorman who he was, but then the man remembered him and let him go up without calling ahead. Michael knew he was staring at him as he walked slowly across the lobby and into the elevator.

Kathy had the door on the chain. 'Who's there?' – from far away, he thought, because he'd walked down the hall too quickly and was dizzy.

'It's Michael.'

She stared across the chained aperture, and he could see how shocked she was at the way he looked.

'Please let me in. I can't go back yet.' That was true. He leaned against the wall. 'Please, Kath.'

She took the chain off and opened the door. He stayed close to the wall, then held her arm across the room to the couch. He half sat, half lay in it while she helped him off with his coat. He was wearing a clean shirt, and a tie, and his suit was pressed. She unknotted the tie and took off his jacket.

'Oh, Michael, oh my darling.' It was over ninety degrees outside, and his shirt was plastered against his ribs that stuck out against the fabric like roots growing around his body. Kathy was sitting next to him, trying to open his collar, so he did it for her. Then she was holding him against her, and he could feel her tears on his cheek, on his neck. He wasn't sure if he'd showered that morning and he was afraid that he smelled. He had shaved, so at least he wouldn't scrape her face.

'What happened?' she asked, still holding him.

'Happened?'

'How long since you've eaten?'

'Yesterday, no, maybe not. We sent out— Maybe it was yesterday.'

'Stay here, Michael.'

He was glad not to move, and glad when she got up so her weight wasn't against him any more. The light was soft through the huge window, and the room was cool. He looked around, then closed his eyes. It was so clean here; he breathed deeply, no smell. How did she keep it so clean and fresh, he wondered.

Then he decided that she never opened the window, that the air was machine-made.

He tried to reach down to unlace his shoes, but that made him dizzy, so he kept his feet on the floor as he lay back against the velvet. She came back and knelt on the floor next to him. He was grateful that she didn't touch him. She had a tray that she put on the coffee table.

'Drink some of the tea as soon as it cools, and eat this.'

It was toast or something – toast. He smiled. It should be custard; he'd never told her that he once cured a patient of cancer by feeding her custard. She held him up, and made him eat some, then drink the tea. It was so sweet it hurt the back of his tongue, but it felt good going down, and he kept drinking. Then the toast again so he could have more tea. This time he didn't mind her near him; she was warm and that felt good because his shirt had gotten cold and clammy in the air-conditioning, and it clung to him. He nestled closer to her, shivered, and closed his eyes. Just before he fell asleep he said, 'If David calls, tell him I'm not here.'

When he woke up, his shoes were off, and he was covered with a soft light blanket. He felt very frail and small, as if his whole body could fit on one pillow of the couch. He thought he was alone. It was sunset and the room was orangy pink; his hand looked ruddy and healthy. He couldn't see her.

'Kathy.'

She was next to him in an instant.

'You won't leave?' he asked.

No, no, she said; she wouldn't leave. He ate some more toast, and this time she added a slice of cheese and he ate that, too. The tea was even sweeter – wonderful stuff. Then she helped him up so he could go to the bathroom. He felt stronger, but it was still a relief to get back to the couch and sit down. But he was getting shaky.

'I'm going to need some pills,' he told her gently.

She got them for him from his jacket, without saying anything.

'You know about it, then?'

She nodded.

'Anders told you, didn't he?'

'Yes. He told me about David, too.' He listened for some satisfaction in her voice that David was in trouble, too, but she sounded tired, as if she didn't care one way or the other about David. Michael relaxed.

'Give them to me.' He nodded at the bottle and she handed it to him, but he couldn't get it open, and she did that for him too. He usually took three at a time, and he shook them into his palm, then he saw her watching and he put two back. She gave him more tea to wash it down.

'You know I was fired?'

'I guess I know everything, Michael.'

'Anders again?' She didn't answer.

'He's your lover, isn't he? I don't mind. I mean – I do mind, but I understand.' She still didn't answer. He'd forgotten how pretty she was; how thin. He touched the inside of her arm; she didn't respond. Then he opened her hand and stroked her palm with his thumb.

He couldn't remember how long it had been since he'd touched her. He couldn't really remember what a woman's body felt like – except strange. She moved her hand to pull the cover up over him, then she stood up. He looked at her waist, the line of her hips, the ridge of bone that protected her soft lower belly, then he closed his eyes.

The phone rang, and he heard her mention John, but the rest was a jumble. Then, much later the phone rang again and he woke up because he knew it was David. Kathy ran across the room and caught it mid-ring.

He listened very carefully, but he wasn't frightened, because he knew she was the only person in the world who wouldn't tell David where he was.

'No,' she was saying, 'I haven't heard from him. Yes, I'll call you if I do.' She was trying to sound sympathetic and concerned, and he grinned, liking the game, then suddenly wishing it wasn't a game, that they lived here together and Kathy still belonged to him.

The sky was dark, and he could see the stars. He recognized the Big Dipper and wished Sam was there so he could show it to him.

But he was at summer camp in the Berkshires. The kind of place he and David could never go to.

'Will you let Sam come to my funeral?' he asked when she hung up.

'You're not that sick, Michael.'

'No. But things happen to people. Will you?'

'Yes.' She thought it was too stupid to argue about. 'Of course he'll be at your funeral.'

He smiled and closed his eyes again, relieved. But he didn't fall asleep.

She gave him some boiled chicken, white meat that she'd shredded into tiny pieces the way his mother used to do for her father when they visited him at the Sons of Zion nursing home on Seventy-third Street. In fact, that was all Michael could remember about the old man – the thoughtful slow way he ate the chicken from his daughter's fingers.

'Would you feed me if I needed you to?' he asked.

'Yes. Is that what you want?'

'No, I just wondered.' He ate the chicken on his own, and she gave him more toast and some Jello. Everything was staying down. He felt neat, compact, in better working order; but still very, very tired.

He asked her to get the Seconal.

'I have to keep taking them,' he told her. 'It's dangerous not to.'

'I know. John told me.'

'You didn't tell him I was here?' Panic hit him. Anders would tell David, any second the phone or doorbell would ring, and he'd be there. Michael would see him, hear his voice; then he'd have to go back to the old apartment, out of the fresh air into the filth. He'd smother . . .

'No,' she said. 'He told me about barbiturate withdrawal a long time ago. When he first knew that . . . about it.'

He took another pill. Then she helped him back to the bathroom to wash. When he took off his clothes, she looked away.

'What happened to your knees?' She was looking at the floor, her hand across her forehead shielding her eyes.

'I fell. Didn't Anders tell you?'

'No.'

'See, you don't know everything after all, do you, Kathy?'
She shook her head. His face and body were so thin he looked almost like a child, and she tried to feel nothing except pity, maybe mixed with disgust, but she still couldn't look at him.

She brought him a robe she kept there for John, and helped him put it on, then she started to lead him back to the living room but he hung back.

'Can I sleep with you?'

'No, Michael.' She started to shake her head.

'Please,' he said. Then he laughed, 'I can't do anything.'

'I don't want you to.'

He slept on the couch. But the next day she let him stay and kept feeding him, and generally looking after him. At noon he called the office and told the new girl to tell his brother that he was fine. Not to worry, but that he wouldn't be back for a day or two. No, there was nowhere David could reach him. Kathy listened to the call, and he wondered if she'd object to the 'couple of days', but she didn't say anything. He kept to the one Seconal a dose, but he added an extra dose. Still it was less than usual and he noticed that he could feel the ache in his knees more, and that the taste and smell of the food she brought him became sharper. David called her three times before noon to see if maybe she had heard from Michael; then the last time he must have said something about coming over, because she told him that she was going to be out. At one he called again, and this time she said she was just leaving to go to Massachusetts to see Sam, and she wouldn't be back until Monday. The phone rang again at two, and then at three, but she didn't answer it. Michael spent the day helping her stretch a canvas and rejoiced at the rough feeling of the sized muslin on the tips of his fingers, at the smell of paint that found its way to the back of his throat and stayed there.

He ate more that day than he'd eaten in a week. She wouldn't let him have anything but the white meat of chicken, and dry toast. She offered plain rice, but he made gagging gestures at her, and she laughed and shook her head. It had been a long time since he'd heard her laugh.

At four the house phone rang. David was downstairs. Michael and Kathy sat and looked at each other. She wondered if his twin looked as bad as Michael did. She was sure he didn't. It was somehow always her image of them – David got the bigger office, the best job, the better clothes, the richest patients. He was still on staff, so he had a job, and Michael didn't. Michael had – what? Her. She smiled at him and he smiled back, while the phone rang and rang. Finally it stopped and she went over to him. He was kneeling, holding the sheet of canvas and the yardstick, measuring for her before they cut.

She knelt next to him and looked at him very closely. He tried to turn his head, but she wouldn't let him. His eyes were clearer, just in one day, but the rest of his face was a ruin of what it had been. His beard looked and felt like black slivers that scratched her fingers as she touched him, and his lips were colourless and dry and the sides of his forehead were shadowed grey triangles. Even his beautiful hair looked dull. She touched it, and he turned his head and kissed her hand. The phone started to ring again, and they waited it out. Then she called downstairs and told the desk she didn't want to be disturbed, that she was out to everyone.

He stayed that night, and all the next day, and she stayed with him. In the afternoon she put on a scarf and big sunglasses while they both giggled at her disguise. She went out the back door to the market and to buy him a pair of wash pants, two cheap wash-and-wear shirts, and some underwear. When she returned, they unwrapped the packages as if they were presents, and he modelled the clothes for her. When she saw how the trousers hung on him, she began to cry. He rocked her in his arms until she stopped, every minute aware of the strangeness of her body. That night she let him sleep in the bed and she slept on the couch. Later he woke up to find her in bed with him. For an instant he was disoriented and thought she was David because she had taken his penis in her mouth. She leaned against him, and he felt her breasts on his thigh. At first he was frightened and wanted her to stop to save them both the embarrassment of failure, but she was patient and gentle. He began to relax and finally to feel that odd, intense relief he always associated with David; then she was straddling him, riding him; and he was holding on to her, reeling with pleasure.

*

When Kathy realized that he finally meant to leave, she started to cry. 'Don't go back. Stay here. I'll see him and explain.'

'I can't do that, Kath. I owe it to him to face him.'

'He won't let you go,' she said. 'You know he won't.'

But how could he stop him? 'How can he stop me?'

'Because he can . . .' He put his arms around her and wanted to tell her that he loved her, but that seemed inadequate. Then he wanted to tell her that she was his life, literally, but he was afraid that such a declaration would frighten her, so he held her without saying anything.

'Stay another day?' she begged.

'The sooner I go, the sooner I'll come back.'

'Call instead.'

Call. Could he do that? *David, I'm sorry. I'm alive. I'm okay, but I can't come back right now. Don't worry. I'm okay.*

Just like that. He let go of her and went to the phone; maybe he wouldn't have to go back into the smell. Maybe he wouldn't have to see David again – or anybody. He dialled. Take care of me, Kathy, he begged her silently. Let me stay here alone with you, we don't have to see anybody for a long time, do we? I'll clean the house and when you come home, I'll have dinner waiting, and I won't have to go out except to shop – and even then I'll wait till dark. Pale Michael, keeping in the shadows. Oh, Kathy, don't let me leave.

He waited. The phone rang and rang, but he knew there would be no answer and there wasn't. 'He doesn't answer.'

'Maybe he's just gone out.' She sounded desperate.

He called the number of the phone in the lobby.

'Tom, it's Dr Ross; has my brother gone out?'

'Not today, Doc.'

'Thanks.' Michael hung up and turned back.

'I've got to go—'

'When will you be back?' she asked.

He smiled. 'If I'm not back in a week, call the cops.'

She shook her head as if she were going to argue some more, and he had to stop her, because she'd ruin everything.

'I can't do it, Kathy,' he said, 'I can't leave my brother alone there without a word.'

chapter twenty-eight

They weren't going to clean the streets again, ever. Maybe it was a holiday. He tried to think. The Fourth of July? Alternate side of the street parking suspended and no garbage collection. But the Fourth was over, and the streets were still filthy. The park was worse than he'd ever seen it, especially now in this terrible heat. There was no breeze and the whole place smelled of dog shit. He stood under a tree and looked across the street at the windows of the apartment. Everything was closed up tight; the drapes were drawn and he could see a line of water dripping down the side of the building from the air conditioner.

'David.' David was up there, waiting. He tried to imagine a breeze, but the air was dead. He faced the river, but it was dead too, oozing like paint in the sun down the island to the bay. There was no point in putting it off any longer and he crossed the street and went upstairs.

The smell was even worse than he remembered, worse than the street, worse than the park. Garbage heaved out to the walls. David stood in the middle of the room. He was bare-chested and his face was red-yellow and oily. He grinned at Michael. 'If I'd known you were coming, I'd have straightened up.'

'What happened to your face?'

'Man-tan. It's supposed to make me look like I've been in Miami. Like it?' David smeared at his cheek, 'Believe it or not, I look better than I did this morning.' He was coming towards Michael, still talking.

'I have to put on a tie and a jacket for my trial, Mike.' He was getting closer; almost to the steps. Michael held on to the railing. 'Today,' David said, 'in just an hour, I appear and tell them that we've been good boys; that we've stopped doing all the nasty things they don't like to think about; and we're getting help . . . Anders' very words . . . "you men have got to get help".' He'd reached Michael, and stood in front of him. 'But now – when I see you – I know I'm not going, Mike. I never want to go back there. I want us to be free of them, both of us.'

He reached out for Michael, touched his cheek, his neck, his hand slid down his back, and he pulled his brother to him. His voice trembled, 'I thought you were dead, Michael.' He whispered, his breath soft, ripe smelling, warm on Michael's face. 'I woke up again this morning without you, and I thought you were dead.'

Michael smelled suntan oil.

They were on the beach. Kiamesha Lake; the hottest day of the year; smearing suntan oil all over each other, while the girls watched because they were twins. Their mother and father were way up near the grass, sitting under an umbrella, and they had a thermos of iced tea. Their father looked up every time a young girl went by. He'd try not to, but he couldn't help himself; and Michael could still see the expression of loss on his father's face. As if something had gotten away from him, before he'd known it. Then he'd look at his sons, wild, running, chasing, and the loss on his father's face intensified, and was mixed with envy, love, pride, too many emotions to keep straight, too many to even feel at once.

'Come with me now,' David whispered. 'It's been so long.' He started pulling Michael down the steps. Michael tried to pull away, but David held on, and Michael wondered where he got the strength. He pulled so hard one of the buttons came off Michael's shirt and David laughed, and slipped his hand inside the shirt.

'Listen, let them have their trial, let them fire me. We'll go north like you always wanted.' Michael shut his eyes. 'We'll go to Vermont,' David whispered. 'People live longer in Vermont than in any state in the union – and shorter in Texas.'

'Get dressed, David. You're going to that hearing. You're going to tell them whatever you have to to keep your job.'

No answer.

'David!'

'Newfoundland's even better,' David said. 'Did you know that in Newfoundland the doctors take helicopters to their patients . . . all the way north . . . above the Arctic Circle . . .'

Michael could see it in spite of himself. A cold clean empty world stretching off the curve of the earth where nothing grew or died.

'It's no use, Dave. I'm leaving you.'

Nothing, no reaction.

'I've been with Kathy since Friday.'

Still nothing.

'I had to try to be someplace else,' Michael said. 'I'm afraid to stay here any more. I can't. Look at it, David. For Christ's sake, look.' David did as he was told. His head turned right, then left, surveying the once fine room, still elegantly proportioned – their father's pride – now five and six inches deep in garbage. The rug stayed damp from spills, and the wet had crept up the brocade drapes towards the ceiling. It had gotten really bad when they started having parties – just the two of them. They'd buy Entemann's marble cake and Louis Sherry pistachio ice cream – their favourite – and they'd pick a small section of the room and have a picnic. But they never cleaned up. The bottles and cartons stayed; and when they ran out of plates and bought paper plates and plastic utensils, they stayed too, until every bit of space had been used again and again. Last spring they'd had a mock Seder with a hard-boiled egg, salt water matzos and wine right in the centre of the room in front of the couch. Then they took Desoxyn and made love again and again with the cold wind blowing across them.

When there was nothing left to cook with or in, they started buying frozen dinners and sending out to Schwartz's Deli on Seventy-second Street. Now the tinfoil pans from the TV dinners sparkled in the room's half light, and the crusts from the corned beef sandwiches Mr Schwartz sent had moulded. Even the bags the sandwiches came in were still there – some empty, some still with sandwich leavings in them.

They celebrated everything. On Flag Day, David brought home a Carvel ice-cream flag, and on Purim the traditional three-cornered pastry. Every party ended with their making love and sometimes they would wait, taking all the time they could – reading to one another about the holiday, or insisting that more food be eaten before they allowed themselves to touch one another. Michael knew he would never forget the first touch of David's fingers sliding across his lips or eyelids, down his cheek.

One night Michael got very high. Too high; and when he tried to get up to go to the bathroom, he found that he couldn't stand. David laughed at him, pointing, yelling, 'Shit in the chair – Ms Field's Bloomingdale's chair – shit in it.' Michael laughed too, but before he knew it, he was doing it, while David watched with a little frown on his face.

Then Michael thought they would rot like the apartment and was surprised that the idea didn't bother him more. At first David insisted that they go to the office, although they seemed to have less time to practise medicine. When he was examining patients he wondered what all the decked out women would do if they knew how their doctors lived, what they did together. He insisted they keep their bodies clean and their clothes clean and pressed, and when he'd call the drugstore for Seconal, he'd have them deliver soap, Arpege dusting powder and toothpaste. And he'd ask Schwartz's delivery boy to bring toilet paper, and rolls of paper towels.

Once David got sick; a virus that was so debilitating he was in bed for a week. And Michael did everything for him. David lay still and Michael washed him, clipped his fingernails and toenails. He noticed the curves inside David's ears and wondered if they were replicated in his own. He even washed and filled an old casserole and brought it to the bedroom to wash David's hair, wondering as his fingers massaged his brother's scalp if they had exactly the same number of hairs – all the same thickness.

'You can't leave, Mike,' David was saying. He wasn't pleading, he didn't even sound unhappy. He was stating a fact.

Michael's head pounded. 'Of course I can leave.'

David shook his head; his high was gone. 'If you leave, I'm coming after you, whether I want to or not. And when I do, you'll go with me. Don't you know that yet? You can't be dumb enough to do that again.'

'Again? What did I do the first time?'

'You married her.'

'And if I hadn't?'

David didn't answer, but came close to Michael and put his arms around him. 'Help me into bed, Mike. I've been up too long.'

'You've got to go to that committee hearing.'

'You call them. Tell them I'm sick.' He looked sick. They both did. Michael hadn't been there an hour, and already the memory of fresh air and clean space was hazy. His eyes were burning again, and he was starting to sweat. David was half-collapsing against him.

'Please, Mike. Help me into bed.' Michael half carried David down the hall and held him steady while he knelt, then lay down on the bed. Michael sat next to him. The image of her was getting faint.

David was lying across the bed, holding Michael's hand. He kissed the back of it, the palm, then David put his arms around Michael and said, 'If I could let you go, I would. But I can't.'

'Why can't you?' Michael whispered.

'I just can't. Besides,' David said, 'even if *I* could, *you* couldn't.'

Michael tried to think of something else to ask, but he couldn't. Finally he said, 'Why can't we just try?'

'It won't work,' David said, absolutely certain. 'Not as long as I'm alive.'

David sat up when he realized what he'd said and they looked at each other for a moment.

Then Michael said, 'Then it's you or me, David; because if I stay with you, I'm going to die.'

David looked wild, the way he had the night they had the fight in the Village. He was full of energy, laughing and kneeling on the bed.

'They'll never guess,' he was almost singing, 'the perfect crime.'

'I won't do it.'

'Don't say that.' David was suddenly serious. 'You've got to.' Then laughing again, 'I swear to God, I'll be disappointed if you don't.'

'I can't. Please, David; please.'

David grabbed him. 'Did you mean it? That you'd die if you stayed?'

Michael didn't say anything. David held on, 'Did you, Mike?'

'Yes,' Michael said softly.

'Then I die anyway, so what are we talking about?' Their father's phrase: 'so what are we talking about?'

'You don't have to die.'

'Yes, I do I don't have any life without you.' David let go of him. 'Now, you remember everything you have to do?'

Michael nodded.

'First?' David prompted.

'I get the Dilantin,' Michael said.

'Don't wait to take it. One convulsion could finish you – even on the street. Then? . . .'

'I get Sustagen or protein supplement . . .'

'Right. Then stay away from here; go to Kathy's – go anywhere. But don't come back.'

'I won't.'

'Good,' he said. 'Don't even stay here long enough to call the cops – just get out. And don't forget to leave the door unlocked' – David grinned – 'so they don't have to break it down.'

'I will.'

'You look scared, Michael.'

'I am.'

'I think they'll let you sign the certificate. You're the only one in the world who'd care enough to insist on a postmortem. And of course you won't. But just in case someone gets really suspicious, the story'll hold. Remember, I was comatose when you woke up, and you force-fed the reds to try and reverse the withdrawal. As long as the killing dose is *injected* – no ordinary postmortem will find it – they'd have to do special tests for that, and I'm sure they won't.'

'But they'll see the needle mark.' Michael thought he'd found something to stop them, but David had an answer for this too.

'Inject the stuff into a haemorrhoid, they'll never find the mark.' He laughed. 'I learned that from a forensic pathologist at Harvard.'

Somehow while they planned – David's plan – their birth order re-established itself. David was older, wiser, knew best. No, he had said, not suicide – that'd be a stigma on both of us, forever; on our parents, and maybe even on Sam.

This way was better; this way was beautiful. They try to kick the habit, and one makes it and lives, and one doesn't and dies.

'There won't be a dry eye in the house,' David said, 'even I wind up looking good.'

They lay down together and stayed there, not moving while the long summer light started to fade.

Michael's face was wet with tears and David wiped them away.

'You might make it,' he said softly. 'You might.'

When it was almost dark, David made Michael get up and get the hypodermic and the Seconal injectable. They kept three 1000 mg vials in case of accidental withdrawal. He brought them into the bedroom and emptied the only bottle they had left – there were five reds in it. Just enough to dull the ache – David's, not Michael's. David talked a little about their father and mother and how easy their deaths had been, both in their sleep, never knowing it was going to happen.

'It won't hurt you, Dave . . .'

'No, no, Michael. It won't.' He looked around the ruined room, then at Michael, and then he scooped up the red capsules and swallowed them.

'Don't wait too long, Michael.' He turned over on his back and looked at his brother, not even blinking much. In a few minutes the drug started to work. 'I thought it would take longer,' he said. Then he smiled and closed his eyes.

Michael sat on the edge of the bed for forty-five minutes watching his brother's chest move with his breath. If he waited any longer the capsules in David's gut would be so disintegrated they'd know something was wrong with the story. He turned David over on his side, filled the hypodermic from all three vials exactly as David had told him to, then slipped the needle in as quickly as he could and pushed the plunger. David's body stiffened, jerked, tried to pull away, but Michael held him until the syringe was empty.

Michael cradled him in his arms until he died, which took about twenty minutes. Then Michael took Louise's brass manta ray, put it in his pocket and left. It was hot and dark outside; the big old drugstore on Broadway and Seventy-third was a dim, cool cave.

The prescription counter was crowded and the pharmacist gave Michael the Dilantin without even looking at him. He got the Sustagen too and went back to the street. Across Broadway old people sat silent on benches in the heat next to junkies and winos who slept or babbled. Behind them, Needle Park was a triangle of paper, cans and bottles. He knew he had to get to

Kathy. He went into the phone booth to call her, to ask her to meet him at Seventieth Street and help him back to her place because he couldn't make it alone. Then he'd call the police, and tell them that something had happened to his brother.

But the phone booth stank of urine, and he was afraid he would be sick if he stayed in it, so he walked on. It was after nine, but there were still children playing on Seventy-third Street. Two drunks lay in a doorway just off Broadway, but the children didn't seem to notice them. He passed the movie house which was showing *Stavisky*. David had read a review of it to him and wanted to see it.

He shook his head and went on. He meant to keep going – across Seventy-second, towards the new apartment building on Broadway, past the McDonald's and then across Broadway to the darker east side of the street where he'd walk in the shadows to Sixty-seventh Street, to Kathy's. But without thinking about it or deciding to, he turned west, and before he knew it, he was at Seventy-second and West End, then Seventy-Second and Riverside, and there was nothing ahead but the park and the river.

He went right into the bedroom, sat down next to his brother's body.

He should have been able to make it, he thought; Kathy had tried so hard. 'But it wasn't enough,' he told her softly, watching his brother's dead face. 'Almost, but not quite enough. I'm sorry.'

Then he found a pair of his shorts and put them on his brother's body. Maybe, he thought, to cover up what he'd done to him.

There was no question of going out again. In fact, he thought, it was a relief to be back – in the dark, the jumble was soft, heaving out to the walls like waves, and the smell was tidal mud on a hot night.

He went back to the door and double-locked it, wondering as he did, how long it would be before someone opened it again, and what they would find when they did. Nothing, he thought. Dust that would blow away out the doors and windows into the air already full of soot. Then he took the bottle of Dilantin into

270

the bathroom, poured the capsules into the toilet and flushed it. A few escaped and bobbed to the top of the water. He flushed again and they disappeared.

Then he waited. The phone rang, he didn't answer it. He walked round a little, but he spent most of the time sitting on their bed near David's body. It took a day or more for the first convulsion to hit, and after it subsided, he lay down on the bed, touching David, to wait for the next one.

He woke up only once after that to find that one of the convulsions had heaved him off the bed and onto the floor. He tried to get back on the bed to be near his brother's body, but he was too weak.

Bari Wood
The Killing Gift 75p

The man who broke into the Gilberts' apartment died brutally.
Dr Jennifer List Gilbert snapped his spine like a drinking straw
without even touching him. For Stavitsky of the Homicide Squad a
highly unusual murder investigation becomes an obsession ...
Because Jennifer Gilbert has the power to kill people just by
thinking them dead ...

'Exceptional ... the tautness and the power of the writing and the
spectacular surprise ending' SPECTATOR

Morris Renek
Las Vegas Strip 80p

Yank Karkov was a renegade with class – a man with a tuxedo and a
golden dream. That dream was a luxury casino in the desert of Nevada
– girls, gambling, and the good life for the big spenders. To build it,
he had to fight the Syndicate, the saboteurs and the soulless desert
itself ...

Colleen McCullough
Tim 80p

She first saw him working on a Sydney building site. From that
moment, a powerful magnetism drew them together – first as friends,
and then as much more. Mary was over forty, a cultured career
woman, living alone. Tim was twenty-five, his god-like body
harbouring the mind of a child.

You can buy these and other Pan Books from booksellers and
newsagents ; or direct from the following address :
Pan Books, Sales Office, Cavaye Place, London SW10 9PG
Send purchase price plus 20p for the first book and 10p for
each additional book, to allow for postage and packing
Prices quoted are applicable in the UK

While every effort is made to keep prices low, it is sometimes
necessary to increase prices at short notice. Pan Books reserve
the right to show on covers and charge new retail prices which
may differ from those advertised in the text or elsewhere.